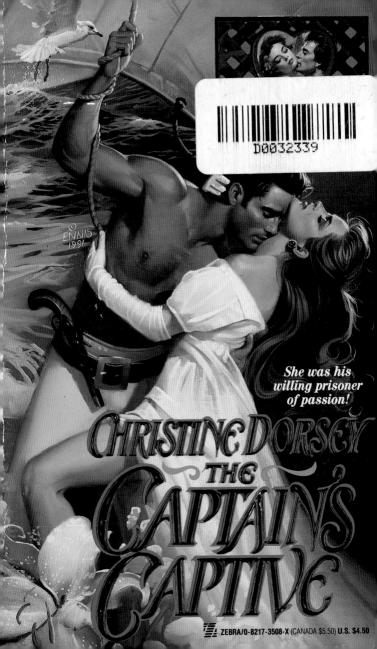

ENNIS
1991

**She was his
willing prisoner
of passion!**

# CHRISTINE DORSEY
# THE
# CAPTAIN'S
# CAPTIVE

ZEBRA/0-8217-3508-X (CANADA $5.50) U.S. $4.50

9 780821 735084

50450

0-8217-3508-X

## PASSION'S AWAKENING

"Don't leave me," Charlotte whispered.

"I have to." The truth of those words hit Jon as he realized how eager he was to lie in her embrace. But she was asleep, damnit, and dreaming of another man—a man he despised.

"Please don't leave me." Her voice was a dreamy siren's song, as sensual as the body that arched toward him.

"Charlotte." Jon tried to wake her. Her only response was a sigh. Steeling himself against responding to that enticing sound, he cupped her shoulders. "For God's sake, I'm not Levid."

Her eyes swept open, and Jon braced himself for her contemptuous stare. But she didn't seem the slightest bit surprised to see him looking down at her.

"I never thought you were," she said with a faint smile. Her arms tightened, pulling him down. "I know who you are. I've always known." His lips bent to hers.

Charlotte thought she'd known exactly how it would feel, this heady thrill of being kissed by him, but her daydreams paled in the heat of reality. His mouth was softer than she expected, more demanding . . . hotter. But the hungry ache, the deep longing, was there. Only stronger, much stronger.

# THE BEST IN HISTORICAL ROMANCES

**TIME-KEPT PROMISES** (2422, $3.95)
by Constance O'Day Flannery
Sean O'Mara froze when he saw his wife Christina standing before him. She had vanished and the news had been written about in all of the papers—he had even been charged with her murder! But now he had living proof of his innocence, and Sean was not about to let her get away. No matter that the woman was claiming to be someone named Kristine; she still caused his blood to boil.

**PASSION'S PRISONER** (2573, $3.95)
by Casey Stewart
When Cassandra Lansing put on men's clothing and entered the Rawlings saloon she didn't expect to lose anything—in fact she was sure that she would win back her prized horse Rapscallion that her grandfather lost in a card game. She almost got a smug satisfaction at the thought of fooling the gamblers into believing that she was a man. But once she caught a glimpse of the virile Josh Rawlings, Cassandra wanted to be the woman in his embrace!

**ANGEL HEART** (2426, $3.95)
by Victoria Thompson
Ever since Angelica's father died, Harlan Snyder had been angling to get his hands on her ranch, the Diamond R. And now, just when she had an important government contract to fulfill, she couldn't find a single cowhand to hire—all because of Snyder's threats. It was only a matter of time before the legendary gunfighter Kid Collins turned up on her doorstep, badly wounded. Angelica assessed his firmly muscled physique and stared into his startling blue eyes. Beneath all that blood and dirt he was the handsomest man she had ever seen, and the one person who could help beat Snyder at his own game.

*Available wherever paperbacks are sold, or order direct from the Publisher. Send cover price plus 50¢ per copy for mailing and handling to Zebra Books, Dept. 3508, 475 Park Avenue South, New York, N.Y. 10016. Residents of New York, New Jersey and Pennsylvania must include sales tax. DO NOT SEND CASH.*

# CHRISTINE DORSEY
## THE CAPTAIN'S CAPTIVE

**ZEBRA BOOKS**
**KENSINGTON PUBLISHING CORP.**

*To my agent, Joyce A. Flaherty,*
*and my editor, Carin Cohen Ritter,*
*with heartfelt thanks.*
*And as always to Chip.*

ZEBRA BOOKS

are published by

Kensington Publishing Corp.
475 Park Avenue South
New York, NY 10016

Copyright © 1991 by Christine Dorsey

First printing: September, 1991

Printed in the United States of America

Huzza for the seamen undaunted by fear,
May they all of 'em find it a happy New-Year,
May the laurels which cluster on liberty's brow,
For a thousand years hence be as blooming as now.


chorus


Columbia's bright name then with glory shall sound,
And the praise of her heroes be sung the year round.


—from "A Happy New Year
to Commodore Rodgers,"
a song composed on December 31, 1812
printed by N. Coverly
author unknown

# Chapter One

*September 1812*

What was she doing here?

Squeezing her eyes shut, Charlotte Winston tried to imagine herself somewhere else. It was a foolish game, she knew, but one that often brought comfort through trying times. Usually she pictured herself in exotic places, places she'd read about in the books lining her father's library, but not today.

Today she dreamed of the peace and quiet of her mother's garden—pictured herself there, sitting on the small wooden bench near the hedge. Sunlight would be filtering down through the narrow willow leaves, dappling the mending in her lap.

Charlotte hated mending, but to be back in her mother's garden she'd do it with a smile. Her mind drifted and she could almost smell the primrose, hear the summer breeze sift through the grasses beyond the garden. Birds twittered overhead, birds that could soar through the heavens. Birds that could fly way beyond the neat brick wall that surrounded the garden.

But Charlotte didn't envy them. No, Charlotte

didn't long to see firsthand the world beyond the garden. She didn't yearn for adventure. She'd learned her lesson. If only she could be back in her mother's gar —

A cannon's thunderous roar shattered her daydream and brought reality crashing around her. Charlotte's eyes flew open and she clutched at the thin ticking on her bunk. Instead of the soft verdant beauty of Oxfordshire she saw the swaying rafters of her cabin on board the *Balfour*.

Last week she'd finally gotten her "sea legs," as the captain of the schooner she'd boarded in England termed her ability to hold down a meal. Then why did she feel the too-familiar swell of nausea, the cold sweat on her upper lip?

Charlotte pressed a lavender-scented handkerchief to her brow and lay back against the pillow. The high collar of her bombazine gown chafed her neck, but she didn't loosen it. After all, it was such a minor discomfort in the scheme of things. Charlotte braced herself for another cannon blast, but heard none. There were the sounds of scurrying feet overhead and sudden jerking movements of the ship that sent Charlotte's stomach into somersaults, but nothing else.

Could it be they'd repelled the attacking ship? Groaning at her own náivete, Charlotte fought back another wave of nausea. The other vessel had eighteen guns—she'd heard one of the crew say that before she and the other passengers were hustled below. By the way he'd accompanied his words with a slow whistle between his yellowed teeth, Charlotte imagined eighteen guns were a lot—at least a lot more than carried by the merchant ship she was on.

Pounding at her door startled Charlotte almost as much as the cannon blast had. She cringed into the corner of the bunk. Her eyes darted about the small cabin searching for something to use as a weapon. Oh, why hadn't she thought of this before? There could be anyone on the other side of that door.

A pirate. Of course, it could be a pirate, tall and dark, devilishly handsome, with a scarf tied around his raven hair and a gold earring dangling from his ear. He'd flash her a wicked smile, haul her into his arms and—

"Miss Winston, are you all right?"

Surprise washed over Charlotte as the door opened and one of the *Balfour's* officers stuck his grizzled head inside. What was in her mind? She had to stop letting her imagination run wild. When the man, who she recognized as Mr. Harley, continued to stare, Charlotte nodded, and he continued. "The captain wants all passengers on deck."

"On deck? What's happened. I heard a cannon." That was real even if her foolish imaginings about the pirate weren't.

"The captain will explain everything when you come above. There's no real cause for alarm." He stepped further into the room. "Are you sure you're not ill? I can send someone if you need assistance to get above deck."

"Assistance?" For the first time Charlotte thought about the appearance she made cowering on her cot. "No. I'm fine." She rose from the bed with as much dignity as she could muster. After all, she was a Winston. One didn't become a general without being able to handle adversity, and she hailed from a long line of British generals.

Charlotte resisted the urge to delay the officer with further questions as he left. She'd find out when she got on deck. Straightening her heavy skirt, she started across the cabin, making it almost to the door before abruptly swerving toward the chamber pot. When her stomach stopped rebelling, Charlotte wet her handkerchief and wiped it gingerly across her mouth. Upholding the family tradition of bravery would be much easier if she didn't feel so horrible.

Taking a deep breath, Charlotte glanced in the small looking glass attached to the wall. Her hair had come loose from the chignon at the back of her neck and she stuffed a damp brown curl behind her ear. Pinching her cheeks didn't do much for her color, which to Charlotte's eye seemed to fade between chalky white and green. But then, she realized, her appearance was the least of her worries.

Hurrying along the companionway, Charlotte realized the other passengers were already above deck. Not that there were that many, but it would have been comforting to face whatever she must face with someone by her side.

Squinting into the bright sunshine Charlotte stepped out on deck. In her haste she'd forgotten her poke bonnet, and now used her hand to shade her eyes as she glanced around. Instead of the death and destruction she'd feared, everyone on deck appeared to be safe. Charlotte's breath left her on a sigh of relief when she saw there were no bloody bodies strewn about.

Except for the obnoxious odor of sulphur she could detect no sign of a battle. The vessel seemed to be in good shape, too. No splintered mast or dangling shrouds. Everything seemed in order—that is, if you ignored the sloop that had attacked them. Which, of course, Charlotte couldn't. It was man-acled to the *Balfour* with grappling hooks, and Charlotte watched in fascination as the sailors on the other vessel hustled about, securing the huge ropes.

"Miss Winston, if you please."

10

Her name blared by Captain Boorstin through his horn grabbed Charlotte's attention and she hurried forward. The other passengers were huddled together listening to the captain. When she joined the group he continued.

"You are all to be transferred to the *Eagle*. Her captain will see you safely ashore at his next port of call. In the meantime you will all be treated courteously, and with the respect due British citizens."

Captain Boorstin droned on about gathering what personal belongings they wished to take with them, but Charlotte wasn't listening. She looked again toward the sloop that had attacked them, wondering what was happening. The vessel was American. Great Britain and America were not on the best of terms, but that didn't give the upstart country a right to attack a peaceful merchant ship.

And what did the captain mean about being put off at the next port of call? She wanted—needed—to go to Montreal. Charlotte tried to gain Mr. Rolling's attention. He was a solicitor from Liverpool who was also traveling to Montreal. On those few occasions when Charlotte had joined the other passengers at the captain's table, he'd been kind, listening as Charlotte told of her mother's death and her reason for traveling to Canada. But now he was too busy complaining to Alfred Smithe, another passenger, to pay her any heed.

All the passengers seemed caught up in their own concerns and paid no attention to Charlotte. Even Captain Boorstin ignored her questions, so Charlotte hurried below when he gave the order to do so. There didn't seem any other choice.

After gathering together a few of her possessions, a change of clothes, her favorite books, and a silhouette of her mother, Charlotte pulled on her bonnet and rejoined the other passengers on deck. There was a great deal of anxiety and speculation about their plight, but apparently nobody knew for certain.

By now, the merchant vessel was swarming with sailors from the *Eagle,* and still no answers were forthcoming. Captain Boorstin had disappeared, and no one else seemed willing or able to explain the situation to her.

*You shouldn't have come. You should have listened to Mrs. Samuels and all the others who told you not to take this voyage.* Charlotte shook her head to dispel these thoughts. What she should or shouldn't have done made no difference now.

Clutching her possessions, Charlotte accepted assistance across to the sloop. Her stomach still seemed to pitch with each movement of the vessels, but she resolutely refused to be sick again, at least not in full view of everyone. But Charlotte imagined the American sailor who helped her knew of her condition. He smiled, offering a word of encouragement. But though he appeared friendly enough, he couldn't —or wouldn't—answer Charlotte's inquiry about what would happen to her and the other passengers.

Acting brave was taking its toll. Charlotte felt small and alone. Closing her eyes, she tried to imagine this was a marvelous adventure, an exciting exploit that was full of daring and romance and . . . Charlotte jerked back to reality. Life was not like her daydreams. *This* was not like her daydreams.

In her imaginings she knew what was happening, knew what to expect. But that wasn't the case with reality.

An apple-cheeked young man introduced himself as Midshipman Taylor and proceeded to tell the passengers from the merchant schooner the same thing their captain had—basically nothing. They were safe, and would be taken to the *Eagle*'s next port of call. He made a reference to the *Eagle*'s captain, motioning toward a group of men standing near the mast.

Charlotte's gaze shifted, and she picked out the captain immediately. She could hear him above the din of activity giving orders to some sailors. His voice was deep and commanding. But his uniform, from the back, which was all she could see, wasn't nearly as impressive as her father's. She supposed that was to be expected from the upstart American Navy.

Charlotte cocked her head, studying the captain as he moved toward the railing. Her father's uniform might be more flamboyant, but his breeches didn't fit near as well as the American captain's. And even without the glittering epaulets that adorned her father's jacket, the captain's shoulders appeared broader. Looking away quickly, Charlotte gave herself a shake. What did she care about the cut of the captain's uniform?

His vessel had illegally attacked hers, and made her a virtual prisoner. And she had no idea what was happening, except that she was supposed to follow along blindly with the other passengers as the midshipmen herded them below. Like so many sheep.

Charlotte began walking, but her footsteps didn't take her toward the hatch. She could handle situations—any situation—if she knew what to expect. Hadn't she said as much to her mother's physician when the elderly gentleman had tried to "protect" Charlotte by not telling her the truth?

"Please, I must know what to expect from her illness," Charlotte had begged years ago, and though the facts had been awful to hear, she'd appreciated the knowledge, and the forewarning.

That same need propelled her toward the captain

13

of the *Eagle*. When she reached him, Charlotte had a moment of doubt. He'd appeared larger than the other sailors, but she hadn't realized how tall he really was. She barely came up to one of his broad shoulders, and Charlotte took a deep breath to bolster her flagging courage.

"Captain." He still faced away from her. The sailors were gone, presumably carrying out their orders, and now he stood staring out toward where the undulating sea blended into the murky horizon. Charlotte cleared her throat and tried again to gain his attention. "Captain!"

He must have heard her this time, for he jerked around, skewering Charlotte with eyes as blue as the cloud-spattered sky. Eyes that held faint traces of sadness. His expression quickly shifted to mild surprise and then annoyance, but by that time Charlotte didn't care.

She'd retreated till she couldn't move any further, and now with her back pressed against a gun barrel, she could only gape, openmouthed.

The captain was her pirate!

Oh, there was no gold ring dangling from his ear, and his cropped hair sported no scarf, but he was the pirate of her imagination. His lean, tanned face was the same, as were the piercing blue eyes.

Charlotte tried to swallow—couldn't. How could this be? When her mind had conjured up the pirate, and admittedly today wasn't the first time she'd fantasized about him, she'd never imagined any real man could look like him. She'd certainly never seen anyone so handsome.

He even had the same expression as her pirate. He scowled down at her, his raven brows almost touching over his straight, aristocratic nose. "Well?"

"W-well?" Charlotte didn't recall her pirate having a parrot, but now she felt like one. All she could do was mimic his word, and even that was difficult. Her voice cracked.

Captain Jonathan Knox's frown deepened, and he scanned the deck for the midshipman he'd put in charge of the passengers from the merchant ship. As Jon suspected, the young man was nowhere to be found. Making a mental note to reprimand him, Jon looked back down at the woman.

She was obviously a *detail* the midshipman had let slip by him. Glad he hadn't put the officer in charge of supervising dangerous prisoners, Jon leaned his hip against the rail. The way she'd crept up on him, Jon could have taken a knife between the ribs before he'd seen her. He guessed he'd have been partly to blame if he'd ended up as fish bait. He shouldn't indulge in useless worrying. It was a waste of time, and he didn't have any to waste.

That reminded him of the woman. She still stared up at him as if she'd seen a ghost, but at least she'd closed her mouth. Jon folded his arms across the deep blue wool of his jacket, then let them fall to his side. His mother had taught him to show respect for the fairer sex, even if this particular specimen was annoying, and for all he could tell behind the yards of heavy black fabric, not especially fair.

Jon softened his expression. She'd probably just gotten separated from the other passengers, and sought directions. He'd have one of the men take her below, and then he could talk with the captain of the schooner. Jon seriously doubted if he knew anything about the *Scorpion*, but it was worth a try. *Anything* was worth a try.

Jon felt the seeds of worry begin to sprout, and shifted his attention back to the woman. He forced a faint smile. "Do you need assistance?"

15

Did she need assistance? What did he think? Her ship had been attacked, she'd been forced to leave most of her possessions, practically dragged onto this vessel going who knew where, and he asked if she needed assistance! Charlotte tried not to notice the way the tiny creases at the corners of his eyes deepened when he smiled. She straightened her back. "I, sir, would like to know who you think you are attacking one of His Majesty's ships and making prisoners of the passengers?"

He was taken aback. Jon couldn't help himself. He expected a shy, maidenly plea for help, and received instead a lambasting. And from this slip of a woman! He folded his arms. Manners be damned. "I, madam, am Captain Jonathan Alexander Knox, and your vessel was attacked because the United States of America and England are at war."

"War?"

"Aye, now if you'll—"

"War's been declared?" Charlotte felt the faint stirrings of her nausea returning.

"I just said as much." Jon was annoyed with himself over his pompous speech. The poor woman's eyes, large anyway, became enormous when he mentioned the war. Now they seemed to dominate what he could see of her delicate face—a face that now had a definite greenish tint. "Perhaps you should go below and lie down."

Charlotte grabbed for the railing, her black-gloved hand clutching the smooth wood. Lying down might be a good idea, though she doubted it would help.

"I can assure you, madam, that no harm will come to you or any of the other passengers." Jon didn't know whether to scoop her up in case she fainted, or get out of her way in the event she became ill.

16

No harm? How could he stand blithely by and say no harm would come to her? Charlotte took a deep breath, trying to relieve the rumblings in her stomach. How was she supposed to get to her father if there was a war? Oh, Mrs. Samuels, her housekeeper, was right. She shouldn't have come.

Jon reached out to touch her arm, thought better of it, and looked around. He needed someone to take this little problem off his hands. But though there were plenty of men on deck, they were all sailors. Rough and ready American sailors who he could count on in most any emergency, but *not* the type to escort a gentlewoman to her quarters. Where in the hell was Taylor?

"I assure you, madam, that my government does not make war on women and—"

Charlotte's head shot up. "Then why did you attack the *Balfour?*"

Jon took a calming breath. Having his motives questioned—especially by a woman—was not something he took well. "I did not 'attack' your vessel." Her eyes narrowed, and to his chagrin, Jon found himself explaining. "We fired harmlessly into the sea. A mere . . ." Jon searched for a good word, grinned when he found it. "*Signal* for your captain to permit boarding."

"And if Captain Boorstin hadn't obeyed your . . . 'signal?' What would your government's position concerning innocent women have been then?"

Trying to suppress his annoyance, Jon scowled back at her, deciding if he ever did make war on a woman, the one in front of him would be a prime candidate. "Since *he* had the common sense to obey my 'signal,' the question is immaterial," he said, his voice growing louder with each word.

He was right. What Captain Knox would or

17

wouldn't have done made no difference. Charlotte couldn't imagine why she stood here discussing it with him. It wasn't like her to be so bold—especially with strangers. Of course, this man didn't seem like a stranger. She had to remember that she didn't know him. He wasn't her pirate. And this wasn't a daydream.

Jon watched the woman sigh. Long lashes fluttered down to form a dark crescent beneath her eyes and he felt a pang of guilt. He shouldn't have yelled. His foul mood wasn't her fault. And she obviously had problems of her own—besides those he'd caused. Her somber attire indicated mourning. He briefly wondered if it was a husband she'd lost.

"Let me take you to your quarters." There was no real need to wait for Taylor, Jon thought. He could take her below deck. He'd feel better when she was safely with the other passengers. There must be someone there to take care of her. A lady such as she wouldn't be traveling alone. Jon touched her elbow and her eyes flew open.

She had to stop it. Charlotte couldn't believe she'd actually stood here and tried to block out reality. And she had. For just a moment she'd been on a pirate ship bound for the Caribbean and romantic adventure. She shook her head to push away the last lingering traces of her dream. It was one thing to let your mind wander when alone, quite another when an enemy captain was staring down at her quizzically. Best to get this unpleasantness over. "Where are you taking me?"

"Below deck. To the other passengers." Was the woman fey? He'd just said that.

"No. I mean your sloop. Where's this port of call you intend to take us?"

"Boston." Jon didn't mention it would be sometime before he headed toward port. He wasn't ready yet to give up the search.

"Boston," Charlotte repeated, wondering how far she'd have to travel to get to her father. The captain began guiding her past groups of sailors loosening the ropes binding the *Eagle* to the *Balfour*. When she looked across at the schooner she noted the crew all wore the uniforms of American sailors.

"Doesn't Boston suit?" She studied the activity around her with such solemn intensity that Jon couldn't resist a little teasing. His sisters complained it was his most vexing quality—at least the one that bothered them the most.

"Suit? Of course it doesn't suit." Charlotte glared up at him. "I want to go to Montreal."

"Well, I sure as hell can't take you there. Unless, of course, we've already captured that fair city."

Charlotte stopped. "Oh, no. Do you suppose they have?"

He was teasing again. There was something about this woman that reminded him of his sisters. He couldn't decide what it was. Certainly not her looks. Libby and Cilla were taller, dark-haired like their parents, and strikingly beautiful. Maybe it was just because she was obviously a gentlewoman, and he hadn't been around many ladies for a while. Come to think of it, he hadn't been around any *women* for a while.

Unlike his sisters, this woman obviously wasn't used to teasing. She stared up at him, concern in her large eyes. Brown eyes, he noticed now that the sun had shifted and her hat didn't completely shadow her face. Brown eyes with flecks of gold radiating from the center.

Jon shrugged. What in the hell did he care what color her eyes were? "I seriously doubt American forces have taken Montreal." Honesty forced him to add, "But the last I heard, it was a goal." Nudging her elbow, Jon started them across the deck again.

"My father won't allow it."

"Your father?" They'd reached the hatch and Jon started down, turning to assist the woman.

"Yes. General Winston would never permit Montreal to be captured." Charlotte knew practically nothing of military strategies, but even as little as she'd been around her father, she knew his stubborn determination would keep Montreal from capture.

Jon's brow arched. "So. We've snagged ourselves a general's daughter, have we?"

Too late, Charlotte realized her mistake. Oh, why had she told him about her father? "Are you going to hold me for ransom?"

"Ransom," Jon laughed. "Now I hadn't thought of that. How much are you worth, do you suppose?"

He was bedeviling her. That flash of insight brought color to Charlotte's cheeks. He had no intention of holding her for ransom or anything else. It was obvious from the amused glint in his eyes that he didn't consider her worth the effort. Not that she wasn't glad. But his attitude galled all the same.

"Listen, Miss Winston . . ." Jon paused as he guided her along the narrow passageway. "Is it Miss Winston?"

"Yes." Charlotte watched his gaze sweep over her black gown. "My mother died two months ago."

"You have my sympathies."

"Thank you." He really wasn't so bad—even if he was the enemy.

"As I was saying, Miss Winston, you have nothing to fear. Neither I nor my men will harm you."

That was comforting—even if she did end up in Boston. Charlotte smiled and told the captain as much.

She had a nice smile. Soft and gentle like her eyes. Jon had a moment of wishing he could yank off that awful hat and get a good look at her. He mentally shook himself. He didn't care what she looked like—at least he shouldn't care. He had more important things to worry about than this slip of a woman. Quickening his step, Jon realized he'd given this matter entirely too much of his time already. He should be with the *Balfour*'s captain right now, gleaning any information the older man had.

Yes, Charlotte decided, if she had to be captured, it was nice her captor was a gentleman. She'd be inconvenienced, of course. Trying to get from Boston to Montreal wouldn't be easy, but she could do it. She had plenty of money sewn into the lining of her skirts. She'd get there.

Charlotte stopped when the captain did, outside a cabin door. The light from a nearby lantern gleamed blue-black in his hair, and again she was struck by how much he looked like her pirate. Even down to the cleft in his square chin. But thank goodness he acted nothing like her pirate. Though he'd been brusque with her at first, he now appeared very mannerly. She smiled again. "My father will appreciate your treatment of me." Wasn't there such a thing as honor among soldiers—even enemies? But then this man wasn't a soldier. He was a sailor.

"My betrothed will also hear of your kindness." Charlotte forced herself not to cringe when she spoke of the man she was to marry—the man her father had arranged for her to marry. But he was a sea captain, like the man standing before her, so they probably understood each other better.

So the little brown wren was betrothed. Jon shrugged. It was probably a good thing. She didn't appear in the first flush of youth. "Are you marrying a resident of Montreal?"

21

"No. He's a sea captain, like yourself . . . but on a different side of this conflict."

"I assumed that." Jon took a step back. He needed to leave. "You may use this cabin," he said, motioning toward the closed door. "I'll have your traveling companion brought here."

"I haven't one."

Jon's brows rose. "You're traveling alone?" At her nod, his eyes narrowed. "Does your father approve of this?"

Charlotte's chin rose. "He doesn't know, but I assure you, I'm perfectly capable of—"

"What of your betrothed? Does he approve of this foolishness?"

Maybe it was foolishness—maybe she'd decided that for herself—but this man didn't have any right to say it. "My intended doesn't know, either." She didn't mention that avoiding his visit to her country estate in England was a side benefit of her trip to Canada. "But I'm sure if he did know, he'd see nothing amiss."

"Then he must be an idiot."

"I assure you, sir, he is not." Actually, her opinion of him was somewhat lower than an idiot, but some perverse loyalty seemed to demand she defend him. "Captain Levid is an outstanding captain and—"

"What did you say?"

Charlotte backed against the rough passageway wall. The pir—captain now loomed over her, his face a mask of threatening intensity. She tried to keep her voice steady and failed. What had happened to the gentleman? "I . . . I said he was a good captain."

"Before that," Jon growled. "His name. Tell me your betrothed's name." He was almost certain he'd heard her right, but had to be sure.

"Levid." Charlotte's voice was hardly more than a

squeak. "Captain Matthew Levid." Even in the dim light, Charlotte saw him pale beneath his sun-bronzed skin. Then color seemed to flood his face. He grabbed her arm, swinging her back along the passageway.

"What are you doing?" She tried to yank away, but couldn't break away from his iron handed grip. "Ouch!" She stumbled, trying to keep up with his long-legged strides, but he simply pulled her to her feet and continued on his way. Opening a door, he pushed her inside, kicking the portal shut with his boot and stalking her as she backed away from him.

"Where . . . where am I?"

"My cabin" came his terse reply.

And when Charlotte stared up at his glowering face she gasped. It wasn't her imagination. He was her pirate!

# Chapter Two

"Answer me, damnit. Where is he?"

Charlotte squeezed her eyes shut trying to conjure up images of her mother's garden. She concentrated on the sweet smell of roses, but could only catch the pirate's masculine scent. His demanding voice, deep and rumbling as thunder, dominated her mind, blocking any attempt to imagine the song of the wood warblers. She tried to see the sunlight sparkling on the fish pond, the—

"What in the hell are you doing?" The pirate's large hands cupping her shoulders brought Charlotte plunging back to reality. "You can't ignore me." Her eyes flew open to meet the pirate's stormy blue stare. "Now tell me where he is."

"Who?" Oh, she wished her every syllable wasn't a mouselike squeak.

"Captain Levid." He seemed to grind the words through his strong white teeth.

"I . . . I don't know."

The pirate captain obviously didn't like her answer for his expression grew even darker. His jaw clinched till Charlotte noticed a muscle twitch in his cheek. "You'd protect the bastard?"

Charlotte didn't understand, but suddenly that didn't seem important. The waves of nausea in her stomach, which she'd been trying to ignore, now screamed for attention. Charlotte swallowed compulsively. "I think . . . No," she groaned. "I *am* going to be—"

Charlotte never got the last word out. With a speed she hadn't expected in a man so large, the pirate grabbed her, yanked a bucket from beneath his cot, and bent her over it, his arm like a steel band around her waist.

His fingers plucked the ribbons of her bonnet, then pulled it from her head. Even as she heaved into the bucket, more embarrassed than she'd ever been in her life, Charlotte was aware of the comforting movement of his large hand on her back. Through the heavy bombazine, through her corset, she felt his gentle touch.

"Better?"

Leaning over his arm, Charlotte took swift, shallow breaths, trying to calm her body. When he asked again, she nodded, too humiliated to raise up and meet his gaze. But the captain didn't seem to notice her discomfort. He passed her a linen towel, covered the bucket with another one, and seated her on the side of the cot while he set the bucket in the passageway.

Charlotte watched him over the top of the cloth, though when he returned to his cabin she covered her face again.

"I know you're under there."

Charlotte didn't know how long the captain had stood over her, but she'd felt his presence, the warmth of his body, for some time before he spoke. Since his voice wasn't unkind, and because she had no other choice, Charlotte lowered the towel.

Jon almost laughed. The woman's antics reminded him of his sister, Cilla. When she was younger, they'd played a game with her blanket. Cilla would hide beneath it and make believe she was invisible. Jon, ten years older, pretended with her.

Jon studied the woman as she looked up at him. Her eyes were large and dark in her pale oval face, but her skin had lost the hint of green. Though she still appeared ill, Jon realized she was prettier than he'd first thought. Not beautiful, but soft and delicate, the way wildflowers that grew along the marches near Oak Hill were pretty.

Her hair had been a surprise, too. When he'd pulled off that atrocious bonnet, curls had fallen, whisper soft, across his wrist. Now from the splintered sunlight shining through the transom window he could tell it was the color of dark honey. It waved around her face, across her slim shoulders, and down her back. Who would have guessed she'd have hair like that?

"Are you feeling better?" Jon forced his attention back to the problem at hand.

"Yes, thank you." Charlotte reached for the mug he offered and took a sip, coughing into the towel as the liquid burned down her throat. Blinking back tears that sprang to her eyes, Charlotte looked up at the captain questioningly.

"Whiskey," he shrugged. "Helps calm the stomach."

Funny, Charlotte thought, during all her seasick days on the *Balfour*, no one had suggested such a cure. Perhaps because it was worse than the nausea, especially for someone who'd never had anything stronger than wine. Still, the captain apparently meant well. Charlotte thanked him as she set the mug on the small stand beside the cot.

The captain merely shrugged. Catching a chair leg with his boot, he scraped it across the wooden deck and sat down. Charlotte glanced down at the wool blanket covering the cot when she caught herself noticing the way the captain's breeches stretched across his thighs.

"It's difficult until you get your sea legs."

Charlotte looked up. Though the anger was gone from his voice, it was still strong, commanding, and Charlotte wondered if anyone dared not respond when he spoke. She swallowed. "I don't think I shall ever get mine—sea legs, I mean."

He shrugged again—an almost indiscernible lift of his broad shoulders—and stretched his legs out in front of him. The toe of his shiny black boot nearly touched her gown. "You'll get used to the motion. It just takes time."

"How much?" To Charlotte's way of thinking, it had already been too long. "I seemed to be improving on the *Balfour,* but now . . ."

The blush that rose as her words faded added color to her cheeks. Jon could tell by the way her hands fluttered that she was embarrassed by her illness. "It will come."

"You almost sound as if you know from firsthand experience." Charlotte noticed the firm assurance in his voice.

The captain hesitated a moment, then as if coming to a conclusion, admitted, "I used to fight the nausea all the time—still do occasionally."

"You do?" Charlotte couldn't have been more shocked if he'd admitted to being the devil himself.

"Aye . . . but only in very rough seas," he added.

Charlotte wondered briefly if he regretted telling her of his weakness. He seemed a bit uncomfortable as he stood and leaned over his desk. He riffled through some papers as she rose, clutching the bedside table to support her wobbly knees. "But you're the captain." Charlotte realized she'd almost said pirate. She had a hard time reconciling this hard, masculine captain who reminded her so much of her pirate with the illness she'd just experienced.

The look the captain shot her over his shoulder had Charlotte slumping back down.

"You act as if you equate captain with God."

"Of course I don't." There was her mousy squeak again. Charlotte cleared her throat. "It's just that I never knew a captain could be seasick."

"I am *not* seasick!" Jon realized he yelled and lowered his voice. "How many captains do you know, besides Levid, that is?"

He might have stopped shouting, but Charlotte heard the contempt in his voice. "None," she said, refraining from adding that she really didn't know Matthew Levid. Not unless you counted one very stilted meeting two years ago, and several equally formal correspondences. "I was just surprised, that's all."

"Well, don't be. Captains are only men. Besides, I got my sea legs when I was young, long before I ever captained a ship."

When he was young? Charlotte wondered how old he was. He didn't look much older than thirty, but she knew she wasn't a very good judge. She'd spent most of her life around older people: her mother, Mrs. Samuels. Charlotte began to think of herself as old—much older than her twenty-one years. That had been one of the reasons for this ill-fated trip.

"Now, Miss Winston." Jon sat back in the chair, spreading a chart across his knees. "What I'd like from you is Captain Levid's whereabouts."

"I . . . I don't know." His question interrupted her

speculation about his age.

Jon's eyes narrowed. "You expect me to believe that." He was attempting to be civil because . . . hell, he didn't know why he was attempting to be civil.

"It's true." He reminded her of the pirate more than ever.

"You were bound for, what . . . Montreal?"

"Yes." Charlotte hoped it wasn't unpatriotic to admit that.

"To meet Levid?"

"N-no."

The chair squeaked as Jon leaned back. He studied the woman as she in turn studied the balled-up towel in her hands. "He's not worth your loyalty, you know."

Charlotte looked up, her eyes flashing. "He's a captain in His Majesty's Navy." Charlotte's cheeks burned from the oath he swore before kicking back the chair and standing up.

He loomed over her, and it took all of Charlotte's willpower not to cower back against the pillow. "You *will* tell me his destination before this is over."

"Wh-what are you going to do?" She couldn't help it—she cringed. So much for hailing from a long line of British generals.

"Keep you here, for starters."

"In your cabin?" Charlotte glanced around the room that the pir— captain seemed to dominate. The Spartan furnishings were austere and functional. The desk was large, nailed to the floor, and from the scatter of charts on top, frequently used. There were several sea chests, a table, several chairs, and the cot where she sat.

She sat on his bed! Charlotte jumped up when he turned on his heel and strode toward the door. "Where are *you* going to stay?"

The wicked grin he shot over his shoulder made Charlotte gasp. "This is my cabin," he said before his countenance sobered. "But you needn't concern yourself about your virtue. Levid only has one thing I want, and it isn't you."

With those words he left, shutting the door, and if the noise on the other side was any indication, locking it. Charlotte started to sink back on the bed, thought better of it, and chose a chair instead. Closing her eyes, she leaned her head back and slowly massaged her temple.

She needed to think, to figure a way out of this predicament. That is, if there *was* a way out. Deciding any escape from this cabin would only be a temporary measure—where could she hide on an enemy ship?—Charlotte concentrated on what to do when the pirate, no, *captain*, returned.

First, and foremost, she had to stop thinking of him as a pirate, as her pirate. This was a vessel of the United States Navy, and Jonathan Knox was its captain. Even if the two countries were at war as he said, there were still rules governing warfare. Women were just not locked away in cabins anymore. This was the nineteenth century.

"Then why are you locked in here?" Charlotte mumbled before she could stop herself. Shaking her head to dispel that negative thought, Charlotte stood and began pacing the cabin.

The captain seemed a reasonable, even friendly, man at times. He got seasick, for heaven's sake. She'd simply force him to be reasonable. A memory of his icy blue stare when she'd mentioned Matthew Levid's name flashed into her mind.

All right, he seemed very *unreasonable* when it came to Captain Levid. But once he realized that she had no intention of betraying her country, he'd

31

accept it. Charlotte bit her bottom lip, thinking again of his steely, determined gaze. Maybe he wouldn't like accepting it, but he'd have to.

She refused, absolutely refused, to tell Captain Knox where Levid was—even if she had known. She thought again of the last post she'd received from Captain Levid, the one that said he'd return to England after his present duty. Off the coast of Brazil. All right, Charlotte conceded, perhaps she did know that much. But Captain Knox would never get her to admit it. No matter how long he kept her locked up.

Charlotte lifted a chart off the desk, glanced at it, then dropped it, unable to decipher any of the graphs and figures on the sheet. Spying for the British was probably out. But she wouldn't be a traitor.

With that decided, Charlotte concentrated on freshening up to await the captain's return. The mirror attached to the wall was too high for her to see in without climbing on one of the sea trunks. When she did, and leaned to the side to see her reflection, Charlotte grimaced. Her hair had come loose from all its pins and hung in curly disarray about her face. No wonder Captain Knox had made it clear he wasn't interested in ravishing her.

*For which I shall be eternally grateful,* Charlotte assured herself as she began to finger-comb her hair. Once she'd straightened the worst of the tangles, she stepped off the trunk and braided her hair. Pulling out the drawer on the bedside table, Charlotte found a piece of twine to tie around the end of her braid.

Satisfied that she looked as neat as possible under the circumstances, Charlotte sat down to wait. Her nausea had passed, which was good, except that now her stomach seemed to realize how long it had gone without nourishment. It growled, and Charlotte shifted in her seat, looking around the cabin for any food she might not have noticed.

Nothing. The pewter mug still sat on the table, but Charlotte didn't think whiskey was what she needed. She was busy trying not to think of plum pudding and kidney pie when the tapping came at the door. Her eyes widened as a boy of around fourteen stuck his head inside.

It appeared as if the sun and salt had bleached all the color from his hair while burning his skin a reddish brown. He smiled impishly as he entered the cabin. "Captain Knox said to bring you some food. Said you'd probably be hungry."

Then Jonathan Knox didn't plan on starving her into betraying her country. As the boy set a food-laden tray on the table, Charlotte regretted she'd misjudged the captain.

"Ain't much," the boy who identified himself as Joey said, but Charlotte's mouth was already watering. The bread, though it bore little resemblance to the fluffy white biscuits and rolls that Mrs. Samuels baked, seemed free of vermin and relatively fresh. Charlotte took a bite, then remembered her manners.

"Is the captain joining me?"

"Nay. He's busy. Said to eat, he'd see you later."

"I see." Charlotte swallowed the bread, wondering what this boy thought of her being in the captain's cabin. She thought about asking him to help her, but thought better of it. He was, after all, an American.

After Joey left, Charlotte finished her meal, stacked the dishes, and continued to wait. When dusk settled outside the transom windows, she lit a candle . . . and continued to wait. Luckily, she found a cache of books—obviously the captain's. His reading taste tended toward the study of astronomy, and naval warfare, but they were better than nothing.

At first she felt guilty looking through his things,

but decided if he intended to keep her locked in his cabin, he deserved no better.

The candle burned lower, and Charlotte closed the *Catalogue of Nebulae* by William Herchel, and glanced toward the door. She thought she'd been ready for another confrontation with the captain, but now was so tired. Could that be his plan? Did he intend to question her when she was weak with fatigue?

Charlotte wandered toward the cot. She was imagining things again. It wouldn't do Captain Knox any good to question her at any time, because she just didn't know anything for certain.

Besides, the captain might have said he planned to stay here with her, but he obviously hadn't meant it. Charlotte sat on the edge of the bunk. She couldn't remember ever being so tired. Not even toward the end of her mother's illness when she'd sat all those nights by her bed had Charlotte felt such fatigue.

A moan escaped her as she stretched. As tired as she was, Charlotte wasn't certain she could sleep. The nausea was back again—not as strong as before, but enough to remind her she shouldn't have eaten so much chowder.

Her gaze caught on the pewter mug, and she leaned forward. Dark-amber liquid lapped the sides of the mug with each rhythmic motion of the sloop. Closing her eyes, fighting back a wave of nausea, Charlotte grabbed the mug and gulped its contents.

She gasped for breath, her fingers losing their grip on the mug handle. The pewter clanged onto the wooden deck, but Charlotte didn't care. She reached for her throat, tugging at the restraint of her high-necked gown, trying to breathe past the fire in her throat.

So this was his plan all along. The pirate was

simply going to kill her. Poison. What a dreadful way to die. Charlotte sank onto the thin ticking, her eyes fluttering shut. Her last thought before falling asleep was that maybe—just maybe—she wasn't going to die after all.

His inability to insert the key into the lock confirmed to Jon what he already suspected. He'd drunk too much. Not a harmless diversion for a captain during time of war. Duty didn't allow for human frailties, and getting drunk was one of them. It also wasn't like him.

Jon pushed open the door and searched the room for the cause of his uncharacteristic behavior. He found the woman sprawled across his bed—in the exact spot where he wanted to be. Annoyance cleared his head, and caused him to kick the door shut. It slammed with a satisfying bang. That didn't seem to disturb his prisoner one bit. She lay there on her side, one small hand curled under her cheek, looking as uncomfortable as he felt.

Flickering light from the lone candle played across her face, and he stepped closer to the cot. Was she always this pale, or did the black dress make her skin look too white?

Jon's gaze wandered down across her gown, past the swell of her breast, the dip of her waist, the crook of her knee where she had it pulled up, and he shook his head. Why in the hell did she wear such a monstrosity? She was in mourning, that was clear. But this particular dress was sadly dated.

He touched the material covering her hip, thinking again that she looked damned uncomfortable in the stiff gown. How could she sleep all bound up like that? Running his finger down the twilled silk, Jon

35

was annoyed that he even cared. "Oh, hell," he mumbled as he began unfastening the buttons that ran the length of her bodice. She wasn't to blame for Levid's acts.

Jon expected her to wake up. He certainly joggled her around enough trying to peel the long, narrow sleeves off her arms. But she appeared unaware of his attempts to undress her, lying there, seemingly quite content, with a sweet smile on her face. An innocent smile.

Jerking on the bodice, Jon heard the cloth tear and winced. But only for a moment. The dress was deplorable. He was doing the woman a favor by rendering it unwearable. He had an easier time removing the gown after that. He'd undressed his share of women, but always with their cooperation. This was definitely different—and harder.

Her corset was next. Why she wore the damnable thing, he didn't know. Once he'd loosened the tapes and removed the whalebone-stiffened material, it was obvious she didn't need it.

The only thing it had done, as far as he could see, was waffle her shift and make it difficult for her to breathe. Jon pulled the corset from beneath her, turning her body to the side and toward him in the process. Her hand came to rest across his thigh. Jon could feel the heat through his nankin breeches.

His blue eyes narrowed, and Jon studied the woman lying in his bed. She really was appealing, soft and smooth-skinned. Her honey-brown hair shone in the dim light, and Jon brushed the loosely woven braid off her neck. It was creamy white and slender and Jon found himself entranced by the faint pulse that beat in the soft hollow.

He touched it, skimming his finger across her collarbone to the rounded swell beneath. Her breasts were small, delicate, like the rest of her, and Jon traced the curve with the tip of his finger. He could see the shadow of her nipple beneath the linen shift, could feel it harden, respond to him as he touched her. Jon shut his eyes and swallowed a moment before he jerked his hand away.

He lurched to his feet, and rubbed his hand down the side of his breeches. What in the hell was wrong with him? He wasn't some lecher who got his thrills from fondling sleeping women. He took a step backward, and kicked something, sending it clanging across the floor. Bending over, he picked up the empty mug, setting it on the table.

Make that sleeping, inebriated women.

Shaking his head, Jon began unbuttoning his tunic. He glanced at the settee beneath the window, then back at his occupied cot. He hadn't seriously considered the sleeping arrangements when he'd put Charlotte Winston in his cabin, and it appeared too late to ponder it now. The settee was too short for him, and he didn't have the heart to move her. She looked very comfortable now.

Moving to the side of the bed, Jon stripped, deciding at the last to keep on his drawers. Gingerly he moved Miss Charlotte Winston to the far side of the bunk and crawled in, pulling the blanket over both of them. He'd be damned if he couldn't control himself around Matthew Levid's betrothed. He hadn't been at sea *that* long.

Stacking his hands beneath his head, Jon watched the play of candlelight and shadows across the wooden ceiling. He shut his eyes, hoping for sleep, but knowing his mind was too active.

He thought about his younger brother, Christopher, wondering how he was doing—what he was doing—then rebuked himself for wasting time worrying about something he couldn't change. Not now. Not until he could find the *Scorpion* and that bastard, Levid.

The woman at his side moaned in her sleep, temporarily taking Jon's mind off Christopher, and he glanced her way. As a key to Levid's whereabouts, Charlotte Winston wasn't much. But she was all he had. If she was heading for Canada, then Levid also might be. Might be. Or he might be anywhere in the whole damn Atlantic Ocean. But she probably could narrow it down for him a bit.

Jon took a deep breath trying to calm his rage. He'd find Levid. He'd get her to tell what she knew. Then he'd get his brother and the other members of his crew the British captain had impressed back.

She moaned again, tossing onto her side, and Jon jerked as her arm flung across his chest. She was not a delicate sleeper. She seemed to want the entire cot for herself. He lifted her hand, determined to show her which side of the bunk was hers, when she snuggled against his side.

He thought she might be awake, but when he scrunched around to look at her, long, dark lashes formed a crescent across her cheeks. She wriggled closer, throwing her leg over his. Jon could feel the soft whisper of her breath against his skin.

"Hell," he mumbled twisting around to blow out the flickering candle. Then he slipped his arm under her shoulders, cradling her closer, and shutting his eyes, fell asleep.

# Chapter Three

It was so pleasant. Charlotte felt warm and safe, and protected. It was a dream. She knew that. For her mother was alive and well. Even in sleep, Charlotte knew that couldn't be. The memory of the past five years, of her mother's suffering and pain, was too vivid to be forgotten.

But as dreams went, this one was wonderful. Charlotte snuggled closer to the fuzzy warmth and breathed deeply. Something tickled her nose and lazily she lifted her head to brush it aside.

It continued to pester, and Charlotte wet her lips tasting something salty—like . . . like seawater. As this filtered through to her groggy brain, her hand touched something warm, hair-roughened, and firm.

Charlotte's eyes flew open.

Just as quickly as she realized she was intimately wrapped around the pirate, her hand on his chest, the events of the previous day exploded back to her.

She jerked away as if she'd touched a stove—or the devil.

"Don't." The protest came rumbling deep and sleep-roughened, from the captain's broad chest. He turned, reached out, and landed his hand on

Charlotte's breast with a satisfied sigh.

She screamed.

Jon woke with a start, searching for the cause of the obnoxious noise. His eyes widened as he found it. For such a tiny thing she certainly could bellow. "Be quiet," he growled, relieved when the screeching ceased.

Charlotte sucked in her breath. "Get your hand off me!"

"My hand isn't—" Jon glanced down, snapped his hand away, and finished his sentence. "On you."

Her breathing came in shallow gasps and Jon couldn't tell if she was angry or frightened. His gaze dropped to her breast. Her nipple still pressed beadlike and hard against the soft linen fabric. He wished it were against his palm.

"You're vile!" Charlotte's gaze had followed his, and now she clutched the blanket to her chin.

Angry. She was definitely more angry than scared. Jon shrugged as she began her tirade.

"How could you? How could you touch me like that, and get into this bed with me?" Her gaze drifted across his naked chest, and Charlotte's eyes widened. "What else did you do? Oh, no." She fought the sob, but it escaped anyway. "How could you?" Her tirade ended as it had begun, except now she appeared piteously close to tears.

"I didn't do anything." Damn, he hated tears.

"Don't deny it." Charlotte sniffed. "Your hand was . . . You touched me."

"No more than you touched me."

"*What?*" Her dark eyes, staring at him across the pillow grew enormous.

"You heard me. If someone should be complaining about touching," which he definitely wasn't, "it should be me."

40

"Why I never . . ." Oh, but she had, and she knew it. He obviously did, too.

"Lady, you not only touched, you sprawled, you crawled all over, you—"

"Shut up!" Charlotte clasped her hands over her ears in case he continued. But he didn't. He stopped, and his expression softened.

"Listen. You were asleep. You didn't know what you were doing. Didn't—"

"Wh-what exactly did I . . . did we do?" Charlotte wished she could remember, but her mind could only grasp filtered images of warmth and comfort.

"Nothing."

"What do you mean, nothing?" The tears were threatening again, and Charlotte blinked. "You just said—"

"What in the hell do you take me for?" Jon's eyes narrowed when she made no response. "I don't make love to unconscious women." He quickly suppressed the pang of guilt that washed over him for touching her last night. "Besides, if I'd made love to you, you'd have known it." Jon glanced toward the empty mug on the table. "No matter how much liquor you'd imbibed."

Charlotte ignored his reference to the whiskey. He'd given it to her, for heaven's sake. "I didn't mean to . . . to imply you'd . . ."

The captain cocked his raven brow.

All right, so she had. But she wasn't going to admit it to him, any more than she'd admit she didn't know exactly what it was they were talking about. She'd heard the cook's helper whispering one day to a shopkeeper, and she'd guessed they were discussing *that*. But Charlotte had only been able to catch bits and pieces of the conversation, for it had been heavily spattered with giggles.

Of course, Charlotte had imagined, usually about the pirate. But her mental images always stopped with kisses, and a vague ravishment.

He denied ravishing her, and she didn't think he'd kissed her. She didn't remember it anyway. And though she hated to agree with the captain, Charlotte had the strangest feeling that if he *had* kissed her, she'd remember. Charlotte lifted her hand, her fingers flitting quickly across her bottom lip.

"Nothing happened," Jon said, his voice sounding uncharacteristically gruff. He watched her fingertips absently outline the curve of her lip. Now that he could see her in full light, without that stupid hat to shadow her face, he noticed things about her. Like her mouth. How soft it looked.

Jon swallowed. He had an almost uncontrollable urge to see if it felt as soft and dewy as it looked. But then he remembered who else must find that mouth enticing. Had Levid kissed her? The thoughts of this woman moaning under Matthew Levid turned his stomach.

All right. She would accept that there'd been no ravishment, no shared kisses. Charlotte tried to remain calm. But why was he in bed with her? Her knuckles grew white as she clutched the blanket. And where was her dress? And corset!

"Captain Knox." His eyes shifted to meet hers, and she felt the impact of his blue gaze. Had her imaginary pirate's eyes been that blue? Charlotte cleared her throat. "May I ask why you found it necessary to sleep in the same bed as . . . as . . ." Charlotte couldn't believe she was having this conversation with him. Not while she was still lying beside him, sharing a pillow. Oh, they were no longer touching, but they were close. Close enough for her to notice things about him, like his smell, so

42

musky and warm, and the black stubble that darkened his jaw and emphasized the cleft in his chin.

His dark brows lifted. "Where else was I to sleep?" he asked logically.

"Another cabin, perhaps."

"I told you yesterday, we were sharing this one until you tell me what you know about Levid's whereabouts."

So he had. "The settee then."

"Too small. I'm not a short man." He stretched, and though he didn't touch her, the movement tightened the blanket across Charlotte's bare legs.

She couldn't keep up this facade of calm any longer. "Where is my dress?" she yelled, blinking to keep back the tears.

He shifted again, glancing over his shoulder, and Charlotte noticed the rumpled heap of black on the cabin floor. Her cheeks reddened when she noticed her corset beside it.

"I want it."

He shook his head, a dark, sleep-tossed curl falling across his forehead. "It won't do you any good."

"Why?"

"It's torn."

"Torn." Charlotte repeated the word as if she'd never heard it before. "Torn?"

He shrugged, that nonchalant lifting of his broad shoulders she'd noticed yesterday, and something inside her snapped. How could he take all that had befallen her—all *he'd* done to her—so lightly?

Charlotte sat up, her hair tangling around her shoulders in wild disarray and glared at him. Compared to the other things that had happened to her, a torn dress was nothing. It certainly wasn't like being kidnapped off a ship and being held captive in a cabin or waking up in bed with a strange man. Charlotte knew that. But then the woman who glared down at the captain didn't feel like Charlotte. At least not the calm, sweet Charlotte who'd been commended after her mother's funeral by the Reverend Haversham for her patience and even temper—her calm, sweet disposition.

"You . . . you . . . *pirate*. You ripped my dress! You . . ." Words failed her. In frustration she balled her fist and hit him in the chest. Hard.

Jon was more shocked than hurt as he grabbed her wrist, stilling her next blow. "What in the hell is wrong with you?" She'd acted almost mousy before, but the mouse was now a lion. She'd given him a glimpse on deck of what lay beneath the quiet, retiring exterior, but it was nothing like this. Her dark eyes sparkled and color flooded her pale face.

"Let go of me, blackguard, cretin . . . bastard!"

She had her voice back with a vengeance. The use of her arms, too. Her vocabulary shocked Jon so, coming from that sweet, innocent mouth, that he dropped her wrist. It took the force of her next blow aimed much lower to make him grab for her again. When he missed the flailing hand he did the first thing he could think of to stop her.

With one quick motion Jon rolled on top of her. Charlotte quieted immediately, the air she could pull into her lungs needed for breathing rather than venting her anger. Her attacking hands stilled also, now drifting like fallen leaves to the ticking.

"Calm now?"

She was anything but calm, Charlotte thought as impotent anger flowed through her, but she nodded. What else could she do with this huge man pressing her into the thin mattress?

"Where did you ever learn language like that?

Your honorable Captain Levid?"

Charlotte nodded again, this time with a defiant jerk of her chin. She glared at him, daring him to guess her admission was a lie.

The one and only conversation she'd had with Matthew Levid had been polite and mannerly—banal . . . boring. But it seemed to annoy Jonathan Knox to think she conferred often with Captain Levid, and right now she wanted him annoyed. She wanted him angry . . . as angry as she herself. Obviously she was no match for him physically—was stupid to even try to hurt him—but she could raise his ire.

He shifted, and though the move relieved her of a portion of his weight, it also reminded Charlotte of her vulnerability. She couldn't move. She could feel every hard muscle from his long thighs, along his flat stomach, to the broad chest that flattened her breasts. Her eyes widened. Though most of his weight now rested on his elbows leaving her free to breathe, Charlotte found that simple task difficult. There didn't seem to be enough air in the room to fill her lungs. Her lips opened.

What was he doing? Just what in the hell was he doing? Jon rolled off her as quickly as he'd rolled on. He was hard, achingly so, and Jon glanced over at the woman—Levid's woman—wondering if she'd noticed. Her eyes were closed, long, dark lashes forming a shadowy web across her high cheekbones. Jon looked away quickly.

My God, there it was again. An almost uncontrollable urge to kiss her. Her lips, the slim column of her neck, the breasts he'd touched last night.

He didn't assault women. Lord knew his parents had reared him with more respect for the gender than that. Jon shoved away thoughts of what his mother would say about his present position. This was different. This was war. And beyond that, he certainly had his reasons for wanting Levid, for using whatever means at his disposal to find him.

But he didn't take women—unwilling women. Jon glanced back at her. Her still-closed eyes gave him the opportunity to let his gaze drift lower. Her chest rose and fell with each breath, clearly outlining her breasts, and her nipples. Her beaded nipples.

Jon swallowed and looked away. There had been a moment when he'd been on top of her, when he'd looked into her dark eyes, that he'd wondered if she were unwilling. Had it been his imagination or were her eyes filled with the same desire that had shot through him?

He had to get out of this bed before he *did* do something. But when Jon started to throw off the blanket, he remembered his state of undress, not to mention the present condition of his lower body. The way she'd slept, sprawled across him, had been bad enough, but lying on her, sinking into her softness . . .

Jon hesitated, then, angry with himself, bit out an oath and jumped from the bunk. This woman had to be at least twenty—certainly old enough to know what happens between men and women. But Jon kept his back to her as he jerked on his breeches.

Finding her someplace else to sleep in his cabin was the first order of business today. He refused to spend another night suffering in unrelieved arousal. Jon threw water on his face, then glanced into the mirror. She watched him suspiciously, the blanket now clutched under her chin. A vision of how she'd looked earlier, the blanket pooled around her waist flashed through his head.

Combing his fingers back through sleep-rumpled

hair, Jon turned. "I'll have another cot brought in here today."

"If you don't mind, I'd prefer a cabin of my own."

"Oh, but I do mind." Jon had to admire her gall. She looked like a cross between a timid virgin and a siren, yet she didn't hesitate to speak up to him. The bunched blanket left one smooth shoulder bare, enticingly so—something he was certain she didn't know. Jon dragged his eyes back to her face. "I thought I'd made myself clear yesterday. You're staying here until you tell me either where Levid is or his destination."

Charlotte let loose her stranglehold on the blanket. "And I told *you* yesterday that I don't know anything." There. She couldn't make herself any clearer.

"Then I suppose you'll remain in this cabin."

"You can't keep me here." What happened to her strong determination? She sounded like a whining child.

"I can and I will." Jon pulled on his tunic, jamming the brass buttons through their holes. "There's no one to stop me. I want Levid. And you're going to help me get him." He turned on his heel and stalked from the cabin.

Charlotte sat staring at the closed door, hearing the now unmistakable click of the lock. What was she to do now? She closed her eyes, but all she could see was the captain.

Had he known what was in her mind? Had he suspected in that one moment when he lay on top of her that she wished he were the pirate? That she wished for the ravishing she knew the pirate would give her? Charlotte touched her hot cheek and lay back against the pillow.

\*        \*        \*

47

"She's refusing to eat."

"What?" Jon completed his sweep of the horizon before snapping shut the spyglass. Dusk was veiling another day of billowy clouds, fair winds, and no sign of enemy vessels. Jon rubbed the ache between his brows. "What's the problem?" he repeated, turning.

"Your hostage," Adam Burke explained, leaning against a belaying pin. "She's decided not to eat anything."

For a moment Jon said nothing, only stared at Adam. They'd grown up together on Maryland's eastern shore, their plantations were close, the ties between the two families closer still. They'd been friends since Jon could remember. Even the years Adam spent studying in England hadn't dimmed that friendship. And when Adam signed on the *Eagle*, they'd continued their accord, discussing philosophies and strategies as earnestly as they'd once contrived ways to make mischief. But Jon hadn't told Adam about Charlotte Winston.

Jon turned to stare out over the water. "She'll eat when she gets hungry."

"Perhaps." Adam shifted, joining his friend in contemplating the spattering of whitecaps that doted the gray waters. "But Joey is worried."

"He come to you?"

"Aye. I suppose he figured as ship's doctor, I could make her eat."

"Can you?"

Adam chuckled. "No, I can't."

"I didn't think so." Jon scrubbed his hand across his whiskered jaw. He'd forgotten to shave this morning because of the woman and now this. "She'll eat when she gets hungry," he repeated. "Or maybe she's seasick. She was yesterday."

48

"That's not what it sounds like to me." Seeing Jon's cocked brow, Adam continued. "If Joey's memory is accurate, her message is pretty clear. She refuses to eat until you mend the clothes you tore off her, cease sleeping with her, and allow her a cabin of her own." Adam ticked the demands off on his fingers.

Both raven brows inched up. "She said that?"

"According to Joey she did," Adam confirmed.

"The woman has a lot of brass."

"I'd say she's not the only one. What's going on here, Jon? I've never known you to take a woman against her will before. Hell, I've never known you to *have* to."

"Well, I have to with this one. And before you lecture me—"

"I never lecture."

Ignoring the interruption, Jon continued. "Let me assure you, this isn't what you think."

"You aren't keeping a woman captive in your cabin?"

Jon's eyes narrowed. Anyone but Adam would take it as a clue to cease this line of questioning. "I am."

"Then you didn't rip her clothes off her?"

Jon just stared.

"Or sleep with her?"

"She's betrothed to Matthew Levid." Jon watched the amusement fade from Adam's face. "She's one of the passengers from the *Balfour*, possibly on her way to meet Levid." Jon paused. "She won't say. But her vessel was bound for Canada."

"You think Levid's there?"

Jon raked a tangle of dark hair off his forehead. "I don't know. The woman's father is in Montreal . . . a General Winston. You ever heard of him?"

"No."

Jon shrugged. "She might be going to Canada just to be with him. But even if Levid isn't there, I'm willing to bet she knows something about where he is."

"But she won't tell you?"

"Hell no, she won't tell me!" Jon lowered his voice, glancing around to see if any tars had noticed his outburst. Looking back out to sea he squared his shoulders. "She will."

Adam leaned against the rail studying his friend. "You know I'd never tell you how to run your ship, but—"

"I don't need your advice, Adam."

"But this isn't really about captaining a sloop. This is personal."

"For God's sake, Adam." Jon pivoted toward his friend. "Levid has Christopher . . . and Belmont, and Andrews, and half a dozen others."

"You think I don't know that? Hell, I signed on with you because I wanted to help get your brother back."

"I know." Jon clasped his friend's shoulder, then let his hand drop. "It's just so damn frustrating. I don't know what to do."

"You are doing all you can."

"Harassing British ships, hoping to run across the *Scorpion*."

Adam brushed back his blond hair. "It's all you can do."

"All I *could* do . . . before I found Charlotte Winston."

"Jon, the woman isn't to blame for something Levid did."

"I know that. You needn't worry. She isn't going to starve to death. I'm putting you in charge of seeing she doesn't." Jon grinned when he heard Adam's

50

mumbled oath. "I'll even help by giving in to some of her demands. Jack can take care of her dress."

"Evans?"

"Sure. He can mend sails, why not a gown? And I've already ordered another cot moved into my cabin. Why don't you go talk to her. Tell her that."

"What about giving her a cabin of her own?"

"No." Jon's reply was abrupt and succinct as he turned on his heel. "She stays where she is."


Charlotte expected the captain and couldn't decide if she was relieved or disappointed when a man she didn't know entered the cabin.

The stranger who introduced himself as Adam Burke was tall, broad-shouldered, and handsome. Not darkly handsome like the captain, but fair, with light hair that shone golden in the candlelight. Like Captain Knox, his hair was cropped short and his skin bronzed by the sun.

Unlike the captain he smiled, a warm, friendly smile that Charlotte couldn't resist returning.

"How are you feeling, Miss Winston?" he asked as he sat in the chair across from Charlotte. "I'm the ship's doctor."

"Quite well."

"Not even a little hungry?"

Charlotte cringed. She'd hoped no one but the captain and Joey would hear of her refusal to eat . . . or of her demands. It had been embarrassing enough to tell them to Joey. But when she'd gotten the idea to refuse food, she decided she needed to let the captain know. Surely he wouldn't let her starve.

Adam didn't wait for an answer. "I realize the ship's fare is not the best, but I do believe it is better than nothing."

"I'm not interested in eating."

"Not even if I come offering compromises."

"From Captain Knox?" Charlotte couldn't keep the excitement from her voice. She was awfully hungry and hoped her growling stomach couldn't be heard all over the sloop.

"Aye. But I see you've already received one of your demands." Adam motioned toward the bed pushed against the far wall.

"I did not ask for a cot. I wish to be free of the captain's presence."

"A separate cabin?" Adam leaned back and crossed his legs.

"Exactly."

"I'm afraid he won't go along with that. You have certain information he wants."

Charlotte sighed. "The whereabouts of Captain Levid. I've explained that I won't tell him that."

"Because of loyalty to your betrothed?"

"And to my country." Charlotte didn't explain that she felt little loyalty to the man himself.

"What if I told you Captain Knox's interest in Levid has very little to do with the war?"

"She very likely wouldn't believe you."

Caught unaware by his voice, Charlotte glanced up to see Jonathan Knox leaning against the doorjamb. Pushing away from the frame, he entered the room, his eyes locked with Charlotte's. Again she was struck by his resemblance to her imaginary pirate. "Well, Miss Winston, am I correct?"

Charlotte raised her chin. "Yes."

"As I thought." Jon continued to stare at her a moment longer before shifting his attention to Adam. "I've sent for some dinner. You're welcome to join Miss Winston and me if you like."

"I won't eat." Charlotte's chin jutted forward and

her eyes dared him to force her. But her defiance seemed lost on the captain, for he never glanced her way. He seemed engrossed in his conversation with Adam Burke, who also refused the captain's invitation, though in more polite terms.

"As you wish," Jon said as Adam stood to leave. "I assume you've assured yourself of the young lady's health and safety."

Adam chuckled. "I don't think there is any immediate danger of starvation."

"Good." Jon walked his friend to the door. "By the way, how many days can she go without food before . . ." The captain paused. "Well, before?"

"I can't be certain. She's rather thin to begin with. Perhaps—"

"Would you stop discussing me as if I weren't present?" Charlotte bolted from the chair, but her theatrics were lost as both men left the room, closing the door behind them without ever looking her way.

She couldn't believe it. They didn't care if she didn't eat. They didn't care if she lived or died.

Charlotte sank back into the chair wishing now she hadn't interrupted the doctor before he said how many days it would take her to die. Oh, God! She didn't want to go this way, alone on an enemy ship. And hungry. She was so hungry.

Closing her eyes, Charlotte imagined a fine roast of beef, glistening in its own juices. She could smell it, almost taste it when she heard the door open again. And then she knew why her imagination had seemed so real. There on a huge tray that dwarfed the cabin boy was a plate piled high with thick slabs of beef. Behind him strode the captain carrying another tray containing pewter plates, a bowl of biscuits, and a jug of wine.

Charlotte felt the saliva pool in her mouth and

swallowed. She would not give in.

"Your merchant vessel was carrying some cattle," the captain said as he cleared a place on the table. "I had some of my crew slaughter one. It's not often we get fresh beef."

He could have been talking to himself for all the attention he paid Charlotte as he went about setting the table for two. When he'd finished, he dismissed Joey, telling him to go to the galley and eat his fill. Then the captain sat across from Charlotte and began filling his plate. Generously.

Just before his fork, laden with juicy beef reached his mouth, Jon glanced up. "Help yourself. You needn't stand on ceremony."

Charlotte tore her eyes away from the meat. She swallowed. "I . . . I won't eat until you set me free from this cabin."

Jon rested his elbow on the table, the meat temptingly near his lips. "Tell me where to find Levid."

"No."

He jammed the food into his mouth, slowly chewing and savoring the flavor before commenting on her refusal. "Then you stay."

Charlotte couldn't believe it. Scraping the chair against the wooden deck, she rose. Arms crossed, she sat on the settee at the far end of the cabin—anything to distance herself from the wonderful aroma of the meat and biscuits.

She glared at him. But the beast only ignored her as he ate his meal, slowly and with relish. Charlotte was certain the appreciative noises he made were for her benefit, but it didn't help as she watched each and every bite he took.

By the time he'd finished—two helpings— Charlotte felt her resolve wavering. What difference did it make if she ate?

"It's late," he said, seemingly to no one in particular, as he pushed his plate aside. Then while Charlotte watched, he stood, stretched, and began undressing. His tunic went first, then his boots. Bare-chested, he poured some water into a small bowl and, cupping his hands, splashed it over his face. Still ignoring her, the captain dried himself, sat down on the edge of the bed—the bed they'd shared the previous night—and blew out the candle.

The cabin was dark, but Charlotte could make out the sound of material against skin—the captain removing his breeches—and the groaning of the cot as he lay down. Then save, for the soft slapping of water against the hull, all was quiet.

How long she sat there on the settee thinking about the leftover food on the table Charlotte didn't know. But it was more than enough time for the captain to go to sleep. She listened for his even breathing, then carefully felt her way to the table.

Food had never tasted so good.

Charlotte stuffed a biscuit into her mouth, chewing as quietly as she could. She ate a slice of beef and two more biscuits before making her way to the cot in the corner.

On the other cot the captain closed his eyes and smiled before turning on his side and falling asleep.

# Chapter Four

Charlotte dropped her fiasco of a fast. There was no reason to pretend any longer. The morning after she'd eaten the leftovers of the captain's dinner, he'd simply looked at her, glanced at the now empty-platter, and cocked a raven brow. Without a word he told her he knew. And Charlotte felt a flush creep up her neck and blossom across her cheeks.

She wasn't very brave or daring.

For years she'd read books about the exploits of others, imagining herself in their place. In her make-believe world she always charged ahead, inspired others . . . saved the day. Even when she fantasized about the pirate, everything worked out for the best. She'd been exciting—captivating—and in the end, the pirate had succumbed to her charms.

But real life wasn't like that.

Taking care of her mother had taught her about life—about the pain and sorrow it could bring. And she'd been strong. Everybody said so. For five years, with the help of Mrs. Samuels, the housekeeper, she'd sat up through the nights when her mother was in pain. She'd read to her on the good days and nursed her through the bad ones.

But this was different. It took a different kind of strength to fight the captain, and apparently she didn't have it. She'd vowed not to eat until the captain released her from his cabin, and she'd folded at the first sign of hunger.

But there was one thing she hadn't done. She hadn't told the captain where Captain Levid might be. He asked her every day, and every day she glared at him, tight-lipped.

He was tiring of the ritual.

It had been four days since the captain stuck her in this cabin, and she could tell he expected her to bare her soul by now—after all, she'd shown him very little but weakness to this point. Each time she saw him, each time she refused to disclose Levid's destination, the captain's jaw clenched tighter, the fan of tiny lines framing his eyes grew deeper.

And he reminded her more and more of her pirate.

He wanted to throttle her. Charlotte noticed the way his long fingers curled into a fist when she jutted her chin forward in defiance. He probably wished he were a pirate so he could threaten to make her walk the plank.

But the truth was, he never touched her. He only paced the cabin, stopping every now and then to glare at her from narrowed steely-blue eyes as he questioned her. He looked dark, powerful, and menacing towering over her, and Charlotte knew she should be afraid. But the truth was, she wasn't.

Perhaps her lack of fear stemmed from the fact the captain reminded her so much of her fantasy pirate. Or maybe it was because she knew he slept on his stomach, burying his cheek into the pillow, or that he had a difficult time shaving the cleft in his chin, or that he snored.

Charlotte knew Captain Knox had put her in his

58

cabin as a punishment, and most of the time she felt duly penalized. But that didn't change the fact that it was hard to fear someone when you could lie awake at night, feeling the gentle sway of the cradling ocean, and listen to him snore.

"What in the hell is all this?"

Charlotte jumped at the sound of the captain's booming voice. The book she was reading—or rather *had* been reading before she'd started thinking about him—plopped to the floor.

"Wh-what are you doing here?" If the captain was anything, he was a creature of habit. She assumed his naval training was the reason for that. And during the four days she'd been here, he followed the same routine. Once he left the cabin in the morning, he didn't return until late, until the second dog watch. But he was here now, and the sun had barely reached its pinnacle. And he didn't look pleased as his scowl shifted from the rope crisscrossing the cabin to Charlotte.

"This is my cabin, is it not?"

Of course it was his cabin. He hadn't allowed her anyplace else except for brief strolls along the deck. Charlotte considered telling him that but decided fueling his anger wouldn't be wise. Apparently it was merely a rhetorical question, for he went on without waiting for a reply.

"Then would you tell me why it resembles the laundry room?" As he spoke, the captain reached for the item draped across the rope closest to him.

Charlotte felt her face flame as he plucked her pantaloons off the line and held them up for inspection. They were still damp, and the ruffled cotton hung limply from his large, dark hand.

"Give me that." Without a thought to the conse-quences, Charlotte snatched her underwear from him, tugging when he held on to it for an instant. "My clothes were dirty so I washed them."

"And hung them in my cabin."

"What else was I to do with them? String them from the yardarm?" Embarrassed by her outburst as well as the intimate apparel—*her* intimate apparel—draped in full view, Charlotte grabbed at her clothes. Whipping the clothes off the ropes made the hemp twirl, slapping a wet petticoat against the captain. It clung to the dark-blue wool of his tunic.

"Oh, my!" Charlotte dove for the petticoat, pausing only when Captain Knox's strong fingers circled her wrist.

"For God's sake, leave them." Realizing she ignored him, continuing to yank wet garments off the ropes with her free hand, Jon batted away the petticoat and hauled her against him. "I said to leave them." He tried to make his voice gruff—the damn woman wouldn't listen—but he found the sound oddly subdued.

"B-but I couldn't." Charlotte tilted her head, staring up into the pirate's—*captain's* bluer than blue eyes. She tried to take a deep breath, but she couldn't seem to fill her lungs. Her breasts were flattened against his hard chest. His scent surrounded her—the same untamed fragrance she'd come to identify as masculine. He smelled of salt air and fresh, brisk winds, and . . . and damp wool. Damp wool?

Tearing her gaze away from his, Charlotte glanced down. Near her hip was bundled the underclothes she'd pulled from the ropes. The dampness had seeped through her gown, and obviously was also wetting the captain's clothes.

When Charlotte first tried to push away, she met with resistance, but then suddenly the captain released her wrist, and stepped back.

60

She could breathe better now, but he still stood close enough for her to notice the cleft in his chin, the disgruntled expression on his face as he plucked at the damp wool. Charlotte opened her mouth to apologize, but he spoke first. "I've seen women's underthings before. Hell, I've seen *your* underthings before."

Oh, he could be so crude! Remarks like this—and knowing he *had* seen her underthings and with her in them—worried her more than any fear she might have of him.

Blinking back tears, Charlotte looked away from him. Washing her clothes had seemed like such a good idea even if she did have to do it in saltwater. Not only would it feel wonderful to have something clean next to her body, but getting the rope from Joey, stringing it, and washing the clothes had given her something to do. She could only read so many books on the stars and navigation and keep her sanity.

Charlotte glanced back at him. "What do you want from me?"

"I think I've made myself clear on that point." The captain didn't miss a beat.

"Matthew Levid," Charlotte sighed. She wished she'd never heard of the man. Of course she'd wished that before ever setting foot on the *Eagle*.

"Precisely. Tell me where he is," Jon interrupted when she began to protest. "Or what you know of his plans, and I will let you leave this cabin. There are several other women we took off the *Balfour*. You may stay with them, never need see me again and . . ." He paused and Charlotte could swear she recognized the same teasing light in his eyes she'd noticed when she first met him—before he knew of her connection with Matthew Levid. "You may hang your clothes all over the ship for all I care."

Why not tell him what she knew? Charlotte inwardly cringed when that traitorous thought popped into her mind. But in all honesty, it wouldn't help him. Of that she was certain. And it would make her life so much simpler.

Charlotte had only received two letters from Matthew Levid since their betrothal. The last, posted from Bristol, had mentioned that he was sailing for the South Atlantic, off the coast of Brazil, and that when he returned to England they would be wed. Though it gave no time frame, it had been sent nearly nine months earlier. And it was one of the reasons she'd left England. She had no desire to wed Matthew Levid.

But she didn't wish to see him captured by Captain Knox, either. Captain Levid *was* in the Royal Navy, and England and America *were* at war. And she would not be a traitor to her country. Her loyalty ran too deep for that.

As if he could read her mind, Jonathan Knox cupped her shoulders, pulled her over to a chair, and gently lowered her into it. He took the balled-up clothes from her and laid them on the table. The dark, damp spot on her gown matched the one on his tunic. It felt cold against her suddenly hot skin as he leaned toward her.

"I assure you . . ." Jon began, "my reasons for seeking Captain Levid are personal, not related to the war." Maybe if he told her why he sought her Matthew Levid she'd cooperate. She seemed like a reasonable person—Jon glanced at the damp underwear hanging across his cabin—most of the time.

"Are you telling me you won't attack his ship?"

"Hell, yes, I'll attack his ship!" Jon forced air through his clenched teeth. What did she think, that

Levid would voluntarily allow his vessel to be boarded? Jon took a calming breath. He wanted to discuss this with her calmly, he really did. But she had a way of making him forget his best intentions. He plopped into the seat across from her and leaned his elbows on the table, willing to try again, then glanced across at her. "Why do you do that?"

Charlotte's lashes fluttered open. "Do what?"

"Shut your eyes like that. I've noticed it before. Are you trying to pretend me gone? Is that the game you play, Miss Winston?"

"No," Charlotte squeaked. She didn't wish him gone. It was herself she pretended had escaped. And she had to stop it. How embarrassing if he ever realized the type of visions her imagination could conjure up.

He studied her with a speculative eye as if he doubted her denial, and Charlotte forced herself to meet his gaze. "It's easy enough to be rid of me. Just tell me what I want to know."

Charlotte raised her chin defiantly. She would tell him nothing. Let him think, as he did, that Levid was headed for Canada. The closer they sailed toward Montreal the better. Besides being unpatriotic to England, telling Captain Knox the truth might lead him to turn his ship south, and Charlotte definitely didn't want that. If nothing more it would prolong her time on his vessel.

She could handle Captain Knox, Charlotte thought as she watched his jaw tighten. Turning on the heel of his boot, he stalked from the cabin. The slamming door drowned out Charlotte's sigh of relief. After a moment Charlotte began rehanging her clothes. With any luck they would dry and she could bundle them away before he returned for the night. Innocent as it was, she didn't want any more reminders of the

63

intimacy they'd shared.

"Whoa, Jon."

Barging around a corner of the aft passageway, Jon bumped into Adam Burke. Grabbing Adam's sleeve, Jon saved his friend from what might have been a painful acquaintance with the deck.

Righting himself, Adam straightened his tunic. "Where are you off to in such a hurry?" Adam chuckled. "If we're being attacked I missed the call to arms."

Throwing the doctor a wry look, Jon continued along the passageway at a more sedate pace.

"Seriously, Captain. Where were you off to in such a hurry," Adam asked, falling in step with Jon. Wooden lanterns swung with each roll of the ship, sending undulating patterns of light across the splintery wall.

"Nowhere."

"Well, for having no destination in mind you certainly were—"

"She's going to drive me to Bedlam."

"Ah." Adam's smile was knowing. "I gather you've been visiting with our Miss Winston."

"Unlike you, Adam, I do not *visit* with Miss Winston. I interrogate her."

"Oh ho," Adam laughed. "I gather your *interrogation* didn't go well." When Jon didn't crack a smile Adam stopped. "I'd planned to take Miss Winston for a stroll on deck, but if her mood is anything like yours, perhaps I should wait."

"Waiting is probably a good idea, unless you wish to lose yourself in the labyrinth she's made of my cabin."

"Labyrinth?"

"Aye. She's done her wash and has it strewn all—Oh, hell, what difference does it make? The truth is, she won't tell me a damn thing about Levid's destination."

"Do you think she knows anything?"

Climbing the ladder, Jon stepped out on deck. He breathed deep of the brisk salt-laden air, then shrugged. "I can't be sure what she knows. She's traveling alone—during wartime—and she's betrothed to the bastard. It's hard to believe she doesn't know anything. But she sure as hell won't tell me."

"Perhaps you're not using the right approach."

Striding to the rail, Jon shook his head. "I've tried everything. I've been calm." He paused, turning toward Adam. "Downright reasonable." Jon shook his head. "Nothing. I even yelled, tried to scare her. She simply shuts her eyes, pretends I'm not there, and clamps her mouth shut." Jon leaned his forearms over the rail.

"You must be losing your touch."

Jon examined his friend through narrowed eyes. "What's that supposed to mean?"

"Nothing really." Adam shrugged. "I just never knew you to have this much trouble wooing a woman."

"I'm not wooing her, for God's sake." A sudden image of how she felt in his arms minutes ago flashed through his mind. "I'm trying to get information out of her." Jon turned, folding his arms across his chest. "And you seem to be taking this whole thing very lightly. You do realize she might hold the key to finding Christopher."

"Believe me, I know." Adam's face lost its amused expression. "I'm just not sure you're going about this the right way."

"The right way? Are you suggesting chains and

torture? Hell, Adam, weren't you the one bellyaching to me about her starving to death? And who insisted that she needed time above deck in the sunshine?"

"She's such a frail little thing."

"Aye. Well, that frail little thing has a stubborn streak as wide as this ocean." Jon shaded his eyes, scanning the hazy horizon.

"Never knew a woman that didn't."

Jon merely grunted.

"Or one that couldn't be persuaded to change her mind . . . given the right incentive."

Jon rubbed his chin. "Hmmm. Maybe torture isn't such a bad idea. I could lock her in the hold, shake out the cat, whip—"

"Would you be serious?"

"Hell, I am serious." Jon raked his fingers back through his wind-tossed hair. "Not about sticking her in the hold . . . I wouldn't do that." Jon sighed, thinking of the last time he'd seen his younger brother. "But almost anything else."

"Seduce her."

"What?" Even as accustomed as he was to Adam's outlandish ideas, Jon was surprised.

"You heard me. I've never known you to fail to persuade a woman once you set your mind on it."

Jon laughed. He couldn't help himself. Clasping Adam on the shoulder, Jon explained the obvious. "She thinks she's protecting her betrothed from the enemy. Hell, she *is* protecting her betrothed from the enemy. That's a little different than convincing a woman to . . . well, you know what I mean."

Considering the subject closed, Jon turned to inspect the rigging. Extra canvas had been added and they were making good time, even sailing against the prevailing winds. He only wished he were certain that northwest toward Canada was the direction they should take. His orders were general—harass British shipping. As long as he stayed in the shipping lanes, and made a general nuisance of himself, he could persue Captain Levid. If he knew where to go.

"Miss Winston is intrigued by you."

Jon snorted. He should have known Adam wouldn't drop one of his crazy notions so quickly—he never did. Well, Jon would set him straight. "She doesn't even like me."

"That's probably true," Adam readily agreed—too readily. "I imagine you've done your best to scare the living daylights out of her."

"She's my prisoner, for God's sake."

Ignoring this last outburst, Adam continued. "But nonetheless she *is* intrigued. When we stroll on deck you're all she talks about."

Jon met his friend's eye. "I'm not goint to seduce an innocent." Jon forced from his mind the disconcerting thoughts he'd had about doing just that. And not even for the noble reason of gaining information about his brother.

"Have it your way, but I don't think bullying her will get her to bare her soul." Adam pushed away from the rail.

Jon didn't have to be told that. As a matter of fact, he rarely began their conversations with the thought of bullying. It just kind of happened. "Maybe you could talk to her. I think she does like you." Jon couldn't imagine his friend being anything but pleasant around any woman.

"I've tried." Adam straightened. "You're right about one thing. She is stubborn."

"As a mule."

Adam chuckled. "I still think you could—"

"I'm not going to seduce her." Jon realized he'd yelled, and jerked around to see if anyone but Adam

67

had heard him. No one was about except the tars scrubbing the smooth deck with holystones. They seemed intent on their work, their backs bent over the wooden sticks.

"Fine."

"Hell, yes, it's fine." Jon strode across the deck toward the quarterdeck, Adam's laughter ringing in his ears. He climbed the ladder, resisting the urge to double back and wipe the smile off his friend's face. It wasn't Adam's fault that Jon's body almost quivered with impotent anger. "And guilt," Jon mumbled as he picked up the quadrant. "Don't forget guilt."

No matter how many times he told himself that his brother's impressment by the British wasn't his fault—no matter how many times his parents and friends told him the same thing—Jon still couldn't escape the guilt. It rode his shoulders like a haircloth shirt, irritating and unshakable. And Jon had the uncomfortable feeling he would wear it until his brother and the other crew members that Levid had taken from the *Eagle* were free.

Not that guilt was all that drove him. Jon loved his younger brother—loved every member of his family. His mother and father, his sisters Cilla and Libby, were all dear to him. But he and Chris had probably been the closest. It certainly wasn't age or temperament that bonded them. Jon was older by twelve years, and had what he considered a much more easygoing personality. Jon shook his head remembering his brother's sometimes volatile temper. He hoped he was controlling it now, because he doubted it would endear him to the officers on an enemy ship.

They both loved the sea. Almost from the time he could toddle along behind, Chris had begged Jon to take him in the small skiff they kept tied to the dock at Oak Hill. The brothers would sail out onto the bay and stay for hours. Jon would tell Chris all the navigating tips he'd read about, Chris nodding his dark head sagely even though Jon was sure he was too young to understand a thing.

Hero worship, his mother had called it. And it had become more pronounced when Jon had returned from the Barbary Coast. He really was a hero then, or so the papers and politicians said. He'd been one of the Americans chosen to accompany Decatur on his raid to burn the captured frigate *Philadelphia* in Tripoli Harbor. It had been a bold and daring act and had won several of the young lieutenants, like himself, appointments as captains.

And Christopher had insisted on joining the Navy as a cabin boy and sailing with his brother. It had been like old times. "Until I lost him." Jon hit the heel of his palm against the rail and forced thoughts of Chris from his mind. He held up the quadrant, checking the angle of the noontime sun. Looking in the *Nautical Almanack,* Jon recorded the angle and converted the *Eagle's* distance from the equator.

They were on course for the coast of Newfoundland, and Jon wondered how close they could get before they'd run into more enemy shipping. Or Matthew Levid.

Jon's laugh was mirthless as he thought about Adam's suggestion regarding Charlotte Winston. Intrigued by him, indeed. She could barely tolerate his presence. Wasn't that the thrust of her demands— to be out of his cabin? Besides, what he'd told Adam was true. Though he rarely lacked female companionship, he shied away from young innocents. And though she might be betrothed to marry Matthew Levid, Jon was convinced Miss Winston was an innocent.

He thought of her lying on his bed, her gown torn

off, her skin smooth and white, and his overpowering urge to touch her. His thoughts had been anything but pure then. Or the next morning when he'd awakened hard and swollen with her all but naked sprawled on top of him.

"I'm only human," Jon mumbled as he placed the quadrant in its wooden box. But that didn't mean he did anything about it, and it didn't mean he'd set out to seduce her, even if he thought he could.

Jon left the quarterdeck and signaled the officer on duty to call the men up for war practice. In the mornings they trained with the guns. Every afternoon, Jon had his sailors and the marines on board exercise with broadswords, muskets, and pikes. The men enjoyed these diversions, and Jon knew it helped with morale. But most of all, he wanted his men ready for anything, and he knew they were. Twice a week, he had target practice with the great guns, occasionally tossing a cask overboard and ordering a particular gun to sink it. And sink it they did. Perhaps the *Eagle* wasn't as large or carried as many guns as some of the other war vessels, but Jon would pit his crew against any of them.

Loosening his jacket, Jon descended toward the main deck. He didn't often join in the exercises, but today he would. He needed something besides studying charts to help him release his pent-up energy.

Hours later Jon sat in the wardroom, his crossed ankles resting on an empty chair. Remnants of his meal of salt fish littered the pewter plate on the table in front of him. The beef from the *Balfour* had been eaten, but the brandy his crew had found on the British merchantman still swirled lazily in his mug. Jon wondered briefly at the course the wine had taken. It had obviously been smuggled out of France, carried illegally into England, loaded on a vessel bound for Canada, and drunk by an American sea captain.

Jon swigged the brandy, closing his eyes as the liquor burned down his throat. He should go back to his cabin. It was late, and his only companions were a pair of midshipmen who obviously felt it their duty to keep the "old man," as all crews referred to their captain, company.

Adam had retired earlier, mentioning he planned to look in on the men occupying the surgery before he went to bed. He hadn't repeated his scheme for getting information from Miss Winston, but that didn't mean Jon had stopped thinking about it.

He was thinking about it now as he dragged himself to his feet and dismissed the midshipmen. He'd obviously had too much to drink because the plan was beginning to seem as if it had some merit. He shook his head to clear the fuzzy effects of the alcohol, and started aft toward his cabin.

Maybe he *should* move Miss Winston out of his cabin and in with the other female passengers. He more than likely wasn't going to learn anything from her, even if he did resort to Adam's idea—which he had no intentions of doing.

And he wanted his cabin back. It wasn't that he didn't enjoy being with the ship's officers, but he wanted some time to himself. And he wasn't getting that with Charlotte Winston constantly underfoot.

She made him uncomfortable. Jon blinked at that revelation. She did. She made him damned uncomfortable. Not just because he felt guilty keeping her locked up in his cabin, but because he did have lustful thoughts about her. Unrequited lustful thoughts, Jon reminded himself. Lustful thoughts that kept him away from his own cabin.

Well, he was tired of it. He'd move her out first

thing in the morning. But first . . . first he'd give Adam's plan a try. Oh, he wasn't going to seduce her, really. But he'd try being nice . . . maybe get a little romantic with her and see if she'd tell him anything.

Even if she didn't tell him about Levid, it would be nice to hold her again. "No you don't, Jonathan," he mumbled to himself, reaching for the latch. "You're doing this for Chris and no other reason, remember that."

Fumbling for the key in his pocket, Jon squeezed down on the iron latch, surprised when the door opened on its own. Had he forgotten to lock it?

The cabin was dark, but Jon could tell the rope-hung clothes were gone, and as he opened the door wider, letting in the meager light from the passage-way, he could tell something else was missing.

Miss Charlotte Winston.

# Chapter Five

Lighting the lantern that swung over the table, Jon took one more quick look around the cabin to make certain she wasn't there, then rushed back through the door. He covered half the distance to the aft hatch before reality set in, slowing his pace. Where was he to look? On a vessel this size she could be anywhere.

"Damn." Jon banged his palm against a low rafter. The dull thud echoed through the empty companionway. How did she get out? Had he forgotten to lock the door this morning? Thinking back, he could remember striding out of the cabin—angry—and slamming the door. But not locking it. Touching the key in his pocket, rubbing his thumb over the cool metal, Jon shook his head. What a fool he'd been.

And now he not only didn't have Charlotte Winston to question—though that hardly seemed any great loss—but he would have her on his conscience if anything happened to her. And knowing her naive state, something could very easily happen.

"Damn," he repeated, scouring his hand down the contours of his face. With determined steps, Jon

73

strode past the hatch toward the surgery. Adam seemed to have some definite theories about how to handle this woman. Perhaps he had some idea of where she might be. If nothing else, he could help search for her.

Sensing movment behind him near the ladder, Jon glanced around—and stopped short. His eyes narrowed, and he turned, leaning his shoulder against the damp wall.

Stepping off the last rung, her black skirts delicately held in one hand, while the other clutched the ladder, was Charlotte. She moved haltingly, pausing to compensate for the boat's sway. Her pale face looked serene in the shifting shadows. She obviously didn't see him.

Pushing himself away from the wall, taking several long strides, Jon rectified that. His hand clamped around her upper arm, evoking a startled gasp and gaining her complete attention.

"Where in the hell have you been?" Jon ignored her indignant protests and futile attempts to free herself as he dragged her along the companionway toward his cabin. He didn't let her go until he yanked open the door. Once inside, he slammed it, giving a satisfied nod when the noise made her jerk. Then, with studied deliberation, he withdrew the brass key from his nankin breeches and locked the door.

"Now . . ." Jon turned toward his captive in time to see her swipe a lock of tumbled hair from her face. "I'd like an explanation." He assumed she was duly chastised, but her next words proved that assumption incorrect.

"You can go to the devil." Charlotte had the pleasure of seeing the captain's face flush with angry color. She resisted the urge to rub her sore arm. Though she thought there was probably a bruise, she refused to give him the satisfaction of knowing he'd hurt her. How dare he treat her this way!

"The devil, eh." Jon moved closer, his gaze steel-hard and never wavering from hers. "You'll wish you only had the devil to contend with if you keep talking like that."

He was the pirate. How many countless times had she closed her eyes and seen the pirate stalk her exactly like this? He'd come nearer till she could see nothing but him, feel nothing but him. Then he'd—

"Oh no you don't." Jon's large hands snaked out, cupping her shoulders, shaking her slight frame until dark-honey curls escaped and cascaded down her back. "Keep your eyes open, damn you. I'm more than tired of speaking to someone who ignores me." Satisfied when her dark lashes parted revealing still darker eyes that crackled with angry sparks, Jon lowered his voice, repeating his question. "Where were you?"

"On deck," Charlotte said, her chin cocked at what she hoped was a defiant angle. But though she tried to sound confident, her voice faltered. He loomed so large and dark before her she had to remind herself that he didn't frighten her.

"On deck," Jon repeated incredulously. Was the woman daft? Did she have no conception of what might befall her wandering about alone on a war-ship? Then a new thought entered his mind, making him feel foolish. "Ah, you were with Dr. Burke?" Jon dropped his hands convinced he'd created a problem where none existed. He *had* given Adam leave to take her from the cabin. When Adam left the wardroom he'd obviously decided to—

"No. Oh, he may have been there," Charlotte was quick to add. "But I didn't see him."

"You mean you went on deck by yourself?"

Charlotte blinked, but was mindful to open her eyes quickly. He didn't like her retreating into her dream world, and, besides, something told her this was the wrong time to do it. The captain definitely looked angrier than she'd ever seen him . . . angrier than she'd ever seen the pirate. "Yes, but—"

"For God's sake, Charlotte." Jon grabbed her shoulders again, dropping his hands when he saw her wince. Turning, he paced the length of the cabin, stopping in front of the transom window. The low-hanging moon skimmed fragile light across the subtle swells, highlighting the pale foam of the *Eagle*'s wake.

Rolling onto the balls of his feet, Jon studied the sky for star formations, letting their order and predictability soothe him before glancing back over his shoulder. He'd gotten himself into this situation by not thinking, by dragging her to his cabin—twice now—but he'd be damned if he'd just let her flit around. "Do you have any idea what could have happened to you?" His men were well disciplined and he wouldn't want anyone else with him in a fight, but they weren't saints. And they'd been at sea for months now.

"I assumed it was all right." When the blue eyes only widened beneath the shelf of raven brows, Charlotte continued. "You didn't lock the door."

"An oversight, I assure you."

Well, how was she to know that? Charlotte resisted the urge to ask, continuing with her explanation. "And when Dr. Burke didn't come, I just thought . . ."

"Well, you thought wrong." Jon's hands clenched behind his back. "I can't be responsible for your safety if you go gallivanting all over this ship alone." Now that he knew she was safe, Jon felt his anger ebbing away. He also realized he had reacted too strongly. He doubted any of his men would have harmed her. A few lewd comments were probably the worst that would happen. Still—

"Oh." Charlotte raised a straight brow. "You only guarantee my safety when I'm in your cabin?"

The steady slap of Jon's clasping and unclasping hands served as his only immediate answer. He took a deep breath, and once again scanned the black velvet sky before turning to face her. She stood backed against his desk, her chin high, a defiant gleam in her large, dark eyes. "I haven't hurt you."

"You've kept me prisoner." The chin notched higher.

"A prisoner with the means to set yourself free." Jon's response didn't skip a beat.

"By committing treason."

The curse mumbled under his breath would have shocked Charlotte had she not heard it from him before. "For the last time this search has nothing to do with the war. Captain Levid's ship forced mine to allow boarders. He—"

"And I'm telling you for the last time that I will tell you nothing . . . even if I knew, which I don't." Charlotte realized she'd hesitated too long in denying any knowledge when she noticed his eyes narrow. She turned away, gasping when his none-too-gentle touch jerked her back toward him. How could he move so quickly and silently?

"Understand this, Miss Winston. I will find Levid. If it takes me the rest of my life, I'll find him. And when I do, and unless you tell me what you know, you'll be at my side." For the love of God, what had she goaded him into saying now?

"But . . . but you said you'd drop me off at the next port of call." She'd asked Dr. Burke how long until they reached Boston and had been counting the days.

77

"That was before I knew of your involvement with Levid." Adam was wrong. Forget any bumbling attempt at seduction. Scaring her *was* the answer. Jon simply hadn't used the right threats before. Apparently she had steeled herself to accept anything, as long as she knew it would end soon. But this menacing threat of spending a lifetime with him was more than she could handle.

Her breathing was rapid and shallow, and Jon wondered briefly if she were going to be sick again. She still suffered from seasickness. He almost felt sorry for her, but quickly suppressed that emotion. He'd release her, as soon as she told him what she knew. Hell, he didn't want her around for a lifetime any more than she wanted him.

"You'll never get away with this." She seemed to recover enough to spit the words at him.

"But I already have." Jon's voice was smooth as silk.

"When they find out you're holding me . . . my father and Captain Levid . . . they'll come after me." Charlotte wasn't certain that was true, but she could hope. That is, until she noticed a satisfied smile curve Captain Knox's lips.

"Excellent suggestion, Miss Winston."

"What do you mean?" Charlotte backed around the desk, knowing even as she did that the furniture offered no defense against the captain.

"I mean you should have been a military strategist. All this time I've been pursuing Levid when I had the means to bring him to me . . . along with a British general." The smile deepened. "It will be quite a coup."

"I . . . I don't understand."

"Oh, come now." Jon crossed his arms. "I think you do."

The problem was, she did, and wondered again why she couldn't keep her mouth shut. If she hadn't mentioned Levid in the first place she'd be relatively safe with the other passengers from the *Balfour*. And now, as if that weren't enough, she had to give the captain the idea to use her as bait. But as far as her father and Captain Levid knew, the bait was still safely ensconced in Oxfordshire. And from what they knew of her, neither would believe her a captive on the high seas. She would simply tell the captain. "They won't come after me."

"Ah but my dear Miss Winston, you just said they would. And I tend to agree with your first assessment of the situation. At first light I shall change our course for the nearest port. There I will send a message to your father. He can inform Captain Levid the next time they meet. It won't be long before they both know of your dire position."

Charlotte swallowed, tearing her eyes away from the captain's hypnotic and self-satisfied stare. Had she inadvertently given him the means to trap Matthew Levid and her father? Somehow she couldn't picture the staid Levid rushing to her rescue even if he did hear of her plight. Despite his proposal of marriage, she didn't think he held her in very high regard. Still it would be a blow to his ego, a figurative slap across the cheek.

And her father . . . Charlotte bit her lip remembering his last visit. She'd mustered her courage and entered his library, hoping to convince him to resign his commission and stay home for her mother's sake. But she'd failed. Her father had been annoyed, assuring Charlotte that she imagined too much, insisting that her mother would be fine, and that remaining closeted away in Oxfordshire was turning Charlotte into an unpleasant companion. That's when he'd told her of the marriage he'd arranged for her. Charlotte shivered at the memory.

She was nearly trembling with fright. Jon had to force himself not to rub his hands together in satisfaction. He turned back toward the window. "You should get some rest. We have a busy day ahead of us." Jon glanced over his shoulder. "Unless you'd rather forget this course and simply tell me what you know of Levid's destination."

Jon noticed the straightening of her head, a flicker of something in her eyes. He hoped she didn't recognize these wild threats for what they were. The entire scheme he'd outlined for her tended toward the ridiculous, but she seemed to believe him, didn't appear to realize how absurd his words were. But perhaps he'd moved too quickly in offering her a way out. He'd back off, give her time to mull over what he'd said.

"First light, Miss Winston. Let me know then what you decide." With the echo of his words still hanging in the air, Jon walked to the table and extinguished the lantern, plunging the cabin into a darkness silvered only by the faint gleam from the moon.

He could hear her moving around the cabin toward her bunk, could even catch a faint shadow of her figure as he leaned against the nailed-down table. She sat on the mattress. He heard her shoes hit the deck, then the sheet rustled as she lifted the blanket and slid beneath it. After that there was silence.

Jon stared into the darkness a moment longer before feeling his way to his cot. She wasn't asleep. He knew because she wasn't moving. The restless sleep habits he'd noticed the first night had continued. Sometimes Jon found himself lying awake, listening to her turn over, hearing the rasp of material over skin . . . remembering how she felt in his arms.

Disgusted with himself, Jon kicked off his boots. They landed on the floor with a thud. His tunic and breeches followed, the shirt topping the heap on the deck. He reached for the tie to his drawers, and stopped. Mumbling under his breath, he dropped the string and climbed into bed.

Hell, he'd keep the damn things on. At least he didn't sleep completely clothed like she did. Ever since that first night when he undressed her, she stubbornly removed only her shoes before retiring for the night.

She probably thought he had designs on her. Jon almost laughed aloud. If he would have followed Adam's suggestion, then she should worry. As it was, she could join the other women at first light—Jon had no doubts she'd see reason this time—and not have to fear for her virtue again.

At least not until she married Levid. Wondering why he didn't like the thought of that, Jon rolled over and fell asleep.

He woke with a start.

Glancing toward the window, he saw only a slight pearling of light. He lay still, listening, trying to discover what had awakened him.

A soft sobbing sound had him half sitting, jerking his head toward Charlotte's bunk. It came again and he lay back, cradling his head on stacked hands. She must be having a nightmare.

Cilla used to have bad dreams. His mother thought they stemmed from the time she'd gotten too close to the fireplace. Her skirts had caught fire, and even though his father had rolled her to the floor, smothering the flames, her legs were burned.

She'd been left with scars and a limp, and

memories that had her crying out in the middle of the night. Jon's heart had always gone out to her, and more times than not he was the one who rushed to her room to wake her and tell her everything was all right.

But that didn't mean he planned to give the same assurances to Charlotte Winston. She sobbed again, and mumbled something that sounded like Mama. So she was calling for her mother . . . her dead mother. That didn't concern him. Jon shut his eyes, trying to close out the sound. But the next whimper had him whipping off the blanket and plopping his bare feet onto the deck. How was he expected to sleep with this going on?

Stubbing his toe on a chair leg didn't help Jon's disposition, but by the time he reached her cot, he'd mellowed. Maybe it was the continued sound of her sobs or the sheen he noticed on the pale cheek not pressed into the pillow. Tears. He reached out, gently wiping at the moisture with his thumb.

Spring's pastel bounty embraced the garden. Charlotte always liked this time of year best. After the long cold winter there seemed to be an awakening of hope. The birds chirped, the flowers opened to the mellow sunshine . . . and Mama seemed to improve. No matter that the recuperation only heralded another decline, it still brought optimism to Charlotte's heart.

The disease was kind today, masking much of its ravishment of her mother's body and spirit, and making Charlotte pray again for it to simply go away and leave them in peace. But it never did for long and today was no exception. The crevices around Mama's mouth deepened as the pain set in, and she only nodded when Charlotte suggested they go inside. But before she could summon Mrs. Samuels there was a thunderous galloping of horses, and they appeared. Charlotte screamed, trying to pull away, but they plucked at her clothing with their clawlike hands and dragged her away. Away from the garden, away from her mother.

She cried out, sobbing, flailing her arms when suddenly she hit something solid. And warm. And strong. His face appeared before her like so many times before, and Charlotte flung her arms around his strong neck.

"I knew you'd come, oh, I knew it."

Jon leaned down into the death grip Charlotte had on him. He tried to unclasp her hands with one of his, but her fingers entwined with each other and the hair at his nape. After a moment he gave it up. He didn't want to hurt her. At least now she wasn't fighting and crying out.

"You came," she repeated, a smile spreading across her still-sleeping face. Whoever she dreamed of made her as happy as she'd been upset before.

"Just rest." Again Jon tried to extricate himself from her embrace. Not that he minded being held by her. The truth was, he didn't mind at all. She felt soft and sweet—just as he remembered. And she smelled like a garden. But he had a strong suspicion she thought he was Levid, and he couldn't abide that. Still, he didn't jerk away as he was inclined when he first thought of Levid. Soothing her brow with his fingers, he tried to inch away.

"No." Her hold tightened. "Don't leave me."

"I have to." The truth of those words hit Jon as he realized how eager he was to lie in her embrace. But she was asleep, damn it, and dreaming of another man—a man he despised.

"Please don't leave me." Her voice was a dreamy siren's song, as sensual as the body that arched toward him.

Jon stiffened. The imprint of her breasts, even through the bombazine, seemed to burn into his flesh. This was madness. He'd wake her. That was the best way out of a nightmare anyway. Wasn't it? But this no longer seemed like a nightmare. And if her movements were any indication, she didn't want out of it.

But Jon did. He wanted to pull away while he still could. While he still remembered who she thought he was. But she held him captive in her gossamer web of dreams.

"Charlotte." Jon spoke her name, trying to wake her. Her only response was a whimsical sigh. Steeling himself against responding to that enticing sound, Jon cupped her shoulders, his fingers biting into the material. "For God's sake, I'm not Levid."

Her eyes swept open, and Jon braced himself for her contemptuous stare. He'd wakened her with the brutality of truth. But she didn't seem the slightest bit surprised to see him looking down at her. Instead, he caught in the grainy light the faintest of smiles, a warm surge of acceptance. "I never thought you were."

Her arms tightened, pulling him down, and this time Jon let himself sink into her. She touched his cheek, a tender butterfly touch. Jon turned to brush his lips against her fingers.

Her smile deepened and Charlotte explored the curve of his jaw. "I know who you are. I've always known who you are." Easy words to say with him holding her, with the whisper of his breath on her cheek. Charlotte only wished it were true. Was he the pirate who always came to save her, or Captain Knox, the man who held her captive?

When his lips bent to hers, she had her answer. They were one and the same.

Charlotte thought she'd known exactly how it felt, this heady thrill of being kissed by him, but her daydreams paled in the heat of reality. His mouth was softer than she expected, more demanding . . . hotter. But the hungry ache, the deep longing, was there. Only stronger, much stronger.

Charlotte gasped for breath as he broke the seal of their kiss only to trail his mouth down the turn of her chin. Her hands tangled in his hair, pulling him nearer, and she nearly cried out with joy as the weight of his body splayed across her.

His mouth found hers again and this time he nibbled gently on her bottom lip until she opened for him. His tongue skimmed across her lips, then etched the line of her teeth before plunging into her mouth to explore the soft warmth.

Beyond analyzing who she thought he was or why she clung to him with such fierce abandon, Jon deepened the kiss. Passion flared in him like the touch of sulphur to wick, stealing away his breath and forcing his hands on a search for a more solid hold on her.

The twilled silk gown was unyielding, but the body beneath it was not. He traced her arms, the gentle slope of her shoulder, her neck, his hands near frantic till one covered the soft swell of her breast. She sighed, arching toward him, filling his palm.

Damn this dress of a thousand buttons! Jon squeezed her flesh, causing her to moan with desire and forcing a groan of frustration from himself. He longed to see her, feel her beneath the gown. He fumbled with the top few buttons, finally opening them, and pushing the material aside with impatient hands . . . replacing his trembling fingers with his mouth.

She tasted as sweet as she smelled.

Sweeter. Jon tracked the slight rise of her collarbone, wet the hollow where her pulse beat frantically. And all the while she pulled him closer, clutched at the back of his neck.

This was lunacy! Jon lifted his head, searching the face a whispered breath from his. Her eyes shone dark and luminous in the shadows, beckoning him back. He needed to leave this cot right now and return to his own. Perhaps if he did, she'd go back to sleep and by morning forget this ever happened. He stared back into her eyes, and knew the foolishness of that. She would remember. And Lord knew he would. But still, he had to—

"Don't leave me."

Her fingers left the depths of his hair to follow the swirl of his ear as she added a whispered please.

"Charlotte." Jon levered himself away, his elbows on either side of her face. Trying to steady his breathing, he said, "You don't know what you're asking."

"I do," she assured, but the truth was, she didn't. But, oh, when he kissed her, when he touched her, she wanted to know. Charlotte's hands wove down his chest, exploring the tangle of hair as it arrowed down his smooth skin. She felt the shudder, the tense bunching of muscles moments before his mouth crushed down on hers.

If this was a dream, then she needed to know how it would end. If it was reality . . . her desire was the same.

He'd wanted before, but couldn't remember it ever being this sharp, this demanding. His legs tangled with her skirts, his swollen body pressed into her stomach, and he ravished her mouth, all thoughts of stopping shoved from his mind.

The hesitant touch of her tongue on his fueled his already exploding passion. She drove him past reason, past caring. Her moans sent his mouth on a molten path down her cheek. He relearned the contours of her slender throat, growled in frustration when his lips met the resistance of twilled silk.

His fingers fumbled, unable to do more than pluck at the stubborn buttons. And she, she writhed against him, her breast nudging the heel of his palm, creating an itch that sent his hand lower. He squeezed, he molded, he imagined the pebbled crown burning through to his flesh. Then with one swipe he tore at the black bombazine, sending buttons flying and rending the silk.

Her skin was warm and pale, her breasts, round and rose-tipped, straining as he took one, then the other into his mouth.

Charlotte cried out, her mouth gaping open as the fire pulsed through her body. He flooded her senses, sent her hands down his back, kneading the muscled ridges that stood out under his slick skin. His buttocks were tight beneath the cotton drawers, and her palms pushed them lower, wanting to know all of him.

His hands tore at her skirt, and doggedly she helped him, eager for his touch. She wanted. She ached.

Lord he wanted her, had never wanted anyone more. He yanked at fabric, sighing when he felt the silken skin of her thigh. His hand traveled higher, and then he cupped her, hot and moist. He felt the pulsing heat travel in waves from him to her.

His touch had her bucking toward him, gasping for breath. How could she burn so, want so? His fingers moved and she moaned, knowing this feeling came from her darkest fantasy, the one she never even admitted to herself.

The waves of ecstasy trembled across her flesh, and she closed her eyes thinking to see the pirate, seeing instead the handsome face of Captain Knox floating above her.

Then stars seemed to explode before her eyes and vivid colors trailed across her vision. And sounds. She heard pounding and wondered if it was her own heart thumping in her chest. It continued louder and more persistent, and Charlotte opened her eyes.

The captain still loomed over her, but he was still. His breathing was shallow and he lowered his head, resting his forehead momentarily against hers before raising it again. His eyes met hers, skittered away before he sucked in his breath.

"What?" he bellowed, making Charlotte realize that the pounding hadn't been her heart but someone outside the cabin door.

"Captain?" came an excited voice that was nearly drowned out by the piping of a whistle and the commotion of running feet overhead.

"Damn it, what's going on?" He rolled off her, heading for the door before Charlotte could fathom what was happening—what *had* happened. When he opened the portal, she jerked the blanket up and around her shoulders. She was exposed from the waist up, covered only by tattered shreds of silk. But she could have saved herself the trouble, for neither the captain nor the messenger seemed to pay her a moment's heed.

"Ship's been sighted, sir," the man said, shifting excitedly from one foot to the other. "It's English. Lieutenant Hull told me to wake you."

"I'll be right there. In the meantime tell Lieutenant Hull to call the men to alert and clear the decks."

Charlotte watched Captain Knox bark out orders then slam the door and pull on his breeches. He didn't seem to remember she was even alive and Charlotte didn't know whether to be upset or relieved by that. Now that space and circumstances separated them she couldn't believe what had happened—what she'd allowed, nay *begged* him to do.

He shoved his arms into his tunic, buttoning it with one hand while moving around the cabin and gathering his sword with the other. Then without even glancing her way he spoke. "You best get dressed. If there's a battle, this room may be needed."

Charlotte propped herself on one elbow, then remembered her state of undress. "Captain, I—"

"If it's an apology you're after, you'll get none from me." Now he did look her way, and his eyes seemed to bore through her for an instant before he yanked open the door and slammed it behind him.

# Chapter Six

Apology indeed!

She certainly hadn't asked for an apology. But in her heart Charlotte knew she wanted one, and her expression, when he finally glanced at her, all but demanded one.

The incongruity of it struck her like the back of a hand. He hadn't started what had happened. She had. She may have been asleep at the beginning, but Charlotte could remember the exact moment she'd awakened—the exact moment she'd reached for him. If anyone should be asking forgiveness, it should be she. But that was ridiculous. He hadn't wanted excuses. He'd wanted her.

And oh, she'd wanted him. Charlotte squeezed her eyes shut, devastatingly aware of what that made her. How could she want a man, an enemy who constantly . . . insistently demanded she commit treason?

Forget that he reminded her of the pirate. It wasn't the pirate she'd kissed, or let touch her . . . or touched. Besides, the pirate wasn't even real. It was all her imagination, her silly, childish imagination.

Moaning, Charlotte rolled onto her side, clutching the scratchy wool blanket to her throat. If only she could forget. Her eyes drifted shut . . .

The loud commotion in the passageway had her jerking up. What had he said? This cabin might be needed? Quickly Charlotte jumped off the bunk, angry at herself for wasting valuable time with useless worry.

The flutter of silk against her skin served as a reminder not only of the passion she'd shared with the captain, but that her only gown was now torn and unwearable. Oh, why hadn't she thought of that when he'd torn at the material? But she'd only been able to think of the way his mouth made her blood heat, the way she'd moaned when he—

"For heaven's sake," Charlotte admonished herself. Was there no end to this lunacy? Dragging at the material she rid herself of the ruined dress and searched about for something to replace it.

The captain had taken her other gown to be mended, but it hadn't been returned yet—and now didn't seem the time to go looking for it. She could hear pounding and thumping—the gun crews displacing the bulkheads between the officers' cabins, readying them to become the gun deck. They were so close she could hear their mumbled curses.

And she stood covered by only a torn shift.

Yanking open the captain's sea trunk she rummaged through it, tossing aside shirts and breeches, finally standing, brushing hair out of her eyes and wondering what she'd expected to find besides that. Angry with herself, the captain, the entire situation, Charlotte pulled on the only thing at hand, one of the captain's white shirts. Its tail skimmed her knees, its sleeves fluttered way past her fingertips and it billowed around her slim body. But it did cover her— for the most part.

A cravat wrapped about her waist helped tame

some of the excess cotton. She kept a pair of his breeches up the same way. Stuffing the gown into the trunk, she closed the lid and slumped down in the chair, glad the cabin didn't contain a cheval glass like her room at home. She didn't want to see how ridiculous she looked.

But at least her ordeal was almost over. A British ship had been spotted on the horizon. A British ship! Charlotte laced her fingers, squeezing her hands together in excitement. She was saved. The thought made her so happy, she refused to acknowledge the pestering question that flitted through her mind. What would her rescue mean to the captain?


"Set more sail!" Jon snapped the glass shut and glanced toward Mr. Hull, his first lieutenant, who hurried to carry out the order. For the past hour the *Eagle* had danced about in the clinging gray fog, jockeying for position, keeping windward of their adversary.

Occasionally the English schooner and the *Eagle* exchanged a short barrage, sending orange-flecked smoke billowing from the yawning gunwhales to be lost in the blanketing mist. But with the range as it was, neither ship accomplished much. Untouched by the bar and rope shot they'd flung at each other, spars and rigging webbed down from masts, still supporting yards of linen that billowed sun-bleached and ghostly against the murky sky.

It was time to commence the battle.

"We're closing to windward, sir." Lieutenant Hull's face shone bright with excitement as he relayed the information.

"Good." Jon kept his squinted eyes trained on the enemy schooner. "Tell the helmsman to continue to

93

tack whenever either beam is perpendicular." Jon paused after giving the orders that would soon bring them upon the enemy vessel, then caught his lieutenant before he hurried off. "And Mr. Hull, have the gun crews ready. I want to rake her stern as we pass."

"Aye, sir." The lieutenant saluted sharply, then scuttled down the ladder backward leaving Jon alone to scrutinize the ever-narrowing stretch of fog separating the two war vessels.

The *Eagle* had the advantage of the attack. Jon had chosen the right moment to move in for the fight. But the Union Jack, visible occasionally through the twirling shroud of mist, flew atop a larger vessel. Jon estimated her at about twenty-four guns, though her position and the curtain of fog made it difficult to tell for certain. Twenty-four to his eighteen. Jon grinned. Certainly odds he could live with, especially when his crew was taken into account.

Scanning the *Eagle*'s sand-strewn deck, noting the sweat-stained intensity of his gunner's faces, Jon felt a thrill of pride. In a pinch they could shoot almost three rounds a minute.

And the rest of his crew . . . Jon squinted into the shrouds, catching sight of the men, muskets at ready, in the fighting tops—the platforms near the junction of the main and topmasts—were just as reliable. If they could see what they were shooting at, that is. He hoped by the time they came within half gunshot distance of the enemy vessel the fog would lift and they could aim their muskets true.

The thunderous roar of the enemy's first volley had Jon spreading his legs against the roll and sway of the deck. His gaze flashed a quick survey as water from the near miss sprayed over the *Eagle*'s rail. Raising his arm, Jon waited. He could feel the tension of his men as they stood by their guns ready to jerk the lock strings, waiting for his signal.

They were nearly abreast—no more than yards apart. The curtain of mist between the two vessels seemed to evaporate and Jon could see the English tars mirroring the actions of his own men. Still he waited. The schooner heeled with the wind, and Jon's arm slashed through the air.

"Fire at will" came his bellowed command as the black muzzles exploded with deafening unity aiming below the water line of the enemy ship. Again with a precision borne of long hours of practice the gun crew swabbed out the bore, then standing to the right, rammed the powder cartridge and ball home before priming the touch-hole.

As trained, some levered their handspike against a carriage step, wedging the quoin to raise elevation and aim at the masts. Others waited for the downward roll of their ship to again rake the enemy's hull below sea level.

Acrid smoke smelling of brimstone and gunpowder fused with the fine droplets of water enveloping the *Eagle*, stinging Jon's eyes, as he peered toward the schooner. The salvo had struck their spars, tangling the sails of their mizzenmast, but the English ship's response had not left the *Eagle* unscathed.

A portion of deck had been riddled with grape shot, leaving a void where men and polished oak rail had once been. Sailors rushed to fill the hole, pulling the dead and wounded along the blood-slicked deck to relative safety beneath the main sail.

A scattering of small fires erupted where the burning metal hit the deck and firemen scurried about hurling wooden-lathed buckets of seawater on flames.

"They're running to leeward, sir!" Mr. Hull's

excited words confirmed Jon's own observation. It appeared the British schooner had decided discretion the better part of valor and planned an escape into the fog.

"Order the helmsman to fill away." Jon noticed the look of surprise cross his first lieutenant's round face and smile. "We aren't giving up the fight, Mr. Hull. I want the *Eagle*'s bowsprit on the enemy's stern. And have the boarders ready at a moment's notice."

Obviously noting what the American vessel was about, the British schooner tried again to out-maneuver the *Eagle*, but without success. By keeping close behind the schooner, the British carriage guns were almost useless, a point that pleased Jon as his marksmen riddled the enemy's decks with musket-fire.

But to be captured, the schooner needed boarding, and every time Jon ordered an attempt to pull along-side her, the enemy ship shied away. But there were other ways to accomplish a boarding.

Ripping off his tunic and grabbing his saber, Jon leaped from the quarterdeck. "Ram her from the rear," he ordered.

The *Eagle* shook and groaned as her bowsprit jammed over the schooner's stern. Her bib-boom pierced the enemy's mainsail as Jon vaulted to the bowsprit. Saber held high, Jon jumped onto the British schooner's deck. Swarms of American marines followed.

The British were caught unawares, but only for a moment. "Repel boarders! Repel board—" Jon heard the beginnings of that bloodcurdling com-mand as he lunged toward the handspike-waving British captain. His fist cut it short.

Jerking around, Jon caught the flash of crimson-edged metal arcing toward his head. He ducked, feinted to the left, and slipped on the wet deck, missing most, but not all, of the deadly swing. Blood from a grazing wound to the side of his head spattered into his eyes and Jon swiped at his face with the sleeve of his sweat-soaked shirt. His vision cleared in time to see his adversary hurtling toward him, sword held high. Clutching at his waistband Jon found the butt of his boarding pistol. Yanking it out, he fired, hitting the sailor square in the chest. A blossom of crimson exploded over his tunic as the lumbering seaman fell on Jon. Pushing the dead-weight aside, Jon bounded to his feet.

All around him men screamed obscenities while slashing through the carnage. Knives and swords gleamed in the sun that had finally burned off the worst of the fog. Noise from the small arms popped in his ears along with the incessant musketfire from the marksmen aboard the *Eagle* who could at last see their targets clearly.

"They've struck their colors!" The quartermaster's words had Jon squinting toward the foretopsail where he saw someone had indeed taken down the battle ensign. Yelling for his men to cease fire, Jon almost missed the strident call from the bowsprit of the *Eagle*. Someone, he thought it was Mr. Adams the purser, had grabbed a speaking trumpet and was now screaming into it.

A warning.

Jon whipped his head around, shaking blood from his eyes as his field of vision widened and he noticed what lay beyond the *Eagle*. "Back to the *Eagle!* Back to the *Eagle!*" Jon dodged among his men who for the most part looked at him like he had gone mad. They'd just captured the ship and a fine catch it was. Why in the name of hell should they—

Jon grabbed one marine's beefy arm, swinging him around till they were nose-to-nose. "You were given an order, damn you. Now move!" Jon gritted the words between his teeth as he flung the man toward the stern.

By now more of his crew had noticed what until just now the fog had hidden. Riding up on the *Eagle*'s windward side, full sails billowing in the wind, was another ship—at least a forty-gun brig by the size of it, British by the strike of her colors.

"Push off," Jon screamed even as his men scurried over the *Eagle*'s bowsprit. "Get these damn ships untangled."

The *Eagle*'s only chance against a vessel of such superior size and cannon power was maneuverability—and shackled to the English schooner, that was her biggest liability at the moment. But that could change. A great rending sound caused Jon to look around as the *Eagle*'s jib boom tore away more of the schooner's main sail. The *Eagle* was moving!

But so were the sailors on the captured English ship. Apparently deciding, in light of the new circumstances, that striking their colors had been premature, they advanced on Jon and the few crew members who'd yet to leap off the schooner.

Firing into the phalanx of men, Jon backed toward the rail. The American sloop was almost free, and a call for him to hurry confirmed that most of his men had already made it across the ever-widening gulf of gray Atlantic between the two vessels. As he turned to leap over the splintered rail, Jon felt the barbed side of a handspike slash against his shoulder. He landed on hands and knees on the *Eagle*'s hard oak deck moments before the two vessels groaned apart.

"Crowd on the canvas!" Jon hauled himself upright, glad to see his order carried out before he'd even given it. But that's the only thing that pleased him. The British brig was nearly alongside the *Eagle*, and her double row of open gunwales promised a devastating broadside.

It came, an explosion of fire and smoke that sent Jon slamming against the rail, the breath squeezed from his lungs. Straightening, he squinted through the brimstone-laden smoke surveying the damage.

God help them. It was all Jon could do to make his way across the tilting deck. His head felt at the same time light and too heavy to hold up. Again he wiped blood out of his eyes, surprised to see that his entire sleeve was sticky red. The memory of the slash to his shoulder came rushing back to him with a trembling clarity and Jon gulped a deep breath only to cough when the smoke stung his lungs.

Jon lunged toward a six-pound cannon, flinging the dead sailor off the scalding muzzle. Taking his place, Jon grabbed the linstock, touching the spark to the powder in the base ring.

The cannon belched flame and iron as it lurched against the breaching tackle. He swabbed and loaded again, not bothering to aim before firing. The enemy brig was so close it was impossible to miss, so close he could see the grappling hooks swinging toward the *Eagle*'s hull.

"Prepare to repel boarders!" Jon tried to scream the order above the din of the wounded's moans and musketfire, but only heard a raspy croak instead. He drew in breath to yell again, but the thud and jerk of the sloop as the hooks found purchase in her railings threw him against the gun. Besides, the men knew. Those sailors who remained in any kind of fighting form grabbed the cutlasses and pikes lashed against the mast and rushed toward the rail only to be driven back by the swarm of English marines.

Ignoring the pain exploding behind his eyes, Jon hurled himself forward. They couldn't lose the ship; couldn't. He grabbed the sword from a fallen marine's hand and swung it with a vengeance. Again and again he hacked, leaving a sea of bloodied Englishmen in his wake.

"Stop him!" On some primitive level of consciousness Jon knew he was being targeted, but it meant nothing till he felt a white-hot pain tear through his left arm.

Jon staggered forward, tried to lift the sword; found he couldn't. Jerking to the side to avoid the point-blank aim of a pistol, Jon stumbled and fell, the echoing sound of his own head hitting the deck the last thing he heard.

"Oh, my God." Charlotte stared openmouthed at the man sitting behind the huge mahogany desk. He stood, and Charlotte took an involuntary step backward, her spine flattening against the cabin door. She'd been ushered into this room moments earlier, thinking her troubles over or hopefully not as acute.

At least she was no longer caught in the middle of a battle with cannons thundering in her ear, or listening with ever-growing dread as seawater sloshed into the hold below her. She'd been rescued from the *Eagle* before it sank; was now safe on an English vessel. Charlotte tried to remember that as the man straightened his tunic, pulling it over the slight bulge of his stomach, and moved around the desk toward her. He should be her perfect salvation, but now, with her initial surprise past, she studied him. The expression in his hard pale eyes gave her pause.

"Miss Winston, we meet again?"

He wrinkled his forehead in that peculiar way

she'd found distasteful the first time she'd seen him, and Charlotte noted the hard edge to his words matched the gleam in his eyes. Why wasn't he greeting her with open arms? Not that she wished *that*, but a small degree of civility would be nice after all she'd been through.

His gaze raked down her body taking in the too-large shirt and breeches, and Charlotte flushed. "You look quite different from the charming young lady I met in Oxfordshire."

"Yes, well, there have been some rather trying circumstances." She would explain what she'd been through to Captain Levid. Perhaps he didn't rate as the person she most wanted to see, but the inevitable was the inevitable. She'd be seeing a lot more of him. Her father had made it clear that she *would* marry Matthew Levid whether she wanted to or not. Even Charlotte had realized this journey had been only a reprieve. But before she could begin, he spoke, his words as icy cold as a blast of wind from the North Sea.

"So I understand. I thought you still in England. You can imagine my surprise when Captain Boorstin of the *Balfour* mentioned your name . . . and your sleeping arrangements. Of course my first thought was that he must be mistaken, but as we spoke, I realized his Charlotte Winston, or should I say Captain Knox's Charlotte Winston and mine were one and the same."

Anger surged through Charlotte. "I don't care for what you're implying."

"Aye, well, perhaps I don't care to be cuckolded, made a laughingstock by my betrothed." His pale eyes sliced over her again. "And I hardly think you're in any position to protest, dressed as you are."

As much as she disliked agreeing with him, disliked *him* for that matter, he had a point—especially when Charlotte remembered the reason she'd been forced to don Jonathan Knox's clothes. Still, there had been mitigating circumstances. "I was abducted."

"According to Captain Boorstin you went with the American captain willingly." He crossed his arms and looked down his nose, his extremely *long* nose, to Charlotte's way of thinking.

She raised her chin. "Captain Boorstin obviously doesn't have all the details."

"Nor do I." He snorted, another habit Charlotte found repulsive. "But I'm counting on you to give them to me." He paced across the Turkish rug, pausing within feet of her. "I was assured you were a young lady with impeccable morals."

"I was . . . am." I think. Charlotte didn't like the way this interview was going—liked even less her own doubts that kept drifting through her head.

"You expect me to believe that after you've spent days with that bastard. And with you dressed like that?" His hand swept down, as if dismissing her garb as too incriminating for words.

Charlotte opened her mouth to explain why she wore a man's shirt and breeches—not just any man's, but Captain Knox's—then closed it. She had no explanation, at least not one that wasn't damning. Besides, she doubted he'd listen if she did. He'd continue with his tirade, telling her that the worst of it was that she'd been seen by many of his officers. The same officers who knew of the American captain's hostage.

Listening to his harangue, but not too carefully, Charlotte wondered if he'd gotten all this information from Captain Boorstin, or if some of it had come from Captain Knox himself.

If he had survived.

Charlotte swallowed, and tried not to worry about that, but it was impossible. She'd seen the death and destruction when she'd come above deck to be transferred to the *Scorpion*. Though she couldn't imagine how anyone could have survived, she knew some had. She had heard their pitiful moans. But most of the men sprawled over the deck or tangled in the spars were dead. They hadn't moved when the British sailors had prodded or kicked at them. They stayed on the *Eagle* when she took her final voyage—to the bottom of the sea.

Was Dr. Burke among them? Young Joey? Captain Knox? Charlotte considered interrupting Matthew Levid's monologue to inquire, but then thought better of it. There was nothing she could do for any of them now.

". . . and you can imagine what your father will say about this."

Charlotte's attention flew back to Captain Levid at the mention of her father's name. She studied her betrothed a moment. The pause in his words obviously meant he expected a reply, but she had none. What would her father think? She decided to respond the way she *hoped* he'd think. "I imagine he'll be glad I survived."

By the grave expression on Captain Levid's florid face, she didn't think he agreed with her assessment of the situation. But then she really didn't feel comfortable arguing the point, not at all certain he wasn't right.

"We'll have to do the best we can. First order of business is to get you out of those"—he snorted again—"awful clothes. Then perhaps we can find a way to make this seem less offensive. We'll—"

"I didn't tell him anything, you know." Charlotte jutted her head forward and stared straight at Captain

103

Levid. She was tired of his insinuations that had no—well, *almost* no—basis in fact. Matthew Levid looked around, his pale eyes questioning, and Charlotte felt her hands drop off her hips. "Captain Knox wanted to know your destination. And I refused to tell him."

"My destination?" Matthew Levid wore his side-whiskers long and curved in toward his thin lips, and he scratched his thumbnail along the arc now.

"Yes." It's about time he acknowledged her patriotism.

"He asked specifically about me?"

"Yes, you. You and the *Scorpion*. That's why he took me to his cabin in the first place to find out where—"

"Why, do you suppose?" He wrinkled his brow again, and Charlotte looked away.

"To make me tell him where you were. I—"

"No, no." Captain Levid dropped into the chair, leaving Charlotte standing by the door. "Did he inquire about anyone else?"

"No. Only you. But I didn't tell him." Levid didn't seem the least impressed by her heroics.

To the contrary, he chuckled, though Charlotte didn't think he seemed amused. "My dear child, you knew nothing to tell him."

"Your letter. You told me you'd be in the South Atlantic, off the coast of Brazil. I realize it's a large area, and he probably wouldn't have found you, but—"

"You don't think I'd divulge my true orders to you, do you?"

Well, yes, actually she had, but Captain Levid didn't seem interested in continuing this particular vein of conversation. He was rubbing his cheek again. As his thumb grated against the whiskers, the pleated lines across his high forehead deepened.

"Why should an American captain concern himself with my whereabouts?"

"I don't know." Charlotte had an uncomfortable feeling she'd said more than she should. But that was ridiculous. She couldn't do any harm now. Could she? Captain Levid's next words proved she could.

"I suppose we'll have to ask the captain himself then, won't we?"

"He's alive?" Charlotte realized her mistake as soon as Matthew Levid jerked his head up and focused those washed-out eyes on her. She shouldn't have acted excited and truthfully hadn't meant to. It was just when she heard . . .

Setting about to correct her error, Charlotte folded her hands and sobered her expression. Of course she was glad he survived. She didn't like to think of anyone dying. Her reaction would have been the same had she discovered Dr. Burke still lived, or Joey.

"Aye, he's alive . . . barely." Levid stood. "Lucid enough for our purposes, though."

Her palms started to perspire and Charlotte unlaced her fingers, wiping them down her breeches—Captain Knox's breeches. "Was he badly wounded?"

"You'll see soon enough."

There was something about his tone that Charlotte found distasteful . . . and threatening. "What are you going to do with Captain Knox?" Charlotte had the feeling she was feeding into his next line, but she couldn't help herself.

"Well, first I want to discover what his interest is in me, of course . . ." He paused, and Charlotte swallowed as she noticed the cruel gleam in the depths of his colorless eyes. "And then find out how well he knows my betrothed."

Before the full implication of Levid's words registered with her, he'd barked a clipped command to someone outside the cabin. The doorway opened and a midshipman entered, pushing another man in front of him.

Charlotte gasped . . . she simply couldn't help herself. If not for Levid's hand that suddenly clamped around her upper arm, she would have sprung forward to help the grime- and blood-encrusted man as he stumbled forward.

But he didn't need her assistance. Dragging a manacled hand up, he grabbed hold of the desk edge and caught himself. He straightened slowly . . . painfully, and Charlotte held her breath.

Though he bore little resemblance to the man who'd strode from his cabin—was it only this morning?—she knew what she'd see when he finally glanced her way. His eyes were as blue as ever, even red-rimmed and glassy as they were, and he fixed them on Charlotte for one unreadable moment before shifting his gaze toward Levid. Then his stare turned murderous, and Charlotte saw his one hand knot in a tense fist.

The other hand could do nothing. It just hung at the end of an arm that bore a ghastly gaping hole and several gouged slashes.

He needed to lie down, not to mention medical attention. But Captain Levid seemed oblivious as he stood, his thumb rubbing up and down on Charlotte's arm, studying his captive.

"Captain." Charlotte's voice was barely above a whisper, but it caught both men's attention. She felt hot then cold, and wondered if she were going to be sick. She tried to keep her eyes off Jonathan Knox's arm—fresh red bled through the rust-colored scabs— but his head was nearly as bad. He'd been cut across the scalp, and she imagined it must throb terribly. She *was* going to be sick.

"What do you want, Charlotte?"

Captain Levid's words and the pinch of her flesh beneath his hand stiffened her spine. She sucked in a gulp of air, and imagined it smelled of blood and pain. "D-don't you think this interview can wait until Captain . . . this man sees a surgeon."

"Does the sight of so much blood upset you?"

Jerking her arm away, Charlotte faced him. "Yes, it upsets me. It would upset any rational person."

Levid traced his sidewhiskers and seemed to contemplate an answer. After a moment he nodded, apparently coming to a decision. "Very well. I will question the prisoner later about everything except . . ."

Charlotte held her breath as Levid turned toward Captain Knox. "What happened between you and Miss Winston in your cabin?"

# Chapter Seven

Standing itself required all of Jon's concentration, without answering some fool question. He swallowed back the acrid bile rising in his throat and met Levid's cold stare.

Ever since Jon realized whose ship he was on, who'd captured the *Eagle*, his fury had raged almost out of control. How long he'd searched for the *Scorpion*, only to find it when victory—when rescuing his brother—was impossible. Jon took a deep breath hoping to clear the pain from his head. It didn't work. What insipid question had Levid asked? Ah, he worried about his betrothed's virtue.

It was almost humorous and might have evoked a laugh, except that would accentuate the drums already pounding at his temple. And then, Jon didn't really feel like laughing. Most of his crew were lost, his ship lay moored on the bottom of the Atlantic, he was bleeding all over the damn carpet, and Levid . . . Levid, the bastard, was worried about a flirtation Jon might have conducted with his future wife.

Shifting his weight, Jon swallowed, surreptitiously eyeing the pitcher of water on Levid's desk. Would he chink the armor of his pride by requesting a drink?

Knowing the answer, and not liking it, Jon forced his gaze from the glistening pewter. But he couldn't stop the painful slide of his tongue over salt-encrusted lips.

Straightening, Jon met Levid's eye. "Where are my men? I demand to see them."

"Demand?" Levid's curved brow arched, wrinkling his forehead. "I hardly think you're in any position to demand anything."

"My men, damnit. Are there any survivors?" A shaft of pain shot through his unbandaged arm. "And is your treatment of them as uncivilized as this?" Jon tried to raise his hand; couldn't.

Leaving Charlotte's side, Levid moved smoothly to the desk. With an evil gleam in his eye, he sloshed water into a pewter mug. After taking a sip, he smiled up at Jon. "There are survivors. As for their treatment . . ." He paused, taking another drink. "They are being cared for. As will you as soon as you answer my question."

Question? What question did he mean? Jon tried to think, but his head felt light, almost as if it weren't there—except for the spot above his brow that ached like the devil. But somehow he knew if anyone had questions to ask, it was he. Like what had happened to his brother and—

"I want to know now!" Levid leaned across the desk, brushing against the mug, spilling the water. Jon watched it bead on the polished surface, then roll lazily to the floor, soaking into the patterned carpet.

"You were alone with Miss Winston, alone in your cabin for five nights, and I will know what happened." Levid's demand pulled Jon's attention from the rug.

A means of revenge clawed at Jon's mind, borne of pain and frustration, it sprouted like an illbegotten

110

weed, choking out rational thought.

Levid wanted to know about Jon and Miss Winston. Well, Jon could tell him plenty. And if some details were only a product of his imagination, who was to know? The lady herself, of course, might deny his tale, but then she'd be expected to, innocent or no. Besides, the story he would tell would not be completely false.

He *had* kissed those pouting lips, touched her velvety skin, had even brought her to a wild frenzy of uncontrolled passion. Had wanted her desperately. Ignoring that thought, Jon forced himself not to search out the woman he knew cowered against the back wall of the cabin. He wasn't doing this to hurt her. It was Levid he hated. Levid who must be punished—punished by the only means available.

He must. Jon thought of his mother, her soft gray eyes tormented by thoughts of her youngest child's agony. And his father, tall and strong, yet unable to save his son. Their hopes had rested on Jon. Oh, they hadn't said that . . . they wouldn't. They'd absolved him of all responsibility, enveloped him in the love that had been his birthright, and told him that life must go on. But Jon felt accountable. He searched. He found. And he failed. But he could still strike out at Levid.

Waves of nausea washed over Jon. He swiped at the sweat crawling down his brow, not surprised to see the back of his hand smeared crimson. His damn head was bleeding again.

Jon sneered at his barbaric treatment. "You want to know what happened in my cabin?" His eyes narrowed, focused in on Levid. "I'll tell you." A small sound made him pause, and forgetting his resolve, he glanced over his shoulder. Charlotte had been so quiet, he'd almost forgotten her presence, and

111

apparently she was trying to forget his. Her eyes were shut in that frustrating habit of hers, her dark lashes a damp tangle across her flushed cheeks.

*Tears*, he thought scornfully. *Damn woman is worried about what I'll say . . . about what her noble betrothed will do once he hears my little story*. Any sympathy he might feel for her plight paled under the weight of his men, his ship . . . his own.

He opened his mouth to speak, to relate a tale of seduction and passion, of debauchery, and her lashes fluttered open. Her gaze locked with his, and though he wanted to think her eyes pleaded with him not to tell, Jon knew that wasn't what he saw.

In the breath of time before she looked away, he saw sympathy . . . for him. Damn it to hell! He wasn't even certain that was the expression he read in the depths of those soft doe eyes, but sure enough for doubts to start nagging at his conscience.

Why didn't she lash out at him—certainly she knew what he planned to do. Or play the coquette and beg Levid not to listen. But no, she simply stood there, huddled in his oversize clothes looking every bit the martyr. A martyr with misplaced sympathies.

Oh, hell.

Straightening his shoulders, Jon glared at Levid, then gave a bark of mirthless laughter. "Happen? What in the hell do you think would happen?" Jon shot a glance behind him and watched as embarrassed color flooded Charlotte's pale face. "Mayhap you find this ragamuffin bag of bones appealing, but . . ." Jon left the rest unsaid, hoping to God she didn't start arguing with him about some of the times he obviously had found her more than appealing. This was no time for vanity.

Levid's glare was scathing, and a vein on his forehead throbbed in cadence with the clenching and unclenching of his fists. Without even the cool comfort of revenge to soothe him, Jon was heaping the wrath of his captor on himself. But the die was cast, nothing left but to make this performance as believable as possible. "I can't say it didn't cross my mind to release some pent-up . . . energy on her. But her penchant for heaving into a bucket every few minutes cooled any ardor I could summon." Jon forced his features into a mask of disdain. "I'm surprised she hasn't soiled this suit of clothing as well as her own." Jon's gaze swept over the shirt and breeches that all but hid her delicate body, wondering how she'd explained her attire, hoping her explanation didn't expose his for the lie it was.

"Is this true, Miss Winston? Have you been ill?" Levid turned his attention to Charlotte.

"Ill?" Charlotte swallowed. Actually, though a queasy stomach persisted, she hadn't been sick since that first day on the *Eagle* but to say that would prove Captain Knox false. And it did provide such an excellent explanation for her attire. She was certain Captain Knox hadn't meant to help her—not after those awful things he'd said—but she'd take advantage of his blunder. "Yes, I have had a difficult time gaining my sea legs." And she had, at first. Would she have to pretend to be sick in the future? A new thought came to her. "I'm certain Captain Boorstin will tell you the same."

"I don't think we need ask him." Levid sat down, examining Charlotte over steepled fingers. Finally, seeming to come to a conclusion, he leaned back in his chair. "You may leave us now, my dear. I've arranged for you to share a cabin with a Mrs. Winthrop. She was a passenger on the *Balfour*, do you remember?"

Charlotte could only nod, amazed by Matthew

113

Levid's near solicitous treatment of her. He acted almost kind. But Charlotte had only to search her recent memory, or look at the bloodied figure of Captain Knox to know that he wasn't.

But would Jonathan Knox have been any more humane were the positions reversed? If the tides of war had shifted, making the American the victor, would he have forsworn the chivalrous behavior of gentlemen? Charlotte had seen the hatred in his blue eyes when he'd spoken of the English captain. More than a declaration of war marred their relationship.

Charlotte tried to imagine Captain Knox as cruel, and couldn't. Oh, she could see him as ruthless in battle, as bold and daring. She could envision him cutting down an enemy with one slash of his silvery sword, but never standing by denying a wounded man treatment. He wouldn't do that.

Charlotte sucked in her breath as the realization hit her. It wasn't Captain Knox but the pirate whom she'd imagined as noble. Though the converse should be true, it was her apparition, a figment, that she knew. This solid man of flesh and blood remained a mystery.

Why had he denied the passion they'd shared? She sensed he'd not escaped the sensual web that had tangled them. Yet he disclaimed any intimacy with her. Why?

She could think of no reason save one, and that was too bizarre to be believed. The captain had no desire to protect her. But was it easier to accept that he merely regretted any liaison they'd had, and really did think of her as unappealing?

Charlotte sighed. The two men were glaring at each other across the expanse of mahogany, obviously assuming she'd been dismissed. It would be heaven to go, to be rid of Matthew Levid's presence and to try and forget the battered form of Captain Knox.

But she couldn't simply leave. Pushing away from the wall, Charlotte approached Matthew Levid. The expression on his face when she cleared her throat confirmed her suspicion that her dismissal was meant to be obeyed. Garnering what courage she could, Charlotte leaned conspiratorially closer to the man she'd be forced to marry.

"You did say Captain Knox could see the surgeon when he'd answered your question, and I believe he—"

"What do you think you're doing?"

Charlotte jerked back at the sound of Captain Levid's ice-coated voice. "I only thought—"

"Well, don't. Captain Knox is none of your concern . . . none. Do you understand me?"

"Yes."

"I didn't hear you."

Charlotte repeated her response, though she thought he'd have to be deaf not to hear her in the first place.

"That's better. Captain Knox has made his opinion of you quite apparent. I should think you'd cease any interest you may have in him."

"I have none," Charlotte insisted, her face blooming with color under the implication.

"As a matter of fact, I'd think his insulting words enough to foster a rather strong dislike of the fellow."

Could it be she agreed with Matthew Levid about something? Charlotte could hardly accept that, but he did have a point. Captain Knox's degrading words were hardly endearing. Admitting it came hard, but Charlotte did. In her mind she'd made excuses for Captain Knox, had made excuses for him because of his resemblance to her fictional pirate. But they

115

weren't one and the same. From now on she'd remember that.

"I do dislike him," she said, suddenly remembering all the awful things he'd done to her, the confinement in his cabin, the browbeating threats. "I care not what you do to him." Charlotte bit her bottom lip. Lord help her, that wasn't true, but it seemed to make Captain Levid happy, and the look of contempt Jonathan Knox shot her only incensed her.

Why should she care? These men were soldiers, their countries at war. How did she know what went on between enemies. She would trust Captain Levid to handle the situation. After all, it was all she *could* do.

With as much dignity as she could muster, clothed in oversize men's clothing, Charlotte retreated from the cabin.

"Well, Captain Knox." Matthew Levid settled back in his chair and studied his captive over steepled fingertips. "It appears you won't have the lady as a champion."

"I never assumed I would." Liar. With annoyance, Jon realized he'd hoped for just that. He would have enjoyed a little solicitude from Charlotte. He *did* feel like hell. But when he'd noticed her hard expression, he accepted that as a foolish wish. Besides, any help for him on her part would simply undo his own chivalrous gesture—if that's what it had been. Insanity seemed more the appropriate term as Jon watched Levid rise and walk around the table toward him, fingering the hilt of his sword.

"Besides complaining of your dastardly treatment of her . . ." Levid paused, and Jon could feel the sweat pooling around his tethered wrists. "Treatment, I may add, that will have to be punished."

Jon's eyes darted around the room, looking for

something—anything—he could use as a weapon. He straightened. He had Levid by at least half a head, and not even the girth of the older man's middle matched Jon's shoulders, but he was wounded and losing blood rapidly and could only separate his hands as far as three iron links allowed. And all the time Levid advanced on him . . . slowly. Caressing that damn sword as if it were a beautiful courtesan.

"As I was saying," Levid continued. "Miss Winston also mentioned that you were very anxious to find me. Me in particular. That piques my curiosity." Levid unsheathed his sword and laid it on the desk, his fingers still molded about the hilt.

"It's no great mystery." Jon tried to keep his voice calm, his eyes off the long, smooth slice of metal. It was an enticement, but the risk wasn't worth it. "Last year you ordered an American vessel boarded."

Levid shrugged and his neck seemed to disappear inside the collar of his ornate uniform. "I've ordered many American vessels boarded. You know the problem we have with desertion."

"This one was the *Eagle,* and it contained no deserters. But that didn't stop you from impressing some of the seamen."

"The *Eagle,* of course. But I recall no Captain Knox. Though you don't make a very good impression at the moment, I rather think I'd remember if we'd met."

"We didn't. I was on shore at the time." Jon couldn't help notice the fingers of Levid's hand growing lax. Should he dive for the sword? Jon had a strong feeling he was going to die anyway; Levid had implied as much. How much sweeter to take Levid with him.

"Then I'm still puzzled by your interest in me. Miss Winston assured me it was obsessive. Surely you

117

didn't mean to revenge a handful of common sailors?''

"One of those sailors was my brother, Christopher Knox." The words gritted through Jon's teeth.

"Your brother?" Levid appeared puzzled a moment longer, then recognition seemed to dawn across his puffy features. "Of course, he would be your brother. Troublesome lot Americans in general, but it seems you Knoxes are particularly annoying."

"He's here, on the *Scorpion?* I want to see him." Where he'd resisted the urge to ask for water, tamping his thirst, the desire to see his brother was more urgent. But the last half hour had given Jon a glimpse of the type of man Levid was.

Slowly shaking his head, Levid leaned his hip against the desk. "Now, now, Captain Knox." Levid's voice sounded tauntingly singsong. "You should know better than to beg for favors . . . in your position."

"I want to see my brother." Reasonable thought demanded a calmer, cooler approach, but at this moment reason escaped Jon.

"Well, I'm afraid you can't." Jon watched as a smile of sorts thinned Levid's already bloodless lips. "Even if I were inclined to grant your wish. And . . ." The hand formerly attached to the sword rose, an accusing finger pointing toward Jon's chest. "Let me assure you, I am not. It would be impossible."

Jon didn't ask why, though he sensed Levid paused for just that reason. Something in Jon feared he didn't want to know. He almost wished he could borrow Charlotte's defense, close his eyes and will everything away. But that luxury eluded him as he stared back at Levid, his heart beating painfully against his ribs.

"You see, your brother was as difficult as you. And

118

like you, he caused nothing but trouble. Being a captain yourself, I'm sure you realize one cannot have troublemakers among their crew. It especially can't be tolerated of someone who had already deserted the Royal Navy."

"He wasn't a deserter. He should never have been on this vessel."

Levid waved that aside as unimportant. "The point is that he was on board, and he didn't conform. So he had to be punished."

Jon's snarl was automatic; as was the tightening of Levid's fingers around the sword hilt. "What did you do to him, you bastard?"

"What any captain would have done in my place. Had him flogged."

Jon came to the unpleasant realization that Levid was enjoying this. It was like a slow, precise form of torture, a torture that Levid controlled and Jon could do nothing about—nothing but play along. He told himself not to participate in Levid's game, but it did no good. He felt like a puppet in one of the shows his parents had taken him to see in Philadelphia, bound and lifeless. But he needed to find out what happened to Christopher.

He asked and noticed a sadistic gleam flash in Levid's pale eyes.

"He survived . . ." Levid paused. "But unfortunately the well-deserved beating did not break his rebellious spirit."

Jon's knees felt weak and he locked them against the sway of his battered body. He would not allow himself to collapse before this man, not as long as consciousness remained.

"He tried to escape," Levid continued, shaking his head. "Bad business that. He was killed in the process."

"You lying bastard." Jon jerked forward, the rattle of his chains an eerie backdrop for his vehement words.

"Oh, but I assure you it's quite—"

Jon's fingers around Levid's throat—or was it the surprise of the younger man's leap—cut off the last word of his testimony. The sword he'd lifted when Jon first moved forward landed on the carpet with a thud, while Levid's hands clawed Jon.

Jon's mind grew fuzzy with hate and revenge. He pressed down into the soft flesh, briefly noting that the hated manacles served a purpose after all as they spanned Levid's neck.

The British captain kicked and thrashed, a wild thrust of his flailing hands catching Jon on his wounded shoulder. For an instant all went black, and Jon's tortured muscles relaxed the pressure.

The moment was all Levid needed to pierce the cabin and beyond with his brittle scream.

Jon didn't notice the cabin door bang open or the marines who lumbered into the cabin responding to their captain's plea for help until they grabbed him. They hauled him roughly away from Levid, pressing his elbows back as far as they could, heedless of the iron cutting into his wrists.

Coughing and sputtering, Levid shifted to his knees. Then, with the assistance of one of his men, he scrambled to his feet, his dignity as crumpled as his uniform. He yanked on his tunic, his face paling when he spotted the blood soaked into the wool, obviously relieved to discover it belonged to his assailant and not himself.

Whirling around quickly, focusing his narrowed eyes on Jon, he tried to speak, cleared his throat, and tried again. "You'll pay for this, Knox. And your payment will be long and painful."

With that Jon stumbled as he was shoved toward the door.

They planned to flog Captain Knox.

Charlotte paced the small cabin she shared with Mrs. Winthrop and her maid. Neither woman had seemed overly pleased to share accommodations, and Charlotte could hardly blame them. With the three cots squeezed into the room, there was barely enough room to move around.

But Charlotte didn't think a lack of space the main concern of the middle-aged woman and her abigail. In their eyes Charlotte was a fallen woman, a woman who'd spent five days and nights in the company of the infamous Captain Knox.

He'd gained quite a reputation on board this ship. Though Charlotte was certain Matthew Levid would disapprove if he knew of the network of gossip, not to mention the tales they conveyed, she'd heard several stories of his daring during the battle—and of his attempt to kill Captain Levid.

Thus the flogging.

Charlotte tired of squeezing between the desk and cot, and with a weary sigh, sank onto the only chair in the cabin. It was none of her concern. None. For the hundredth time today Charlotte told herself that.

What happened to Jonathan Knox did not affect her. She'd been his captive, nothing more. The only problem was, it didn't seem to matter how many times Charlotte told herself that, she still couldn't stop the nagging concern that crept over her.

She tried to convince herself it stemmed from his resemblance to the pirate, but knew that wasn't it. She even doubted it had anything to do with the passion she'd found in Captain Knox's arms. If anything, that should make her want to purge him from her mind, because she couldn't understand how she could have been so wanton.

Burying her face in her hands, Charlotte closed her eyes and tried to think of the peaceful garden. She concentrated on the sounds, the flowery fragrance, the gentle breeze . . . but all she knew was the sway of ship on swells and the faintly nauseating smell of bilge water.

She couldn't forget about him.

She didn't understand.

And there was nothing she could do about anything, even if she did.

The knock at the door made Charlotte straighten her shoulders. With a soft groan she stood and opened it. The sight of her visitor didn't surprise her.

"Are you ready?"

"Captain Levid, I don't understand why it's necessary for me to attend this . . . this—"

"I thought we discussed this last evening." Matthew Levid's tone was impatient.

"Discussed, yes . . ." Charlotte paused, not sure how, or even if, she should continue. Conversations of this sort did not endear her to Captain Levid, and though that was hardly her goal, she'd found he could make things very unpleasant for her when angered. "It's just . . . well, Mrs. Winthrop isn't attending." Charlotte knew the other female passengers; those rescued from the *Eagle* were having tea in Captain Levid's cabin.

"Quite true, Miss Winston. But then the other ladies have nothing to prove, do they?"

"Nor do I."

"We shall see, my dear. Now do get your shawl. There's a stiff breeze this morning."

Charlotte considered digging in her heels, literally

122

and figuratively. She didn't think Matthew Levid would drag her kicking and screaming onto the deck. But then she wasn't entirely sure. So in the end, she complied, wrapping a borrowed shawl around her shoulders and following the captain into the passageway.

Here the odor of pitch and bilge water grew stronger, and Charlotte felt her stomach tighten, then lurch. What little breakfast of dried toast she'd managed to eat now threatened to make a reappearance. Though she hadn't been ill for nearly a sennight, it seemed evident that she had not entirely overcome her malady.

"Captain Levid." His pace had taken him several feet beyond her, but he stopped at the sound of her voice. "I think I'm going to be ill." He covered the distance between them quickly, grabbing her arm and jerking her up against him.

"You are going to watch this, Charlotte, if I need take you topside strapped to a bunk. So let's have no more talk of illness."

His threat delivered, Levid let go of Charlotte with such force that she fell back, only avoiding a fall due to the narrowness of the passageway. But Levid didn't even bother to see if she stayed upright. He continued down the corridor as if naught had happened.

Sucking in her breath, Charlotte followed, her mind racing furiously. What was she going to do?

Blinding sun assailed her when Charlotte stepped through the hatch. Captain Levid had been right about one thing. A strong wind whipped through the sails and slapped at Charlotte's skirts.

Both watches had been piped on deck. Charlotte, with her elbow now firmly grasped by Levid, made her way through them and quickly maneuvered the steps to the quarterdeck. From there Captain Levid asked if the entire ship's company was present or accounted for. A positive response from one of his officers prompted his signal for the prisoner to be brought forward.

The staccato rapping of the drummer seemed to match the wild cadence of Charlotte's heart as she searched down through the crowd and found Jonathan Knox.

Though barefoot, his dark head rose above those of his guards, his close-cropped black curls ruffling in the wind. He looked cleaner, his white, flowing-sleeved shirt free from bloodstains. Charlotte imagined this was for appearance' sake rather than any proof of humane treatment he'd received. His pace was steady, firm, but his left arm still hung limply at his side and Charlotte thought she could notice, even at this distance, the creases at the corners of his eyes and the lines bracketing his mouth etched deeper into his skin.

The procession of marine guards and prisoner stopped on the deck, directly below them, and Charlotte watched Jonathan Knox's eyes lift. They were as blue as the azure sky that formed his backdrop, but he didn't look at her. Instead, his defiant stare remained locked on the man beside her.

The quartermaster recited the charges. "Attempted escape. Attempted murder. Two dozen lashes."

Charlotte tried not to gasp, but she noticed Levid's sharp, reproving look and realized she'd failed. Amazingly enough, she no longer felt like throwing up. Now she was quite certain she would faint. But somehow or other she remained upright as Captain Levid ordered the prisoner seized up.

Jonathan Knox walked to an iron grating, removed his shirt, and stood spreadeagle as the guards tied his wrists and ankles. Exposed, Charlotte could see the wounds on his arm. They had obviously healed some, but still looked red and swollen. She couldn't begin to imagine how it must feel to have that abused arm tied.

But in the next moment as the leather cat lashed through the air, planting its kiss on the broad expanse of Captain Knox's back, concern for his existing wounds seemed almost misspent.

Charlotte lost track of the count. She wanted to look away, yet couldn't. With each hissing snap of the whip she forced herself to watch, to see it welt and cut the rippling muscles.

Officially Jonathan Knox suffered this punishment for trying to escape and attempted murder. At this point Charlotte could only imagine that anyone would attempt escape. As for attempted murder . . . Why did Jonathan Knox hate Levid so much?

Not that she didn't dislike him herself, but that was because she knew him. Captain Knox hadn't. But he knew him now. Knew the pain of his revenge.

Mercifully, the flogging stopped. The American captain was cut down. His shirt flapping from his breeches, he turned. His eyes met Charlotte's and locked, the expression of undisguised contempt hitting her with as much force as the cat had struck him.

# Chapter Eight

Charlotte stiffened as the midshipman paused beside her. She continued to stare out over the blue waters of the St. Lawrence River, but she couldn't help noticing the way he leaned forward, resting his forearms against the rail. Under her lashes she noticed him crack his knuckles, the sound making her own joints ache in sympathy. This sign of nervousness was all that belied his casual stance, his seemingly nonchalant indifference to the woman beside him.

But Charlotte knew different. It was no accident that he'd chosen this spot, or this particular time, to approach her. There was no one on deck to notice them. Charlotte didn't even have to glance around to be certain of that. She'd dealt with Mr. Grey long enough to know he took no chances.

The coins slid in Charlotte's palm, and she closed her fingers more tightly over them before turning toward the midshipman, a forced smile thinning her lips. "How far are we from Montreal?" She already knew the answer, or at least when the *Scorpion* would reach the island, but it was a little game they played—a game of innocent conversation.

But apparently Mr. Grey tired of the game, for he wasted no time in launching into the reason for this unscheduled meeting. "I can no longer get extra food to the prisoner."

"Why?" In her shock Charlotte forgot her pose of indifference and gripped the railing. "Our agreement was—"

"To hell with our agreement. It's become too dangerous. I'll not risk my career for a few pounds."

Charlotte decided against pointing out that he'd done just that for more than a week. Nor did it seem prudent to mention that one word from her and Mr. Grey could forget about the Royal Navy, except possibly for its brig. But then they both knew she couldn't carry out such a hollow threat.

Her well-being hung in the balance as well as his. Charlotte couldn't even imagine what Matthew Levid would do if he knew what she'd been up to. Just the thought of his anger made Charlotte shiver with trepidation.

The midshipman apparently misread her shutter. "The American won't starve to death in the next few days." He angled his body toward hers, smiling when she backed away. "Of course I can't guarantee what will happen to him once he reaches Montreal."

Charlotte's lips pursed and she looked away. She'd worry about that when they reached their destination. Certainly her father would listen to reason about Jonathan Knox. She needed to believe that. Because if her father would be understanding about him, then maybe he'd also listen to reason about Matthew Levid. Closing her eyes, Charlotte prayed he'd reconsider forcing her to marry the British captain.

"You still owe me money."

Mr. Grey's harsh words brought Charlotte back to

the present. She turned and studied her paid accomplice. He stood not much taller than she, had sandy hair cut short and combed forward, a ruddy complexion, and eyes that made her uncomfortable. But, in truth, it had been his eyes that had drawn Charlotte to him. They were restless, shiftless, and in their dark depths she'd thought she'd seen a touch of avarice.

And she'd approached him about getting more food to the prisoner. Charlotte still couldn't believe she'd done it. She'd half expected Mr. Grey to report her to the captain in a frenzy of patriotic zeal. But he hadn't. Instead he'd smiled, baring teeth that overlapped one another, and asked how much she would pay.

Quickly Charlotte slipped the money into his hand. She watched as he counted the coins, wondering why his frown deepened.

"This isn't enough."

"What do you mean? We agreed—"

"I told you before, the agreement is off." The words hissed through his teeth and Charlotte wished, not for the first time, that she'd never gotten herself into this. She wasn't even sure why she had. "It has cost me more money than I thought to buy off the guards," he continued. "We don't want them running to Captain Levid, now do we?"

"No." Charlotte wet her suddenly dry lips. "I suppose I could give you more." She mentally calculated how much was left from the stash she'd yanked from the hem of her gown before the *Eagle* sank. Again she wondered why she was doing this. It certainly wasn't as if she owed Captain Knox anything—not after his callous treatment of her. But she couldn't stand by and watch anyone starve to death, and after she'd heard Captain Levid order the American placed on half rations, she knew that was a possibility.

"Aren't his wounds and the bloody welts on his back punishment enough?" she'd asked Captain Levid before she could curb her tongue. His only response had been a contemptuous stare and an alteration of his order. "Make that quarter rations, Mr. Webster," he'd told his quartermaster, while never taking his eyes off Charlotte. Fighting back tears, Charlotte had stumbled from the cabin. She hadn't seen Captain Levid since.

"Be on deck tomorrow morning. We should be able to see Montreal by then. And bring more money."

Before Charlotte could ask how much more would satisfy him, the midshipman walked away. Calling him back didn't seem prudent. Besides, his presence disgusted her, made her feel dirty. The thought of a British officer committing treason for money appalled her. But then, if he hadn't, Jonathan Knox might be dead now. Grudgingly Charlotte admitted she owed Mr. Grey. He had done what she asked, even giving her short reports on the American's condition.

Biting her bottom lip, Charlotte watched the tree-lined coast skim by through eyes blurry with tears. Captain Knox was still alive. The ship's surgeon had apparently seen the American, for Mr. Grey reported the musketball removed from his arm, his wounds stitched, and ungent spread on his ravaged back.

Charlotte closed her eyes, trying to imagine Captain Knox—the pirate—as she'd known him before, standing tall and proud, his face dark and wickedly handsome, a grin tugging at the corners of his mouth. But she couldn't. Try as she might, the only vision that surfaced showed him clutching the iron rails, his knuckles white, the tendons on his neck standing out in bold relief as he suffered each lick of the cat across his bloody back in agonized silence.

Her only escape from reliving this scene in her mind was the equally disturbing memory of him turning, his eyes locked with hers. He knew his treatment, so severe even in war, was because of her.

The next morning as early as she could, Charlotte made her way onto the deck. A wispy mist rose from the river and she watched it curl around the beach of Montreal Island. The town stood shining in the eastern sun, its tin church spires dwarfed by the mountain in the background.

She was finally here. Charlotte could hardly contain her excitement. She'd soon be ashore—oh, to stand on something that didn't tilt and sway—and she'd see her father.

Clasping her fingers, Charlotte gave a sigh of relief. Her ordeal was almost over. She'd tell her father everything. They'd never been very close, but Charlotte was certain that was because he was forced to be away so much. Now she'd be here with him. He'd help her forget about her mother's last years, the pain and suffering. She'd also speak to him of Jonathan Knox's punishment. Her father was a military man . . . strict but fair. He'd never condone such treatment. She was sure of it.

Horace Winston would probably insist Captain Knox be detained for a while, and then perhaps a prisoner exchange could be worked out.

From rumors she'd heard, that had already been accomplished for most of the Americans taken off the *Eagle*. Two days off the tip of Newfoundland, the

*Scorpion* had encountered a British schooner. The two vessels had maneuvered alongside each other, exchanged signals, then apparently the crew from the *Eagle* had been rowed across to the other ship.

Mrs. Winthrop had come back from the captain's cabin that evening—a place Charlotte refused to go—with the story that the prisoners would be taken to the nearest port and paroled. Certainly something of that nature could be worked out for Captain Knox.

But the first thing she intended to discuss with her father was Matthew Levid. Once Charlotte told him how horrendous her betrothed was . . . Well, Charlotte was certain her father would never sanction such a marriage, let alone insist upon it.

Charlotte was so deep in thought she didn't notice the man who moved to her side until he cleared his throat. Expecting Mr. Grey, she couldn't stifle a cry of surprise when she noticed it was instead the very man she'd been thinking about. Evidently her wish to never set eyes on Matthew Levid again was to be denied.

"I've arranged for a longboat to take you to shore . . ." Levid began when he had her attention.

"Thank you." Charlotte averted her eyes. They hadn't spoken or even seen each other since she'd left his cabin the day Jonathan Knox was flogged.

"Tell your father I will be along directly, as soon as I've seen everything taken care of here."

"Of course." Secretly she hoped that after she'd spoken to her father, he'd refuse to even receive Captain Levid again.

"Captain Levid, sir." The arrival of Mr. Grey near them interrupted what Charlotte thought a very tense silence.

"What is it?" Captain Levid shifted, returning the salute.

"We have the prisoner, sir. He's ready to transport to shore."

Charlotte stiffened at the midshipman's words, and she slowly lifted her lashes, bracing herself for the sight of Jonathan Knox. It didn't help. Her breathing became shallow, and Charlotte tried to suck more air into her lungs.

He stood taller than the marines guarding him, though his arms were shackled across his stomach. And he stared straight ahead, his expression shuttered beneath the heavy black beard that shadowed his face. From what she could tell, he favored his left arm, though the absence of fresh blood on his shirt implied some healing. The cut on his head still looked angry, but again, Charlotte could see signs of healing. She could see nothing of his back, but his movements were fluid so she assumed the surgeon's care had helped.

Gradually, as she studied Captain Knox, Charlotte became aware of someone's gaze on her. She turned her head in time to see Matthew Levid glare at her with undisguised disdain. Swallowing, Charlotte turned her face away.

"Tell your father I will have the prisoner put in the gaol." Levid's words were clipped and his fingers punishing as they circled Charlotte's elbow. "Come, my dear," he said, sounding for all the world like a doting lover. "I'll see you to the boat."

As much as she disliked his touch, Charlotte had no choice but to follow. The sooner she left this boat, the sooner she could be away from his presence. But she couldn't keep from glancing over her shoulder, even when the pressure on her arm increased.

He'd been watching her. Charlotte could tell by the jerk of his head when her eyes touched his face. But what he'd been thinking as he observed her walk away on Levid's arm, she could only guess.

Charlotte let the brass knocker fall from her trembling fingers. She was nervous, and wasn't certain why. Her father wasn't expecting her, of course, and would be upset by the news she brought, but surely he would understand her need to come.

A young soldier opened the front door of the stone house on St. Paul's Street where she'd been brought. His uniform shone bright and crisp in the morning sun.

"I've come to see General Winston."

Charlotte barely had the words out before she was ushered into the hallway of the large, two-story house. "You're Miss Winston, are you not?" The soldier's tone was pleasant, though he didn't soften his expression with a smile.

"Yes, I am. But how did you—"

"The general received a message this morning from the *Scorpion* informing him of your arrival." He led her to a large, handsomely furnished drawing room and indicated she should enter.

Charlotte had thought to surprise her father, but apparently Captain Levid had prevented that. Walking to the window, looking out over the narrow, winding street, Charlotte wondered what else Matthew Levid might have said in his message.

"I'll tell the general you're here."

Charlotte nodded, running her fingers down the ball fringe on the drapes as the soldier left the room. Did her father know about his wife?

Several minutes later, when General Winston opened the parlor door, Charlotte still didn't know the answer to that question. He stood tall and straight framed in the doorway, dressed in full uniform. It was the only way she always thought of him—stiff and distant. But surely that would change now that they were together.

Wiping her damp palms along the skirt of yet another borrowed gown, Charlotte stepped forward. "Hello, Papa."

"Charlotte." General Winston hesitated a moment before entering the room. He stopped short of meeting his daughter. "This is a surprise."

Knowing better than to expect a hug, yet feeling the lack of it just the same, Charlotte forced a smile. "I understood you knew I was coming."

"As of this morning, yes. But before then, I'd never have thought you'd do such a thing. Even when I received Captain Levid's message, I couldn't understand—"

"Mother died." The blunt words tumbled from her lips, and Charlotte bit back the sob that followed. Her strength seemed to melt away like so much sun-scorched mist, but she knew of nowhere to turn for comfort.

The color had drained from her father's face, but instead of reaching for her, he'd turned away. Charlotte locked her knees, resisted the urge to shut her eyes, and forged ahead.

The general said nothing as he reached for the decanter on his desk.

"She died peacefully . . . in her sleep . . ." Charlotte began, not mentioning the endless nights that pain had kept her mother awake, when even the laudanum had lost its power to numb. Shaking her head when he offered her the glass of wine he poured, Charlotte stepped closer as her father upended the glass himself. "You knew she was very ill."

"Yes, of course. We all did. But I never expected this."

Charlotte reminded herself that everyone dealt with grief differently. Some became hysterical, some melancholy, and apparently some acted as if they'd never considered the possibility—even though she'd tried to tell him on his last visit home. Tentatively she touched his hand, pulling back when his body tensed. Recognizing the too-familiar sting of tears against her eyelids, Charlotte turned away. "At least now she has no more pain."

"You're right, of course." Another drink followed the first. "I know it wasn't easy for your mother."

"No, it wasn't." Folding her hands, Charlotte walked back toward the window. How had she expected her father to take this news? She wasn't certain. But Charlotte knew now she'd longed for someone to share the pain with. She'd hoped that person was her father.

"Why did you come here, Charlotte?"

The fact that her father's question mirrored the one spinning in her own head made it no easier to answer. *To share our grief, and somehow make it bearable* hardly seemed an appropriate answer. Nor did she think he'd understand her need to get away from Oxfordshire, to taste, if only briefly, the freedom so long denied her. Nor did this seem the time to discuss her hoped-for release from Captain Levid. "I came to tell you about Mother" seemed the simplest reply.

"A letter would have accomplished the same thing, I should think."

Charlotte said nothing, only stood wondering if this was it. Was there to be no more discussion of their loss? Did he not wish to know of her last words? Her funeral? The life she'd lived since his last visit?

Her father's next words convinced her that discussion of her mother was indeed over, at least for the present. "I understand this foolish endeavor of yours has caused some problems."

Foolish endeavor? Charlotte bit her lip, glancing toward the window. "Our ship was attacked."

"And you were taken prisoner."

His words were more accusation than question, and Charlotte turned back toward him. "All the passengers and crew of the *Balfour* were."

"But not all of them were confined to the captain's cabin."

Anger shot through her, but she took a calming breath before responding. "I see Captain Levid's message contained more than news of my arrival."

"For God's sake, Charlotte, how could you?"

Charlotte's eyes widened. Her father *could* show emotion. He was showing it now. Intense anger raged in his eyes, the same dark brown as her own, in his voice. Perhaps it was only love and grief he was incapable of demonstrating.

"Do you have any idea of the difficulty I went through to see you betrothed. Men were not exactly lining up in the lane to offer for you. And now . . ."

Swallowing, trying to pretend she hadn't heard the cruel words, Charlotte asked, "What are you talking about?"

"Captain Levid." Her father bit out the name. "He wants to discuss your betrothal. He implies that he may withdraw his proposal."

Relief made her weak. Charlotte reached for a chair back, wrapping her fingers around the polished mahogany. "But that's wonderful."

General Winston stared at her as if she'd lost her mind. "Wonderful? A fine man like Matthew Levid threatens to withdraw his suit and you say it's wonderful. Perhaps you didn't hear me when I said you had no other prospects . . . and that was before your disgraceful behavior with the American." This speech seemed to take its toll, for her father turned back to the sideboard to refill his glass.

Charlotte's hand stopped him. "Let me tell you about your *fine* Captain Levid." Her father pulled his hand away, but Charlotte continued. "He had a severely wounded man flogged, and then put on quarter rations."

"A man that had tried to kill him . . . and I may add had compromised you."

Silk swished against her leg as Charlotte stepped back. How could she argue with what he'd said? She didn't know if Jonathan Knox had tried to kill Captain Levid, but she'd witnessed the American's expression when talking about Levid enough to know it was possible.

As for the other, all Charlotte could do was deny it again. "Captain Knox did not . . . did not . . ."

"We won't discuss this, Charlotte!"

"But you said he did, and he didn't." *Ah, but he would have,* a small voice whispered in her ear. *And you would have let him.*

"That's enough." Horace Winston slammed his hand against the sideboard, spilling the wine. "You'll go to the room I've had prepared for you and stay there till summoned."

Backing away took all Charlotte's concentration. She'd never seen her father like this before; didn't know he could become so angry. But Charlotte realized she really knew very little about the man who'd fathered her. He stared at her now, anger contorting his aristocratic features, and she turned, reaching for the doorknob.

"And Charlotte . . ."

She paused but didn't glance around.

"Captain Levid will be joining us for our evening

meal. I hope by that time to have convinced him that he should honor his obligation to you. I'll expect your cooperation."

When Charlotte didn't answer, but continued to finger the smooth brass, his voice rang louder . . . nearer. "Do you understand me, Charlotte?"

"Yes. I understand completely," she whispered before leaving the room.

But Captain Levid didn't come that evening, or even the next. Concerns on his ship kept him away, Charlotte's father assured her as they sat staring at each other across the expanse of Irish lace tablecloth.

It was morning of the third day since Charlotte's arrival in Montreal, and she'd joined her father for breakfast. Though she'd become thoroughly familiar with the inside of her bedroom, she'd seen little else of the city. That was to end today.

"I've arranged for you to go shopping today," General Winston said as he spooned jam onto a toast wedge.

Charlotte glanced up without responding. This was the first pleasant thing her father had said since sending her to her room. She'd taken most of her meals there, asking for a tray when her father sent word that Levid would not be joining them. But this morning he'd requested her presence at the morning meal.

"A Madame Ramezay will accompany you," he continued as if he hadn't noticed her lack of response. "She has excellent taste and will soon have you fitted out properly."

The motion of his fork toward her gown made Charlotte glance down. Mrs. Winthrop had loaned her two dresses. Today she wore the plum silk. Neither gown fit, as Mrs. Winthrop's figure contained many more curves than Charlotte's. But as

139

Captain Levid had pointed out to her, anything was better than displaying herself in men's garb.

Though the clothes did not belong to her, and she'd already decided they must be returned, Charlotte did not feel inclined to shop for finery. "I'm in mourning," she reminded her father.

"We'll have none of that. Your mother's death was unfortunate, but Captain Levid doesn't wish to see you draped in black, and neither do I. Nor will there be any talk of postponing the wedding. If he'll still have you, that is."

If he'll still . . . Charlotte found her father's attitude unbelievable. She opened her mouth to tell him so, but a servant's announcement of a guest stopped her.

Madame Ramezay swept into the room in a flurry of beflowered chinz. She brushed a kiss across the general's cheek, and apologized for her tardy arrival. "Ah, but you know me, *ma chère*. I can barely function before noon. It is only because of my deep desire to please you that I have torn myself away from my boudoir this early."

Before Charlotte could fully appreciate her father's attitude toward the woman—he smiled and actually preened as she spoke—Madame Ramezay turned her attention to Charlotte.

"Oh, but this must be your daughter, Horace. You never told me she was such a beauty. But isn't that just like a father, so inclined to overlook the roses in his own garden."

"Charlotte . . ." Her father rose and proceeded to make the introductions, not seeming to mind when Madame Ramezay stole the obligation from him.

"But please call me Desirée. It is so much more charming than Madame Ramezay, is it not? And you shall be Charlotte. Such a pretty name for a pretty girl. Are we ready to go, Charlotte?"

Arguing seemed useless. Besides, Charlotte doubted she could manage to wedge in a word of protest. And, despite the older woman's apparent ability to talk without taking a break to so much as breathe, Charlotte found herself liking her. She imagined Madame—Desirée's age to be approximately forty, though she acted much younger.

"I have lived in Montreal forever," Desirée said as they walked north on St. Paul Street, toward the retail district. "You must let me show you around. We shall attend the concerts and parties."

"I don't really think I should. I'm in mourning. You see—"

"Ah, yes. Your poor mother." Sadness momentarily sobered the dimpled face. "Such a tragedy. I am so sorry. But you see, I know how you are feeling. My dear François died not three years ago."

"I'm sorry."

"Of course." Desirée touched Charlotte's cheek. "Death is part of life, is it not? That's why we must take what happiness we can. Your dear mother would not want you to be sad. You've been sad for so long. Now you must be happy. Enjoy life, little one."

"How do you know about my mother?"

"Your papa told me," Desirée stated matter-of-factly while fingering a length of rose-colored silk. "Do you like this shade? I think it would look wonderful on you."

And to Charlotte's surprise, it did. The dusty pink seemed to make her dark eyes shine brighter and her skin take on a becoming blush. Still she tried to explain why she couldn't have a gown made of it, but Desirée wouldn't hear of it.

"Your papa gave me my orders, and like a good

141

soldier, I must obey, *n'est'cé, pa?*"

And if she were truthful with herself, Charlotte realized she was having such a good time she didn't want to resist the Frenchwoman. Charlotte had never had much interest in clothes. Her mother's illness had occupied so much of her time, and Kennington, the nearest village to her home, had such few shops. And truthfully, there'd never been another woman to show much interest in what she wore, outside of being certain her clothing was proper and tidy.

But Desirée changed all that. She did indeed seem to know every place and everybody. Clothiers and shopkeepers greeted her—and thus Charlotte—with a smile and a willingness to help. Before she knew it, Charlotte had ordered a new wardrobe, and had more hats being delivered to the house on St. Paul's Street than she'd owned in her entire life.

"And now we must find something already made for tonight." Desirée turned to the shopkeeper, a lady near her own age. "Miss Winston is receiving her betrothed this evening and must look her very best."

The pleasure of the day faded, and Charlotte faced reality. Of course this was the reason she needed all these clothes. Matthew Levid. Her expression must have mirrored her feeling because as soon as the shopkeeper disappeared behind a curtain, Desirée drew Charlotte to the side.

"What is it *ma chère?*"

"Nothing." Charlotte picked up a ribbon, and mimicking Desirée's earlier actions, lifted it to her hair. "What do you think?"

"I think you are not being truthful with your new friend."

Charlotte dropped the ribbon, realizing Desirée saw through her attempt to change the subject.

142

"You are not pleased with your father's choice."

It was more statement than question, and Charlotte could do nothing but nod her agreement. But she didn't want Desirée to think she had no reason. "I think he's cruel."

"Ah, cruel men are the worst," Desirée said, then smiled. "But perhaps you can soften his ways."

"I don't want to soften his ways. I don't want to have anything to do with him." Charlotte realized her voice had risen, and quickly turned away, catching her lower lip between her teeth.

"This is because of your American, I think."

Shocked that Desirée would know that, too, Charlotte swirled around. "That's part of it," she admitted.

"Perhaps more than part?"

"I . . . I don't know what you mean."

Linking their arms, Desirée walked Charlotte to the window. When they'd moved as far away from the shopkeepers hearing as possible, Desirée sighed. "I've never been blessed with a daughter, *ma chère*, but if I had, I'd give her the advice I shall give you now. Forget this American. Thinking of him will cause you nothing but grief."

She seemed to sense Charlotte's resistance, for her hand reached out, stroking her cheek. "So young," she said under her breath. "And a little in love, I think." She smiled sadly, ignoring the negative shake of Charlotte's head. "But nothing can come of it. The American is doomed."

"What are you talking about?"

"Nothing. I have said too much." Desirée started to turn away, but Charlotte caught her shoulder, spinning the older woman back to face her.

"No. You said doomed. I want to know what you mean." But nothing Charlotte said could change

Desirée's mind. She simply refused to speak of it again.

The rest of the shopping was accomplished quickly. Desirée proclaimed the gown she picked out for Charlotte for that evening perfect, but Charlotte had lost her appetite for shopping. Nothing really interested her until on the walk home, while pointing out to Charlotte different landmarks in the city, Desirée mentioned the gaol.

Immediately Charlotte's gaze flew to the large stone structure. Behind one of those many barred windows was Jonathan Knox. Was he doomed as Desirée said? Charlotte decided to ask her father again even if it did create another row. But she steadfastly refused to believe that love had anything to do with her concern.

Still, as she studied herself in the mirror, that evening, amazed by the transformation that Desirée had brought about in her appearance, Charlotte had to admit she was willing to sacrifice a lot to ensure the American's safety. She'd concocted her plan this afternoon, as Desirée cut her hair so that light-brown tendrils now curled beguilingly about her face.

She'd make a deal with her father. He wanted her to marry Levid. She would. Without protest. Charlotte couldn't help the shudder that ran through her. But then she really wasn't giving her father anything that he probably wouldn't get anyway. He seemed determined for her to marry Levid, but she'd help the process. Staring into the mirror, she almost believed she could.

Desirée had assured her that she looked lovely. With a sigh, Charlotte turned away. If she could make Captain Levid want her, so much the better.

And in exchange for acting the seductress—again Charlotte cringed—she only wanted Jonathan Knox returned to America. She couldn't believe this wouldn't be done anyway. So was it too much to ask for her cooperation?

Charlotte didn't think so, nor did she think about why she was willing to do this.

Doomed. The word gave her little rest, and hurried her step as she descended the stairs. Her new silk slippers made nary a sound as she walked across the carpet toward the drawing room. Her father's expression of admiration when he saw her gown and hair might have warmed her heart before, but now it only strengthened Charlotte's resolve to strike a bargain with him.

He raised his goblet of wine. "Desirée did well."

"Father, I need to speak with you." Turning, Charlotte closed the drawing-room door, shutting her eyes and taking a deep breath before facing him.

"What is it?" he asked impatiently. "Captain Levid will be here soon."

"That's what I want to discuss. I—"

"And I thought I made myself clear on that point. You *will* marry Levid if he'll—"

"Have me," Charlotte interrupted. "I know what you said. "I'm just . . . I'm willing to do my part to ensure he will have me," she finished.

"Meaning?"

Charlotte's eyes cut to her father's face. She swallowed. Certainly he knew what she was saying. But he continued to stare at her, his expression disdainful. "The dress, the hair," Charlotte explained. "I'll strive to be a pleasant companion."

"I should think that might help." General Winston emptied his goblet and turned back to the sideboard to refill it.

"There's just one other thing." Her father glanced over his shoulder and Charlotte wiped her palms down the side of her skirt. "I want something in exchange for my cooperation." His eyes narrowed and she rushed on. "Captain Knox. I want him released and sent back to his country."

"Why you little . . ." His last word was lost in the sound of his glass crashing against the far wall.

Charlotte could only stare openmouthed as he stalked toward her. He grabbed her arms, shaking her hard before letting her go. "You will do your best to charm Captain Levid . . . and there will be no more talk of this American. Is that understood? Is it?" he repeated when Charlotte said nothing.

"Yes." Charlotte fought to keep her voice steady.

"All right then." He yanked on the lapels of his jacket and crossed the room, reaching for another glass. "I should have paid more heed to Desirée when she mentioned your attachment to this American captain." He poured more wine.

"Who is she?"

"Who?"

Still quaking inside from his earlier display of anger, Charlotte knew she shouldn't provoke him again. But something, perhaps it was loyalty to her dead mother, compelled her to seek an answer. She braided her fingers. "Desirée. What is she to you?"

He took a swallow of wine. "None of your damn business."

"She's your mistress, isn't she?"

"Charlotte, I'm warning you . . ."

He was coming toward her again, but she didn't care. "All that time when mother was ill, you were here with her. How could you?"

A knock at the door saved him from replying, saved Charlotte whatever punishment he meant to give. He opened the door after grabbing her elbow and giving her a telling look, and together they went to meet

146

their guest.

Charlotte didn't know how she made it through the meal. She sat at her father's side, across the table from Captain Levid. She supposed she was charming, though she couldn't remember a word she said.

Captain Levid made several comments about her appearance, and his gaze seemed permanently fixed to her bodice, but Charlotte didn't care. She just longed for the moment when she could retire.

It came at the end of the meal. She stood, locking her wobbly knees, and announced she had a headache and was going to her room. Before anyone could say a word, she left the room.

Once in the hallway she closed her eyes and leaned against the flocked wallpaper. How she'd love to escape into her dream world, but she couldn't. Only reality swam behind her lashes when she tried. The door to the dining room was ajar and she could hear voices—her father and Captain Levid. They were talking about her, but she didn't care.

Charlotte pushed away from the wall and took a step toward the stairs, then stopped. One of the men—her father—mentioned Jonathan Knox's name.

She glanced around quickly, thankful the entrance hall was empty, and pressed her ear toward the shaft of light escaping the dining room.

"I want him gone." That from Captain Levid.

"Believe me, no more than I." Her father's tone was angry. "And by the morrow it will be accomplished."

Gone? Could they plan to send him to America, Charlotte thought, only to berate her náiveté as her father's next words came drifting through the open space. "I've arranged for Captain Knox to escape this evening. When he does, my men will kill him."

147

Charlotte's breath caught, and she jammed her head against her mouth to catch any sound that might escape. But it was a useless precaution. Matthew Levid's laughter drowned any noise that might come from the hall. When he finished showing his appreciation for her father's scheme, Levid asked, "How can you be certain Knox will attempt an escape tonight?"

Charlotte stayed only long enough to hear her father's reply before turning on her heel and escaping through the front door.

# Chapter Nine

A gray misty rain fell, chilling the air and covering everything with a fine sheen. Charlotte's mind raced as her silk-slippered feet slid over the wooden sidewalk. She needed to think, to come up with a rational plan, but only one thought surfaced, and it pounded through her head with each step she took.

Murder. Her father and Captain Levid were conspiring to murder Jonathan Knox. This was no military justice or honorable fight to the finish. This was a malicious, cold-blooded taking of life. And if things her father had said were any indication, she was part of the cause.

Well, she wouldn't let them succeed. But how could she stop them?

The scheme was already set in motion. Even now as she made her way along the narrow street, Captain Knox might be lying in the dirt, mortally wounded. That thought made her ignore the pain in her side and quicken her pace.

Oil lamps spilled puddles of light that did little to chase away the night shadows. Earlier, in the light of day, with Desirée by her side, Montreal had appeared lively and gay. Now each sound, every whiff of air drifting off the river, seemed sinister.

"Stop it," Charlotte admonished herself as she approached Rue Notre Dame. She would not let her imagination get the best of her. She passed the Seminary of St. Sulpice, and still had no idea what she could do to warn Captain Knox. Her father had said the guard would leave his post and Captain Knox's cell door would be "accidentally" left unlocked. Who could resist such temptation? Certainly not a man like Jonathan Knox.

Though their unconventional acquaintance had been short, she knew enough about him to bet he'd do anything within his power to escape. Perhaps if she could sneak into the gaol and—

A rifle's report shattered the evening silence.

"No." Blood pounded in Charlotte's head as she rushed toward the gaol. Were they shooting at him? Had the soldiers her father positioned near the back door already killed him?

For whatever reason, no streetlights burned in this area; nothing dispelled the heavy cloak of night. One more shot sounded, then another, and Charlotte paused, not knowing what to do. She'd reached the gaol. Even in the twilight she could make out the huge stone building—a black shadow looming from the darkness. With trembling fingers she reached out, clasping the damp wrought-iron fence she remembered from that afternoon. It felt solid beneath her palm, and she pressed her body against it, clinging as sharp claps of gunfire burst behind her.

Charlotte squeezed her eyes shut, trying to string together snatches of prayers running through her head together. *I shall not want . . . Leadeth me . . . his name sake . . .*

"Jesus!" The name exploded from out of the darkness as an unseen force barreled into her. Charlotte's grasp on the rails failed and she flew to the wet grass, landing hard on her back. A heavy weight flopped on top of her, driving the air from her lungs, stifling her feeble attempt to scream.

"What the hell?"

Charlotte stiffened. She knew that voice. But how was it possible? "Captain Knox?"

The man atop her grew rigid, the harsh breathing close to her ear caught. Slowly the weight shifted, rising slightly. Charlotte could barely make out bright eyes shining in a dark, whiskered face when another blast from a musket sent him sprawling.

Now the only competition to the night sounds was the duet of their rasping breath, the pounding of their hearts. Charlotte hesitated, almost afraid to ask. "Did they hit you?"

"No." He hissed the word close to her ear, his breath fluttering the newly cut curls.

Thank goodness. Perhaps her father's plan hadn't been foolproof. "You shouldn't have tried to escape. It was a trap." Charlotte's words were no more than a whisper, but she guessed under the circumstances that was appropriate.

"I figured that out," he responded dryly. Jon lifted his head, his face inches from hers. "Why in the hell are you here? Come to watch the trap clamp shut?"

"No, I—"

Again gunfire sounded, much closer, and Jon flattened himself as best he could, crushing down against Charlotte. She tried not to notice the way his hard body felt pressed so intimately to hers. He was in mortal danger, for heaven's sake. This was no time to think about his broad chest flush with her breasts, or the musky smell of his skin. But she couldn't help the memories that assailed her, flashing her back to a place and time when he had held her in his arms.

But apparently his mind didn't have this annoying habit of leaping from the present. As soon as the musket fire stopped, he jerked to his feet. "Come on," he said huskily, grabbing Charlotte's arm and dragging her up behind him.

"No, I can't—" Charlotte's protest was lost as he yanked her along. After that, it was all she could do to keep up with the captain as he ran around the side of a large stone building and down a side street. This one had no wooden sidewalk, and their feet sank in the mud as they ran along. Charlotte's lungs burned, and the pain in her side threatened to send her sprawling to the ground with every step, but he kept going.

She could hear the pounding feet behind them, but had no idea if their pursuers had spotted them. She herself could see almost nothing, and was relying on Captain Knox to steer the way. "They're getting closer," Charlotte gasped, but he paid no attention, only continued running down the street, dragging her behind.

When he reached a crossroads, he stopped so abruptly that Charlotte's momentum sent her crashing into him. She'd have fallen if two strong hands hadn't clasped her shoulders. He shoved her in front of him. "Where in the hell are we?" he demanded.

Glancing furtively up and down the street, Charlotte shook her head. Rows of wooden buildings with light shining through iron-shuttered windows appeared to be homes, but she had no idea the name of the street or even which direction they'd come. "I . . . I don't know."

The expletive that escaped him would have shocked her had the situation not been so dire—and if she hadn't heard him use it before. Charlotte hazarded a glance over her shoulder, and what she saw made her gasp. "They have torches," she whispered. She felt him look around, knew he could see the dozen or so flames bobbing in the darkness, sending spirals of pale-gray smoke floating into the air. She squinted, trying to see if all the soldiers carried torches, but she couldn't tell. Regardless, they had the unarmed captain greatly outnumbered.

"This way," he ordered, and Charlotte wondered why he bothered. It wasn't as if she could do anything but follow, since he'd again manacled his hand around her wrist and was dragging her behind him.

They headed toward a huge building that looked like a church. Charlotte tried to remember if she'd seen it, on her brief tour today. Could it be the Nôtre Dame de Bon Secius, or the Scotch Church? She wasn't sure, and she had no time for speculating as she tried to keep up.

The captain jerked on a gate, found it locked, cursed under his breath, then swerved around the side of the rough stone building. This must be the front of the building, for it opened out onto a wide square. By now Charlotte could hear barked commands shouted to the soldiers. "Spread out and find the prisoner." They weren't to the church yet, but Charlotte didn't think it would take them long.

Apparently the captain didn't think so, either. He pulled her forward, and Charlotte hoped they weren't going to run anymore. She honestly didn't think she could move another step. But instead of dragging her along with him, Captain Knox shoved her into a deep crevice formed by an angle in the architecture. Sharp-edged rock snagged her clothing and gouged at her skin as he wedged himself in after her.

His broad back blocked any view of the outside square, but she could hear the footsteps drawing closer. Within minutes the soldiers would be upon their hiding place.

The captain must have had a sudden change of heart, because he shifted, momentarily affording her a glimpse of the soldiers outside their cramped alcove. Before she knew what he was about, Charlotte felt a large palm clamp over her mouth.

She tried to protest. After all, why would she want to give him away now? She had come to the gaol to warn him. But he didn't know that, and taking her weak struggles as an attempt to reveal their location, he tightened his grip.

The soldiers were so close she could hear their breathing, the creaking of their leather boots.

In front of her, pressed tightly against her, Charlotte could feel Jonathan Knox's tension. It seemed to seep from his body through hers. Though the evening was chilly, they were both sweating profusely, and the captain's hand slipped for a fraction of a minute before he regained his concentration and squeezed even tighter.

Charlotte wondered if he realized that she could have screamed in that instant, but guessed by the way he held her now, that he didn't.

Besides, he was too absorbed with watching the two men standing right in front of their hiding place to think about anything else. One soldier held his torch aloft, grunting into the shaft of light he created in the drizzly darkness. "We'll never find the bastard now."

The other leaned against a stone pillar. "Got better things to do tonight than chase some Yank."

The hoot of laughter sent chills up Charlotte's spine. "What better have *you* got to do?"

Obviously disgruntled, the second man growled. "Anything is better than being out in this. I'm damn well soaked to the skin."

"I'll grant you that. But the sergeant isn't going to let us head for the barracks until we find the bloke, so we better get to it."

Charlotte held her breath as the soldiers stalked away, speculating on how the sergeant knew the prisoner would attempt an escape tonight.

"Interesting question, don't you think?" Jon whispered, his voice dark and accusing as he leaned down toward his captive. The lack of light made it difficult to see her, but he caught a glimpse of huge eyes staring at him over his hand. Of course she couldn't answer him, but her lack of response angered him all the same. His fingers tightened, biting into soft flesh, hurting her. Her eyes widened, and she trembled. He could feel the delicate bones of her jaw, her soft breath on his hand. He released her, hoping to God he wasn't making a fatal mistake. But all she did was let out a low sob that made him feel guilty as hell. He was the victim in all this. Why should he feel guilty?

Inching forward, Jon peered out into the square. He caught sight of torches disappearing around the corner of the building. Trying to steady his breathing, he pressed his shoulder into the damp stone, then looked back toward Charlotte. He could barely make her out in the darkness. "Where is he?"

"Who?"

"Don't play games with me, damnit. In case you haven't noticed, I'm not in the mood," Jon snarled. "Now tell me where I can find Levid."

"Why do you want to know?" Charlotte had a frightening idea she knew why, and the evil grate of Jonathan Knox's laugh did nothing to dispel her theory.

"I plan to invite him to tea. Why in the hell do you think I want to know?"

155

"You want to go after him again." Charlotte's voice was breathless. "Wasn't one attempt at killing him enough?"

"No." Jon leaned back toward her. "Because I didn't succeed. And now he's after me. He was behind my little escape tonight wasn't he?"

Perhaps he did have something to do with it, but the idea was her father's. And the plan had failed—at least for now. But if the captain insisted on seeking revenge, he would be caught. He needed to get off the island and back to his own country, but Charlotte didn't think he'd leave if he knew where Levid was. "Captain Levid left." The lie escaped her lips before she could stop it.

She couldn't see him, but Charlotte could imagine him narrowing his eyes. "What do you mean left?"

"Left. Sailed away." The lies were coming fast and furious. "He only stopped in Montreal long enough to deliver me to my father, and to deliver you, of course, and then he went back to sea."

His hands found her shoulders, his fingers none too gentle. "You expect me to believe—"

"I don't care what you believe." Twisting away in the confined space, Charlotte knocked her elbow into a jagged stone.

"If you're trying to protect him . . ."

"I'm not." This Charlotte could say with complete candor. It wasn't Matthew Levid she was trying to protect. Apparently the sincerity of her words had some effect, for his hands slid down her arms and she heard him sigh.

"You have to get out of here. The soldiers could come back anytime. Go." She gave him a small shove. He didn't budge.

"You'd like that, wouldn't you? Well, I've got news for you. I'm not going anyplace without you."

156

"Me?" She couldn't go with him. She had to get back to her father's house before he discovered her missing—before he put two and two together. Besides, it didn't make sense for her to go with him. "I'd only slow you down."

"I'll see that you keep up." With those words, the captain hauled her out of their hiding place. "Besides, if your betrothed didn't plan this attempt to get rid of me, I'd bet your father had something to do with it. That means I should be pretty safe as long as I have you with me."

She was being abducted! Oh, how did she get herself into these situations? All she'd wanted to do was warn him for heaven's sake, not go running off with him. When the soldiers were chasing them, she had no choice. He hadn't given her a choice. But now he was relatively safe. And she wasn't. How could she get away? He didn't leave her long to ponder as he grabbed her wrist and pulled her, forcing her to keep up with his long strides.

He had to get off this damn island, Jon thought. But how? All he'd seen of the town had been a quick trip from the *Scorpion* to the gaol, not much of a tour. But while he'd been cooling his heels in the gaol, his companion had been free as a bird. And unless he missed his guess, the little wren had seen enough of the city to know a way out. "Which way to the river?" he demanded, stopping at the intersection of two streets.

"I don't know." St. Paul's Street was close to the St. Lawrence River, but they'd twisted all around in their escape so she had no idea how to even get there.

"You don't know?" He sounded incredulous. "What have you been doing with all your time since we got here, attending soirées?"

"Not that it's any of your business, but no." Oh, he

157

could make her so angry. At the moment she couldn't imagine why she'd bothered to save his life. Well, she hadn't actually saved it, but she'd been going to.

Drawing herself to her full height, Charlotte stared at the dark shadow that was the captain. "I've only been out once and that was on a shopping trip. At the time I didn't realize I should be making a mental map of the city." Lacing her words with sarcasm was not something Charlotte usually did, but this situation called for it.

He either didn't notice her tone, or thought nothing of it. "You should have at least taken note of where you were."

"I did." Maybe she should point out that she found the gaol because of this afternoon's shopping trip, but decided he wouldn't be very impressed anyway. Besides, wasn't he a navigator? "Why don't you read the stars or something."

"That would be rather difficult through the clouds."

Though it had stopped drizzling, the sky was overcast with only an occasional sliver of moonshine to soften the night.

"Come on." Again the words were useless as his strong fingers gripped her arm, dragging her along behind him. "And if you're tempted to scream for help, just remember I can break your neck without working up a sweat." For emphasis he wrapped his fingers of his free hand around her throat, dropping it when he felt the flutter of her pulse.

He frightened her, truly frightened her for the first time. On the *Eagle* he'd reminded her of the pirate, and he'd overwhelmed her. There had been threats—threats she'd believed—but she still hadn't been frightened . . . not of him. Her reaction to him had been the scariest part. But things had changed. Even though she'd been on an enemy ship before, it had somehow seemed civilized. Everything had seemed civilized until Matthew Levid.

His actions had changed everything. Now they were all suffering.

Charlotte tripped over the torn hem of her gown, but before her knees could hit the stone road he'd hauled her up. She guessed he saw this action as an escape attempt or a ploy to slow him down, for his voice was rough with anger when he warned her to be more careful.

She wanted to rail at him, to yank her arm free and confront him. Granted he'd suffered, and suffered severely at Levid's hands, but she was not to blame. And if she'd wanted to see him dead, she could think of a lot easier ways than being yanked through the dark streets of Montreal. She could have done nothing when she heard her father and Captain Levid talking. That would have served the arrogant American right.

But she couldn't tell him this. What little she had left of her energy was needed to stumble along behind him, and she couldn't have broken the iron grip of his fingers even if she'd had two times her strength.

So she just kept dragging one foot in front of the other, hoping her captor had some destination in mind and that they reached it soon. Charlotte longed to see where they were, but the captain kept to the back alleys, studiously avoiding the wider streets with their oil lights and occasional groups of people.

And with good reason. Charlotte could only imagine what they looked like, but then her imagination had always been good. Her new gown, the one that she'd admired in her mirror—was it only hours ago—now hung in dirty, damp shreds. Her hair hung in fitful tangles down her back, the carefully curled and twisted style Desirée had coaxed it into ravaged beyond recognition.

As for the captain, he must be in worse shape still. She hadn't gotten a good look at him, but several times when he'd leaned close to her, she'd felt the bristle of beard. And she was certain he still wore the clothes he'd worn on the *Scorpion*.

The sharp yap of a dog sounded behind her moments before Charlotte felt a sharp, hot pain shoot up from her heel. She shrieked, clutching toward the captain, and still the pain continued. His curse sounded above her screams and for an instant Charlotte thought he might drop her arm and run, leaving her to the mercy of the growling, biting dog. But he didn't.

Deftly he swung her around, his body jerking in what Charlotte thought were kicking motions. Each movement brought her face rubbing against the dampness of his linen shirt as she clung to him. Her screams had subsided to loud, gulping sobs, but she heard the dog yelp then whimper away.

She tried to stop making noises, knew his palm would clamp uncomfortably over her mouth any second, but she couldn't. She'd kept her feelings pent up inside her and now the dam had burst. Tears streamed down her face, and she didn't try to stem their flow as another dry, hiccupy sob trembled through her.

He spun around and Charlotte stiffened, but instead of an unyielding hand flattening across her jaw, she was hauled up against him, her cries muffled in the soft folds of cloth covering his hard chest. His heart beat a fast, steady cadence beneath muscle that heaved in and out, and Charlotte realized he was as out of breath as she.

"Are you hurt?" His question rumbled deep and

low against her ear. When she didn't answer, only continued the pitiful sobbing, she seemed unable to control his hand that soothed down the length of her hair, coming to rest on her back. "Did he hurt you?" His voice was more insistent now, and to Charlotte's displeasure, he unplastered her from his shirtfront and held her at arm's length.

For the first time this evening, Charlotte was thankful of the darkness. She could tell he strained to see her, but unless his eyes were more adept in the dark than hers, he could only make out a dark shape, not the pathetic creature she must appear. With a reserve of strength Charlotte didn't know she possessed, she sucked in her breath, wiped her hand under her runny nose, and let out a strangled squeak. "I'm fine."

"Are you sure? Did he bite you?"

"No. I don't think he broke the skin." Charlotte twisted her foot about, checking for damage. "He scared me more than anything," she admitted.

Jon pulled her back into the shelter of his embrace. "It's all right now."

What was he doing? Just what the hell was he doing? Jon dropped his arms and turned around, remembering to grab hold of Charlotte Winston's hand before he started out of the alley. He had no business comforting her, no business at all. He didn't even know why he did it. If anyone in this mess needed comforting, it was *he*. He'd been shot and stabbed and flogged, for God's sake. Then stuck in a prison only to be tricked into escaping and shot at again.

For all he knew, half of Montreal was looking for him—at least the residents who wore British uniforms—and if they found him, he could forget about any future. And here he was worrying if Charlotte

Winston, the cause of a goodly portion of his troubles, had been bitten by a dog. By the feel of it when he'd kicked it, it had been a runty little mutt anyway.

They were getting close to the river. Jon could smell it. Charlotte faltered and Jon slowed his pace. He was going to have to go out into the open to reach the river. Moving cautiously, Jon left the cover of a warehouse and stepped out onto the steep shore that served as a natural wharf for the city. If the soldiers were laying in wait for him, this, or down on the beach, would be the perfect spot.

Dragging Charlotte up beside him, Jon leaned toward her. Somehow she'd known of the first part of the plan to kill him. Maybe she knew more. "Are they waiting for me down there?" He motioned toward the beach with their linked hands.

"Who?" Charlotte was half afraid she was going to start wailing again.

He made an exasperated sound that convinced Charlotte of his annoyance with her, and hissed in her ear, "In case you haven't noticed, your pretty little neck is at much at risk here as mine, should there be any more shooting."

His words sent chills down Charlotte's spine. She thought they'd escaped the soldiers, had hoped he'd soon release her. But apparently he suspected further trouble, and more, thought her privy to whatever it was. Charlotte started to protest, but his hand clamping over her mouth stopped her.

Charlotte heard the voices, and stared up at the captain, just making out his silhouette, before he shoved her back into the shadows. Almost afraid to breathe lest she give away their presence, Charlotte cowered behind him.

162

But the commotion came only from a pair of drunken sailors who wandered on the quay.

"All right . . ." Jon began when the sailors were out of earshot. "We're going to go down to the beach and hope we can find a boat or something. Stay behind me, and for God's sake, try to keep up."

"Can't you just leave me here? I won't tell them where you've gone. I promise."

"Why?" Jon loomed over her in the darkness. "Is there some reason you don't want to go down on that beach? Are there soldiers down there waiting for me, Charlotte?"

"No . . . I don't know. Just let me go."

"Can't" is all he said before pulling her back out into the open.

They climbed down the slope of land onto the beach. It was sandy beneath her shoes and Charlotte could hear water lapping against the shore and see the outline of several vessels lying off in the harbor. She'd walked across the beach earlier, when the longboat had brought her ashore. How different things had seemed then.

"Stay down." The whispered words came to her about the same time her arm was jerked, and Charlotte found herself moving along bent at the waist.

"I can't . . ." she began to protest, but stopped, realizing it would do no good. She obviously was moving in this awkward position.

When they reached the shore, cold water inched over her feet, sending shivers across her skin. Still they sloshed on. "What are you—" His insistent shush quieted her. What was his plan now? Surely he didn't think they could swim across the St. Lawrence River. But then they were walking along the shore, not into the river.

"Ouch. Damnit!"

Charlotte fell against his hard back. "What is it?"

"Be quiet," Jon warned, gingerly rubbing his aching shin. "I found us a boat." He didn't need to specify that he'd found it the hard way.

"*Us?* You mean you aren't going to let me go now?" Charlotte couldn't believe he planned to drag her out onto the river. But then everything since she'd met him seemed somewhat unreal.

Suddenly Charlotte realized he'd let her go, intent upon examing the small boat she could just make out in the darkness. Without stopping to think of the consequences, she started off across the sand. She'd made it maybe ten rods before she heard his clipped oath. The next thing she knew, Charlotte was sprawled facedown on the beach, spitting sand.

"Oh no you don't, Charlotte, my love. You're coming with me." Without another word, he picked her up, ignoring her struggles, and deposited her unceremoniously in the small, flat-bottomed boat.

It wasn't much as boats went, Jon thought, but it should get them across the river. "Sit still," he ordered as he shoved off from shore and then settled in beside her.

Charlotte fought back a sob and shut her eyes. If ever there was a need to escape from the present, it was now. But not even that luxury was afforded her, for the captain's voice, sharp and angry, ripped her back to reality.

"You lying bitch!"

Charlotte's eyes flew open and she stared about her to see what had caused his outburst. The clouds had finally cleared away leaving the night flooded with reflected moonlight. She could see fairly well now. And there, as she followed the captain's hard stare, was a ship, its name clearly distinguishable on the stern. *Scorpion*.

But before Charlotte could think of a way to explain her deceit, a new threat arose. A shout rang out from shore. "There he is!" And that was followed by the too-familiar sound of a firing musket.

# Chapter Ten

"Get your head down!"

The captain's shouted command broke Charlotte's trancelike gaze at the *Scorpion*. Why hadn't she realized that he'd see Captain Levid's ship in the harbor? A second report sounded, and Charlotte realized this was no time to worry about a little lie. Frantically she threw herself to the bottom of the boat, her hip sloshing in a puddle of pooled water.

Another shot zinged past, and Charlotte covered her ears. "Are they shooting at us?" she called, raising her voice above the sound of water hitting the side of the boat.

The captain didn't answer, merely grunting as he dragged the oars against the current. Then, leaning forward, he plunged the wooden oars into the water. From her spot huddled in the bottom of the boat Charlotte watched his shirt strain across his shoulders. Plastered to his skin by the rain and splashing spray, it shone bright in the moonlight that now shone through the dissipating clouds. It made a perfect target, Charlotte thought as yet another cracking sound shattered the air. She no longer needed a response to her question. The answer was obvious.

"Shouldn't you duck?" Charlotte grabbed hold of the seat as he suddenly turned the boat, throwing her toward the side.

"And who in the hell is going to row?" he growled, tossing a quick glance over his shoulder before taking another long pull on both oars. The maneuver straightened their course, and put them in the shadow of a merchant ship anchored in the harbor. Damn, he was glad to be out of the brightness of the full moon. Why did the clouds have to pick that moment to scatter?

Jon slapped the oars into the river again, putting his full weight behind the drag. He fought the current, sending the small boat out of range of the soldiers shooting at them from shore. He hoped the night watch on the ships in the harbor didn't take up the gauntlet. So far, all seemed quiet.

Charlotte shifted, trying to squirm away from the water sloshing around in the flatboat bottom as the captain rowed up the river, staying as far as possible from the brigs and schooners anchored there. Her feet were soaked, and even though it seemed to be the norm for the night, this water differed from the damp, chilly rain. It was frigid. It was also getting deeper by the minute.

All manner of reasons came to mind as to why water slowly filled the boat, and were quickly dismissed. There *was* some water slopping over the sides from the oars and the play of the boat on the swells, but not near enough to cause this ever-deepening pool of dark, cold liquid. Sucking in her breath, Charlotte inched up on the seat. "Captain."

Jon moaned when he heard her voice. He'd almost forgotten she was in the boat. He *wanted* to forget she was back there. For the moment, he wanted to forget all about her. Jon strained forward. His back hurt like hell, but he hadn't felt this alive in a fortnight.

He was escaping. He was escaping!

A week ago, he wouldn't have thought it possible. He'd been shackled hand and foot, his arm bleeding, his temple throbbing, and the skin on his ravaged back burning like hell. But here he was, rowing up the St. Lawrence River, moving farther and farther away from his pursuers with each stroke. Sure he'd have to pull over to the shore soon and find his way through some Canadian wilderness, but he'd do it. He'd gotten this far, hadn't he?

"Captain?"

And no thanks to the lying wench sitting behind him. No, all she cared about was protecting that whoreson she was betrothed to. Out to sea indeed. She probably thought he'd sneak up on Levid and wring his plump neck. Jon gripped the oars, his fingers itching to do just that. But not now. No, now that he'd had some time to think, Jon knew the odds were stacked against him. But he'd get Levid. The bastard would pay dearly for killing Christopher.

"Captain Knox!"

The voice was more insistent this time and Jon jerked around, making the boat pull to the right. "What?"

"We're sinking."

Jon's eyes flashed down to the water shimmering blue-black in the shadows, then up to where his hostage sat, knees doubled up to her chest, sodden feet curved over the edge of the seat. He would hardly say they were sinking, but they were taking on water. Now he realized why the boat grew heavier to pull through the water. He'd thought it was just fatigue setting in. Not very observant of him, he mused. But, of course, he'd had other things on his mind while the lovely Miss Winston had just been along for the

169

ride. "Why in the hell didn't you tell me?"

"I just did." Oh, the insufferable, arrogant man. First he ignored her, then he howled because she couldn't get his attention. Well, let him sink. Let him! She hoped he drowned. Wished she'd never, ever worried about him. And especially wished she'd never tried to save him.

But if he sank, so would she—like an anchor. Swimming had never been something she'd wanted to try. Truthfully, she'd never been overly fond of water, and to date it hadn't seemed to like her too much, either. If she wasn't seasick, she was stranded on a sinking boat in the middle of a dark river. Charlotte looked toward the shore, but could see nothing. She'd never make it. She closed her eyes in despair.

"Take it, for God's sake."

Charlotte's eyes snapped open and snagged on a rope-handled bucket held inches from her face. Visions of tropical islands faded. "What . . ?" she began before he interrupted her with one rough-edged word.

"Bail!"

"Me?" Charlotte grabbed for the pail. He gave her no choice as he swerved back around, all but tossing it at her.

"Well, I'll do it if you'd rather row" came his sarcastic reply.

Charlotte bent down, scooped the bucket across the bottom, then tried to lift it. The water-filled container was deuced heavy. She couldn't budge it, perched as she was on the seat. Resignedly Charlotte thrust her legs down, plunging her feet into the freezing water. Bracing herself, ignoring the chattering of her teeth, she hauled the water up and over the side.

The muscles in her back burned, but she bent over again and again, emptying bucketful after bucketful. If she kept a brisk pace she could keep ahead of the water that filtered into the boat. All right, she could handle this until they reached the shore. How wide could the river be anyway?

Leaning back, promising herself just the tiniest of breaks, Charlotte swiped a tangle of hair from her eyes. She glanced about and made a disturbing discovery. Dropping the bucket, she stood as it splashed to the bottom of the boat. "Where are we going?"

"Sit down before you capsize us!"

Reluctantly Charlotte obeyed, clutching hold of the boat's sides as it swayed. But that didn't mean she'd be diverted. "Why aren't we headed for shore?" They'd left Montreal Harbor behind them, but the captain was rowing up the river, making no attempt to shorten their distance from either bank.

"Bail," he commanded, shooting a fierce look over his shoulder.

She wanted to refuse him—more than anything. But the water had inched up the side during her short reprieve. Snatching up the hemp handle, Charlotte scooped. "I want to head for the shore," she reiterated.

"I don't doubt if given your choice, you'd opt for returning to Montreal," Jon said as he bent over the oars. "But that doesn't mean we're going to do it."

"But I can't keep up with the water, and—"

"You can, and you will," Jon interrupted her whining lament. "Now bail!"

Biting her lip, Charlotte dragged the pail across the bottom and heaved it over the side. He was right. She could. But that didn't mean she liked it. Charlotte didn't think she'd ever been so physically miserable in all her life. She'd come close in the

171

weeks since she'd met the arrogant captain, but as a splinter of hemp slivered into her palm she decided this was the worst.

"That's better."

Better? How could he say *anything* was better? Charlotte looked up to see the captain half turned on his seat, watching her. She stared back at him, her expression full of anger.

"We need to get one thing straight here, Miss Winston. You may have had the upper hand before, but things have changed. You're the captive now, and I'm the captain." He used one ore to straighten the boat before continuing. "That means I give the orders, and you do what I say . . . whatever I say."

Well, she'd see about that. Granted, he might have the upper hand now, but there would come a time . . . Just let her get off this stupid river. It would be light soon, and then she'd get away. Her father would probably send soldiers after her.

Charlotte's mind tripped over that thought. Her father didn't know she was gone, and probably wouldn't until morning—maybe not even then. They hadn't been spending much time together, and he might not notice until she didn't come down to the evening meal.

And what would he think? Charlotte leaned back and bit her lip. Would he connect her disappearance with Captain Knox's escape? She didn't know, but—

"Are you still bailing?"

His strident question interrupted her thoughts, and she glanced down guiltily at the deepening pool of water and at the pail in her hand. With a resigned sigh, she bent forward, making a face at his broad back before sloshing water into the bucket. He didn't even look around.

Sooner or later they had to stop. They had to!

Forget about her. Forget that she thought her back would snap if she bent over one more time. Forget that the muscles in her arms screamed in pain. Forget that she was tired—beyond tired—and wet and cold. What about him?

He was only a man made of flesh and bone, for heaven's sake. She knew that. She'd seen his flesh torn by Levid's whip. Why wasn't *he* tired? She watched the corded muscles of his back and arms bunch, relaxed for a moment, then strained again. He had a musket wound in his arm, welts across his back. How could he go on this way?

"Are you bailing?"

It wasn't really a question. He knew she wasn't. It was just his annoying way of letting her know she better start.

Charlotte reached down, stifling a cry of pain. Tears stung her eyes, but she fought them back. "I'm tired. I can't do this anymore."

Something in her tone must have touched him, or maybe his body, too, had reached its limit. Slowly he turned, pulling the oars in.

At that moment he reminded her more of the pirate than ever before. Charlotte had to force herself to remember he wasn't.

The breeze off the river caught in the dark curls and played in the folds of his white shirt. He did have a beard, she could see that plainly now, and though the pirate never had one, it seemed to fit the circumstances. All Charlotte could do was stare at him as the water inched up her ankles.

Jon shifted, looking over Charlotte's shoulder at the night sky. "It will be dawn in a couple of hours," he announced. "I'll make for the shore. We can rest a while before we start out again."

Rest. The word sounded wonderful to Charlotte's

ears. She latched on to it, embraced it, and then realized how foolish she was.

While he slept would be the perfect time to escape him. She certainly couldn't do it while he was awake. Charlotte almost moaned as she imagined herself fighting off the sleep that her body craved. But she'd do it. Hopefully.

With a meaningful glance toward the bucket, the captain twisted back around on his seat and dipped the oars. They splashed into the water, sending moon-silvered droplets spraying into the boat across Charlotte's ruined gown.

Why hadn't she thought to grab a cloak before running out of the house on her silly rescue mission, Charlotte wondered as a fresh crop of goose flesh covered her bare arms. Because she hadn't thought at all. That much was obvious. If she'd thought, she wouldn't have gone to warn him and she wouldn't be in this predicament now.

"For God's sake—bail or we'll not make it to shore."

She wanted to scream, but instead she flung the bucket down, dragging it across the bottom of the boat and dumped water, all the while watching the shoreline. They'd passed villages and an occasional farm on their journey up the river, but the spot they approached didn't look the least inhabited.

There was no beach. A shadowy thick woods reached to the very edge of the shore. It looked impenetrable, dark and sinister.

The captain maneuvered the boat close to the coastline, but didn't land it, instead paddled farther upstream. She supposed he was searching for an ideal place to pull the boat ashore, but to Charlotte, one spot looked as desolate as the rest.

A gaggle of geese exploded above the trees, frightening her and forcing a shrill squeal. For the first time, Charlotte had serious doubts about tramping through the forest to escape him.

Resolutely she stiffened her aching back. She had only to stick to the shoreline, heading east till she came opposite Montreal or one of the villages they'd passed. She could do it.

Before she knew what he was doing, the captain jumped from the boat and sloshed knee-deep through the water, pulling the boat onto a small moss-covered spit of land.

Slowly, stretching her aching muscles, Charlotte climbed over the side, stepping onto the spongy earth.

She looked around for the captain, could find him nowhere, and had the strongest desire to bolt. But she didn't. He'd be back any minute, and she needed a longer head start.

As if to prove her point, Charlotte heard a rustling of underbrush, then Jon emerged from the shadows between two trees, his arms piled high with twigs and small branches.

"We need a fire," he announced, dropping the kindling and hunching down.

A fire sounded heavenly. Charlotte couldn't remember ever being so cold. At first the running, and even bailing, had kept her a little warm, but now . . . The October air was crisp and biting and Charlotte was still chilled to the bone. But he seemed to be forgetting something. "How are you going to start one?" She didn't have a flint—another thing she would have brought had she realized she'd be stuck in the wilderness—and she doubted he did, either.

Charlotte saw a grin split his whiskered face. "You'll see." While she watched he used his thumbnail to peel bark from a twig, then began twisting it around in a groove of another. For a long time, as he rubbed the stick between his large, long-fingered hand, nothing happened. He bent forward and blew gently, and suddenly a faint wisp of smoke floated up from the spot where the two sticks rubbed together.

"Hand me some of that." Jon motioned with a jerk of his head toward a pile of dried grass he'd gathered. He fed the tiny spark that sprang forth, nursing it with more gentle puffs of air until an orange-gold flame crackled and danced in the darkness.

After adding a few twigs to the fire, Jon hunched back on his heels, his forearms resting on his thighs, and glanced around. His eyes finally came to rest on Charlotte. "I don't suppose you have a weapon of any kind on you."

The way he said it, as if it would be a major flaw in her character if she didn't, which of course she didn't, made Charlotte clench her teeth. Raising her chin, using a haughty tone she didn't know she possessed, Charlotte responded, "Actually I meant to bring my musket, but I must have mislaid it."

Shrugging, Jon let his fingers dangle between his knees and tugged at some thick grass growing there. "You could have a knife or something."

"Where?" Charlotte dragged her hands down across her gown before she realized her mistake. She was right, of course, there was no place to hide a weapon or anything else under the ruined material. It clung to her body, molding every curve and hollow, revealing more than an acceptable amount of skin through its rips and tears.

But though she felt vindicated in pointing out her obvious inability to conceal anything, the expression on the captain's face as his gaze drifted over her made her cheeks grow warm. Stepping back, Charlotte caught her heel on a rotting log and grabbed at a low-hanging pine branch to keep from falling. Righting herself, folding her arms across her breasts, which had become the focus of the captain's attention, Charlotte cleared her throat. "What are we going to do now?"

Jon's eyes snapped to her face, and he shook his head in disgust. How in the hell could he feel any desire for her—or worse, feel sorry for her? She certainly hadn't had any sympathy for him. And the way she was looking at him now, as if she were afraid he was going to jump up and strip what was left of her dress off her, annoyed the hell out of him.

He stood, stretching the stiffness from his legs. "Take your clothes off."

"What?" Oh, she hated it when her voice squeaked. She couldn't have possibly heard him right. Could she?

"Your clothes," he repeated, convincing her that she hadn't misunderstood him. "Hang them over a branch here by the fire and they'll be dry when you wake up."

"They're not wet." A blatant lie if ever there was one, but a lie she intended to stand by. It didn't matter what he did, she would refuse to shed her gown. He could—

"Suit yourself." Reaching down, Jon began unfastening his breeches.

"What are you doing?"

"*I'm* not sleeping in wet clothes." Bending over, Jon removed first one soppy boot, then the other.

"Oh." Charlotte whirled around, suddenly very interested in the dark-lacy shadows thrown upon the water by the pine branches overhead. "Aren't we going to eat something?" Charlotte didn't look around, but she thought she heard the slide of his wet shirt across his skin above the sound of chattering birds.

"Any suggestions?"

"Well, no I . . ." Charlotte turned, then caught her breath. How could she have forgotten his state of undress? And why did she feel compelled to look at people when she spoke? Charlotte swallowed and continued, fixing her stare on a branch of an oak tree above the captain's head. "I thought you might catch something . . . like a rabbit." She was hungry, and didn't like the idea of starting back toward Montreal without something to eat. She didn't think the possibility of finding food for herself very good.

Jon kicked a stone out of the way and lay down next to the fire, stretching his legs out before him. "I might be able to snare something later, but I have to get some rest first. Besides," his eyes fixed on hers and turned an icy blue, "if anyone should be hungry, it is I. Food wasn't foremost on my captor's mind on the *Scorpion* or in the gaol. Hell, all you've done is miss your morning chocolate."

"But didn't you . . . ?" Charlotte stopped, her teeth biting into the soft swell of her bottom lip.

"Didn't I what?" Jon's eyes narrowed.

"Nothing . . . nothing." She almost blurted out something about the extra food she'd provided for him, but realized now he'd probably never received it. Looking at him, really looking at him, Charlotte noticed that he'd lost weight. His chest was still broad and deep, his shoulders brawny, but there was a hollow beneath his ribs, where his drawers hung on his hip bones. Oh, what a fool she'd been to trust Mr. Grey. She was thankful that he'd never had the chance to collect any more money from her.

"Better lie down and rest while you can." Jon added a few sticks to the fire, and indicated the spot beside him. "We'll start back upstream in a few hours."

"Upstream? You mean we're going in that boat . . .

178

that leaky boat?''

The captain's noncommittal stare only made her angrier. "But it has a hole in it."

He shrugged again. Charlotte was beginning to think she hated shrugs. "With you bailing, it stays afloat."

"But . . ." Charlotte sputtered and stopped. What was she arguing about? She wasn't going to be here when he woke up. Let him find someone else to bail for him—a neat trick in this wilderness.

Reluctantly Charlotte sat on the ground, grimacing when her cold, sodden gown stuck to her legs. Plucking at it did no good, and when she glanced to her right and noticed the captain watching her feeble attempts, her hand froze.

"It would dry much faster hanging up," he remarked before stacking his hands beneath his head and closing his eyes.

Well, maybe it would, Charlotte admitted, looking to where his breeches and shirt swung from a branch, but that didn't mean she planned to do anything about it. Besides, she wouldn't be here long enough for her gown to dry. She inched down, keeping a wary eye on the captain.

He'd stretched out on a bed of pine needles and moss, and seemed comfortable enough. For all his talk of drying his clothes, he'd kept his drawers on, and they were still damp, molding boldly over his lower body. Charlotte jerked her gaze away when she realized where it had settled.

His chest. That's what she should watch. As soon as his breathing grew steady and even, as soon as she knew he was asleep, she'd start hiking back down the river. Charlotte turned her head and watched his hair-covered chest rise and fall. The chill in the air made his male nipples hard. Charlotte bit her lip in vexation when she noticed that. His breathing, that's what she needed to concentrate on.

Her eyes slid up to his armpit, then around to the bunched strength of the arm bent under his head. His face looked relaxed under the week's growth of beard, and very handsome despite the scar at the edge of his hairline. If anything, it made him appear more dangerous—more piratish.

With a sigh, Charlotte shut her eyes. Her cheeks were hot, and a small coil of something warm and wet was growing in the pit of her stomach. She wouldn't look at him. Time. That was all that was needed. Time for him to get deeply to sleep. For the sun to come up. For her to daydream about the pirate . . .

Charlotte jerked awake.

She was inches from the captain—about ready to roll onto him! If something hadn't awakened her, she'd be snuggled up to his warm, hard body by now. Oh, how could she?

Wriggling away, Charlotte kept her gaze fixed on the captain. He was definitely asleep now, snoring softly. Carefully, as quietly as she could, Charlotte stood. Her damp gown felt clammy and cold, awful, but she ignored her discomfort as she glanced up. The trees were so dense she couldn't make out the sun's position, so she had no idea how long she'd slept. But she did know it was time to leave.

With a small smile, and a last look at the sleeping captain, Charlotte started off, wishing she had something other than silk slippers, with which to protect her feet against the uneven rocky ground.

Jon woke by degrees, first noticing his uncomfortable position, and stretching to relieve it, then remembering that he no longer resided in a vermin-infested gaol. His yawn turned into a smile that disappeared suddenly as his eyes opened.

"Charlotte?"

No answer. Just the chirping of birds, and the lazy drone of insects, blended with the soft lapping of the river.

"Charlotte!"

Jon hitched up on his elbows and looked around, his blue eyes narrowed. If she'd gone into the woods to answer nature's call she'd hear him and respond. Nothing.

"Damn woman," he muttered, jumping to his feet and jerking on his breeches and boots. "Damn stupid woman," he repeated as he grabbed his shirt. Tracking her wouldn't be hard, but it *would* take time, and he wasn't interested in heading back toward Montreal. Jon didn't need the trail of broken underbrush and footprints to tell him that's the way she'd head. Right back to her Captain Levid.

So let her.

Jon turned away from her trail and returned to the clearing where he'd slept. He could make better time without her, even if he didn't have her to bail water from the boat. He'd only decided to travel by water because he didn't think she could make it across country.

He still didn't.

But that was *her* problem. Jon buttoned his shirt. *She* decided to leave.

Jon looked toward the south, and home, then back over his shoulder toward the heart of British Canada.

"Hell."


She'd always liked trees. They were pretty and

181

green and made shade in the summer and gave refuge to small animals and birds. But those were civilized trees, not these monstrosities that seemed to tear at her clothing and hair. Charlotte glanced toward her left and made out the glimmer of sunshine on the river. Good. She was still heading in the right direction. Marshy land and steep rocks had forced her inland, but she couldn't lose sight of the river.

Charlotte tramped through some underbrush, trying to avoid the brambles on a bush. She was so hungry and tired, but she had to keep going. At least it was warmer now. Charlotte looked up at the dark canopy of leaves blocking the sun, and then at the thick, rough trunks that seemed to press in on her from all sides, and suppressed a shiver. She *had* to keep going.

"Ouch, damnit!" Charlotte pricked her finger trying to untangle her skirt from a briar bush. Sticking the wounded digit in her mouth, she shook her head, amazed by her language. A fortnight ago she'd never spoken such a word as damnit. Now all it took was a tiny pinprick of pain to send it tumbling from her lips.

No doubt about it. She'd been around Jonathan Knox too long. But no more, she reminded herself as she yanked on her gown, giving the skirt yet another rip. Fatalistically she lifted her shoulders, then stopped. Oh, no. She wasn't going to start shrugging, too.

But Charlotte couldn't help wondering about the captain as she trudged along. Had he awakened yet? If he had, what did he think about her absence? He'd probably be glad he didn't have to put up with her anymore. Fine. That was just fine with her. She was equally glad. She certainly hadn't wanted to come with him. She just wanted to make sure he wasn't killed.

He'd be all right now, she knew. He'd make it down to his country, be given another ship to command, and maybe even meet Captain Levid again. And this time Jonathan Knox would win. Charlotte bit her lip, annoyed by her disloyal thought.

Oh, what did she care about Matthew Levid. She might have told her father she'd marry him, but she wasn't going to. Besides, he definitely wouldn't want her after this . . . this . . . Charlotte threw her hands up, not knowing exactly what to call this.

And she certainly wouldn't wed anyone who plotted to murder someone.

Charlotte's thoughts drifted to her father. He'd disappointed her, that was for certain. She'd come to him hoping to share their loss, to grow closer through that sharing . . . and she'd found out he was capable of murder.

When she reached Montreal . . . Charlotte stepped on a sharp stone and another oath escaped her lips. *If* she reached Montreal—no, *when*—she would get there. She'd see about obtaining passage back to England, to Oxfordshire, where she could live a quiet, secluded life.

The meadow was such a relief after fighting her way through underbrush and trees that at first Charlotte couldn't believe her eyes. Covered with thick brownish-green grass, it appeared almost dreamlike.

Charlotte stepped into the sunlight. She wanted to rest. Every cell of her being cried out for it. But she couldn't. Traveling would be easier now, at least until she reached the wall of trees at the far end of the meadow, but if she didn't keep moving she'd have to spend the night in the wilderness—alone.

She'd made it a few rods into the clearing when Charlotte heard rustling behind her. She jerked around, her heart beating a frantic tattoo. If it was a wild animal, she'd never be able to outrun it.

What she saw made her cry out. Looking more savage and angrier than any beast she could imagine, the captain emerged from the forest. Arms flying at her side, Charlotte started racing through the knee-high grass. Blood pounded loud in her ears, but it was the sound of pursuing footfalls that was deafening.

# Chapter Eleven

Running was useless, escape impossible, but Charlotte tried anyway, carving a jagged path through the wild grass and fall flowers. Her breath burned, coming in ragged gulps, then exploded from her altogether as she hit the hard ground. Kicking at the arms that bound her legs—another exercise in futility—only trapped her more firmly beneath the captain's restraining weight.

She squirmed, trampled grass and bits of dirt scratching her face as he inched up her body. "Let me go!" Her plea sent a blue jay chattering overhead, but had no effect on the man pinioning her to the ground. He grabbed her shoulders, jerking her round till she lay trapped beneath two powerful thighs.

Again Charlotte tried to protest. She opened her lips, gasping and spitting the bitter blades of grass from her mouth. Thinking to swipe the debris away, she raised her arms only to have them grabbed and stretched above her head. "Get off me!"

Her cry brought a mirthless grin, a steely expression, to Jon's eyes. "Oh, I think not," he said as his legs pressed against her hips.

"Beast!" Charlotte wriggled and bucked, sending

her body against the V between his legs. The heat, the answering warmth between her own legs, made her pause, then flatten herself into the nest of crushed grass.

He didn't seem to notice the contact or her reaction as he stared down at her, his eyes as blue as the cloudless sky above him, as hard as the ground that pressed into her back.

"A beast, am I?" he questioned, his fingers tightening around her wrist. "Perhaps you've the right of it there. But then you must have a taste for the breed. Your Captain Levid more than fits the mold." Jon shifted, anger smoldering within him. "That is where you were headed, right, back to him?"

Charlotte never wanted to see Captain Levid again, wished in her heart she'd never heard of him, but something perverse took over her voice as she lay sprawled beneath the captain. Hurting him as he was hurting her became her primary goal. Her hands were bound, her feet and legs useless against him, but her words could inflict pain. And as she spoke, she knew hers were. "Yes, I'm going back to Montreal"— the devil took hold of her tongue—"to him."

Jon thought he'd known anger before, but now it burst to flame, the inferno devouring any rational thought. Levid was the man who'd impressed, nay kidnapped, his brother and others of his crew. He'd taunted Jon about Christopher's death, then used the whip to deepen the pain, to ensure that Jon would never forget it—as if he could.

The bite of the cat still stung his back, and as he looked down at this woman—Levid's woman—Jon could easily conjure up visions of her standing beside Levid, watching each flaying crack of the whip, knowing the sweet taste of revenge.

For Jon had no doubt that his punishment was not

186

for attempted murder; he'd escaped the penalty for that when he'd fled Montreal. The degradation he'd endured had been revenge for his treatment of Charlotte Winston. What he couldn't decide for sure was whether she'd turned Levid on him because of what Jon had done to her . . . or what he hadn't done.

Jon's eyes narrowed and he lowered his body, his face a heartbeat from hers. "I'll send you back, if that's your wish." His voice deepened. "But first I think we have some unfinished business."

"I . . . I don't know what you mean."

"Don't you?" Jon's grin was demonic. "I've stripes on my back that say otherwise."

It wasn't his back, but the hard, engorged muscle pressing into her stomach that had Charlotte's attention. That and the unbridled sensual gleam in his hooded eyes. "You can't mean to . . ." What? He reminded her of the more lusty daydreams of her pirate, the ones where he ravaged her until she could barely speak. But there was something else in the captain's expression—a hard edge of rage that simmered close to the surface. He had every right to be angry. But not at her.

Again Charlotte arched, straining against the binding manacle of his fingers. But this time the press of her body to his couldn't be ignored. It sent Charlotte's heart racing, pounding in her chest and scorching her skin the way no sun could, and melting her insides.

Retreat accomplished nothing, for his long, hard body followed hers, ground down into her softness. Charlotte's moan escaped her, was followed by the tickling of his breath against her cheek. His voice was barely a whisper, a lover's sigh, but the words delivered like the sensual slide of silk over skin held the cutting edge of truth.

187

"I shall not disappoint your fine Captain Levid. He expects you've been used by me, and used by me, you'll be. We wouldn't want to waste that delightful punishment he inflicted."

"No, please don't." Charlotte tried to wriggle away, but his body blanketed hers, making each movement more caress than denial. His intentions were perfectly clear. Charlotte would have known even if she hadn't had a prelude to lovemaking in his cabin. His lips skimmed above her chin, the curve of her jaw, the soft-rough whiskers of his beard the only point of contact. It felt delicious, a promise of things to come, but Charlotte steeled herself against the sensation, ignoring the shivers running the length of her spine.

"You can't do this." Her breathlessness had naught to do with fear. He did nothing until she began to protest again. Then his mouth crushed down on hers, demanding her silence.

Jon drove his tongue into Charlotte's mouth expecting resistance, but found none. She opened for him as unabashedly, as sweetly, as she had on the other occasions he'd kissed her. But this was to be different. This time he would not stop.

This was his revenge, and Charlotte Winston was his vehicle.

She meant nothing to him, Jon reminded himself as he tasted her honeyed, sweet mouth. He wanted Levid to suffer, to suffer as he had, and at the present Charlotte was the only means of doing that. When Levid took his bride, when he searched in vain for the maidenhead Jon would rent, then the revenge would be complete. But it wouldn't stop there. Every time Levid came to his wife's bed, he'd know, and he'd remember.

Charlotte whimpered deep in her throat and a new

thought came to Jon. She would remember, too. A sweet and subtle revenge.

Transferring his hold on her wrists to one hand he slid the other down her arm, noticing the slight trembling in the wake of his fingers. He traced a tear in her sleeve, his mouth sensitive to her tension when he did. Breaking the bond of their kiss, his eyes sought the cause. He pushed aside fabric when he spotted the crimson scratch marring the tender white flesh.

It wasn't a deep cut. She probably wouldn't have noticed it except for his roving hands. But the sight of it crossing the porcelain skin tightened the knot in Jon's stomach. His gaze flew to hers, and in that moment, Jon knew this was not revenge he sought.

He wanted her—would want her if he'd never heard the hated name of Levid. And as his lips gently touched the tender skin torn by some wayward branch and the tightness in his stomach loosened, he knew he would have her.

She wished for her hands to be free, and they were. Free to descend slowly, sensually, cocooning his face in the arc of her elbow. Charlotte knew she should push him away before the chance was gone, but something in her said it was already too late. She didn't want him gone.

His words were cruel, and if words were all she believed, Charlotte would have thought her mind gone. But there was more, so much more. Things that belied his claim of punishment.

His kiss might border on pain, but it was the sweet prologue to passion that coiled inside her causing it. Never his touch. Never the way he used his mouth to caress her skin, her lips.

As if to prove her thoughts, his mouth claimed hers again in an earthy kiss that had her fingers sifting

189

through his thick, midnight-black hair. The hair of the devilish pirate. The hair of the captain.

Could her mind have conjured up the texture and sun-warmed feel of his hair? Never. This was no aberration, no figment of her imagination, but a man of flesh and blood. A man who haunted her day and night.

Charlotte's fingers snagged on a twig knotted in the short curls, and her mouth beneath his tilted in a smile.

"What?" Jon lifted his head but a breath from hers and studied her face. Was it possible that she smiled? Acceptance he could understand. Whatever was between them, whether hatred or revenge, had been tempered from the beginning by a strong dose of lust. He'd felt the pull from the first time he'd gazed into her deep brown eyes . . . the first time he'd touched her sweet body.

And though her awakening to the joys of sensual delights might have been slower, it was still there. She seemed as incapable of denying his touch as he was in withholding it. The last night in his cabin proved that. Her fingers in his hair proved that.

But he couldn't imagine her happy about this affliction they shared. Yet, unless his eyes deceived him, she was smiling up at him as if sharing a great joke. "What?" he repeated, unable to stop himself from skimming his tongue across her moist lips.

What indeed? How could he purge everything from her mind with so simple an act? Her hands tightened, fingers digging deeper, impervious to everything but the feel of this man until he shifted and something whisper-soft fell on her arm. Pine needles. Charlotte ruffled his hair, laughing out loud as a small shower of pine tags drifted across her.

Realizing the reason for her mirth, Jon shook his

head, loosening another spattering across her chest.

"You're dirty," she whispered, her tone more sympathetic than accusing.

"It comes from sleeping on the ground." He plucked a pine needle from her golden-brown curls, letting the end of it trail ever so softly down her neck and across her collarbone. "So are you."

Charlotte swallowed, felt her nipples tighten painfully beneath the muslin shift. Why was she allowing this? If there was to be pain, it should come from fighting him, defending her virtue, not begging him with her eyes to take liberties with her.

But her lips parted and her breath caught as she watched him follow the path of the pine needle with his smoky-blue gaze. Down it went, catching momentarily on the torn lace at her neckline, then curving out over her breast.

The ache grew.

Charlotte heard a sound, a foreign sound mingling with the warbling of the grosbeak. Its call was sensual . . . earthy, and she realized with a start it came from her.

A mating sigh as old as time drew Jon closer. His hand covered her breast, the pine needle forgotten as her puckered nipple, hard through the separating fabric, burned into his palm. Whatever they might be to each other at another time—captive, captor—for now they were two people trapped in the desires of the flesh.

Charlotte arched, filling him with the softness of her body. His touch, the squeeze of his long, dark fingers, assuaged the sweet pain in her breast. His masterful caress sent another smoldering ember erupting into flame.

Deep in the core of her woman's body a want—a need—blossomed. It grew rapidly, scorching her skin

191

and making her breath escape in rapid gasps. Each exquisite thrust of his tongue, each grinding movement of his palm, sent her deeper into the labyrinth of her passion.

He was driving her wild. Slowly and sensually mad.

His mouth left hers and scorched a path down the fine column of her neck, pausing to feast on the pulse beating frantically beneath her skin.

Charlotte's eyelids drifted down, shutting out the glaring sun, closing in the wonderful sensations he unleashed in her. Her mind, so trained to skitter to fantasy remained anchored in reality. Who needed fanciful dreams when the real thing was so achingly sweet?

Her imagination could never reproduce the smell of crushed grass, of wild autumn flowers, and musky man scent that wafted about her. It inundated her senses, heightened them.

Oh, she burned. Desire raced to every cell of her body, but pooled, swelling, at the apex of her legs. Shifting, unconsciously seeking relief, Charlotte moved till his rock-hard manhood rested firmly in the cradle of her body. He moaned, his mouth tearing from hers as he drew a ragged breath, and Charlotte felt a dizzying spear of victory. She could drive him as wild as he drove her.

For a while she rode the crest of her discovery, savoring the thought, luxuriating in the knowledge, but then his restless hands skimmed away her bodice and his mouth covered her nipple. His tongue seared the puckered peak, teasing it to prominence, and her body responded the only way it knew how.

Arching toward him, forcing her breast more fully into his mouth, Charlotte spread her legs—or tried to. Muslin skirts bound her, tangled around her ankles and thighs. But not for long.

# MORE PASSION AND ADVENTURE AWAIT... YOUR TRIP TO A BIG ADVENTUROUS WORLD BEGINS WHEN YOU ACCEPT YOUR FIRST 4 NOVELS ABSOLUTELY *FREE* (AN $18.00 VALUE)

Accept your Free gift and start to experience more of the passion and adventure you like in a historical romance novel. Each Zebra novel is filled with proud men, spirited women and tempestuous love that you'll remember long after you turn the last page.

Zebra Historical Romances are the finest novels of their kind. They are written by authors who really know how to weave tales of romance and adventure in the historical settings you love. You'll feel like you've actually gone back in time with the thrilling stories that each Zebra novel offers.

## GET YOUR FREE GIFT WITH THE START OF YOUR HOME SUBSCRIPTION

Our readers tell us that these books sell out very fast in book stores and often they miss the newest titles. So Zebra has made arrangements for you to receive the four newest novels published each month.

You'll be guaranteed that you'll never miss a title, and home delivery is so convenient. And to show you just how easy it is to get Zebra Historical Romances, we'll send you your first 4 books absolutely FREE! Our gift to you just for trying our home subscription service.

## BIG SAVINGS AND FREE HOME DELIVERY

Each month, you'll receive the four newest titles as soon as they are published. You'll probably receive them even before the bookstores do. What's more, you may preview these exciting novels free for 10 days. If you like them as much as we think you will, just pay the low preferred subscriber's price of just $3.75 each. *You'll save $3.00 each month off the publisher's price.* AND, your savings are even greater because there are never any shipping, handling or other hidden charges—FREE Home Delivery. Of course you can return any shipment within 10 days for full credit, no questions asked. There is no minimum number of books you must buy.

GET
FOUR
FREE
BOOKS
(AN $18.00 VALUE)

He either realized her frustration or his own desire and reached the same frenzied point, for he worked the gown down her ribs, following its descent with his lips. Jon breathed in the smell of her fevered flesh, pushing the fabric below her hips.

Pausing when she lay naked beneath him, Jon lifted his head, his eyes raking her, seeing her clearly for the first time. Sunlight made her skin glow with creamy radiance against the carpet of brilliant green. He touched her, softly as he'd done that first night while she slept, and remembered the twinge of guilt.

But there was no shame now.

Charlotte's hand covered his, pressing it down before she reached for him. His eyes were dark, nearly all the blue overshadowed by desire. Dark whiskers, dark sun-bronzed skin, dark eyes. He looked dangerous and erotic and Charlotte didn't know what she'd do if he didn't ease this longing in her.

Jon's clothes quickly followed hers, and when he nestled down on top of her again, it was glorious skin against skin.

Charlotte's arms wrapped around his powerful shoulders, her finger played in the hair at his nape, and then roamed lower crossing the ridge of a scar.

She froze, a reaction he mirrored when he felt her tense. Jon stared down at her, his hand splayed over her stomach.

"Does . . . does it still hurt?" Charlotte felt as if she'd been splashed with cold water, her emotions so hot one moment cooled with the memory of what had happened to him.

"No." Jon's jaw clenched. "It's healed."

But her fingers were gentle as they traced the raised welt. Her eyes never left his, not even when his hand began to move, tangling in the thatch of curls above her legs.

"Ooohh." Charlotte writhed against him as his

finger slid inside.

She was warm and moist, trembling every time he nudged the tiny nub, and Jon thought he would burst. He pressed against her, her heat drawing him like a magnet. "This may hurt," honesty forced him to warn her. For an instant reality shot through him like a lead ball. This was Levid's woman he was about to claim. Levid's woman.

But when he looked down at flushed face and kiss-reddened lips he only saw Charlotte Winston. A woman he was about to ruin. A woman who . . .

Charlotte arched, driving him deep inside her, catching her breath when his manhood tore the tiny membrane.

"Are you all right?" Jon lay perfectly still, his body burning as her moist heat enveloped him.

"Yes." Her voice sounded strange and far away. All thought vanished as he moved, slowly at first, small, testing strokes, then, as her body accepted all of him, deep, probing thrusts.

Charlotte grabbed his sweat-slicked arms, clutching him to her as waves of pleasure washed over her. Shallow at first like the St. Lawrence lapping the shore, then wild and savage like a mighty temptest at sea.

With one last thrust Jon collapsed, his arms giving out as a great weakness overcame him. His heart raced, and his breathing was shallow, but not so shallow that he couldn't smell the scent of sunshine clinging to the soft curls beneath his face. Pressing a final kiss on her temple Jon rolled to his side onto the grass. She came willingly when he wrapped his arms around her shoulders, and the feel of her sweet love-warmed body kept reason at bay.

\*     \*     \*

The tropical sun was hotter than Charlotte realized. So very hot. She'd been kidnapped by the pirate and taken to his secret cove where he'd made passionate love to her and then . . .

Charlotte's eyes sprang open.

She was with the pirate . . . but it really wasn't the pirate. It was Captain Knox. And they weren't on some imaginary Caribbean island.

But the part about making love was real. She could feel the captain beside her. Feel his strong arm across her stomach. Her naked stomach. Her eyelids drifted shut as all the vivid memories came rushing back. Glorious memories. Unbelievable memories. What had she done?

Charlotte tried to move and groaned. Her skin felt tight, too small for her body, and it hurt. Carefully she lifted her head, looking away in embarrassment when she saw his muscled thigh wrapped intimately about her legs. Steeling herself, Charlotte glanced down, searching for the source of her discomfort.

She was red . . . burned by the autumn sun that glared overhead. All her years of wearing a bonnet and using a parasol had been for naught. She'd lain exposed to the sun—all of her—for goodness knew how long.

Careful not to awake the sleeping man beside her, Charlotte slipped from under his weight. He barely stirred—testimony to the little sleep he'd had lately. Stifling a yawn, Charlotte realized she, too, was tired, and if it hadn't been for her discomfort would probably still be asleep.

Standing and reaching for her clothes, Charlotte gave the captain a quick inspection. Years of exposure to the sun and sea had turned his skin a deep bronze—above the waist, that is. His lower body had suffered from lying in the sun, but it wasn't as burned as hers, as his skin appeared naturally darker.

Charlotte winced as her chemise slipped down over her body. A sunburn was the least of her worries, she told herself as she pulled down her gown. Hunger and abduction and her wanton behavior with the captain—now that was something for concern. And getting back to Montreal . . . and the fact that she felt a genuine regret about leaving the captain.

"Stop it," Charlotte admonished herself, careful to keep her voice low. He made it perfectly clear why he was making love to her, and just because she'd been carried away on the wings of passion, just because she temporarily forgot proper decorum—Charlotte bit her lip to keep the tears at bay—didn't mean she cared about him.

She stuffed her bruised feet into the torn silk slippers. Nothing had changed—not really. She would still go back to England, to Oxfordshire, and live out her days in quiet solitude. Her books and her imagination were all she really needed, but now she had a healthy dose of reality to spur that imagination.

Resolutely Charlotte started off across the meadow.

"Where do you think you're going?"

His voice stopped her in her tracks, but she didn't turn around. "Back to Montreal." Charlotte was proud of her firm voice.

"I don't think so."

"But you said—" Charlotte spun back around, her heart pounding. Why had she looked around? Didn't she remember his state of undress? Didn't she reason that he might have stood up? And why should the sight of his body do such strange things to hers? Taking a deep breath, Charlotte began again. "You said I could go back."

196

"I didn't mean now." Jon grabbed for his breeches and jammed his legs inside, cursing when the rough material scraped against his reddened hip.

"Well, now is when I want to go."

"That's too bad, Charlotte." Jon's hand around her upper arm halted Charlotte's continued trek across the meadow. His voice lowered dangerously and his eyes narrowed as she looked around. "Captain Levid will just have to wait a while for the pleasure of your company."

"Why?" Charlotte's eyes met his, searching for an answer. She didn't care a fig about Matthew Levid, but Jon's motives for what happened between them had been clear. She'd think the sooner Levid found out, the better the captain would like it.

"Why?" Jon dropped her arm and moved back to his disheveled pile of clothing. "Because at this moment it isn't in my best interest to return you to Montreal. Too many of the residents seem to want me dead."

"I can find my own way back." She spoke the words with more confidence than she felt, and the cynical lift of the captain's brow didn't help. "I can," she insisted. "I got this far, didn't I?" Charlotte's chin jutted up when she noticed the beginnings of a grin forming at the corners of his mouth. Memories of what that mouth had done to her sent it higher.

"You only covered about a tenth of the ground we traveled upstream. And though I've no way of knowing exactly when you departed our little camp, by the looks of you I'd say you traveled for some time."

"By the looks of me?" Charlotte's hands flew to her hips. "If I appear less than perfectly groomed, it's not because of my attempted escape. It's because you . . . you . . ."

"What?" Jon paused in the process of putting on his shirt and caught her flitting gaze, forcing it to meet his. "I *what?*"

Charlotte knew how a bird must feel ensnared by a predator cat. Summoning all her strength, she turned away from his hypnotic stare. "I'm going back," she whispered, starting again across the meadow. This time it wasn't the cold clasp of his hand that stopped her, but his equally frigid words. "It wasn't rape."

Her feet refused to move. Shutting her eyes, Charlotte shook her head. "I know that."

"But that's what you wanted to say, isn't it?"

How could his deep gravelly voice sound so vulnerable at times? "I wanted to," Charlotte admitted, turning back toward him. "But I didn't."

This time it was he who seemed reluctant to meet her eyes. He busied himself with his boots. "Good," he mumbled, and Charlotte wasn't certain at first whether he referred to the fact that he'd pulled on his boot or that she'd not called it rape. Then he looked up, and she knew. "Lord knows the thought of raping you, of killing you, crossed my mind more than once as the whip stung or—"

"Why would you want to kill me?"

"Actually," Jon worked on the second boot, "you weren't my first choice."

"Captain Levid . . . Why are you so obsessed with him? I mean, I understand why you hate him now . . . after what he did, but—"

"It doesn't matter now." Jon straightened. "But I will have my revenge."

"But not by raping me."

His eyes pierced hers, and Charlotte was sorry now she'd pushed him. His expression spoke clearly that he didn't have to, and she could hardly contradict that. Every time he touched her she opened for him willingly, nay eagerly. Charlotte swallowed, at a loss for words.

"Tell Levid what you will," Jon said, starting toward the river.

"You mean he might accept rape better than . . . than . . ." What could she call what she'd done?

"I don't give a damn about his acceptance, but I thought you might." And he shouldn't give a damn about that, either, Jon thought, annoyed with himself. Maybe he should just let her go wandering off toward Montreal. She might make it. And Lord knew he didn't need this millstone around his neck. She caught up with him and he found himself automatically slowing his pace.

"Where are you going?" He appeared to be finished discussing their lovemaking and Charlotte was just as glad. He wasn't paying any attention to her, and she supposed she really should just start off toward Montreal, but . . .

"To the river," he answered without glancing her way. "I told you before, in my cabin, I wouldn't apologize, and the same goes for now."

He stopped and Charlotte, who was climbing over a log, bumped into him. Goodness, he was back talking about what happened in the meadow. First he told her he'd thought about rape, and now, even though he argued to the contrary, he appeared apologetic. "I . . . I didn't ask you to," Charlotte reminded.

He studied her a moment before continuing. When he did, his voice was even lower than usual. "As much as I'd like it otherwise, there seems to be something between us. Something . . ." Jon's words trailed off, and he shook his head as if to clear his senses. "Are you hungry?"

It took Charlotte a moment to follow what he'd asked. One second he acted as if he shared this strange obsession she felt for him, and the next he mentioned food.

Charlotte glanced around. This area must be filled with game, but they had no weapon, nothing to use to catch anything. That didn't seem to stop the captain.

Searching through the underbrush he found a long stick and used a sharp rock to shape the end into a point.

"What are you going to do with that?"

"Go fishing," he said with a grin. Charlotte had forgotten how exciting that grin could be, even hidden beneath a fortnight's growth of whiskers.

He shucked his boots, rolled up his pants, and waded into the shallow waters by the river's edge. Fascinated, Charlotte sat on a fallen tree to watch, all thoughts of escaping back to Montreal losing importance next to the prospect of food.

Cold, sparkling water rushed between legs planted wide, and he appeared to study the clear swirling liquid intently. Minutes passed, and still he stood.

"What are you waiting for?" Charlotte shinnied over the rough bark, trying to get a better look. Her perch extended out over the water, and she bunched up her skirt to keep it dry.

When he didn't answer, continuing to lean over, his pointed stick hoisted in front of him, Charlotte inched out further on the log. "Is there a fish down there?" she asked just as he thrust the stick into the water.

His muttered curse and the glare he flashed her had Charlotte biting her bottom lip. "For God's sake, would you be quiet?"

"I just wondered what you were doing," Charlotte mumbled.

"I'm trying to spear a fish," he told her before

bending back to his task.

"Can you do that?"

Charlotte watched him straighten slowly, and fought the urge to scramble off the log and run away. But when he turned toward her, though he looked a little impatient, he spoke calmly, after an exaggerated sigh. "I used to catch fish like this often, when I was a kid. My father taught my brother and me, and we used to make a contest of it. Seeing who could catch the most."

"Did you win?" Charlotte didn't have to close her eyes to imagine him a strapping youth, with shining black hair and bluer than blue eyes.

"Usually," Jon admitted.

"Because you were quicker?"

"More than likely because I was twelve years older . . ." Jon paused. "But that never stopped my brother from trying to beat me."

"Oh." Charlotte smiled, realizing how little she knew about Jonathan Knox. "Is your brother a man of the sea also?"

"He was."

"Was?" He sounded so final.

"My brother is dead," Jon said, looking back into the water. "Now please be quiet so I can catch us something to eat." He glanced around quickly. "And be careful on that branch."

With that warning he lifted his stick and ignored her. Charlotte bent forward, trying to see beneath the surface of the water. A sliver of silver caught her eye— a fish—and she wriggled out farther to get a better look. The fish looked large, maybe a foot long, though she couldn't tell for sure, and he was swimming straight for the captain.

Charlotte wondered if he saw it, decided he must, and that calling now wouldn't be the most prudent thing to do. But she wanted to see him spear it. If she could just move out a little farther . . .

The fish swam closer, and Charlotte leaned farther. Jon stood tense, his concentration trained on the shimmering fish. He raised his arm. Charlotte tilted her body, then grabbed for the branch as she heard a loud crack.

The fish darted away and Jon's body shot up and twisted around, his face a mask of shock. That was the last thing Charlotte saw before she splashed into the cold river.

# Chapter Twelve

"What the hell?" Jon dropped the stick, giving only a fleeting thought to the fish that got away, and waded downstream. The water deepened, creeping up his pants by the time he reached a sputtering, splashing Charlotte. Silt swirled up from the bottom, clouding the water as he reached down and grabbed beneath her shoulders, hauling her up.

She coughed, sucking in more water from her dripping hair before Jon swiped it off her face. "I . . . I can't swim," Charlotte said, relief pouring through her that she could breathe.

"All you had to do was stand."

"Stand?" When the water had rushed over her head she'd had a horrifying image of herself drowning, nobody ever knowing or caring what happened to her—nobody but the captain. But he had saved her. Though by the expression on his face—part amusement, part annoyance—she hadn't really needed his efforts.

Charlotte glanced down. Sure enough her feet were firmly planted on the sandy bottom, with no more than half of her below water. She straightened, pulling away from the captain's loose embrace, steadying herself as the current caught her skirts. The reddish tint of her face, begun by the sun, heightened by her sputtering for breath, deepened.

Seeing her embarrassment, Jon felt something akin to anger with himself. And that annoyed him. She made him miss spearing the biggest fish he ever saw, with him hungry enough to eat it scales and all. He'd told her to be quiet, and what did she do? Make enough noise to scare away every living thing in a two-mile radius. And then . . . then she has the nerve to look up at him with those big brown eyes and make him feel like a veritable bastard. "Come on." He wrapped an arm around her waist, ignoring the halfhearted slap she gave his hand.

She dragged at her sodden skirts, then stumbled, and Jon scooped her up in his arms. Gritting his teeth over the stones at the river's bottom, he climbed up on the bank. Her shivering made him hold her tighter and hesitate before lowering her onto a smooth rock.

"You should get out of those wet clothes before you catch a chill," he said, grimacing when she began shaking her head. "Don't play the modest maiden with me now. I've seen all of you. Remember?"

How could she forget? But that didn't mean she planned to make a practice of undressing for him. Except that her teeth were chattering so badly she couldn't even tell him so. The sun might be warm, but here under the trees the air held cold. And the water, a lot of which ran in rivulets down her back and chest, was freezing.

Besides, he didn't seem particularly interested in her. He had already turned away and was busy building a fire.

"We'll need this to cook the fish," Jon said, never

taking his eyes off the stick he twisted. And the sooner he got her dress dry the better. She might as well be wearing nothing the way the filmy fabric clung to her, and the things the cold water did to her breasts . . . Jon rubbed harder.

"Do you think you'll catch another?"

"Fish?" Jon glanced up to see her nod, then wished he hadn't. How could he want her again? They were . . . Lord knew where. Jon wished he'd paid more attention to his geography lessons and not been so cocked sure that navigation by sea was all he needed to know. He hadn't eaten in almost two days, weeks longer if you meant something decent. He had no shelter, no weapon . . . no nothing. And here he was getting aroused by Charlotte Winston—again— the woman that helped put him in this predicament.

Jon swallowed, forcing himself to keep his eyes off her as he fed the flames. "I'll get us something to eat. But you stay here."

Charlotte thought he gave that last command with more emphasis than needed, but she supposed she did deserve it. Grabbing fabric, Charlotte wrung out as much water as she could, then tried spreading the blue material around her legs to dry. It felt cold and clammy, wretchedly uncomfortable. With a groan the captain appeared not to hear, Charlotte grabbed the hem and pulled the gown over her head. Then she inched closer to the fire, leaned back against the rock, and fell instantly asleep.

The delectable fragrance of food nudged her awake. She'd been dreaming of Christmas three years ago. Her mother had seemed better, and Mrs. Samuels had outdone herself with the dinner. There was roast goose and kidney pie. Plum pudding, dried fruits, Charlotte took another whiff, realized that wasn't what she smelled, and opened her eyes. It wasn't roast goose, but Charlotte didn't think she'd ever seen such a culinary delight.

Maybe fish had never been high on her list of favored foods, but at this moment she ranked it at the very top. Charlotte's stomach gave an unladylike rumble and she glanced around to see if the captain noticed, but he was nowhere about.

Scrambling to her feet, Charlotte brushed at the soil and leaves stuck to her damp chemise, then reached for her gown.

It wasn't there.

She clearly remembered laying it out on the rock to dry. A flutter of blue caught her eye, and she turned to see her gown hanging from a tree branch. With a sigh of relief she snatched it down, and was pulling the still-damp material over her head when she heard someone moving through the woods.

The cloying fabric seemed to fight her every move, and though Charlotte jerked and tugged, by the time her head popped through the gown's neck, the captain stood leaning against the silvery yellow trunk of a birch, watching her.

His blue eyes raked down her body, and Charlotte rued removing her gown in the first place. Knowing full well the absurdity of her action, she turned away and finished squirming into her dress. Wet or not, she wouldn't remove it again—not until she was safely back in Montreal.

By the time she looked back, the captain was crouched beside the fire. He reached out toward one of the slabs of fish and jerked his fingers back. Removing his shirt and using the bunched cloth to protect his hands from the heat, the captain took all four sticks with their skewered hunks of fish off the spitlike contraption he'd fashioned out of four Y-shaped branches.

"I'm afraid we'll have to eat off the rock," he said, and it was testimony to Charlotte's hunger that she didn't care in the least. If not for his warning that it was hot, she might have attacked the food, devouring it straightaway. As it was, Charlotte tried to keep some semblance of decorum as she ate, though she couldn't help an occasional sigh of satisfaction.

"I do believe that was the best fish I ever ate," she raved when there was naught left but a pile of slivery bones.

"Really?" The captain's chuckle sounded skeptical. "You've either had poor luck with cooks or you were hungrier than I thought." His eyes met hers. "When *was* the last time you ate?"

Earlier he had accused her of missing her morning chocolate. Was he now doubting that assessment? More important, did she want him to know how little she'd eaten recently, especially at the last dreadful meal with Captain Levid? "Yesterday," she murmured, standing and starting down toward the river to wash her hands.

Now that she'd eaten, Charlotte felt revived. Maybe she could make it down the river to Montreal. She glanced back at the captain. He appeared unconcerned with her whereabouts, but she imagined his facade of nonchalance would evaporate quickly enough if she bolted.

Besides—Charlotte studied the sky—it wouldn't be long until dark. She didn't want to be out in the forest by herself at night. Scooping her hands, Charlotte drank her fill of the clear cold water. Tomorrow morning would be early enough to leave.

"We'll stay here tonight, and start out first thing in the morning," Jon said when she returned from the river.

"Start out for where?" Charlotte couldn't help

asking. It really made no difference, since she hoped to be heading east toward Montreal.

"South." Jon fed more twigs into the fire. "I'm trying to picture in my mind where we are in relation to New York, and I think it's almost due south." Jon shifted and looked around. "I don't suppose you know any geography, do you?"

"No."

"I didn't think so."

"Well, actually I do. I mean, I know about England, Scotland, too." For some reason Charlotte didn't want the captain to think her ignorant.

"Remind me to look you up the next time I've lost my way on the British Isles," he said, standing and brushing his hands on the side of his breeches.

"You needn't be sarcastic." Charlotte rose, not liking the advantage his height gave him. It didn't help. She still had to tilt her head to look him in the eye. "I'm not the one lost in my own country."

"Correct me if I'm wrong, but I believe we're in Lower Canada, not the United States. And," Jon took an intimidating step forward, "the reason I'm here in the first place is because of your Captain Levid."

"He's not *my* Captain Levid." Charlotte ignored his snort of disbelief. "And even if he were, it wasn't my idea for you to try to kill him. On board *his* ship. With your hands shackled." Reaching out, Charlotte poked his chest with her finger. "Whatever possessed you to act so irrationally?" She jabbed, anger ruling her thoughts until she glanced up at his eyes. They were steely blue and narrowed.

Realizing she'd gone too far, Charlotte tried to snatch her hand away, but his grip on her wrist locked it in place, prevented her retreat.

"Whatever possessed me? Do you really want to know?"

He had her back against the rough bark of a pine, and all Charlotte could do was nod.

"I'd say a lot of it had to do with the illustrious Captain Levid's treatment of his prisoners. But then maybe you don't remember his refusal to grant me even the very basic of medical care. And maybe you don't remember why his treatment of me was so harsh."

"I . . . I don't know."

"Oh, come now, Miss Winston, jog that pretty little head of yours. Think back." Jon's words snarled through his clinched teeth. "Remember running to your betrothed and pouring out your heart? Telling him what a beast I'd been to you."

"But I didn't." His eyes narrowed to fiery blue slits. "I didn't!" Charlotte insisted, then twisted away when his expression continued to show his disbelief. "Fine." Charlotte turned away from him, her fingers twisted in the folds of her skirt. "I don't care whether you believe me or not. I should have urged him to do his worst."

"He certainly tried," Jon said, his words harsh with the memory of the lash.

"And why not?" Charlotte whirled around on the scattering of pine needles. "You deserved it. You kidnapped me!"

"Don't forget the ravishment."

He loomed over her again, and rather than retreat further, Charlotte turned her head, choosing simply to not look at him. But he'd allow none of that. His fingers clamped around her jaw, forcing her face around. "There's one thing I never could understand, Charlotte. Were you angry because of what I did to you . . . or because you enjoyed it so much?"

"You bastard," Charlotte whispered as tears blurred her vision. She blinked to keep them from spilling over her lashes, but it was a lost cause.

Oh, hell! He hated tears. But in truth Jon knew he deserved these. Raking his fingers through his raven hair, Jon sighed, then reached for her. She jerked away, but that only made him the more determined to hold her.

Her shoulders and back were stiff as the pine mast on his schooner, but he wrapped his arms around her anyway, feeling the dampness from her crying seep through his shirt.

"You're right, you know. I really can be a bastard." She sniffed.

"You accused me of acting irrational with Levid, and maybe you're right. But I've also had a hard time with logic since I met you."

More sniffles.

"Take this morning, for instance." Jon could feel her shaking her head, but he continued. "I'm the last person to criticize you for liking what happens when we touch. I seem to lose all sense of reality."

Charlotte's breath came in a hiccup. Tentatively she pulled away and searched his face for any sign of mockery. She found none. "You do?" she questioned, wondering if he could possibly have the same feelings as she.

"Isn't it obvious?" Damn if he wasn't going to kiss her again. And after this morning there was no question where that would lead. Hadn't he been angry, blaming her for this predicament just moments ago? Jon wasn't certain. He was only sure of one thing. He *was* going to kiss her again.

How could she want the touch of his lips so much? Hadn't she just decided to hate him forever because of his cruel words?

His tongue probed and she opened for him, her arms clinging to the solid strength of his ribs. The kiss deepened and Charlotte found herself swirling

210

away on the wings of heady sensations. The sound of her sigh mingled with the incessant hum of evening insects, the whisper of wind through the trees, the scraping of wood against pebbles.

"Er, excuse me, but I was wondering if you'd mind sharing your camp for the night?"

Jon jerked around, simultaneously reaching for his sword, which wasn't there, and shoving Charlotte behind him. "Who in the hell are you?" Jon asked, staring at a huge bear of a man striding toward them. Behind him, pulled onto the shore, was a bundle-laden canoe.

"I am Henri DeFleur, a trapper." He motioned toward the canoe, "On my way to Montreal, I saw the smoke from your fire and thought I might have some company tonight."

Jon took in the rifle slung across the stranger's back and the knife strapped to his calf, and decided this was not a man he wanted as an enemy. Besides, if he rejected the trapper's request, he'd only move a ways downstream, and Jon would rather have the mountain man where he could see him.

"I'm Jonathan Brown," Jon lied, "and this is my wife, Charlotte. We'd be glad to have you join us, but we have little to offer. Our boat capsized two days ago and I'm afraid we weren't able to save much," Jon improvised. He draped his arm around Charlotte's shoulders, hoping she had enough sense to keep her mouth shut.

"That's too bad." Henri rubbed his grizzled beard, then let loose with a stream of tobacco juice. "Don't have much room in the canoe, but I could probably take the missus with me tomorrow. Send someone back for you when we reach Montreal."

"That would be—"

"Unnecessary," Jon finished for Charlotte, his

211

fingers tightening on her upper arms. "My wife and I will manage . . . together."

"But of course." Henri gestured with his hands. "I meant nothing by my offer but to be of some help."

"And we appreciate it. Don't we, Charlotte?"

This would be the perfect time to protest, to scream out the truth. She'd been abducted and held against her will. Charlotte hadn't missed the weapons Henri had at his disposal. If she told him the truth, she might end up with a bruised arm—she might have that already—but Henri would prevail. How could he not? The captain had no gun, no knife, nothing to protect himself.

And that was exactly why she couldn't do it. Oh, Charlotte was determined to leave tomorrow morning with the trapper, but she'd speak with him privately, make him understand that she wanted no harm to befall the captain.

Smiling first at the captain and then the trapper, Charlotte agreed with her "husband." "Your offer was most kind, Mr. DeFleur, but I couldn't leave Jonathan."

By the time the deep, resonant voice of the horned owl dominated the early-night sounds, Charlotte began to wonder if she'd have a chance to speak to the trapper alone. He'd gone down to his canoe to unpack his blanket—a perfect opportunity for Charlotte to explain her predicament. But when she started down to the beach the captain grabbed her arm, pulling her off into a stand of beech.

"Where do you think you're going?"

Charlotte yanked her arm free, and turned away. "I wanted a drink."

"Stay away from him, Charlotte."

"I don't know what you mean. I . . . oh, what are you doing?" He cupped her shoulders and spun her around to face him. Lowering his head, he waited until their eyes met, his probing and serious, surrounded by the bronze of his skin, the ebony of his hair and beard.

"You seem unaware of how serious this is," Jon hissed into her ear. "He has a musket and knife, and he has us—"

"Us?" Charlotte ignored the bite of his fingers in her flesh. "There is no 'us.' You dragged me out of Montreal, and all over this godforsaken wilderness, and I want to go home." Anger faded from her eyes, replaced by a silent plea. "Let me leave with him in the morning."

"I can't do that."

"Why?" She gripped his arms. "You don't want me with you. I cause nothing but trouble, falling into the river, running away whenever I can. You said you couldn't take me back. Well, now you don't have to. I can go with Mr. DeFleur."

"No."

"You're just being stubborn. Give me one good reason why I shouldn't go with him. Just one."

Jon started to turn away, stopped when her hands tightened on his arms. "All right, you want a reason. I don't trust him, and I don't like the way he looks at you."

Taking an involuntary step back, Charlotte's fingers fluttered to her throat. "That's silly. He doesn't look at me any way at all." Though she didn't have a mirror, Charlotte had some idea how she must appear with her hair curling wildly, her clothes torn and her face burned by the sun. She never considered herself one to turn heads on her best day, and she certainly couldn't credit the captain's assessment. "You're imagining things." Goodness, was she rubbing off on him?

The captain said nothing, only stared at her in that way that seemed anything but fanciful. Charlotte tried another tack.

"What do you care if he does look at me strange? You only brought me along to help you out of Montreal. You don't need me anymore."

Apparently he didn't think this worth arguing about either for the captain merely turned on his heel, heading back toward the camp. Almost as an afterthought he paused, and glanced over his broad shoulder. "You're not going with him" was all he said.

"We'll see about that," Charlotte mumbled before following him. She was tired. Tired of the captain telling her what to do. Tired of being dirty. Tired of being hungry and wet. And tired of this "adventure."

All Charlotte wanted was to be back in Oxfordshire, snuggled in her own bed, safe and sound. Her gaze fell on the captain's muscled back as he bent over the fire, and she grimaced. Maybe she'd miss him—at first. But certainly she could forget him.

The captain volunteered to take the first watch, telling Henri DeFleur he'd wake him later. Charlotte had serious doubts that the captain would keep his promise. He motioned for her to lie down close to him, and Charlotte curled up on the blanket the trapper had given her. That gesture in itself had been an act of goodwill, but the captain had seemed unimpressed earlier when she'd caught his eye.

Charlotte lay awake watching the intricate pattern of moonlight sift through the trees overhead. Henri DeFleur slept soundly across the fire from her. She could hear his loud, rumbled snoring.

Now what was she to do? Though she couldn't see his face without shifting about, Charlotte sensed that the captain still watched. She'd never get an opportunity to speak with the trapper alone. Never. Frustrated, she shut her eyes, willing her frenzied mind to think of something. But nothing came to her, and soon the fatigue of the day bore down upon her, forcing her into a fitful sleep.

Dawn's arrival had already sent the birds chattering about, searching for a meal, when again Charlotte's eyes opened. She groaned, the tortured sound only partly due to the discomfort of sleeping on the packed ground.

She'd missed her chance to return to Montreal, to England. From what she could see, the trapper's bedroll—and the trapper—were gone. Charlotte lay alone in the small clearing, bundled in a rough blanket that had done little to protect her from the cold. And more . . . Charlotte reached down, scratching furiously at a small welt on her arm; the wool seemed both home and breeding ground to a host of vermin.

Sighing, Charlotte stood up, wondering where the captain was. Her gaze strayed to the river, and a smile broke across her chapped lips. The trapper leaned over his canoe, strapping in the few things he'd removed last night.

She wasn't too late!

Bolting toward the incline in the beach, at first Charlotte didn't notice the low growl of a question tossed her way. But when the captain repeated it— "Where are you going?"—Charlotte stopped and looked back at him.

He emerged from a stand of trees, and stood staring at her. She could run to the trapper, screaming the truth. Charlotte swallowed, her glance drawn to his bare chest, the slashing scar across his upper arm. She wanted no part of inflicting more pain on him. Whatever she did would have to be done secretly . . .

and quickly.

"I have to . . . to . . ." Charlotte paused, unable to say the words that would give her an excuse to leave his presence. But the captain apparently recognized her dilemma. With a sweeping bow, he motioned for her to go through the trees the way he'd come.

Her head lowered, eyes refusing to meet his, Charlotte nodded, then started to move past him. The shirt he held sacklike in his hand caught her attention. "What's in there?"

"Some berries. I scouted around a bit this morning." His eyes narrowed as they found the figure by the water's edge. "Not out of sight of camp."

"Are they edible, do you think?" Charlotte backed slowly toward the underbrush, disappearing into the thick foliage, but not before she caught his quick grin.

"Hurry up and we shall see."

She planned to hurry, all right, but not back to eat berries. Gathering up her skirts, Charlotte scurried through the brambles, skirting the camp and heading for a spot downriver to where the trees grew to the shoreline.

Nagging prickles of guilt speared through her, but she carefully reasoned them away. The captain would be better off without her. He wanted to reach his home, get another ship, and rejoin the war.

And she . . . all she wanted to do was go home. Charlotte fought back another thought . . . a frightening thought. She also had a strong desire to stay with the captain. But that could lead to nothing. He didn't want her. Staying with him would only place her in a strange land, surrounded by people who were her enemies.

No. The only thing to do was go home. And the

only way to do that was to travel with the trapper to Montreal.

Charlotte peeked around a tree trunk and spotted Henri. He stood, hand shading his eyes, looking out over the sun-sparkled water. His arms were even brawnier than the captain's and were encased in some type of animal skin. His way of dress made him appear very barbaric and the captain's warning sprang to her mind. But Charlotte ignored it.

"Mr. DeFleur," she hissed, motioning to him to come her way when he looked up. She watched him throw a quick glance over his shoulder toward the camp before walking slowly along the bank toward her.

Charlotte's heart pounded in her chest, and her trepidation increased with each step that brought him closer. Was she making a mistake?

The trapper didn't seem to think so. He didn't even seem surprised that she hid in a stand of trees beckoning him. His walk was cocky, his smile, showing badly yellowed teeth, confident.

"Ah, Madam Brown," he said as he approached, causing Charlotte's finger to fly to her lips in an attempt to shush him. If they hurried, and were quiet, they could be gone before the captain noticed anything awry.

But the trapper didn't seem to realize that speed was of any concern as he sauntered toward her. He appeared even taller, larger, in the strong morning light. The captain stood well over six feet, but this man seemed a mountain in comparison. His grizzled strands of hair hung limp and filthy from a nearly bald pate as he tore off the weathered fur hat.

"I knew you'd find a way for us to meet."

Charlotte stepped further into the stand of trees.

217

"What?" She skittered to the side when he reached for her.

"Now's no time to play the coquette." His beefy hands closed over Charlotte's arm and she stifled a scream.

"You don't understand . . ." she began as calmly as she could. "I want to go with you to Montreal."

"Montreal?" Apparently that gave him pause, because he hesitated before wrapping his arms around her in a bear hug that stole the breath from Charlotte's body. "I don't think that man of yours is willing to let you go."

"He's not my man . . . Would you please stop it?" Charlotte used all her strength to shove at the smelly bulk pressed against her, but nothing happened, except for Henri giving her a questioning look. "Not your man?" His arms loosened.

"No." Taking a deep breath, Charlotte continued. She had an uncomfortable feeling she might be making a mistake, but it was too late to turn back now. "I left Montreal with . . . Mr. Brown, willingly, you understand. But I've changed my mind, and wish to go home."

A smile split the trapper's scraggly beard. "He run out of ways to please you already, did he?"

"Of course not." Charlotte jerked her head to the side to avoid his slobbery lips.

"That won't happen with me, *chérie*. I know how to please a woman . . . again and again."

"I . . . don't . . . want . . . pleased." Charlotte knew for certain now. She'd made a horrible mistake! Opening her mouth to scream proved another error. The trapper's lips clamped down on hers in a suffocating, disgusting kiss.

Charlotte wriggled and squirmed, pushed and shoved, but it did no good. His mountainous body

218

held hers in the claws of a huge trap.

She felt helpless.

Charlotte's eyes drifted shut, transporting her to another place, another time. Trade winds rattled giant palm fronds and stirred the fragrance of tropical blossoms, surrounding her with sensual delights. Squinting against the bright sun that rode in the sky like a fiery ball, she searched the horizon. Suddenly sails split the hazy line where sky met sea. He came for her. He came . . .

"Get your hands off her!"

It was the pirate! No. Charlotte's eyes flew open when Henri turned from her. She stared with a mixture of disbelief and relief at Captain Knox's handsome face.

He stood tall and straight not ten rods from her, and stared at the sun gleaming off the edge of the knife Henri pulled from his boot. Undaunted, he motioned toward Charlotte. "Come over here."

She wanted to, with all her being. But her feet simply wouldn't respond to the message her brain sent, no doubt because the trapper still had a firm grip on her arm.

"But the mademoiselle wishes to stay with me."

"Well, that's too damn bad, because she isn't going to," Jon said before taking a menacing step forward.

"I don't," Charlotte murmured, but she wasn't certain either man heard her.

The trapper shoved her aside, and shifted the knife in his hand, a daring grin on his face. "Is she worth dying for, monsieur?"

Jon didn't have time to ponder the question—and in his present frame of mind that probably was for the best—before the trapper's crouching form sprang forward. Dodging to the side, Jon narrowly missed being gutted by the deadly blade.

Henri's laugh sent chills down Jon's spine. "Ah, so you want to play. But that is all right with Henri. It just makes the victory that much sweeter, no?"

The trapper lunged forward again, but this time Jon not only feinted to the right, he stuck out his foot and tripped the giant man. Unfortunately the Frenchman proved more agile than Jon had given him credit for. He caught himself against a tree and turned, all mischief gone from his eyes. "You will pay for that, my friend."

This time his bellow rang out through the forest, sending a flock of blackbirds soaring skyward as he leaped. Jon's attempt to sidestep failed when he tripped over a rotting log. The slice of the blade burned through the flesh of his arm. But that wasn't the worst of it.

Henri dove on top of him, only momentarily deterred by the fist Jon sank into his beefy jaw. Jon punched again, a hard thrust to the trapper's throat, but though that jab stunned, Henri recovered quickly, grinning as he swept the hunting knife toward Jon's throat.

# Chapter Thirteen

With a primal grunt, Jon summoned his strength and tried to shift from under the ever-lowering knife. Beads of sweat pooled on his brow and his muscles stood rigid, but he couldn't stem the downward force of the glistening blade.

His last thought. Dear God, he was thinking his last thought on this earthly plane, Jon realized with a clarity that belied the situation. It should be of his mother, or father, or home. Why in heaven's name was his mind fixed on Char—

The thud came out of nowhere, cracking loudly in Jon's ears. The weight that crashed on top of him nearly whooshed air from his lungs. But it was dead-weight.

Nonthreatening.

Heaving the trapper aside, Jon stared up into Charlotte Winston's frightened face. She still clutched an arm-thick branch in her clenched fingers. "Are you planning to bash my head in, too?" Jon asked when she continued to gaze down at him, the club held high.

"No. Oh, no." Charlotte dropped the branch, apologizing profusely when it landed on Jon's foot.

"Are you all right?"

Jon wasn't certain if she were referring to his arm, where blood dripped down puddling on the leaf-strewn ground, or his foot. But he levered himself up, assuring her he was as good as could be expected.

Kneeling beside him, Charlotte tore strips from her chemise to fashion as a bandage. She lifted large, dark eyes to his. "I thought he was going to kill you."

Jon managed a grin, gritting his teeth against the pain in his upper arm as she tied off the binding. "So did I." His expression sobered. "He would have, if it hadn't been for you."

A soft rose blush crept up Charlotte's cheeks. "I didn't— "Oh my goodness, is Mr. DeFleur dead? Did I kill him?"

Jon hadn't given the fate of the other man much thought and admittedly wasn't too concerned. But he reached over with his good arm and gave the trapper a shove, glancing up at Charlotte when the trapper moaned.

"Looks like he'll live. Anyone that big has to have a tough head."

"Do you think we should bandage it?"

Jon stood, and glared down at her. "Not unless you want him to take up where he left off when I interrupted him."

Charlotte looked away. "No," she breathed. "I don't want that."

"Then I think we should get out of here." Jon started down toward the beach. "Pick up that knife and come on."

"The knife?" Charlotte glanced toward the captain, but he'd already sauntered off toward Mr. DeFleur's canoe. Hesitantly she bent over, gingerly picking up the knife handle between her thumb and finger. It was heavier than she thought. Gripping it

222

more firmly, she noticed the blood smeared on the blade.

The captain's blood.

Charlotte's knees were weak, and she bit her bottom lip to keep it from quivering. Taking a deep breath, she wiped the blade across a patch of grass and turned down toward the shore.

She found the captain bent over the trapper's canoe. "What are you doing?"

Jon glanced up. "Looking for the powder and ball for that musket." He motioned toward the long gun leaning against a birch tree.

"Are you planning to . . ." Charlotte hesitated to use the word steal, decided instead on, "*take* Mr. DeFleur's gun?"

Apparently the captain didn't think that question warranted an answer because he just stared at her a moment and then bent back to his task.

Charlotte stood, the knife hanging by her side, throwing occasional nervous glances over her shoulder to where the trapper still lay sprawled on his back. She sighed. "Are we taking the canoe?"

Jon slung a powder horn over his shoulder. "Back to Montreal?" Their eyes met. "Hardly. I told you yesterday we're heading south." Either expecting no argument, or caring little if he got one, Jon motioned Charlotte over. "Give me the knife." He stuck it in the top of his boot. "I'm leaving your friend his pistol and enough powder and shot to last him until Montreal."

"He isn't my friend," Charlotte mumbled before falling into step beside him.

Jon shrugged, wincing at the pain in his arm. "I wasn't the one kissing him."

"I wasn't kissing him. I was trying to get away!"

The captain shrugged again, and picked up his

pace, heading back onto the meadow. It was all Charlotte could do to keep up, let alone argue in her defense. Besides, if the captain wanted to believe she'd enjoyed the trapper's caresses, let him. She'd saved his damn life. She didn't owe him anything else.

His arm was bleeding again. Charlotte brushed hair out of her eyes and tried not to notice. But there it was, fresh blood darkening the wrapped cotton. He must know it—feel it, for goodness' sakes. But he kept going, his pace only slowing down to step over the occasional fallen log.

Charlotte thought she'd been tired of forests yesterday, but today was worse. For one thing, she was hungrier. That fish last night hadn't really filled the emptiness inside her. For another thing, she didn't like the silence between them. And she didn't like watching his stupid arm bleed.

"Don't you think we should rest a while?"

The captain made an impatient sound before turning, hands on his lean hips. "Are you tired?"

Charlotte considered lying, then decided it wasn't worth the effort. What he thought about her made no difference. "Yes, I'm tired. We've been traveling for . . ." Charlotte lifted her hands, realizing she had no idea how long they'd been tramping through the forest. "For a long time," she finished. "Besides, you're bleeding." Might as well make this partly because of him.

The way he looked down at his arm made Charlotte wonder if he knew it needed attention. He sank down, leaning his head against a tree trunk, and closed his eyes.

"Are you all right?" Charlotte crouched down beside him, trying—with scant success—to keep her skirt pulled down while she reached underneath for a fresh section on her chemise.

"I'm fine." His dark lashes fluttered up; his gaze settled on her exposed leg, then lifted to meet hers. "Maybe we should rest a little, though."

Why did he have to look at her like that? Charlotte jerked at her gown, then began untying the soaked bandage. The wound wasn't particularly deep, but all the jostling around had kept it from clotting. After binding it and rolling down his shirtsleeve, Charlotte tore away more of her undergarment to fashion a sling.

The captain smiled his thanks, and Charlotte felt herself grow warm all over. She scrunched back against a nearby tree, and shut her eyes.

"I never thanked you properly for saving my life."

Charlotte rolled her head to the side, her expression registering surprise. She hadn't expected him to say that. Swallowing, she lifted her hand. "It was nothing."

"Well, maybe you think so, but I'm rather fond of my life . . . and I do thank you."

Charlotte picked at the moss growing near along the thick roots of the tree. "You saved me, too."

Jon leaned his head back. "From the trapper?"

"Yes." Crumbling bits of moss onto her skirt, Charlotte looked away. "I *was* trying to push him away."

At first Charlotte thought his snort of disdain directed at her, but when she searched his face, she realized differently. He met her eyes, his appearing more than a little contrite.

"You knew I was fighting him."

"I suppose I did," Jon admitted.

"Then why did you say what you did?"

Jon shrugged, but that wasn't sufficient answer for Charlotte. Rising to her knees, scattering crumpled bits of moss, Charlotte faced him. "Why?"

"Hell, I don't know." He thought back to the moment he'd come across them, had seen the burly trapper's arms enfolding her, and his jaw clenched. "I was angry."

"Angry?"

"Yes!" Jon stood, reaching down for her hand. "I think we should get moving."

Sighing, Charlotte allowed herself to be pulled upright. He obviously considered the discussion closed. But as much as she'd prefer it also, she had something to tell him.

"I did go to Mr. DeFleur." No surprise registered in the captain's expression. Charlotte continued. "I wanted him to take me back to Montreal." She tilted her head and watched the captain's whiskered face for any show of emotion. There was none.

"I told you not to trust him."

"I know, and it didn't take me long to realize you were right." Charlotte took a deep breath. "But I had to try."

The captain only nodded, and shouldering the musket, started out again. Charlotte fell in beside him, helping to push some of the brambles and branches out of the way.

"This isn't like England," she finally said when they stopped by a crystal-clear stream to drink. "It's wilder." Jon only looked at her as he wiped at his mouth with the back of his hand. "Not at all what I expected."

Jon leaned back on his heels. "We should run across civilization soon."

Charlotte smiled. "I'm not very good at this." The wave of her hand included the stream and canopy of trees.——

"You're doing all right." Jon stood and reached

down for her hand.

"All those years when my mother was ill, I thought I wanted an adventure, but—"

"You've had a little more than an adventure," he said, tossing her a look that made Charlotte laugh.

"I suppose you're right." She followed him up the sloping bank. "But nothing is like I thought it would be." Her expression sobered. "He has a mistress."

"Who? Levid?" Besides being a cruel bastard, the man was crazy.

"No . . ." Charlotte paused. "Oh, I don't know if *he* does or not. I mean my father. My father keeps a mistress." She stepped over tangled root. "That may be part of the reason he was angry I came to Canada."

So her father hadn't welcomed her with open arms. Jon found himself disliking the man, but for Charlotte's sake he offered an excuse. "He probably was worried about your safety." With good reason, Jon added silently.

Charlotte shrugged. "Maybe, but I don't think that was it."

Jon took her delicately boned hand and helped her over a gully. "A lot of men keep mistresses."

"Do you?" She stopped and gazed up at him, her dark eyes serious.

"What? Keep a mistress?"

"Yes. You said a lot of men do. I just wondered if you have one."

Jon met her stare a moment before nudging her forward. How did this conversation twist around to him? "No, I don't," he answered firmly, hoping she'd drop the subject.

"Why not?"

He should have known better. "Hell, I don't know . . . I'm at sea a lot."

"Oh. So if you were, say a planter, you'd probably

have one?"

"Charlotte . . ." Jon drew her name out in frustration. "I have women . . . friends, but no one in particular. Now can we just keep moving?" He didn't give her time to respond before he surged on ahead.

Charlotte had no idea how long they walked this time. She hoped the captain knew where he was headed, because she'd hate to think they were walking in circles. Resting for a moment, she leaned against a tree. She'd held back for some privacy and knew she should hurry before he got too far ahead. But she was simply too tired to rush. Charlotte squinted toward the trail he'd made, muttering under her breath when she realized he'd disappeared from view.

Pushing away from the tree trunk, Charlotte began to follow when she heard an excited yelp. She froze, not knowing if she should proceed or not. But the captain yelled again, and this time he called her name. Picking up her skirts, Charlotte ran toward his voice.

She broke through the trees, slid down a small incline, and came to a stop beside the captain. Right in the center of a road.

"What's this?" Charlotte had been so sure they were wandering around in the deepest wilderness she could hardly fathom what she saw.

"It appears we've stumbled upon a road."

Using her hand to shade her eyes, Charlotte looked first one way then the other. "Where does it go?"

"North, I imagine, would take us back to Montreal." Jon studied her as if he expected her to bolt up the road at any moment.

"And this way?" Charlotte pointed south.

"I'm not sure." Again Jon wished for a chance to relive a lost geography lesson. "Lake Champlain maybe."

"Are we in Canada or the United States?"

Jon shrugged, and Charlotte found herself mimicking the gesture. "Well," she said. "It shall be easier to walk on this road than through the forest."

"It also makes us more vulnerable."

Charlotte turned, her hands jammed into her hippockets. "Don't tell me we have to go back into the woods."

"No." Jon couldn't help grinning at her vehemence. "We just need to keep a close watch. Come on."

Walking was walking, Charlotte decided after they'd been doing it for a while. To be certain, the road was easier to traverse than the forest . . . but not much.

Where were the wagons that had rutted the road? Charlotte had almost given up on any relief coming her way when she heard a rumbling of horses' hooves and wooden wheels. She looked around only to see the captain motion her toward a thicket beside the road. "Captain Knox, I—"

"Get yourself hidden, Charlotte."

Reluctantly she obeyed, crouching behind an uprooted tree and batting away a horde of flies. She glanced up, expecting to see the captain squatting beside her, but he still stood by the side of the road. Charlotte opened her mouth to call to him, but the wagon—she could see it plainly now—was almost upon him.

The driver, a slumped-over man in rough clothing, reined his team of workhorses to a stop. Taking off a wide-brimmed felt hat, he wiped at his damp forehead with his shirtsleeve. Eyeing the captain, he nodded his head in response to his greeting.

"You one of them soldiers from down the lake?"

Jon shook his head, wishing he knew the man's allegiance, or even what country they were in. "I'm from west of here. Me and my missus been traveling a while. Got ourselves robbed by a trapper a few days back."

"Your missus, huh?" The man stretched in his seat making no attempt to disguise his survey of the area.

Jon ignored him. "Name's Jonathan Brown. I'm heading for New York."

"You and the missus got a long way to go. There's a war on now," he added, settling down on the wooden seat.

"We heard. And who might you be?" Jon didn't know whether to trust the man or not, but at this point he wasn't sure he had a choice. In any case he was glad he'd taken the trouble to load the musket.

"Eb Riker. Got me a place down a ways. Welcome to ride along if you like."

"Appreciate that." Jon glanced back toward the trees to call Charlotte, but she was already scurrying out from the shadows. "This is my wife, Mrs. Brown."

"Ma'am." The man lifted his hat and offered Charlotte a seat beside him, but after her experience with the trapper, she opted to climb into the back. There she settled amid dusty burlap bags and slatted barrels.

She must have dozed because one moment she was listening to the captain spin a concocted story about their life on the frontier, and the next thing she knew the wagon halted in front of a small weatherboard cabin.

"Like I said," Charlotte heard Eb Riker explain as she yawned and stretched her stiff legs, "you're welcome to stay the night and travel with me tomorrow to Plattsburg." Charlotte smiled when she heard the captain accept the offer. Tonight they'd sleep indoors, and they'd eat. She was certain Mr. Riker

230

would include supper in his invitation.

After their introduction, Mrs. Riker eyed Charlotte with distrust, and it occurred to Charlotte how she must look. Not that the other woman had too much to recommend her, but at least she appeared reasonably clean and her clothes, though homespun and faded, were in one piece. Charlotte fingered the torn sleeve of her gown and stared down at the dusty toes of her slippers.

"My wife's had a rough time of it," Jon offered, wondering if either of the Rikers believed his story.

"You look like you had your share of problems, too." The woman inclined her head toward Jon's arm.

"I took exception to a trapper stealing all our possessions," Jon grinned. "Not that it made much difference in the end."

Neither the woman or her husband seemed to see the humor in his remark, but the woman did holler for two of her children who led Charlotte away, offering her a bath. Jon watched her go, hoping she had enough sense to keep to his story.


"I don't like this."

Jon climbed through the opening, then closed the trap and scanned the loft. Most of the space was taken up by a large quilt-covered mattress. Charlotte stood beside it, holding a stub of a candle. The flickering flame sent splashes of light across the roughhewn walls and the billowy nightdress Mrs. Riker had lent Charlotte.

"I don't know," Jon said, rubbing his freshly shaven chin. "I don't see anything wrong with it. Isn't the bed soft enough for you?"

Charlotte gritted her teeth. "That's not what I

mean, and you know it." She placed the candleholder on the small wooden table. "We shouldn't be up here together."

"But the children volunteered to sleep in the barn so we could have it."

"That's because they think we're married," Charlotte whispered.

"What else was I going to tell them?" Jon sat on the edge, testing the mattress. "This isn't bad."

"You could have said I was your sister," Charlotte insisted, ignoring his reference to the comfort of their bed.

"I don't think so." Jon shook his head. "You don't look anything like either of my sisters."

"They don't know that," Charlotte hissed before she caught the gleam in his eye and realized he was teasing her. With a sigh she backed away from the bed. "This just isn't going to work."

"Sure it is." Jon kicked off his boots, then reached for his shirttail. "The bed's plenty big enough for two. You stay on your side, I'll stay on mine." He pulled the shirt over his head. "Besides, it's not as if we haven't—"

"All right," Charlotte interrupted, catching the drift of what he planned to say. "I suppose it will have to do."

Climbing gingerly into her side of the bed, Charlotte settled beneath the faded quilt, pulling it to her chin. She shut her eyes, trying to block out the sounds made by the man beside her—clothes sliding over bronzed skin, his sigh when the mattress sank beneath his prone weight—but it was impossible. Where was her imagination, her haven of escape, when she needed it?

All she knew was him. Even the smell of the strong lye soap he'd used to wash and shave filled her senses, mingling with the captain's own unique scent to drive her crazy. Clutching the quilt to her breast, she wriggled, trying to find a more comfortable position, and searched her memory for a distraction. The only one that came to mind featured a meadow of wildflowers and swaying grass, a pair of strong arms, and the captain's passion-filled eyes looking down at her.

Charlotte gritted her teeth, determined to think of something else . . . anything. She'd—

"Charlotte?"

"What?" she snapped.

"I didn't mean to wake you." The captain leaned up on his elbow.

"You didn't." Charlotte forced calmness into her voice.

"I was wondering if you'd . . ." he began, and Charlotte dug her fingers into the fabric. Here it came. He couldn't stop thinking of it either, and he was going to ask her to make love with him. But she wouldn't. Oh, no. She'd explain the situation to him logically. Explain how the other time had been a mistake, and it couldn't happen again. Not if it killed her.

She opened her mouth to tell him, then noticed the peculiar way he looked at her. She'd seen him in the throes of passion, and this wasn't it. His expression seemed more puzzled as he stared at her.

"Are you all right?" he questioned, leaning forward to brush a lock of hair off her forehead.

"I'm fine," Charlotte insisted, trying not to let him see how his touch affected her. "What were you going to say?" He'd ask, she'd say no, and that would be the end of it.

Jon shrugged. She was really acting strange, but maybe it was just fatigue. He knew *he'd* never been so tired. "I wondered if you'd blow out the candle."

"The candle?" Charlotte glanced over at the partially gutted taper, the flame swimming in a puddle of melted tallow, then back at the captain.

"Yes, though I'm so tired I could fall asleep with a hundred candles burning, I think it would be safer to extinguish it."

"Of course." Charlotte rolled over, taking the quilt with her, and blew out the candle, watching the lazy spiral of smoke rise into the air. By the time she lay back and let her gaze drift toward the captain, he'd fulfilled his prophecy and fallen asleep—on his back, the moonlight filtering through the cracks in the eves making sensual designs and shadows on his bare chest.

*He* wasn't kept awake by erotic memories. *He* didn't even seem to notice that they were in bed together. *He* was almost naked. Charlotte's eyes drifted down his broad chest over his thin cotton drawers, trying to ignore the well-defined bulge, to his long muscular legs.

How *could* he just lie there sleeping? He snored, a deep resonant sound, and Charlotte whipped off the quilt. Obviously he could, so there was no reason for her to defend her virtue, such as it was.

She needed to get some sleep. But the nap she'd taken in the wagon . . . and the man lying beside her . . . made that impossible. Charlotte tossed and turned, wriggled and thrashed, finally falling into a fitful slumber.

The arm thrown across his chest hadn't awakened him, but the thigh over his groin had. Smiling into the darkness, Jon turned his head, breathing in Charlotte's sweet fragrance, and inched his hand up her hip. She could wake him like this anytime.

When he'd first crawled into the bed, he'd been so exhausted, too tired to even think about the woman lying beside him. But now that he had some rest, she was all he could think of.

She shifted, rubbing her leg across his hard manhood, and Jon groaned, running his fingers down her thigh, tightening his hold to halt the movement. She moaned, whispering something in her sleep, and Jon forced himself to stop caressing her leg.

He throbbed for her, but he wasn't such a cad as to take advantage of a sleeping woman. Damn, he wasn't. Jon dropped his hand onto the quilt and whispered in her ear. His breath fluttered the fine hair curling around her face. "Hmm." Her face muzzled into his, her small nose brushing against his jaw.

"Charlotte."

Jon's breath caught, but he resisted the urge to touch her again—barely. "Charlotte, honey, wake up." He could tell the exact moment she left her dream world and joined the real one. Her body stiffened, and he felt the flutter of her lashes against his cheek.

She must have realized where her arm and leg were, for she slowly removed them, eliciting another groan from Jon as her thigh skimmed across his groin.

"Oh . . . I'm sorry."

"Don't be. It's all right." Jon reached for her hand when she tried to leave the bed. "Where are you going?"

"I . . . I better just sit here on the edge of the bed for a while."

"Why?"

"Why?" Charlotte repeated, sounding as if he asked the silliest question she could imagine. "Because I can't stay on my side of the bed. Because

I'm all over you," she finished, feeling a heated flush climb up her face.

"I don't mind."

Charlotte shot him a look over her shoulder she imagined he missed in the dim light. She also couldn't see the expression on his face. "Are you laughing at me?"

"No. Well, maybe a little," Jon admitted, grabbing her around the waist as she bolted from the mattress and flopping her onto her back.

"Let me up," Charlotte hissed, her arms flailing against his chest as he loomed over her.

"Not until you stop this nonsense. And keep your voice down. Do you want to wake the Rikers?"

"No," Charlotte whispered. "But I don't want to lie here with you, either. I bother you."

"You're damn right you bother me." Jon caught her hands in one of his, ignoring her gasp. "But it has nothing to do with the way you crawl all over the bed in your sleep." Jon lowered his body onto hers, letting her feel exactly what he meant. "You've bothered me since the first moment I saw you."

Charlotte felt her body soften, melt around the hardness pressing into her belly. She swallowed. "You hated me. I caused you trouble."

"You did that." His deep chuckle rumbled up through his chest. "But I never hated you. And I always, always wanted you."

His kiss began as a soft blending of breath, but quickly changed, deepened. Charlotte arched against him as his tongue plunged into her mouth, driving sanity from her head.

"We shouldn't," she whispered when their lips parted. Her breathing rasped as shallow as his, their hearts pounded in frantic accord.

Jon released her hands, trailing his fingers down

236

her cotton-covered arms. "Tell me to stop and I will." Taking a deep breath, he amended, "I'll try." He couldn't stop touching her. Her face, her hair, everything about her beckoned him.

"I can't. I can't."

Jon barely heard her, searched for her meaning. "Can't what?" His mouth skimmed under her chin, found the softness below her ear.

"Can't tell you to stop." Her arms wove around his neck, drawing him closer. "I don't want you to stop."

The words were the ones he wanted to hear, yet her tortured tone reached a similar chord within him. They shouldn't do this. Before, he'd told himself revenge was the reason he wanted her. But now he knew different. This hunger had nothing to do with Levid, or his brother, or the war. Only desire ruled his passions—ruled hers. A desire that seemed to feed upon itself. A desire that could lead to nothing.

Jon took a painful breath, and stared down at her. His forearms bracketed her face, and he shifted a finger to sift through a strand of soft brown hair. "I want you more than you can imagine. But this doesn't change anything."

Charlotte wet her suddenly dry lips. "I know that. There's nothing it can change." It was as simple as that, yet as complex. This portion of her life was like a fantasy, a fantasy come true. But it would end when she went back to England.

His lips brushed hers and Charlotte thanked providence her real world hadn't claimed her yet. Like a spiraling vortex, his touch drew her in, took her places that shamed her imagination . . . her memory.

Their legs tangled as he slowly worked the borrowed nightrail above her knees, her thighs, and past her throbbing heat. His hand cupped, soothed, worked Charlotte to a fevered pitch of excitement and hunger. She writhed, whispering his name on an erotic moan, and Jon lost all semblance of composure.

The billowing nightrail fluttered to the loft floor like a windless sail, his breeches discarded in no less a hurry. Now satiny skin caressed his body and he sank into it with a groan of satisfaction.

She was soft and sweet, melting around him as only a woman could, as only this woman could. Jon's mouth moved down her exquisite throat, tracing the subtle line of her collarbone, then closing with moist heat over her straining breast.

She burned for him, her body tight and aching . . . longing. Charlotte's fingers braided through his hair, loving the clean smell of him, the tingling heat of his mouth and tongue on her nipple. She arched, wanting to feel more of him, sighing when his swollen staff teased her. Lifting, stretching off the mattress, Charlotte pushed toward him, but he stayed her with a sweep of his hand down the side of her hip.

She gasped as his finger skimmed over the sensitive nub of flesh, moaned deep in her throat as his body slid lower, using his tongue to drive her insane.

His strong hands grasped her hips, levering her up and open to him. Charlotte's breath hissed through parted lips. Her body jerked in frenzied ecstasy, and still he continued his wicked delights, driving her still higher.

His tongue stroked and she cried out, digging her hands into his hair and biting her lip in wild abandon. The waves crashed over her, tightening her knees against his head, sending her body into uncontrolled spasms of sensual pleasure. She crested, then started the upward surge again as his hard length slid slowly, sensually into her wet, heated body.

He thrust, the tendons in his powerful arms standing out in bold relief, then withdrew, only to begin the exquisite torture again.

Charlotte clutched his shoulders, feeling all control slipping away, feeling the coil inside her tighten. The spasms began again, stronger, longer, and this time she didn't ascend the spiral alone. The captain stiffened, then thrust into her, the shudders multiplying as they crashed over them again and again.

Charlotte lay, her fingers tangled in the curls on his chest, listening to the steady beat of his heart. There seemed to be so much to say, yet she couldn't think of a thing. Maybe there really was nothing to be gained by speaking of this. Maybe it was best to just accept and go on. The only problem was, Charlotte wasn't certain she could do that. But then what choice did she have?

Perhaps if she— The captain's snore cut off her thought. Snuggling into his arms more comfortably Charlotte gave in to reality. There would be no discussion tonight.

However, things would be different tomorrow.

# Chapter Fourteen

But there was no chance to talk things through in the morning.

When Charlotte awoke, well past dawn, the captain's side of the bed was empty. Only the rumpled quilt and the faint smell of the captain proved the reality of the previous night.

Hurriedly, Charlotte pulled on the borrowed dress, and slipped her feet into her own torn shoes. She braided her hair, catching the curled end in a ribbon taken from her chemise. Hoping for a moment alone with the captain, she opened the trap and backed down the ladder.

But only Mrs. Riker and two of her children were in the kitchen preparing breakfast. The older woman looked up and smiled when Charlotte's feet touched the puncheon floor.

"Your man's helping mine pack the raft. Eb's been meaning to take a trip down the lake to Plattsburg," she said, gathering up her skirts and using them to insulate her hand against the frying pan's heat as she grabbed the handle.

"But isn't Plattsburg an American town?" Charlotte asked after apologizing for sleeping so late. She hoped the color she felt flood her face didn't give away the real reason she'd overslept.

"They pay for supplies same as the British," Mrs. Riker replied, not bothering to glance up.

Charlotte had discovered last night they were still in Canada, but apparently this family had no strong ties to either side during the present conflict. And when the youngest of the Riker children, a babe in arms, started crying from the cradle in the corner, Charlotte decided other things in life did take priority. Mrs. Riker moved to the cradle, asking Charlotte to look after the frying potatoes.

Leaning over the smoking fireplace and copying Mrs. Riker's movements, Charlotte tried to hide her lack of cooking skills. Mrs. Samuels, along with a cook's helper, took care of preparing the meals at home, and though Charlotte had enjoyed visiting with them, she hadn't learned even the fundamentals of cooking.

When the potatoes were turned out onto a large ironstone platter, that flaw in her education was obvious to everybody. Still Mrs. Riker said nothing, and when the men came after washing their hands in the bucket by the door, they crunched through the charred potatoes without comment.

After breakfast the captain announced to Charlotte they would be accompanying Mr. Riker to Plattsburg. He draped his arm about her shoulders in a way Charlotte supposed was meant to keep her from arguing. But she had nothing to say about it one way or the other. She didn't imagine this was the place to make a stand anyway . . . that is, if a stand could be made.

"Take the shawl, too. The days are getting colder." Mrs. Riker, babe on hip, pulled Charlotte aside while the men tested the ropes on the raft.

"But I can't take all this from you." The woman had already given Charlotte the gown she wore, and though it made no pretense at style, it covered more than the torn rag of a dress Charlotte had on upon arriving.

Mrs. Riker pushed the woven shawl back into Charlotte's hands. "I have another. Besides, your man traded his knife for your things."

"He did?" Charlotte shaded her eyes and glanced down the bank in time to see the captain leap onto shore. She shouldn't let the knowledge that he'd given up the knife affect her—after all, it wasn't really his knife—but it did. Charlotte smiled at the older woman and gave her a hug, then scrambled down the hillock toward the lake.

The trip down Lake Champlain was pleasant enough for her. Of course she wasn't working the raft along the placid sheet of water. Charlotte leaned back against a barrel and let her gaze drift. The captain and Mr. Riker kept the raft hugging the western shore and Charlotte looked out over the undulating countryside. Occasionally she'd catch a glimpse of civilization, but for the most part the area appeared uninhabited. Forests of firs, pines, birch, oak, and ash spread toward the interior.

They reached Plattsburg Bay late afternoon of the second day. After helping Eb Riker unload the raft, Charlotte and the captain bid him farewell and headed for the mud fort occupied by what she estimated to be thousands of troops.

"Let me do the talking," the captain advised, and Charlotte stopped in her tracks. This was almost the first thing he'd said directly to her since they'd spent the night in the Riker's loft. She told him so, ignoring the cock of his brow when she referred to the night they'd spent together.

"There's been little time for talk," Jon reminded her.

"I know. Please forget I mentioned it." At this moment she didn't know why she had. The captain acted as if the times they'd made love never happened, and she had a feeling she should follow his lead in this. Pretending it didn't happen, that she'd never lain in his arms, seemed the best approach.

Especially now that the seeds of a plan were forming in her mind.

It was ridiculous for her to go any farther south. The captain didn't need her as a hostage anymore. He was safe in his own country. And though he had obvious objections to taking her back himself, or even trusting the trapper, Henri DeFleur, to do it, he shouldn't mind her staying here. Staying, that is, until she could find an escort back to lower Canada. And from there home to Oxfordshire. Away from the captain.

Charlotte sighed, then coughed to cover the sound when the captain looked down at her. Leaving him was the best—the only—thing she could do.

An unsettling suspicion stayed with her that she was falling in love with Jonathan Knox. Charlotte tried to tell herself it was the pirate and her silly imagination playing her false, but she didn't really believe that, any more than she thought the captain loved her. And she couldn't stay with him feeling as she did, knowing it wasn't reciprocated.

Stifling another sigh, Charlotte followed the captain to a rough wooden building guarded by two sentries. The captain gave his name, and though the soldiers seemed skeptical, looking them over with open disdain, one of them entered the building. He turned moments later with a surprised expression on his face and a request that they enter.

After seating Charlotte in one of the chairs lining the room and admonishing her to stay put, Jon followed the militia private through another door. He entered a small, cluttered room obviously used as an office. Any reservations he felt about trying to explain all that had happened vanished when a tall redheaded man stood and moved toward him.

"Jon, is it really you?"

"Jacob Anderson?" Jon blinked, and spearing his fingers through his disheveled hair, he strode around the desk. The man standing before him was one of his family's oldest friends. His parents had known Jacob for over thirty years, since the early days of the Revolution. Jon's mother had nursed the redhead in a Philadelphia prison, and his father, at Jacob's insistence, had taken him to New York to spy for General Washington. Jacob had even been there when Alexander Knox, Jon's father, was captured by the British.

Jon's parents always told the story that if Jacob Anderson hadn't brought word to Jon's mother about the capture, she wouldn't have rushed to New York to help Alexander escape and Jon would never have been born. Why, Jacob Anderson was even Jon's godfather. But the last Jon had heard, Jacob and his family were living in New York. Jacob ran a successful, though at times controversial, newspaper, where his strong Democrat views often had him at odds with the Federalists of the city.

Clasping the older man by the shoulders, Jon shook his head in disbelief. "How long has it been . . . and what in the hell are you doing here? Thought you'd given up on the Army."

"I had." Jacob Anderson slapped Jon's shoulder. "A lot of us had before this mess broke out. But when they called up the militia . . ." Jacob lifted his hands.

"I've been up here about a month now. General Dearborn has plans to attack Canada. But if he doesn't get to it before the snow flies, it will be too late this year."

"Going up through Montreal?"

"That's the plan. Part of it anyway." Again his hands lifted in a sign of confusion. "Hell, I don't know what he's got in mind. I don't think *he* knows. It's not like the old days when your father and I— What are you grinning at?"

"Nothing." Jon tried to sober his expression. "It's just . . . you sound a lot like father."

"Well, I should think so. Anyone in their right mind— Oh, bother." Jacob jerked a chair forward for Jon. "Now don't let me get on my soapbox about this war." He folded his long frame into the chair opposite Jon's. "How is your father? And Elizabeth?" He paused and seemed to look at Jon, really look at him, for the first time. "And what are you doing up here? Dressed like that?"

The joy of seeing his old friend evaporated like a puddle on a blustery day. Jon looked across at Jacob. He must be near fifty, Jon thought as he took in the gangly arms and legs that made him appear more youthful. It had been near two years since Jon had seen him, but he still seemed the same. If only things were the same.

"Did you hear about Christopher?" Jon's words were low, painful.

Jacob rubbed the back of his neck. "Your father wrote me about it a couple of months ago. Damn shame about him being impressed into the British Navy." He glanced up. "How's Elizabeth taking it?"

"Mother's strong." Jon shifted in his chair. "She's going to have to be." Jacob's stare met his. "Because there's more. I'm afraid Chris is dead."

Jacob's chin fell to his chest, and he heaved a sigh. When he looked up again, his eyes were bright with unshed tears. "How did it happen?"

"I don't know . . . not exactly." Jon suddenly felt tired, like everything that had happened was happening once again. He wanted nothing more than to lie down and forget. But he couldn't. Forearms on thighs, he sucked in a lungful of air. "He died on board the ship that impressed him." Catching Jacob's eye, he continued. "You know Christopher. He wasn't going to take this atrocity without fighting back. Apparently he did it once too often."

Jacob leaned back in his chair. "Accidents happen. They just—"

"Hell, this was no accident." Jon leaped from the chair, unable to stand the confinement another minute. "Chris had no business being on the *Scorpion* in the first place. And I've firsthand knowledge of the son of a bitch who captains her." With a savage jerk Jon tore his shirttail from his breeches and flung it up, revealing the web of scars on his back.

"My God!" Jacob's exclamation came out as a gasp of air. "What happened to you?"

Jon let the linen fall from his fingers and turned to face Jacob. "I managed to find Levid." At the questioning expression on Jacob's face, Jon explained. "The captain of the *Scorpion*. Unfortunately, I also managed to lose my ship and get myself captured."

"He did that to you?"

"Aye." Jon slumped back into the chair. "He wasn't exactly without provocation. I tried to kill him." Jon shrugged, then dropped his head into his hands. "He'd just told me about Christopher."

"Oh, Jon. I'm so sorry."

Sitting up, embarrassed by his display of emotion, Jon continued. "I'm going to find him again. And this time . . ." His fist clenched. "This time things will be different." Jon shook his head, trying to pull himself together. "I need to get to Washington, get a new command."

"I can help you there," Jacob said, standing and searching through some papers on his desk. "At least in getting to Washington. A horse, some supplies . . . You should get there quick enough."

Jon stood, clasping his hands behind his back. "There's more." Jacob looked up, and Jon shrugged. He'd almost forgotten about Charlotte in the last few emotional moments, but she couldn't be overlooked now.

The husband-and-wife ruse wouldn't work with Jacob. He knew Jon wasn't married. Besides, Jon wouldn't lie to him. Which only left the truth. "There's another complication," Jon continued. "I'm traveling with a woman."

Jacob leaned against the edge of the desk. "I see."

"I don't think you do." For some reason he couldn't tolerate Jacob's simple words, simple acceptance. "I escaped from the gaol in Montreal, and . . . and brought Charlotte with me." Jon rubbed his fingers across his chin and plopped back into the chair. "She's the daughter of a General Winston in Montreal, and is engaged to marry Captain Levid."

"The one who—"

"Aye. One and the same."

"Then what's she doing with you?" Jacob seemed genuinely perplexed, and Jon wished he could explain it to him, but the truth was, he didn't even understand it himself. He just knew he didn't like the idea of Charlotte going back to Levid. And that knowledge annoyed him more than Jacob's expression of bewilderment.

Jon shrugged, slapping his palms against muscular thighs. "I brought her along."

"Ah." Jacob's hazel eyes lit up.

"It's not like that." Or at least it wasn't. Jon would be hard-pressed to tell just exactly what it was right now. "She didn't come willingly."

"You abducted her?"

Jon winced at the sound of that, but he guessed it pretty accurately summed up the situation and told him so.

"What are you going to do with her?"

"Hell, I don't know . . ." Jon began, then immediately contradicted himself. "She doesn't know it yet, and I've my doubts if she'll like the idea, but I guess I'm taking her home with me."

"Are you sure that's a good idea?"

"Well, I told you . . . showed you what her betrothed is capable of. He—"

"But there's a war. He may be—"

"It's not just the war with him, Jacob. I saw the way he treats people. Charlotte wouldn't fare any better."

"Are you planning to wed the girl?"

"No." Jon shot out of his seat and paced to the window. "Who said anything about a wedding. I'm not going to marry her, just—"

"Take her home with you?" Jacob couldn't quite suppress the grin that split his freckled face.

"Aye," Jon agreed, not seeing the humor in the situation.

Charlotte liked Colonel Anderson. He'd come out of the other room and taken her hand, smiling down at her with sparkling eyes that held a hint of sadness. When the captain introduced them, Charlotte realized Jon and he were acquaintances from before, and that didn't bode well for her plan. But since then, Colonel Anderson had been so nice, and she had renewed hope.

Colonel Anderson insisted Jon and she share his accommodations while in Plattsburg, and because the captain said nothing, Charlotte assumed it was decided. She didn't, however, wish to share a room with the captain and had opened her mouth to say so when she remembered his admonition to let him do the talking. Besides, she realized, the captain had given her name as Charlotte Winston. Apparently the farce of their marriage was over.

"Is the fowl to your liking, Miss Winston?"

Charlotte glanced up when Major Anderson spoke. He sat across the table—the table that took up much of the main room of his quarters. To his right was Captain Knox. The captain didn't seem much concerned if Charlotte enjoyed her meal or not. He was studiously ignoring her, as he'd done since they'd followed Colonel Anderson to his cabin.

"It's excellent, thank you," Charlotte responded, returning his smile. He seemed genuinely concerned about her welfare, despite the fact that he was an American. This bolstered her resolve even more.

The captain's attitude made it easier, too. She couldn't fathom why he'd sulked and scowled since meeting with Colonel Anderson. She couldn't understand his attitude, since the colonel was doing everything he could to make them comfortable. Well, it was fine with her. This way, leaving him would not cause her any regret. Charlotte took a deep breath. Well, almost none.

For Charlotte was determined to stay in Plattsburg when the captain started south tomorrow morning. All she needed was a moment alone with Colonel

Anderson to explain her dilemma. If he agreed to let her stay, she was confident Captain Knox would agree. He'd probably be glad to be rid of her. Again Charlotte took a deep breath. Why should she care? Just why should she care?

Later that evening Charlotte heard the front door close. She ran to the window of the bedroom and peeked through. Moments later she saw the captain, limned in moonlight, striding away. He had on a borrowed coat, his hands jammed into the pockets, and he was alone.

Before she changed her mind, Charlotte rushed toward the bedroom door and threw it open, startling Colonel Anderson. Charlotte could tell she'd done that by the way he quickly straightened from unrolling a pallet on the floor.

He and the captain had insisted they'd sleep in front of the fire so she could have the bedroom. Actually, Colonel Anderson had insisted. Jonathan Knox had just looked at her with those cerulean eyes of his and said nothing. But she knew what he was thinking, because she'd been thinking the same thing. My goodness, how had she ever let passion for him take over her thoughts . . . practically her life?

"I thought you'd be asleep, Miss Winston."

Colonel Anderson's words brought Charlotte's mind back to the present. She smiled shyly, glancing down at the clothes she still wore. "I'm not tired." This sounded lame indeed, as fatigue was the excuse she'd used earlier to retire. The colonel didn't seem to notice the contradiction. He just stood there, holding a pillow and staring at her. He finally broke the silence that seemed to have a stranglehold on Charlotte.

"Jon just stepped out."

Charlotte swallowed. "Yes, I know." She hesitated. "I wished to speak to you . . . alone." Ignoring the questioning furrow between his brows, Charlotte rushed ahead. "I don't know what the captain told you, but I'm not traveling with him . . . well, exactly willingly." The furrow deepened and Charlotte realized nothing in her actions had implied anything of the sort. "I . . . I'm not exactly unwilling, but . . . What I'm trying to say is that I want to go back to Canada."

"And you'd like my help?"

"Well, yes." It had sounded so simple when she'd rehearsed what she wanted to say, but now . . . "I just need a place to stay until I can arrange a way to return."

"You are aware there's a war." Jacob dropped the pillow and cocked his head.

"Of course I know that." Charlotte looked up from her contemplation of the chairback she'd grabbed. She wasn't certain from his words what he planned to do, and now his silence was unnerving. "How do you think I got here in the first place?" Charlotte felt tears threatening and tried to blink them back. Her voice faltered, but she had to continue, had to make him understand. If she could only explain. Charlotte took a deep breath and started. Like a floodgate released, the words spewed out.

"While I was held captive, Captain Knox found out about my betrothal to Captain Levid, and he was so angry. He tried to make me reveal Captain Levid's location, but I wouldn't. And then in the battle he lost his ship and I think he tried to kill Captain Levid, though I don't know why. But then they flogged him and I couldn't do anything. I paid for more food, but he probably didn't get it. And he was wounded . . ."

Charlotte paused for a breath and her eyes

implored. "There was blood everywhere and I thought he would die. But then they tried to kill him. They were going to shoot him when he escaped. I tried to warn him, but it was too late. And then he grabbed me and brought me here. And I want to go home."

She stopped on a pitiful note, her bloodless fingers digging into the wooden chairback. Jacob wasn't really certain what she'd said, but he did know that this woman and Jon had been through a lot together—and he wasn't entirely sure they didn't wish to go through a lot more. Jacob cleared his throat, and she looked up, her bottom lip clamped between two rows of white teeth. "You say you want to go home?"

She nodded, sending spirals of hair curling around her face.

"Is it Captain Levid you wish to return to?"

Charlotte looked at the tall redheaded man as if he'd spoken blasphemy. She knew her explanation had been inadequate, but had he not understood a word she'd said? "No," she assured him. "I don't ever want to see Captain Levid again. It's England . . . home." Charlotte shook her head. "Don't you see, I can't stay here with Jon." Tears filled her eyes. "He . . . I . . ." Tears spilled over her lashes and through the blur, Charlotte saw Colonel Anderson move toward her. "It's just too complicated," she mumbled before his arm wrapped around her.

"I know. Don't cry. It will be all right."

Charlotte tried to be strong and pull away, but it had been so long since someone tried to comfort her. Her mother had been the one who needed consoling, and Charlotte had been glad to do it. When she'd hoped for support from her father, he'd given none. And the captain . . . There were times when she

253

glimpsed his gentleness, when it soothed over her like a balm. But most often he kept her senses in an upheaval. Unlike Colonel Anderson, Jonathan Knox's touch excited rather than calmed.

Leaning into the arm curved around her, what was left of Charlotte's composure evaporated. She heaved a sigh, then let the tears fall unimpeded, dampening the front of his uniform jacket. "I just don't know what to do."

"Have you talked with Jon about this?"

The sobs were coming in earnest now, and Charlotte hiccuped, sucking in a gulp of air. "Oh, he won't listen. He's—"

"What the hell is going on here?"

Charlotte tried to jerk away—she'd recognize that deep, resonant voice anywhere, especially spiced with anger—but Colonel Anderson wouldn't let her. His arm tightened possessively. With his free hand he retrieved a handkerchief from his pocket and dabbed at Charlotte's face before answering Captain Knox's bellowed question. "Your friend and I were having a discussion."

"It looks like a damn sight more than a discussion to me." Jon couldn't imagine why he was so angry, but it took all his composure to keep from pulling Jacob's arm off Charlotte.

"Well, you obviously aren't seeing things straight in this instance."

Colonel Anderson's words weren't having a soothing effect on Charlotte, and as she peeked out over the linen handkerchief, she noticed they weren't diffusing the captain's anger, either. If anything, as he stood with balled-up hands planted firmly on his lean hips, he looked more enraged. But he managed to keep his voice level, as he jerked his head toward the door he'd just entered. "I'd like to speak with you,

Jacob . . . outside." His last word was little more than a barked command, and Charlotte imagined he'd perfected the tone during his years at sea.

But he wasn't at sea now . . . he wasn't even in command. Colonel Anderson was. Yet when the captain slammed out the door, nearly yanking it from its leather hinges, Jacob Anderson let his arm drop from Charlotte's shoulders and moved toward the door.

Charlotte gripped his arm, trying to slow his pace. Though strong, Colonel Anderson wasn't nearly as large as the captain, and he appeared a good twenty years older. She'd seen the captain fight. Colonel Anderson didn't stand a chance. "Let me talk to him. He's—"

To her amazement, Jacob smiled when he turned back to her. Touching her cheek, he shook his head. "It's me he wants to see."

"But he'll hurt you, and it's all my fault." Charlotte's fingers gripped tighter, then fell away completely when Colonel Anderson laughed.

"I've known Jon since he wore leading strings. Nothing's going to happen."

Charlotte just wished she had the same confidence as she watched Colonel Anderson follow the captain outside. For herself, she couldn't decide whether to listen to the older man and stay put, or join the two men outside. Telling herself her choice had nothing to do with cowardice, she dropped into one of the chairs beside the fireplace.

Jacob caught sight of his friend standing some twenty rods from the cabin, his hands spread down his hips, his head thrown back studying the night sky.

"What was that about inside?" Jacob asked as he came up on him.

Jon's head snapped around, and he sighed, his shoulders drooping. "Hell, I don't know." Jon motioned toward the cabin. "Is she all right?"

"About now she's worried you're going to tear me limb from limb."

Jon laughed. "Maybe I should go inside and ease her mind."

"Just a minute." Jacob touched Jon's arm. "Miss Winston's upset. And I don't just mean about the little scene inside." His voice gentled. "You want to tell me what's going on here?"

Jon blew out a breath that frosted in the night air. "I told you."

"She wants to go back to Canada, eventually England."

"And that bastard she's betrothed to," Jon spit out.

Jacob rubbed his hands together to warm them. "She has a father back there, too."

Again Jon studied the heavens, the orderly array of stars. "He's not much better. And to tell you the truth, I don't think he cares about her."

"But you do."

"No." Jon's head whipped around. "I mean, I don't dislike her . . . At first I thought I did, but . . . Well, for chrissakes, she saved my life—of course I care what happens to her."

Jon ignored the amused chuckle Jacob sent his way and went on rambling to himself, as if sorting out his feelings. "She needs someone to look after her now, and you know how good my mother is at doing that. Aye, Mother is just what she needs, and it will take my mother's mind off what happened to Christopher once I tell her."

"By having his killer's betrothed under her roof," Jacob pointed out logically.

Jon swore into the night air. "Charlotte didn't have anything to do with it." He ignored his earlier

256

recriminations of her. "And Mother isn't vengeful."

"But you are."

"What in the hell is that supposed to mean?"

Jacob let out a puff of air. "You told me yourself, you want revenge on Levid for what he did to Christopher."

"And you wouldn't?" Jon's tone was incredulous. "That's not the point."

"Then kindly tell me what is." Jon was tiring of this discussion.

"I think you need to examine your motives for keeping Miss Winston with you."

Jon shook his head. "Didn't I just tell you—"

"*All* your motives, Jon. She's not Levid, and I'd be willing to wager she had nothing to do with what happened to Christopher . . . or you." Jacob stepped closer. "She's a woman with feelings, Jon. Not a doll for you to take here or there because you feel like it."

Jon rubbed his jaw, his hand scraping down over his bristly chin. "I know what I'm doing, Jacob. She's going with me to Oak Hill."

Watching Jacob walk away, Jon clasped his hands behind his back and rocked backward on his heel. Jacob said he'd be gone for a while, back to his headquarter's office. This was the perfect opportunity to tell Charlotte of his decision. Jon started toward the cabin, then stopped. He wished he could be certain Jacob hadn't hit on a bit of truth.


Charlotte bolted to her feet, her eyes enormous in her pale face, when Jon opened the door. He stomped his feet and sloughed off the coat, staring at her all the while.

Charlotte laced her hands. "Where's Colonel Anderson?"

Jon shrugged. "He had some work to do."

"You didn't . . . ?"

"Fight?" Jon supplied, giving her a crooked grin when she nodded. "No. And I apologize for . . . for . . ." What was he supposed to call it. When she nodded again, he decided he didn't have to call it anything. Jon sat, motioning her to do the same. "Why don't you tell me what you told Jacob."

She should have known Colonel Anderson would go straight to the captain and that he'd react this way. He'd . . . Charlotte paused. The captain wasn't acting like she expected. Not at all. He sat, calmly waiting for her response. Maybe they *could* discuss this. After all, it would be better for both of them if she returned to Canada. Wouldn't it?

Looking him in the eye, Charlotte said, "I'd like to remain here until I can return to Canada, then get passage home to England."

"To Levid?" Now why did he have to ask that? Jon pretended not to notice the widening of her dark eyes.

Why did he care? "I assume Captain Levid is gone by now," Charlotte hedged.

Jon's lips thinned in a facsimile of a smile. "You mean the way he supposedly left earlier, after dropping you off in Montreal?" Pleased to see she had the good grace to blush, Jon folded his arms across his chest.

"I told you that so you wouldn't go after him."

"That hellbent on saving him, were you?" Jon's teeth hurt from clenching them.

"Not him . . . you." At the captain's arched brow, Charlotte continued. "I knew you'd never get out of Montreal if you tried to find him. Killing him isn't worth it."

Jon stood. "It is to me." He noticed her blanch at his words and went on. "That's not what I want to speak with you about." Hunkering down in front of her, Jon lifted her hands from her lap. They were cold. "Listen, it's not safe for you to stay here. I want you to come home to Maryland with me."

Charlotte's gaze met his and she studied him so intently she wasn't surprised when he broke the stare and looked down.

"You can stay with my family," he continued. "That is, until it's safe for you to go back to England."

"Why?"

Jon dropped her hands and stood. "What do you mean, 'why?'"

"I think it's a pretty straightforward question . . . Why are you doing this?" Charlotte rose and started pacing the floor. "You abduct me . . . twice. Risk my life along with your own dragging me all over the countryside. And now you want to protect me, keep me safe and sound at your home. And I . . . I want to know why."

"Hell." Jon raked his fingers through his hair. "Maybe I feel bad for all that's happened to you." She turned, giving him a look of pure disbelief. "I didn't have a lot of choices, you know. When I was trying to escape from Montreal you were just there."

"I'd come to warn you. To tell you they planned for you to escape so they could kill you."

Jon shook his head. "All the more reason for you to come with me to Maryland."

"I don't want to go."

Damn stubborn woman. "Well, you're going." Jon turned to stare out the window at the blackened sky.

Damn stubborn man. Charlotte's chin notched higher. "I won't make love with you again."

Jon twisted around and his jaw dropped open. That was the last thing he'd expected her to say. But

259

she certainly seemed adamant about it.

"I mean it, Captain. I'll kick and fight and scream if you try to touch me again."

Jon considered pointing out that had hardly been her reaction the other times, but decided he wasn't that much of a bastard. Besides, how could he fault her when he seemed to have no control over his actions with her, either. Instead, he nodded. "All right. If that's the way you want it—"

"It is," Charlotte insisted.

"As I was saying," Jon continued, "that's the way it will be."

"Good."

"Fine."

"All right then. I'll go with you."

"Fine." Hadn't he just said that? "Get some rest. We'll leave first thing in the morning."

Charlotte nodded, and turned toward the bedroom door. She flopped down on the cornhusk mattress wondering if she'd be able to keep from wanting him, touching him.

In the other room, Jon slammed his hands against the stone fireplace. Why did he ever agree to such a thing? No way in hell he was going to be able to keep his hands off her.

# Chapter Fifteen

Captain Jonathan Knox was true to his word.

He not only didn't initiate any lovemaking, he barely spoke or looked at her. They rode now, as they had since leaving the ferry across the Chester River, along a rutted, deserted country road. The captain seemed oblivious to her. It was quiet except for the melody of birds singing overhead and the steady plodding beat of horses' hoofs. Charlotte sighed, deciding this was preferable to the hustle and bustle of the rest of their journey south.

The trip from Plattsburg to Albany had seemed to take forever. They'd rowed down Lake Champlain in the company of several soldiers, then ridden on horseback to Albany. There they'd departed company with the militiamen, and boarded a steamboat to New York. Charlotte had the misfortune to be seasick without actually being at sea. She spent most of the time in the cabin the captain had arranged for her to share with two elderly women traveling together. Jon remained on deck, mostly conversing with the vessel's captain.

After two days of this torture—to Charlotte's way of thinking—they arrived in New York. The captain took the time to deliver a letter from Colonel Anderson to his wife, a plump, apple-cheeked woman that Charlotte liked immediately. But he declined Mrs. Anderson's invitation to stay with her for a few days.

Instead, Captain Knox secured them seats on a stagecoach heading down the Lancaster Pike. For days Charlotte bounced around in the stuffy, dust-laden coach. Her rump became intimately acquainted with the surface of the firmly padded seats as she tried to remember what she had against travel by water. With each engraved Franklin stone they passed marking off the mileposts, Charlotte's limbs grew stiffer.

She rarely saw the captain. Though he was courteous and always treated her with respect, he kept his distance, erecting an invisible wall between them that left Charlotte feeling morose. He rode outside, with the stagecoach driver, during the days, saw her safely to her room at an inn each night, then fetched her in the morning. All without uttering more than ten words, and certainly nothing that wasn't necessary.

The trip gave Charlotte time to think and, to her frustration, to daydream. It wasn't till her mind had wandered far from the discomfort of the bone-bouncing ride and the sound of whirling wheels that Charlotte realized how long it had been since she'd escaped into her fantasies.

Lately the captain's presence had made imagination unnecessary, but with his emotional withdrawal from her, Charlotte found her fertile mind filling the void with fanciful thoughts. And they no longer centered around a mythical pirate or peaceful garden.

Jonathan Knox so consumed her thoughts that Charlotte had trouble knowing where fantasy faded into memory. She could close her eyes and be back in his arms again, his mouth molded to hers, their bodies straining toward release.

It was a beautiful daydream and one that softened the lonely hours. But Charlotte knew she had to force herself to stop when the coach rolled to a halt in front of the Eagle Hotel near Philadelphia and the captain opened the door to hand her out. She'd been thinking of him—graphically—when he appeared before her in flesh and blood.

His raven hair tossed by the wind around his sun-bronzed face looked better than any dream. His body loomed bigger, broader, taller than her memory recalled. And his eyes, those stormy blue eyes that seemed to reach down and read her soul, stared at her with such unleashed desire that she knew he answered the longing he saw in her.

The two of them remained motionless, his powerful hand enveloping hers, their eyes locked, until the overweight gentleman who'd crowded Charlotte on the seat harumphed and said something about wishing to leave the confines of the coach.

The other passenger jostled Charlotte's arm and she swayed toward the captain, her trance broken when his other hand reached up to steady her.

The captain seemed to regain his perspective at the same moment Charlotte did, for he quickly dropped her hand, reached into the coach, and dragged her out, setting her down with such force, Charlotte's teeth clamped together.

After that, he didn't touch her, not even to guide her into the inn. He saw her to her room, ordered dinner sent there, and left her without a word.

But long after the door slammed behind him, Charlotte sat on the Windsor chair, staring at the hand lying limply in her lap. It still tingled from his warmth. But she couldn't help wondering how much

263

of what happened was real and how much her imagination.

That night she slept poorly, dreaming of the captain and wanting him with a near painful ache.

But she'd told him there would be no more intimacy, and she couldn't fault him for his adherence to her request. Damn the man anyway!

When the journey became a ride on horseback between the rural burgs of Maryland, his withdrawal continued. He rode his big bay he'd bought in Philadelphia with money loaned him by Jacob Anderson ahead of her, glancing over his shoulder only occasionally to see if she kept up.

But now Charlotte sensed he wanted to distance himself not just from her, but from everything. The captain still functioned competently, leading them along the narrow dirt road, but he seemed to do it by rote.

What could cause this change? Before, he had seemed so anxious to get home. Now, as he slowed his horse to a walk, he acted almost afraid to face what lay ahead. But that was ridiculous. The captain never shied away from anything.

Yet, there could be no mistaking his reluctance as he drew the bay to a halt at the entrance to an oak-lined lane. He sat there so long, the birds chattering in the brush, the late-afternoon sun filtering lazily through the brown-edged leaves that Charlotte nudged her mare forward.

"Captain?"

It was proof of the depth of his inner thoughts that he initially didn't seem to hear her. Charlotte took a deep breath, repeating his name, and this time he looked up, the sorrow in his eyes so poignant, she wanted to reach out and touch him, make whatever caused this suffering to disappear. But she didn't, and then the moment passed. The captain almost visibly shook off his depression.

"This is the lane to Oak Hill," he explained before prodding his horse into motion. Now it seemed he couldn't reach his destination quickly enough. Charlotte struggled to keep up, still wondering what had caused that moment of reluctance, and why he'd been so sad.

*He* was coming home, for heaven's sakes. And though he'd made it clear his visit was only temporary, it must be such a relief after all he'd endured.

Charlotte stifled a pang of homesickness. Her life, too, had been riddled with disappointment and frustration for so long. But nothing was gained by dwelling on her problems. Besides, at that moment they rounded a bend in the lane, and Oak Hill's manor house came into view.

It surprised Charlotte, though she couldn't say what she'd expected. Certainly nothing so large . . . or welcoming. The whitewashed two-story house had a deep, gabled roof, black against the cloud-puffed blue sky. Smaller additions, symmetrical in size and shape, bowed in on either side of the main house, bending toward the crushed shell drive. The outbuildings, from what she could see, were well kept, but Charlotte had little time to examine the grounds before the front door opened and a woman strolled out onto the porch.

She was tall, her thick, dark hair shot through with silver, and it only took her a moment to notice the horses galloping toward the house. Charlotte saw the captain's chest heave before he threw himself from the bay and started toward the woman. At the same time, she squealed his name. Her hand to her mouth she flew off the porch to be caught in his steely embrace.

"Jon! Oh, Jon, is it really you?" The woman

framed his face with her hands and laughed, tears shining in her gray eyes as the captain twirled her around. Gone was the mask of gloom he'd worn. Now his grin deepened the creases at the corners of his eyes.

"It's me all right," he assured, scooping the woman up again in a bear hug that had her batting playfully at his arms.

"I knew you'd be all right. I just knew it. Adam said—" The woman didn't have time to finish her explanation before the door flew open again and two other women bounded through. They were followed by two young girls, and they all propelled themselves down the porch steps, hurling themselves at the captain. And they all received the same kind of welcome he gave the older woman.

During all this, Charlotte remained seated on the mare, not knowing what to do. She was happy for the captain, surrounded by the love of his family, but she'd never felt more an intruder or more lonely. If she'd had any idea where she was or how to get home, she'd have turned the horse around and galloped away. But she didn't. So she sat, ignored, watching the scene of family love develop before her.

Arms clasped with his, the three women, chattering so in unison Charlotte couldn't understand them, started pulling the captain toward the house.

"Wait a minute," he laughed. The captain turned to Charlotte, a smile of apology on his lips that nearly melted her heart. "I've brought a guest."

Disentangling his arms, Jon stepped around the horse and reached up for Charlotte. "Don't let them overwhelm you," he whispered near her ear before drawing her forward.

Easy for him to say, Charlotte thought. He was a head taller than these women; Charlotte felt insignificant by comparison. But the captain squeezed her waist before letting her go, and Charlotte couldn't help but feel better.

"This is Charlotte Winston," the captain said to the older woman whom he introduced as his mother, Elizabeth Knox. The two others he named as his sisters Libby and Cilla.

"It's Priscilla," the younger of the two sisters corrected. "How many times must I remind you of that?"

"Till I get it right, I suppose," the captain chuckled at the dark-haired woman, who, Charlotte noticed, walked with a limp.

"Stop it, you two," Elizabeth Knox chided lovingly as her younger daughter opened her mouth to keep the banter going.

"Sorry, Mother," Jon said, his eyes still twinkling with mischief. "And these two," Jon reached down to tug gently on the little girls' raven curls, "are Libby's twins, Sarah and Rebecca."

The girls, whom Charlotte imagined were about eight years old, curtsied and she smiled, wondering how she'd ever tell them apart. They looked, not only like each other, but like their mother, aunt, and grandmother. All of Captain Knox's family shared the same dark-haired good looks.

"I apologize for ignoring you earlier." Elizabeth Knox smiled at Charlotte as she took her hand and led her into the house. "We were all just so surprised and happy." She reached back and clasped his hand. "To see Jon, I mean. I'm afraid we weren't looking anyplace else."

"I understand." Though Charlotte had never experienced a homecoming like this, she could easily imagine the other woman's feelings. Jon's mother squeezed Charlotte's arm much the same way her son had squeezed her side, and Charlotte again felt better.

The front hall they entered was wide and airy, with a door at the far end opening out onto a garden. The open stairway to one side spiraled to the upstairs, and it was there Elizabeth led her. "You must be tired, child. How far has this son of mine brought you?"

"I'm not certain how far," Charlotte hedged, not knowing exactly how to answer the question. How *was* the captain going to explain her presence?

"From Montreal," Jon provided, simply shrugging when his mother turned, an inquiring lift to her straight brow. "Where's Father?"

"Oh, my goodness, Alex." The captain's mother dropped Charlotte's hand. "I'd forgotten in all the excitement. He'll be so glad you're home. Sarah and Becca." She turned toward the little girls who hadn't let go of Jon's hands. "Run down to the stable and fetch your grandfather. And mind, don't tell him who's here." Her gray eyes caught her son's. "I want to see his surprise."

Charlotte had the strange feeling they'd forgotten her again, but she could hardly fault Jon's family. They seemed so genuinely pleased—and relieved—to see him. She heard them mention the name Adam, and wondered if they spoke of the captain's doctor friend from the *Eagle*.

Apparently the captain noticed it, too, because he touched his mother's arm. "You said something about Adam."

"Oh, yes, he—"

But before Elizabeth could explain, the front door banged open and a tall, gray-haired man burst through. "The twins said I better get up to the house quick. What's wrong?" Alexander Knox demanded of his wife. Then his focus broadened, and a smile replaced his expression of concern. "Well, I'll be damned."

"No doubt if you don't watch your language," Elizabeth countered, but she wore a broad smile as Alex clasped his son in a huge hug.

"Where have you been, Son? You had your mother worried."

"Oh, I was not. I knew he'd come back to us."

Alex reached out to throw an arm around his wife and pull her into the hug, chuckling deep in his chest. "I guess she did say that. Well, come on in the parlor and tell us what's happened. When Adam stopped over, he didn't hold much hope for you."

"Alex." His wife's voice stopped her husband, whom Charlotte thought looked like an older version of the captain. "We have a guest." Elizabeth nodded toward Charlotte, and for the first time the captain's father looked her way. Charlotte was beginning to wonder if she were invisible in the dark-blue riding habit the captain had bought her in Philadelphia.

"Father, this is Charlotte Winston."

Again there was no explanation, and Charlotte wondered what his family must think of her. But no one said or did anything to indicate they disapproved of her being there. The captain's father smiled at her, and there was no doubt where Jonathan Knox got his good looks. Even with his thick hair mostly white, the older man exuded a potent appeal much like his son.

Charlotte glanced at the captain, wishing he would say something to explain her presence, but now he seemed distant. His blue eyes, so like his father's, held that expression of deep sorrow she'd noticed earlier, and again Charlotte had the strongest urge to cushion his head to her breast and make everything all right.

But she had no chance to even discover what caused his pain. In a tone that left no room for argument, he turned to his sisters and suggested they accompany Charlotte upstairs and show her to her room. Charlotte noticed his mother and father exchange a look, but neither said anything as she followed the younger women and two little girls up the curved staircase.

As soon as Charlotte disappeared around the landing, Jon turned to his parents. "I know you have questions." He jerked his chin toward the staircase.

"What's wrong, Jon? Are you all right?"

Wrapping his arm around his mother's shoulders, Jon walked toward the library. The moment he'd been dreading was here. He'd dwelled on this for weeks, trying to think of the best way to tell his parents about Chris. But there were no words that could ease the pain of the truth . . . their son, his brother, was dead.

Jon closed the paneled door behind him. He noticed his father pouring three glasses of Madeira and realized they knew something was terribly wrong when his mother accepted hers rather than wave it away. She never drank more than one glass with dinner.

"What is it, Son?" It was his father who spoke, spoke in the same deep voice Jon remembered from his childhood. From the days they'd all been so happy. The days Christopher had followed him around like a puppy dog.

Jon swallowed, setting his own goblet aside. "I found the ship that impressed Chris . . ." he began, his heart sinking when he noticed his mother's gaze flit to the door as if she expected her younger son to come bounding in.

"Adam told us as much. But he said you were captured . . . or dead."

Jon's gaze jerked up to meet his father's. "I came

damn close . . . too close." Dropping into a chair, Jon rested his forearms on his knees.

"What is it, Jon? What's wrong?"

His mother's softly spoken question coupled with her hand resting lightly on his bent head brought the sting of tears to his eyes. Reaching up and covering her hand with his, he lowered it to his lips—and found he couldn't say the words that needed to be said.

It might be different if he knew for certain they were true. But he didn't. Levid's leering face swam before his eyes as he taunted Jon with the news of his brother, but the truth was, something didn't sound right to Jon. It had been eating at him for a fortnight, and suddenly it hit him.

Would the captain of a ship know immediately the names of all the common sailors he impressed, *and* be able to tell something about them at a moment's notice? Would Levid? He hadn't hesitated to tell Jon his brother was dead. Yet . . . Yet Levid had wanted to hurt Jon, hurt him more than physically. What better way than with news of his brother's death?

Jon squeezed his eyes shut. His theory made sense in a sadistic sort of way, but was he simply making excuses because he couldn't face the truth? He didn't know. He honestly didn't know. But there was enough doubt in his mind to keep him from breaking his parents' hearts.

Jon took a steadying breath. "I didn't find Chris." Not a lie—not entirely the truth, but not a lie, either.

Jon heard their combined sighs and realized by his failure to answer immediately that his parents had feared the worst. Was he helping by not confirming their fears?

"Jon, we never expected you to. I told you from the beginning that searching wasn't going to help. Chris

271

will find his way back home." Alex took a healthy swig of wine.

"But I was on the *Scorpion*. I was on the damn schooner myself, and—"

"Stop torturing yourself like this." Elizabeth's words were firm, but her hand on his head was gentle. "We've told you before, none of this is your fault."

"Your mother's right, Jon. Chris went to sea because he wanted to—"

"Because of me." Jon's head shot up as he interrupted his father. "He went to sea because of me. He was on my damn ship when he was impressed. It is my fault."

"No. It was in his blood, just like it's in yours. He'd have joined the Navy with or without you."

Jon said nothing. He wished he could accept what his father told him, but another haunting memory filled his mind. Christopher. He was twelve years old, all arms and legs, and he was hurrying to keep up with Jon's longer strides. "I want to be just like you, Jon. Just like you." The words rang in his ears as clearly now as they had those many years ago.

Standing, Jon looked around the book-lined room, the room that held so many perfect memories. "I'm going to find Levid again. And this time, I will find Chris." *Or at least proof of what happened to him.* With those words he left the library.

"Jon, no."

"Let him go, Elizabeth." Alex came up behind her, touching her hand when she would have opened the latch.

"But he's hurting," Elizabeth pleaded. "He needs us."

"And he knows where we are. Right now, I think he just wants to be alone."

The linen of her husband's shirt felt warm and comforting as he drew her closer.

Charlotte closed her eyes and breathed in the tangy scent of the twilight-shrouded autumn garden. Her head fell back against the wooden-slatted bench and she allowed her mind to wonder to her mother's garden in Oxfordshire. It wasn't nearly as large as this one at Oak Hill, but it had always been such a peaceful place. Is that why she'd sought out this spot as soon as the captain's sister left her to dress for dinner? Did she seek peace for her troubled soul?

Shaking her head, Charlotte reached out to touch a delicate blossom. The rose, one of the last that clung to the garden before frost shriveled its petals, felt whisper-soft. As soft as the touch on her shoulder.

Charlotte twisted around on the bench, her breath catching when she saw Jon standing beside her. Dressed in gray breeches, his broad shoulders filling his dark-blue coat, and the cravat snowy white contrasting his sun-bronzed skin, he looked impossibly tall and masculine. So out of place in the dainty garden.

"I didn't mean to startle you. I thought you heard me call you."

Had she been so lost in her imaginary world she'd failed to hear him? Charlotte shook her head again. "It's all right. Please sit down." She brushed aside the skirts of a pale-blue gown lent to her by Cilla. Was she always to wear borrowed clothes? she wondered.

"I really just came out to tell you we'll be eating soon," Jon said, at the same time accepting her invitation to sit. It wasn't a good idea. He knew that as soon as his thigh brushed against her skirts. These weeks of holding himself apart from her while they traveled hadn't done a bit of good—not one damn bit. He still wanted her more than he'd ever wanted another woman.

Jon shifted away. "I'm leaving tomorrow morning. I'll stop at Adam's plantation and then go to Washington."

Charlotte swallowed. "Oh." She'd insisted upon him keeping his distance. Charlotte remembered that very well. And he had. Then why did she feel this overwhelming desire to melt into his arms? But he didn't want to hold her. She'd noticed his movement, slight as it was, away from her.

"Aye." Jon cleared his throat. "I shall seek a new command, a new ship."

"And then you'll go back to the war?"

Jon tried to stare straight ahead, to watch the twinkling candlelight shining through the tiny windowpanes in the back of the house. But he turned, his eyes inescapably drawn to her. "Yes, I'll return to war."

"And you'll continue searching for Captain Levid?" Charlotte knew she shouldn't question him. She was better off not knowing, but she couldn't seem to stop herself from asking any more than the hapless moth could help fluttering toward the flame.

"Until I find him."

"But this time he might finish what he started before." Charlotte's voice dropped to a whisper. "He might kill you."

"Or I him."

His eyes, in the fast-fading light of evening, shone with an intensity Charlotte couldn't comprehend. She wet her suddenly dry lips. "Is it worth it, this hate you harbor? Is taking his life worth the chance of losing your own?"

Jon thought of the boy who'd shadowed him, the

274

evil in Levid's eyes when he bragged about snuffing out the life of that boy, and he could answer only one way. "Aye, it's worth it. That and more."

"I don't understand you."

Jon had no answer for that, so he gave none. Besides, her loyalties were elsewhere. Even if she were shocked by the cruelties of her betrothed, she'd blame them on the times. And Jon didn't think he could bear to hear her defend Levid. Better to not tell her of his brother.

He leaned back, his shoulder grazing Charlotte's. "I've always liked it out here."

"In the garden?" Charlotte shifted toward him.

"Yes, in the garden. You sound surprised."

"Well I . . . I'm not. Not really. It's just . . . well, you seem a little out of place here."

"Oh, and where do you think I belong?"

Why had she said something so stupid? Just because she'd been thinking him too blatantly male for the garden didn't mean he didn't belong here, for heaven's sake. But he looked at her now with a puzzled expression on his face so she had to say something. "I see you on the bow of a ship or maybe hacking your way through the forest."

If she accomplished nothing else with her silly reply, she had made him laugh. Charlotte smiled as she watched him. It had been so long since she'd seen him happy. Again she wondered why he'd seemed so sad earlier. He turned to her then, his arm resting along the back of the bench.

"Well," he said. "You appear right at home here."

"Not on a ship or in the woods," she teased, sighing when he arched his brow. "I suppose you're right. My mother had a garden, very much like this one. I spent a lot of time there."

"I'll see that you get home, Charlotte." His fingers

brushed a strand of golden-brown hair behind her ear.

Charlotte forced herself not to lean into his hand. He spoke of home, and that should be her only thought, but when he touched her she could only grieve that home was so far away from him.

"We better go in."

His words spoken so briskly made Charlotte wonder if he'd read the desire strumming through her. He must think her strange. First demanding he stay away from her, then practically begging him with her eyes to ignore her request.

"Wait." Charlotte's hand grabbed hold of his sleeve. The feel of his muscular arm beneath the wool made her pull away. But she could not shy away from the question burning in her mind. If she thought their relationship strange, what must his family think? "I'd like to know what you've told them . . . about me."

Jon settled back into the seat. "Not much."

"Not much?" Charlotte threw up her hands. "Didn't they think it odd that you'd brought home a woman?"

"Actually I told them you are an acquaintance of Jacob Anderson and that I brought you here for safe-keeping until you could return home to England."

"And that didn't concern them?"

"What, the fact that we traveled alone together?" A mischievous light shone in Jon's eyes, and he chuckled softly when he noticed her blush.

"No," Charlotte breathed. "The fact that I'm English."

"Oh, that," he said in a way that made Charlotte know he'd realized her concern all along. "They're very enlightened."

"Perhaps they don't share your hatred of the

enemy." Charlotte couldn't help the teasing tone that crept into her voice.

"Perhaps they don't know all that I do," he said, making Charlotte wonder if he spoke of his experience on the *Scorpion*, and if he had mentioned it to his parents. "But then . . ." Jon's tone lightened. "I never professed to hating *all* British citizens." His finger traced, feather-soft, across her cheek.

"Do they know about . . . about what happened between us." A flush heated Charlotte's face as she looked down at her hands.

"No, they don't . . ." Jon paused. "Nor do they know who your father is . . . or your betrothed. I'm afraid their enlightenment may not go that far."

"I see." Charlotte took a deep breath. "You seem to have this all arranged. I say nothing, and I remain an honored guest in your home."

"You needn't sound so put off by it." Jon stood, clasping his hands behind his back. "This *is* what we decided."

"Actually, *we* never decided anything." Rising, Charlotte turned about to face him. *"You* decided what I would do and where I would go."

Jon stared at a spot over her head. "This was the best I could think of to do with you."

*"Do* with me!" His eyes flashed down at her tone and she returned his stare, her own eyes bright with anger. "I'm not some . . . some possession that you *do something with.*"

"I didn't mean—"

"You most assuredly did!" Charlotte saw the captain's eyes widen and she didn't know whether it was she or Jon who was more surprised by her outburst. Turning away, she lowered her voice. "You've been domineering and arrogant from the first, forcing me to do things—"

277

Grabbing her arm, Jon whirled her around to face him. "Just what things are you referring to?"

Charlotte tried to yank her arm away, but his fingers only tightened. "Treason. You tried to get me to tell you where Captain Levid was."

"Which you never did," Jon pointed out.

"You . . . you abducted me. Forced me to come with you across half the country." There, let him try to deny that. But he didn't. He simply lowered his head till they were nose-to-nose.

"Well, you've had your share of calling the shots, too, lady."

"I have not." Indignation surged through her. Hadn't he told her that he was the captain and she the captive? How dare he say she'd had any control over what happened to her.

"What about your decision before we left Platts-burg?" Charlotte felt her face burn red, but he refused to let her go. "You said no more making love, and I . . . I stuck to it."

"Hardly a sacrifice."

"What?" Jon straightened, looming over her. "What did you say?"

Oh heaven's, why were they discussing this? Charlotte twisted her arm again in a futile attempt to free herself from him and flee into the house. Closing her eyes in frustration, she gave up. "I said it was no sacrifice for you. It doesn't count as me ordering you around if you didn't want to do it anyway."

"Are you daft?"

He let go of her arm now, but Charlotte couldn't move. The intensity of his stare held her as securely as any grip. She could only shake her head, but he ignored her denial.

"That's it, isn't it? You're crazy and you're trying to make me crazy." He jerked his fingers back through his freshly combed hair. "You think I don't want to make love to you?"

"Well, you didn't try to—" The rest of Charlotte's explanation halted when his lips crushed down on hers.

How long had it been since they'd kissed? Charlotte couldn't remember. It seemed like forever, yet then again, only yesterday, as his powerful arms pulled her up against his hard, unyielding body. She moaned, finding the hair at his nape with her hands, braiding her fingers through the raven curls.

His tongue found hers and she sighed, open-mouthed. Oh, she had missed the feel of him, the smell, this pleasurable want that zinged through her veins. He shifted, his palm closing over her breast, and Charlotte arched into him.

She could feel him hard and throbbing against her stomach, moved with him as he rubbed against her. His kiss was hungry, his hands were hungry, and she wanted nothing more than to quench that desire. To satiate him . . . herself.

Passion exploded within her, and she clutched his jacket, trying to hold on to some shred of reality. How could this happen so quickly? One moment they'd argued, the next . . .

His lips rasped down her chin, following the curve of her jaw before she let her head fall back. "Never," he said, the vibrations quivering the skin on her neck. "Never think I don't want you."

How could she think that? How could she think at all with the delicious things he did with his hands and mouth? He inundated her senses. He was everything she felt, saw, smelled, tasted, heard . . .

"Jon! Did you find her, Jon? We're all waiting to eat."

She was wrong. He wasn't everything Charlotte

could hear. Because she certainly heard that, and it definitely wasn't him.

The captain heard it, too. He pulled away slowly and looked down at her, his eyes questioning.

"Jon, can you hear me?"

Charlotte recognized Cilla's voice, and thought she heard a rustle as if the woman were moving through the garden. Panic seized her, must have shown in her expression, because the captain smiled, touching the tip of her nose before cradling her head against his shoulder.

"I hear you, Cilla. I found Charlotte and we're coming in."

"We're waiting dinner for you." Charlotte couldn't tell if her voice was any closer or not.

"So you said. We'll be right there."

When the echoes of the slamming door died, Jon stepped back. What the hell had come over him? Maybe—all right, there was no maybe about it—he got hard just thinking about Charlotte Winston. But he had no business, no damn business, doing anything about it. Especially not in the garden behind his house. Jon caught himself. Not anywhere.

He glanced down at Charlotte. She looked as shaken as he felt. "Are you all right?" Stupid question. She was probably no more all right than he was. But she gave him a half smile, and he shrugged. There seemed no help for it but to go in. It wasn't going to be easy convincing his parents she meant nothing to him now.

# Chapter Sixteen

Spring had come to Oak Hill. Though it was only the beginning of March, it seemed overnight that the grass grew greener and the buds of oak leaves unfurled, pushing away the remnants of last year's growth. They formed a sanctuary for the robins as they went about the task of nesting. Charlotte rested her forehead against the cool windowpane in her bedroom and smiled. She felt, like the birds, the strong desire to nest, to stay in this peaceful place, surrounded by people she'd grown to love.

Charlotte sighed, then drew a small design on the misted glass. Though she'd been here over four months she must remember it couldn't last. No matter that Elizabeth and Alexander treated her like a daughter, that Libby and Cilla regarded her as a sister, or that she adored Libby's children, she was still only a guest in their house.

"It's only temporary," Charlotte whispered. Only until the captain could arrange a way for her to go home. Home. Charlotte shook her head. The word brought only visions of loneliness. But she had no choice. For as much as the captain's family might want her, it seemed the captain did not.

When she spotted Elizabeth and Cilla on the front lawn, looking up at her window and waving, Charlotte pushed thoughts of the captain from her mind. She nodded and laughed when they motioned for her to join them. Grabbing her shawl, she left the room, her step light. For now she would indulge the fantasy that she was part of this family, part of the love that flowed so easily from them . . . from all but one of them.

"I didn't think you'd ever wake up," Cilla chided as Charlotte stepped into the buttery-soft sunshine. "And then we couldn't get your attention. I wanted to throw pebbles at the window, but Mother wouldn't hear of it. Whatever were you thinking about?"

Elizabeth opened her mouth to comment on her daughter's manners, but seeing the laughter in Charlotte's eyes changed her mind. "Cilla wants to go riding and I have other things to do."

"Don't think from what she said you were my second choice," Cilla assured, linking her arm with Charlotte's and moving toward the house. Jon's sister had a limp—caused by burns she'd suffered as a child, Cilla had told Charlotte not long after she'd come to stay at Oak Hill—but it was hardly noticeable this morning. "Actually," Cilla whispered dramatically, catching her mother's eye, "you were my first choice. Older people can be so slow."

This brought peals of laughter from the three women. It was a well-known fact that Elizabeth was an accomplished horsewoman, and could, if the spirit moved her, outrace any of her offspring with the possible exception of Jon. "He's so blasted good with the horses," Cilla had confided to Charlotte once. "I think Father expected him to stay and run the farm. But . . . Jon's always had a mind of his own. Even though sailing used to make him sick, he made up his mind he wanted to be a sailor. And nothing can stop Jon once he's done that.''

"Will you go?" Cilla asked, bringing Charlotte's thoughts back to the present.

"You know I will." Cilla was twenty-four, and though Charlotte was close with both sisters, she spent more time with Cilla. Libby, her husband, Edward, and the twins lived on a plantation a few miles farther down the Manakin River from Oak Hill. She and the girls often rode over for the day, and at Christmas they all came for an extended visit. It gave Charlotte a glimpse of how joyous those times could be. And they'd been made more so by the unexpected visit of Jonathan Knox.

He arrived early one morning two days before Christmas, arms full of presents. He even brought Charlotte something, a length of yellow ribbon, and though it wasn't near as elaborate as some of his other gifts, Charlotte cherished it. Stupidly, she assured herself, because during the whole of his visit he'd spoken no more than ten words to her, and those in the company of another person.

"Good." Cilla squeezed her arm. "You better change into your riding habit. I'll go down to the stables and have them saddle our horses." She took a couple of steps, then turned back. "Are you certain you don't want to come too, Mother?"

"I'm sure. You two go on." She started toward the house, Charlotte by her side. "There are some letters I need to write."

"To Jonathan?" Charlotte winced. She hadn't meant to ask that, but Elizabeth didn't seem to think the question unusual. Of course she couldn't know how often her son invaded Charlotte's thoughts, or that the reason Charlotte slept late some mornings was because waking from dreams of him left her tossing and turning way into the night.

"I've very little hope of a letter reaching him because of the way he moves around, but I'll post one," Elizabeth sighed.

When he came home at Christmas, the captain had hope of commanding a new ship and breaking through the British blockade of the Chesapeake Bay. "Will you please send him my regards?" Charlotte asked, her eyes fastened on the Turkish carpet in the hall. These postscripts were the only communication Charlotte had with the captain except his Christmas visit since he left home in November, the morning after bringing her to Oak Hill.

She knew how he fared because he often sent letters to his family. And always at the end, as if it were an afterthought, was a message to her. It was never anything elaborate. Just a line or two inquiring of her well-being, or sending his best wishes.

So she responded in kind. Wanting to say, wishing to hear, so much more. But glad also that they kept their correspondence to a few unimportant words.

One of her biggest fears, that the captain's parents would suspect just exactly how well she knew their son, had not materialized. They hadn't said or done a thing when she'd entered the parlor on his arm that autumn evening after kissing him in the box garden. The talk around the table had been lively, with the captain relating his recent experiences, though Charlotte noticed he glossed over the more drastic things that happened to him.

And the next morning he was gone. Without another word for her. And since then she'd lived for his letters, to learn how he was doing . . . and to read his stilted message to her.

"Are you all right, Charlotte?"

Glancing up, Charlotte realized she'd paused at the bottom of the stairway, her hand resting lightly on the oak newel.

"Don't be embarrassed, dear," Elizabeth said when she noticed Charlotte's blush. "There's not a thing wrong with woolgathering."

"I tend to do it too much, though."

"We all have our ways of coping."

Charlotte looked up in surprise. "I don't understand—"

"My son," Elizabeth smiled, taking Charlotte's arm and pulling her down on the bottom stair with her. "You miss him very much, don't you?"

Dropping her gaze, Charlotte swallowed. "I . . . I miss him, of course. We all do, but—"

"But not the same way as you."

Charlotte's jaw dropped. It simply dropped and she sat on the steps staring at the captain's mother, who smiled at her as if they shared a great secret.

"You needn't look so shocked, Charlotte. Jon's father and I were young and very much in love during the last war. I know what you're going through."

Denying her feelings for the captain seemed useless, besides, Charlotte didn't think she could get the words out. But there was one difference between Elizabeth and herself. "Your son doesn't love me." The words tasted bitter on her tongue, but Elizabeth only laughed.

"And what makes you think that?"

"I . . . I just know. He hardly mentions me in his letters," Charlotte blurted out.

"You're right," agreed Elizabeth, and Charlotte would have felt good had this been an argument she wanted to win. "He inquires more about the kitchen cat than he does you."

"You noticed that, too?" Charlotte asked slowly, dejectedly.

"Of course," Elizabeth chuckled. "How could anyone miss it."

Charlotte grimaced. "Well then . . ."

"How old are you dear?"

"Twenty-two." Charlotte folded her hands in her lap, not understanding what her age had to do with anything.

"Hmm." Elizabeth bit her bottom lip. "That should be old enough to understand men, but then I'll wager you haven't had much experience because of caring for your mother. And maybe Knox men are just different."

"Different? How?"

"Well, not in any way that counts. They're just stubborn and prideful. Ah," Elizabeth continued when she saw Charlotte's eyes light up. "I see you've noticed that."

"Actually, there have been a few times when he—"

"A few?" Elizabeth laughed heartily. "Remember, I'm his mother. I love him dearly. But I know what he can be like." She raised her finger. "Just like his father. He thought it was best for me if we didn't become involved." Elizabeth threw up her hands. "What the dear man didn't know was I'd fallen in love with him the moment I saw him." She shrugged. "It was too late even then."

"What did you do?"

"I convinced him it was too late for him also." Elizabeth reached for the banister and stood. "Don't worry. I saw the way Jon looked at you when he thought nobody else noticed." Bending over, she patted Charlotte's hand. "Everything will work out."

But Charlotte wasn't as sure of that as Elizabeth.

She wasn't sure at all. The captain planned to send her back to England, and though she certainly liked it here, Charlotte wasn't certain she didn't belong back in Oxfordshire.

But it was too nice a day to worry about that as she and Cilla rode toward the river. The sun warmed her skin through the wool riding habit Jon had bought her in Philadelphia as the horses plodded through the sandy soil, and Cilla chatted merrily.

She spoke of many things, but Charlotte couldn't help noticing the regularity with which she mentioned Adam Burke's name. Nor was this the first time this thought had passed through her mind. But now, maybe because she'd had a similar conversation with Elizabeth concerning herself and Jon, Charlotte turned toward her friend.

"You're in love with Adam Burke, aren't you?"

Cilla shrugged, not bothering to deny it. "I suppose so. But nothing can ever come of it."

"Why not, for heaven's sake?" Now that she thought of it, Adam, who'd come home with Jon at Christmastime, had been very attentive to Cilla.

"It just wouldn't, that's all." They'd reached Oak Hill's wharf, and Cilla slid from the saddle, walking away when Charlotte did the same.

Charlotte could tell Cilla didn't want to talk about Adam, but something kept her going. Even if her own affair of the heart was doomed to failure, she wanted Cilla to be happy. Tying her horse's reins she followed Cilla onto the wooden wharf reaching into the Manakin River. Water lapped against the shore and the supporting piles which were sunk into the river bottom.

"Cilla, I think you're wrong about this. Adam seems very fond of you. I wouldn't be surprised if he asks for your hand as soon as the war is over."

Charlotte knew Adam was with Jon. Both men spent their time petitioning for a ship in Washington while working at the Navy Yard.

"He won't ask," Cilla stated.

"But you can't know that for certain. He might—"

"He already did, Charlotte, and I declined his offer."

Surprise made Charlotte's eyes open wider. It wasn't that she'd never heard of denying a suitor—goodness knows she'd have done it with Captain Levid given the chance—but obviously Cilla didn't feel toward Adam the way Charlotte did about Matthew Levid. "But—"

"Don't ask, Charlotte. Just don't ask." Cilla turned and walked back toward the horses.

She had to. Charlotte took a deep breath and followed. She'd never seen the fun-loving Cilla look so heartbroken. Though Charlotte felt a novice at this business of having a friend her own age, she imagined sharing pain was one aspect of it. "Why can't you just tell me why you turned him down?" Charlotte begged as she caught up with Cilla.

Cilla's shoulders drooped as she let out a sigh. "Because I don't want pity."

"Pity? I don't pity you."

"Not you." The corner of Cilla's lip twitched in humor, then her sulk returned. "Adam," she said as if the one word explained everything. When Charlotte still looked at her in wonderment Cilla continued. "He only asked me because he felt sorry for me. My legs," Cilla said when a puzzled expression remained on Charlotte's face.

"Your legs?" Cilla had told Charlotte about the accident when she was a child. About stepping too close to the fireplace in the large summer kitchen and stumbling over the cat. About her skirts catching fire and her father grabbing her and smothering the flames. She'd stated it matter-of-factly, a simple explanation for the limp she couldn't hide. But Charlotte didn't think her stilted gait reason enough for Adam's pity, and told her so.

"Believe what you like." Cilla gathered up her reins. "But even if he wasn't motivated by sympathy I couldn't bear to see the disgust in his eyes when he saw the scars."

"Cilla." Charlotte moved toward her, shaken by the sorrowful expression on her friend's face. "Don't you know that if he loved you, nothing of the sort would bother him."

"But you haven't seen them, Charlotte." Cilla's voice beseeched her to understand. "They're horrid."

"But *you* are not," Charlotte countered. "And I believe you do Adam a great injustice to assume he would ever find anything about you less than wonderful."

"Pretty words." Cilla looked up, scrubbing at the tears spilling from her eyes. "But I can't accept them. Besides," she sniffed. "It isn't as if Adam refused to take no for an answer. He's made no mention of it since."

"Maybe he's afraid of another rejection." Charlotte ignored Cilla's skeptical expression. "I saw the way you treated him at Christmastime. You all but ignored him."

"No more than you ignored Jon."

"Jon?" Charlotte was taken aback by Cilla's comment. "I didn't ignore anyone. I didn't," she insisted when Cilla's brow arched. "Besides, we were not speaking of me." There was no need to point out that her brother was the one who'd all but acted as if Charlotte was invisible.

Cilla sighed. "I don't want to talk of this anymore.

It's hopeless."

"It is not. If you'd only—" It took Charlotte a moment to realize Cilla wasn't listening to a word she said. Instead, her gaze was fixed on something over Charlotte's shoulder. Swirling around, shading her eyes to squint out over the sun-dappled river, Charlotte tried to find the source of Cilla's concentration. "What is it?"

"A shallop." Cilla motioned toward the small boat sailing up the river toward them. "I don't recognize it."

Charlotte experienced a fleeting pang of anxiety before spotting the boat. All winter the British had enforced a naval blockade at the mouth of the bay, and rumors ran rampant that come spring they'd begin an invasion up the Chesapeake. Word recently reached Oak Hill that British ships had been spotted from the Virginia shore.

Talk of this sort always made Charlotte wonder what she'd do if the British did invade this far north. Where did her loyalties really lie?

But the question needed no answer today. The one-man sail boat headed their way was no invasion.

"That looks like . . ." Cilla hurried to the edge of the wharf, Charlotte close at her heels. "It is!" she said, smiling. "It's Jon." Standing on tiptoe, Cilla began waving, an excited yelp escaping her lips when the boat's occupant signaled back. "I wonder what he's doing home?" Cilla asked rhetorically before turning and limping back to her horse.

"What a minute." Cilla had mounted by the time Charlotte roused herself from her study of the boat. Her heart was racing when she reached Jon's sister, but it had nothing to do with her run back the wharf. "Where are you going?"

"Back to tell the family." Cilla turned her mare's

head. "They'll be so excited."

"Well, wait for me." Charlotte reached for the reins she'd tethered around an oak sapling.

"You stay here." Cilla shrugged. "Somebody should meet him. He's already seen us." With those words she nudged her horse toward the road leading back to the manor house.

"No! Don't leave me here . . ." Charlotte stopped, realizing only the chattering jays were left to hear her. Turning back to face the river and the ever-nearing shallop, Charlotte sighed. What difference did it make if she saw Jon now or not? If he was home for any length of time, she would see her fill of him. All she needed to do was treat him in the same distant manner he treated her.

With that in mind Charlotte returned to the wharf and watched his approach. The shallop tossed gently on the lolling waves, the snappy spring breeze filling the sail, bringing him ever closer.

Charlotte could see him clearly now; the wind-swept ebony of his close-cropped hair, the chiseled perfection of his tanned face, the symmetry of his powerful body as he grasped the rudder, steering the fast-moving boat toward shore.

When he stood to trim the sail, Charlotte's breath caught and she twisted her hands together. How could she ever keep herself from him?

But as he leaped to shore, straightening from tying the sailboat to the wharf, and glanced at her, a reserved expression in his blue eyes, Charlotte decided her task might be easier than she thought.

She cleared her throat as she stepped forward, feeling awkward. "We didn't expect you."

"I hadn't realized myself I was coming until a few days ago." Jon shrugged into his tunic, more to give himself something to do than because the towering

291

loblolly pines shaded the sun. He definitely wasn't cold. Just seeing Charlotte had sent heated blood racing through his body.

Her mouth felt dry, her lips parched, but licking them didn't help. If only she could think of something to say, but as he stood, feet apart, hands clasped behind his back, all rational thought left her mind. "Cilla noticed you on the river," Charlotte said, feeling silly even before the words were completely out.

"Is she here?" Jon forced his gaze away from Charlotte, but not for long. Whatever had possessed him to think he could ignore her?

"No. She rode back to Oak Hill . . . to tell your family."

"And you stayed?" Jon's black brow quirked.

"She told me to," Charlotte assured lest he think it had been her idea. But his expression, the slightest hint of a smile, left her wondering if he thought she lied or thought her quickness to explain her presence amusing. Turning, Charlotte led the way off the wharf. "I suppose we should hurry. They'll be waiting for you."

Charlotte stopped suddenly when she spotted the gray gelding munching contentedly on some winter dried grass beside a holly tree. Why hadn't she thought of this before? There was only one horse— and that one sported a side saddle—to carry them back to the manor house.

Her eye caught Jon's and she noticed the grin spreading across his face. Charlotte couldn't help but respond.

"I suppose I could run along beside you," he said, leaning his arms against an overhead branch.

"It's nearly three miles."

Jon shrugged. "I've done it before." He moved

over toward the horse, and Charlotte stepped out of his way. "But I don't think it necessary this time." Reaching under the gelding's body, he unbuckled the cinch.

"What are you doing?"

"Well, I'm sure as hell not riding sidesaddle." His grin deepened. "We can double up."

"Oh, I don't think . . ." Stepping backward, Charlotte came close to tripping over a tree stump; if not for the quickness of the captain she would have.

"It's the only way," Jon insisted, pulling his steadying hand away from her arm.

She knew exactly what he meant. Either could walk back to the house, and make it without trouble. But it would only invite a wealth of questions—questions neither wanted to answer.

But moments later when he pulled her up to sit in front of him on the horse's bony back, Charlotte realized there were worse things than answering unwanted queries. Like trying to resist the maddening feel of his arms bracketing her body, or the sensual smell of tangy salt air that surrounded her.

Jon nudged the gelding with his knees, smiling at the ramrod stiffness of Charlotte's back. If she didn't loosen up she'd bounce right off the damn horse. But if she did relax her seat she'd slide more firmly against him . . . Jon gritted his teeth and forced the thought aside. He didn't come back to cause trouble, or kindle sparks better left banked. But as they jogged along the path, and her body of its own accord slipped back, her hip nestling into the V between his legs, Jon knew the fire simmered much too close to the surface to be ignored.

Only the sight of his father galloping down the path, leading Jon's own horse, kept him from snuggling his nose into the collar of her riding jacket. As it was he settled her back more intimately against him as he reined in the gelding.

Charlotte tried to swallow, but her mouth felt cotton dry. All the moisture in her body seemed to have settled between her legs, forced there by the feel of the rock-hard bulge slowly swelling against her hip. She didn't dare seek his gaze; knew he stared straight ahead, having no more control of himself than she did.

"Jon! Cilla said you were home." Alex pulled his stallion up beside his son. "Thought you might be needing an extra horse."

"Thanks." Jon tried not to squirm. "But I think we can make it back to the house all right."

"Are you sure? It would be no problem for me to go back to the wharf for the sidesaddle," Alex's glance fell on the horse's back. "Be a sight more comfortable."

"We're fine" came Jon's succinct reply. Seeing the startled expression on his father's face, he grinned. "I'm in a hurry to see if there are any of Mother's molasses cookies in the larder. Been thinking of nothing else since Christmas." As blatant a lie as he ever spoke, Jon decided. He may have a sweet tooth, and he did love his mother's cookies, but it was the woman perched in front of him that filled his thoughts—and he didn't like it one bit.

But the story about the cookies seemed to appease his father. He turned his horse in a tight circle and started back up the road toward the house. And Jon tried thinking of every cold plunge he'd ever taken in the river, trying to get a particularly unruly part of his body back under control.

"Think we've got some cookies in a tin, but Charlotte baked them. They're pretty good, too."

Charlotte's face grew warm with those words of praise from the captain's father. She also sensed Jon looking down at her. She could imagine him recalling the charred potatoes she put in front of him, and wondering if these cookies were equally burned. Charlotte shifted, her eyes rising to meet his. "Your mother and Cilla have been teaching me to cook. Lydia, too," she added, including the indentured servant who did most of the food preparation at Oak Hill.

"Hmm," was all he said, but a grin played around the corners of his mouth, and Charlotte had a wild urge to stuff a whole batch of molasses cookies down his throat and make him eat his "hmm."

By strictly keeping his mind on the reply of naval battles he'd fought, Jon was able to dismount without embarrassment when they reached Oak Hill. Right before Cilla hurled herself into his arms, Jon noticed Charlotte slip into the house.

"How long do you think they're going to be in the library?" Cilla tossed down the sock she was knitting and limped to the window.

"Till they're finished, I imagine," Elizabeth responded without looking up from her mending.

"Well, I don't think it's fair. Jon comes all the way from Washington City full of news of . . . of the war, and he goes straight off with father."

Charlotte hid her smile as she ripped out her last three stitches. She didn't doubt that Cilla's interest in a certain naval doctor far outweighed her desire for an accounting of the war. But Charlotte could hardly fault her impatience. Regardless of the vow she'd made to herself when she jumped from the horse and ran upstairs to toss water on her burning face—the vow to stay as far away from Jonathan Knox as possible—she wished for him to join them in the parlor. Just to hear news of the war, Charlotte tried to convince herself, as she stifled a curse over yet another tangled stitch.

When he did enter the parlor by his father's side a few minutes later, Charlotte gave up all pretense of sewing. Cilla, on the other hand, settled back into her seat and picked up her needles, slipping easily back into the row of chain stitches. Her only outward sign of impatience was a mumbled, "About time."

"Now, Daughter," Alex said before settling his hip against the arm of Elizabeth's chair. "Jon has a proposition for us, and if you're in agreement, Lizzy, I'd like to give him the schooner."

"The *Freedom?* But we haven't used her in years. Not since we started sending our produce to Baltimore. I seriously doubt she's seaworthy."

"I intend to make it more than seaworthy, Mother." Without realizing what he was doing, Jon sat on the arm of Charlotte's chair. "You know I've been frustrated all winter trying to get a new command. They're building vessels for the Great Lakes, but the Chesapeake is all but being ignored." Charlotte watched him lean forward, his face intense, and realized how important this was to him.

"The British have bottled us in, and if they gain control of the bay . . ." He spread out his hands, palms up, and leaned back. His arm rubbed against Charlotte's shoulder. He looked around, and their eyes locked. Taking a deep breath, he broke the stare and leaned forward.

"Washington City's vulnerable," Jon continued. "Though finding anyone in power to accept that is difficult. And then there's Baltimore. If that falls, the British have only to march a short way to Philadelphia." Jon sighed. "There isn't a whole hell of a lot standing in their way."

"But I don't understand what you want want to do," Elizabeth said, reaching up to grab her husband's hand.

"Captain Gordon, the naval commander of Baltimore, is putting together a fleet to protect the upper bay," Jon explained. "Captain Barney will be in charge of the flotilla. The Secretary of the Navy has authorized him to appropriate private schooners, to incorporate them into the Navy. I've taken the liberty of speaking to him, and he'd like me to captain one of them. He's trying to find one for me himself, but I thought of the *Freedom*. She's basically sound, with a sharp hull that promises speed."

"You'll need more than speed against the British, Jon," Elizabeth warned.

"And I'll have it. The Dorsey Works in Baltimore will fit her out with guns . . ." Jon paused, his smile for his mother alone. "I won't sail her till she's ready."

"I know." Elizabeth shook her head, laughing. "And I think you *knew* there was never any question of your father or me refusing you. Even if you weren't our son, we both worked hard to get this nation started. We don't want anything happening to it now."

"Great!" Jon leaned back again, and Charlotte felt her pulse quicken as his sleeve rubbed against her. "I'll ride down to Jessup Creek in the morning and check her out. If she's not in too bad a shape, I'll get some men to help sail her into the river. Crew members might be a problem with Maryland paying a bounty of sixteen dollars per recruit, but I'm hoping I can find some sailors among the watermen around here."

He continued talking of his plans, and Charlotte wondered how he could be so oblivious to her. Every part of her body responded to his nearness, and she hoped she could hide that fact until he sailed away.

# Chapter Seventeen

She'd have to leave. There was no other choice.

Charlotte tossed a pinecone into the water and leaned back against the loblolly's rough bark. Watching the pinecone dip and swirl, she rested her chin on the bend of her knees and wondered how she could make good her escape.

No, escape wasn't a good word. That implied she didn't like Oak Hill. And the truth was, she'd grown to love it. Not just the plantation with its gentle terrain and large telescoping house; the people who lived here were dear to her.

Elizabeth and Alex, Libby and Cilla treated her like family. What more could someone who'd grown up without such nurturing want?

"Jonathan Knox," Charlotte whispered so softly the tern feeding along the shoreline couldn't hear.

Hunching her shoulders, wrapping her arms around her legs, Charlotte sighed. This time the tern took flight, protesting the disturbance with an angry kip kip sound, and Charlotte lifted her head to watch him, then dropped it back on her knees.

She could forget about Jonathan Knox—maybe— if he weren't around all the time. But she couldn't continue seeing him almost every day . . . pretending.

Charlotte laughed aloud. Pretending used to be the area in which she excelled. Pretending the handsome pirate swept her away. Pretending her mother would get well. Pretending her father would come home . . . would care.

Biting her lip, Charlotte linked her fingers. Yes, pretending was what she did best. Then why couldn't she pretend now? So Jon had stayed at Oak Hill for nearly a month refitting his new ship. Certainly she could imagine him someplace else. It wasn't as if he paid much attention to her.

Not that he took much notice of anyone. He was much too involved with the schooner he'd renamed the *Revenge*. But he was loving with his parents and sister, displaying a teasing warmth Charlotte had glimpsed before—had experienced before. But no more. Now he seemed cold . . . remote.

She sighed again, catching herself and twisting around when she heard the footfall. Jonathan Knox stood tall and still, watching her, the momentary flash of surprise gone from his eyes. Charlotte could tell he wanted to turn on his heel and leave the secluded spot by the water's edge, and something inside her wished he would. But he didn't.

Clasping his hands behind his back and squaring his stance, he muttered something about believing her up at the house.

Charlotte almost laughed. Did he imagine she thought he came looking for her? For the past month, since he'd come to Oak Hill, the captain made it a practice never ever to be anywhere alone with her.

But now they *were* alone. Alone and separated from the reality of the world by the gurgling waters of the Manakin River and the newly unfurled leaves of oak trees.

Why was she staring at him like that? Jon shifted his gaze across the river, then back to her. Some of the surprise had faded from her eyes. They appeared dark in the shadows, but he knew if he moved closer they'd be a soft brown. His shoulders stiffened. "I didn't mean to disturb you."

"No." Charlotte's voice stopped him from retreating. "You're not bothering me. Really." She slid to the side, motioning toward the blanket she'd brought from the house to sit upon.

Shrugging, Jon lowered himself to the ground, sitting near, but not on the blanket. If he kept his distance he could control himself. Hadn't he done an admirable job—a damn admirable job—so far? He glanced her way, glad that she was looking out over the water. It gave him a chance to study her profile. It was pretty. *She* was pretty.

Jon's brow creased as he pondered why it took him so long to realize how much he liked her looks. Oh, he'd known she had a certain appeal—he caught on to that right away—but because of her awful mourning clothes, her seasickness, their journey through the forest and down to Maryland, there'd been little opportunity to see her at her best.

Now he did, and he couldn't help liking what he saw. The generous sweep of dark lashes, the small, freckle-spattered nose and gently curved mouth were irresistible. He wished she'd turn toward him, and when she did felt a warmth spread through him. She looked like she belonged here, surrounded by the cattails and holly. It took Jon a moment to remember she didn't.

That thought made his voice harsh. "I'm leaving tomorrow to pick up the *Revenge* in Chestertown.

From there we'll head across the bay."

"Then you've enlisted enough men?" Just because he didn't usually talk to her didn't mean she wasn't fully aware of what he did. She'd sat quietly while he spoke to his parents about the difficulty in finding men to work his ship.

"We're still a little short, but I'm hoping to hire on a few more in Baltimore."

Charlotte nodded, then looked away. She knew he'd be leaving soon—goodness, how many times had she wished him gone—but now that the time was upon her, she felt . . . she wasn't certain how she felt. Glad, certainly. Perhaps now she could begin to forget him. But another part of her wished she didn't have to.

Suddenly Charlotte forgot about herself and thought of Cilla. She turned to face him, her eyes wide. "Does this mean Adam is leaving, too?"

She couldn't care about that. But the grasp she had on his arm made it obvious she did. "Aye," Jon answered. "He's part of the crew." Then letting curiosity and another feeling he couldn't quite name get the better of him. "What do you care?"

"I don't." Charlotte noticed the skeptical lift to his brow. "I mean I don't want to see him . . . or anyone go off to war, but . . . Well, I know Cilla won't like him gone."

"Cilla?" A grin lifted the corners of Jon's mouth. "Cilla wants him to stay?"

"Well, of course she does. And I think he feels the same."

The grin broadened. "Are you playing matchmaker?" Jon thought back over the past month. Adam had visited Oak Hill often, but like a dunce Jon thought it was because of him. Of course he'd been so busy with the *Revenge* he'd had little time for his friend—and apparently hadn't been missed by him at all.

"No." Charlotte's fingers plucked at a stalk of marsh grass. "No," she repeated. "I just like Cilla." She paused. "I like your whole family."

Jon didn't know how to respond to that so he said nothing, the silence broken only by the harsh call of a gull.

"Jon?"

Glancing toward her, Jon smiled. It was only recently that she started calling him his given name, and he assumed it was because it might sound strange in front of the family to refer to him as Captain. But he still liked to hear her say it.

"How many brothers do you have?"

"What?" Jon didn't know what he'd expected her to ask, but bringing up Christopher wasn't it. "One, why?"

"Because . . . well . . ." Now that she started Charlotte wasn't sure how to continue. But this had preyed on her mind for near a fortnight. "Cilla told me she had a brother who'd been impressed by the British."

"Aye."

"And you said once that your brother was dead."

His only response this time was a hard stare, but Charlotte went on. "Is he?" A mask of sadness lifted over his features and Charlotte rushed on. "I don't mean to intrude, but . . . but Cilla didn't act at all as if her brother were dead. Just forced to sail on a British ship. And though I realize in time of war there's always that possibility, I . . ." She was rambling and couldn't seem to stop herself. She probably would have continued if Jon hadn't interrupted.

"He's dead." Jon shut his eyes to the pain, opening

303

them when he realized what a relief it was to share. "At least that's what I was told."

"But Cilla doesn't know." It was more statement than question, and by the expression in Jon's blue eyes when he looked at her, Charlotte knew no answer was necessary.

His parents didn't know, either—Charlotte was sure of it. Elizabeth often spoke of her sons coming home . . . of having them all safe and happy at Oak Hill again.

But why would Jon keep this secret? What would be gained by keeping the truth from his loved ones? Wasn't false hope worse than no hope at all? Before she could imagine a reason for him, he spoke, pain etched in his words.

"I don't know my brother is dead for certain, and until I do, I don't want them to know." With that he got up and walked down toward the shore.

"But how will you ever find out?" Charlotte's voice followed him. "Who told you in the first place? Oh, Jon, you may never know for certain. You might—" She'd been going to say *die yourself trying to find out*. But then she realized he almost had. Because in that instant she knew—knew who captained the ship that impressed Jon's brother, knew who had said he was dead. The evidence had been before her all the while. In his search for Captain Levid. In his hatred.

And she knew why Jon had renamed his schooner the *Revenge* even though his parents had initially protested the change. He might say he didn't know the truth of his brother's death, but in his heart he believed it, and he meant to have his revenge.

But at what cost?

He stood, hands clasped behind his back facing out across the river, and Charlotte rose and moved toward him. Her riding boots left imprints in the moist, spongy soil. She thought to touch his arm, but didn't, merely took a stance near him.

"Don't do this," she whispered, thinking perhaps the soft gurgling of the water, the cries of the gulls, had drowned out her words when he didn't look around. This time she did touch him, clutching his sleeve and forcing him to look down at her. "Don't go after Captain Levid. No good can come of it."

Jon wasn't surprised she figured out who he spoke of—he never thought her stupid. Still, his jaw clinched and he pulled his arm away. A derisive snort prefaced his words. "No good can come of it. A noble sentiment. But tell me, Charlotte, is your concern for me . . . or him?"

The smack of her palm against his cheek surprised her as much as him. One moment Charlotte felt the unfair sting of his words and the next . . . the next she reacted. Her hand tingled. She glanced at it, then up to the lean cheek that bore a reddening print.

His lips thinned in anger, the flash of his eyes, now the deep shade of a churning squall at sea, bore into her, frightening in its intensity. Turning, her skirts swirling about her legs, Charlotte stepped away from him. But his hand shot out clutching her shoulder and whirled her back to face him.

"Dramatics aside, Charlotte, I want an answer. Whom do you wish to protect?"

His fingers held her in an iron grip and Charlotte's hands flattened against his chest to keep herself steady. She could feel the agitated thump of his heart and knew her own beneath her heaving bosom matched his. She looked up at him, her eyes wide, thinking it impossible for him not to know whom she cared for, whom she wished to protect, yet unable to voice the words.

305

Their eyes locked. The air around them, so spring-soft one moment, now seemed charged, electrified like the prestorm heat of late summer. He yanked her closer, pressing her breasts into the unyielding strength of his chest, lowering his head till no more than a breath separated them.

"Who?" he said, his whisper-soft voice a sensual counterpoint to the heat and hardness she felt everywhere their bodies touched.

Charlotte arched her foot, standing on tiptoe, striving for the moment when their lips met. But though she stretched, though his hand dropped from her arm resting lightly on the curve of her bottom, he kept them apart. "Who?" he demanded again, and Charlotte had no choice but to answer.

"You." She breathed a heartbeat before his mouth crashed down on hers.

Oh, she loved the feel of him, the taste. He was like every fantasy she'd ever had, only better. In the months since he'd touched her, Charlotte's memory and imagination had twined, braided, to create a mental image she feared shamed reality. Now she knew it didn't even come close.

Nothing could simulate the brush of his fingers across her skin, the mingling of breath, the desire that sprang to life, like the man himself.

A tiny sound escaped her as his tongue tipped the corners of her mouth, then wet the quivering seam. She opened for him freely, fully, wanting the sensual slide of his tongue over hers.

He should stop . . . and in just a moment he would, Jon told himself, long after that moment passed. Charlotte didn't want this, she'd made that quite clear in Plattsburg. And he'd tried to stay away from her . . . Lord knew he had. Not only because of her, but because of Captain Levid, of what he planned to do to Levid.

But none of that seemed to matter when she wrapped her arms around his neck, digging her fingers into his hair. Her breasts flattened against his chest, her thighs against his, and his body caught fire.

Any question about what they should or shouldn't do quickly evaporated. This was happening. This was real. And neither wanted it to stop.

Jon sifted his fingers through her hair, dislodging the pins and sending them scattering among the pine needles. He cupped her neck, angling her head to accept his kiss more fully. She moaned, arching her body into his, and a deep throbbing ache washed over him.

When Jon's palm flattened over Charlotte's breast, then trailed down her stomach, he abandoned any thoughts of stopping. Whatever was between them, whatever spell she wove whenever they touched, was beyond his control.

Charlotte skimmed her fingers across his cheek. The mark of her slap had disappeared, faded into the deeply bronzed skin. His whiskers felt rough, excitedly so, and Charlotte's touch moved across his jaw and down his neck, relearning the masculine contours. But her mind could not concentrate. She loved the feel of him, yet what he did to her made her hand fall away, her head drop back, and her eyes close.

She didn't see Jon watching her as the heel of his hand pressed between her legs. She didn't see his smile of male satisfaction as her bottom lip caught between rows of pearl-white teeth.

"Oh . . ." The tortured moan escaped her as her knees weakened. Charlotte was bent over his arm, the strong arm that kept her from crumpling to the ground. His palm rubbed, cupped, abrading her through the thin layers of cotton and silk.

"Open your legs." His words vibrated against her neck as he bent over her, his lips and tongue making erotic designs on her skin. Charlotte didn't think she could make any conscious movement, but his command, the continued pressure of his searching hand, had her spreading her legs to the limits of her skirt.

And now he moved, down . . . around . . . between. The gown inched up, and then there was only skin, hot, hard, and calloused against her.

She was so soft and wet, so incredibly woman against his hand that Jon thought he'd burst. His breeches bound him uncomfortably and he ground himself against Charlotte's hip.

The pressure built higher and stronger, and Charlotte wondered how she'd ever lived without these marvelous sensations. Before she'd known the captain she'd only had fleeting glimpses of what pleasure might be. Since his touch she'd known, and she'd missed the wondrous pleasure they shared. The trembling vibrations that began low and spread through her body. That made her tighten and quiver and rub herself against him wantonly.

"Jon. Jon." Charlotte grabbed for his shoulders, her nails digging into the heavy wool, as wave upon wave swept over her. Charlotte's legs gave way and she felt herself falling, drifting through space. And then she was against him, bundled next to his hard chest, tasting the essence of his open mouth.

Jon's heel caught the corner of the blanket, and he kicked it from beneath the pine tree into a clearing. With deliberate haste he lowered Charlotte, his movements made awkward by the need to keep his mouth locked to hers. He'd had her before, had never forgotten, and now couldn't wait to bury himself in her again.

308

He straddled her, his fumbling fingers groping with the buttons. His lips tore away long enough to allow a quick perusal of her riding jacket closure, and then he was kissing her again, deeply, hungrily.

A salt-tinged breeze blew off the river, caressing Charlotte's skin as Jon tore away her chemise. Her nipples tightened, beaded almost painfully until his warm hand covered her. Her breast swelled to fill his hand, molding to the cup of his palm. She still ached, but now the torment traveled lower, consuming her body with a longing she understood . . . remembered from other times.

She needed him.

Unfastening buttons had always seemed such a simple task. Now Charlotte couldn't accomplish it fast enough. She fought the engraved brass discs on his uniform jacket, urgently trying to get to him.

But she failed, failed so completely that a tiny whimper escaped. His fingers joined hers, twined momentarily while his deep-blue eyes searched hers, then made quick work of the buttons. He dragged the tunic from his arms, bunching the sleeves, and tossed it into the underbrush.

Charlotte reached for the linen shirt covering his flat stomach, and again their eyes locked. He whipped the garment over his head. Now she touched hot, vibrant, hair-roughened skin. His hand covered hers, but this time he nudged gently but firmly downward. She could protest, though she wondered if the cotton dryness of her mouth made speech impossible. Her tongue slipped from between her lips, and Charlotte saw Jon's gaze follow the movement. The raw passion and hunger in his eyes filled her with wanting and her hand slipped lower.

His groan sounded primitive and sexual as she touched him. He still stradled her, his knees pressed into the moist soil, his firm thighs squeezing her hips. Dappled sun shone through the newly emerged leaves, making sensual patterns on sweat-slick skin. His back was straight, his head thrown back, teeth clinched, and Charlotte marveled at the power she had over him. Each movement of her hand caused a deep intake of breath, caused his broad chest to expand even more. His nipples pearled and Charlotte longed to touch him there. But that would mean losing her other hold and she could not do that.

Thick and throbbing and so incredibly hard, Charlotte learned his contours. He moaned when she tried to close her fingers around him, tightened his legs when both hands began working the buttons free.

Now Charlotte learned he was also soft and smooth and so hot her stroking fingers burned. But the heat felt wonderful and Charlotte arched her body toward the flames, quickening her touch till he grabbed her hands, flattening them firmly against him.

"Stop! My God if you don't cease this . . . I shall . . . embarrass myself." With a final squeeze he jerked her hands away and began stripping off Charlotte's skirt and petticoats.

His lips followed the descent, and soon Charlotte lay writhing, hot and aching, beneath him. His lips touched her as she clutched the midnight-black curls covering his head. Reality faded, fantasy filled the void. But it wasn't the fantasies of before. This one was firmly based. This one was Jon.

By the time he slid into her, his throbbing heat filling her, Charlotte could do naught but experience the sensual delights around her. Her hands thrown wide of the blanket, dug in the soft dirt, filling the air with a pungent smell that mingled with the brackish odor of the river, the musky smell of him.

His breathing quickened, as did hers, with each powerful thrust, with each accepting arch. The ragged sound rang in her ears blotting out the chattering birds and the rattle of wind through the cat-o'-nine tails.

Charlotte's arms wrapped around his shoulders, her legs around his hips, and she clung to him as she soared above the marsh. She called his name again and again until his mouth clamped over her and the thrust of his tongue matched the erotic rhythm of their entwined bodies.

Charlotte wasn't certain how long she lay there, his big body pressing her into the soft bed of pine needles, and she really didn't care. Oh, she knew she should. She should care a great deal.

What respectable lady would lie with a man in the bright daylight? In the open? What lady would revel in the feel of his naked body, run her fingers down the curve of his hip? Want him again?

Her fingers skimmed lightly, lovingly, over his body, memorizing the feel of him for when he was gone. Soft and warm, she sighed her pleasure. And then her fingers inched higher.

Charlotte felt him stiffen or she might not have noticed the first ridge of scars. Till this moment she thought he was asleep, so contentedly he rested atop her. But now he shifted, turning and sitting up.

"We'd better get back." He reached for his breeches.

Embarrassment tinted Charlotte's cheeks. Moments ago, lying naked beneath him had not elicited this reaction, but now with his back turned, she felt a blush spread over her like a cloak. Biting her bottom lip, Charlotte grabbed up her skirt. Her eyes never left his back as her gaze traced the web of crisscrossing scars.

She couldn't imagine the pain he'd endured . . . nor the humiliation. Matthew Levid had done his worst. Then Charlotte remembered Jon's brother. Not his worst at all.

"Jon." She touched his back, not pulling away when he again stiffened, his shoulders squaring. "Your brother wouldn't want you to sacrifice your life in vain."

"How do you know what Chris would want?" His narrowed blue eyes met hers and again Charlotte felt the heat of embarrassment, but she shoved it aside. Moments ago they'd been so close, and now . . . now because of Levid they were like strangers. It seemed so unfair.

"You're right . . ." Charlotte began, then hesitated. "I don't know your brother. But I've become very fond of your parents and sisters, and I can't imagine anyone in your family wanting you hurt. Including your brother."

"We're at war, Charlotte. I'm simply going off to fight." His voice sounded tired, as if he grew weary of explaining such fundamentals. But Charlotte wasn't fooled.

Rising to her knees, she ignored the flash of desire that sprang to his eyes. "In a ship named *Revenge*."

"Damnit, Charlotte, I had to name it something." He shook pine needles from his shirt and yanked it over his head.

Charlotte turned away and pulled on her torn chemise, letting the ends flutter open in the spring breeze while she reached for her riding jacket. "I don't want you to be reckless." She thought of the tales she'd heard on the *Scorpion* about the intrepid American captain, and tears stung her eyes. "Just don't be reckless," she repeated.

He came to her that night, in the darkness of the midnight hour, and Charlotte was not surprised. Nor did she send him away. She could no more do that than he could give up his quest for Captain Levid.

Now with him standing before her, moonlight streaming through the window to brighten the open-throated white shirt he wore, Charlotte wondered what would become of them. At supper that evening the conversation had been light and witty . . . and forced. Everyone knew Jon was leaving and that he might not come back.

The British were on the bay in full force. Their ships seemed to be everywhere, and word of American losses reached Oak Hill every day. Tales such as that had spurred Jon on to complete work on the *Revenge*.

Adam had come to Oak Hill for the evening and he planned to leave with Jon in the morning. Charlotte thought she noticed several meaningful glances pass between Adam and Cilla. Or maybe she only hoped she did. Hoped someone would find love and happiness.

For no matter what their encounter by the river had meant—and Charlotte couldn't begin to explain it—she knew it wasn't a declaration of love. Desire, lust, obsession. These things she could believe. But he didn't love her. And at times, as when he was reminded of the stripes on his back, Charlotte wasn't certain he didn't blame her.

Not consciously. Charlotte knew he was too reasonable for that. He knew now that she would never hurt him. But in the recesses of his mind, how could he help but link her with Matthew Levid? And how could Jon help hating him?

Still, he came to her, perhaps drawn by the same force that compelled her to open the door, and her arms.

They lay in the high tester bed, their naked bodies linked, and laughed when the rope springs groaned, the sound echoing above the soft spring night sounds. Jon buried his face in her hair as she muffled her giggles against the solid strength of his shoulder.

"Do you think anyone can hear us?" Charlotte whispered, her eyes large and shining in the dim silvery moonlight.

Jon shrugged, thrust, and the laughter stopped—but the noise of the bed did not. "Damn thing. How come it's so loud?"

"You might not notice it if your parents weren't in the next room," Charlotte observed.

"You're probably right." His mouth, hot and moist, covered her straining nipple.

"Jon?"

"Hmm?"

"Is that why you never came to me before?"

He lifted his head, his blue eyes boring into her. His fingers feathered from her temple. "No. My staying away from you had nothing to do with them." Brushing his lips over the tip of her nose, he explained. "We decided there would be no more of this." His kiss defined exactly what "this" was.

"We did, didn't we?"

"Aye, and it was a very sensible decision." His hand drifted down her body, tangling in the curls where their bodies met.

"But not one . . . , oh . . ." Charlotte's voice faltered as he began moving again. "We can keep."

"No," Jon agreed, and Charlotte couldn't tell how he felt about his admission. But he paid no further attention to the squeaking ropes as he made love to her well into the night.

He liked watching her sleep, Jon decided as he lay in the tester bed, chin propped in hand. The pearly morning light caressed her skin and highlighted the light-brown hair that tangled on the pillow. She smiled in her sleep, but Jon resisted the urge to lean over and kiss the slightly parted lips.

He didn't want to wake her. As quietly as he could Jon slipped from the bed. Waking her would only mean saying good-bye, and Jon found that something he couldn't deal with right now.

Besides, he didn't know what to tell her. Because he didn't know how he felt about her. His emotions were so wound up with Christopher and Matthew Levid that he couldn't see Charlotte—just Charlotte. And he didn't like that one bit. But there it was, and now was not the time to muddle through the mess, so he sneaked from the room, hoping the good-byes from last night would last them. Feeling like a thief in the night, he pulled the door shut quietly behind him—and turned to face the surprised countenance of his mother.

"I . . . I thought to see you off." Elizabeth Knox had obviously just come from her room.

"There was no need for you to rise so early." Jon forced himself to meet her eyes. How could her catching him leaving Charlotte's room make him feel more like ten than thirty-one?

"It's no problem." She skirted around him. "Finish dressing." She paused and Jon glanced down at his open shirt, the boots he clutched in his hand, and nearly groaned. "I'll fix you some breakfast."

By the time Jon gathered his sea chest and roused Adam, he decided for Charlotte's sake to bring up last night's sleeping arrangements. When he found his mother in the dining room pouring coffee into a china cup he cleared his throat. "I don't want you to think less of Charlotte."

Elizabeth Knox looked up at her son and smiled. "Why would I do that, dear?"

Was she playing games with him? He leveled her a look that clearly stated he had no time for it if she was, and his mother had the decency to flush. "Well, if you insist upon discussing this, Jon, let me say that you've had no one fooled, least of all your father and me."

"What are you talking about?"

"All that talk of helping out Jacob Anderson by bringing her here." She pointed her finger at his chest. "We knew differently. You haven't done a very good job of hiding your feelings for her since you brought her here . . . and I may add, neither has she."

His feelings? How could he hide them when he didn't know what they were? But his mother seemed convinced that he and Charlotte were one of the great love matches of history, and to argue would only bring up his questionable motives for being in her room, so Jon let it pass.

He did wonder about her assessment of Charlotte's feelings, but decided his mother read into them what she wanted to believe. At least Charlotte wouldn't suffer any recriminations while he was gone. As a matter of fact, his mother seemed to approve of their relationship.

As he left the house his mother stayed him with a hand on his arm. "I do hope you plan to do the right thing by that sweet girl," she whispered.

Jon nodded, wishing he knew what the right thing was.

# Chapter Eighteen

"Is it thoughts of Adam that has that smile on your face?" Charlotte grinned when Cilla shot her a glance so like her brothers. She laughed aloud at Cilla's reply.

"Adam Burke is the furthest thing from my mind. He is," she insisted. "Oh I should never have confided in you after he left in the spring."

"Don't say that." Charlotte nudged her horse closer to Cilla's mare. "I was only teasing."

"I know." Cilla glanced at Charlotte through her lashes, and a blush stained her cheeks. "And you were right, of course. I was thinking about him." They trotted on in companionable silence toward the river until Cilla sighed. "It's been so long."

"Four months," Charlotte said quickly—too quickly. She shrugged when Cilla glanced her way. She couldn't help it. She'd counted the days as conscientiously as Cilla. The day Adam left was the last time she'd seen the captain. *Jon*, she amended. He hadn't been the distant captain, but a flesh-and-blood man when he'd come to her that night.

"Well, however long it's been," Charlotte continued the thread of the conversation. "I doubt Adam has changed his mind about you."

"Let's hope not." Cilla grinned, revealing her dimple. Charlotte had noticed one just like it denting Cilla's father's cheek. But not Jon. He had inherited the cleft in his mother's chin.

"I'm glad you had a talk with Adam." Charlotte guided her horse along a trail that led along the mouth of the Manakin River.

"He didn't give me much choice, cornering me in the garden like he did." She eyed Charlotte skeptically. "Are you certain you didn't goad him into talking to me?"

"As I've told you numerous times, I didn't. I only saw Adam in the company of the rest of your family, and I certainly wasn't going to 'goad him,' as you call it, in front of them." Charlotte didn't mention her conversation with Jon, or her belief that he might have spoken with his friend. Besides, she couldn't prove it, and everything had worked out for the best. Adam had declared his love, stating he didn't give a fig about Cilla's scars and that he was tired of her refusals.

"Well, you can't blame me for being skeptical. We had . . . What's wrong, Charlotte?"

Charlotte's stare had wandered out over the sun-sparkled water, where the mouth of the Manakin River emptied into the Chesapeake Bay. Color drained from her face, and she glanced quickly at Cilla, then back toward the west. "Ships," she said, fear tightening her throat.

Cilla turned, a gasp escaping her at what she saw. Sun-bleached white sails billowed in the late-summer breeze, skimming a dozen or more boats north along the bay. "Do you think they're ours?"

Charlotte shook her head. Though she couldn't be certain which side of this conflict was hers, she knew what Cilla meant. No one at Oak Hill—except Jon—questioned her loyalty to the United States. But then no one else knew anything about her. Pushing that uncomfortable thought aside, Charlotte shaded her eyes. "I don't think our Navy has that many ships all together. They must be English."

"And they must be heading north toward Baltimore . . . toward Jon and Adam."

That realization made Charlotte's blood run cold. The *Revenge* had joined a small flotilla of vessels under the command of Commodore Joshua Barney. By the end of May, the last anyone at Oak Hill had heard was that the four schooners and one gunboat were patroling the bay between Annapolis and the Potomac River. They were all privately owned boats, captained by United States naval officers and extremely patriotic. They were also no match for the English fleet headed their way.

Closing her eyes, Charlotte whispered a short prayer for Jon. But when her lashes lifted, she realized she had more pressing and personal problems. One of the ships had broken away from the others and was heading toward the mouth of the Manakin—the river that bordered Oak Hill.

Cilla noticed it, too, and together they turned their horses in a tight circle, sending sandy soil flying as they galloped toward the plantation.

Since early spring word had spread throughout the bay of the British atrocities. Admiral Cockburn had raided the islands of the Chesapeake. He'd burned the towns of Havre de Grace, Georgetown, and Fredericktown. And all along the way, the British fleet had sacked and pillaged plantations.

"Thank God, you're back!" Elizabeth Knox rushed down the porch steps as Charlotte and Cilla raced into the yard.

"British ships are heading up the river," Charlotte yelled as she slid from the saddle.

"We know." Elizabeth hugged Charlotte and then Cilla. "Word came to us, but we didn't know where you were. Come." She hurried them into the house.

Charlotte paused in the doorway to the front parlor to watch Alexander Knox load his gun. "You can't be thinking of fighting them." Her voice rose almost hysterically.

Alex looked up, his face grim. "I fought the British in the first Revolutionary War, and by God, I'll fight them in the second." His voice lowered. "Don't worry, Charlotte, I'm not going to do anything foolish."

But as Charlotte climbed the stairs she wondered what he considered foolish. She couldn't imagine Alexander Knox standing idly by while the British destroyed his home.

*Maybe they won't stop here.* But even as she thought it, Charlotte feared the worse.

"I can't believe this," Cilla moaned, her balled-up fist clinched against her mouth. "British soldiers at Oak Hill. If you'd only heard the stories my father can tell about the first war." She stood at the window watching the cloud of dust settle around the regiment of marines marching up from the river. "Awful." She shook her head. "But even then, they never came here."

"Hush now, Priscilla." Elizabeth pulled her daughter from the bedroom window. "I want you and Charlotte to stay here."

"Where are you doing?" Charlotte was frightened, and as unbelievable as it seemed, of British soldiers. Somehow it didn't seem right, yet she couldn't help it.

"Downstairs with Major Knox," Elizabeth answered, closing the door behind her.

Charlotte glanced at Cilla. "My father was a major in the last war."

Peeking through the curtains Charlotte saw the officer at the head of the column of men stop and hail to the house. His straight-legged pants gleamed in the sunlight, and he stared straight ahead, as did the men behind him. They were British soldiers, like her father, and Charlotte wondered that she felt no surge of patriotism at the sight. She was on American soil, an innocent bystander to this war, but certainly her loyalties were clear. Weren't they?

As she watched, Alexander Knox, with Elizabeth beside him, stepped through the door. Alarm shot down Charlotte's spine. These were the people who'd been so kind to her. The people she'd grown to love.

They stood tall and intrepid in the shadow of their home, but they were two against many. And though Alexander cradled a rifle in his arms, it meant nothing. The sweep of Charlotte's gaze across the armed marines proved that.

An officer stepped forward, a lieutenant, and Charlotte pressed her nose to the wavery glass.

"Are you Alexander Knox?" The question, spoken in a clipped military accent, drifted through the open window.

"I am. And you're trespassing on my property."

"We've come to buy horses. I understand you raise the best around." Charlotte saw the British lieutenant glance toward the barn and the stable beyond.

"I've none for sale," Alexander replied, his eyes steady. Charlotte felt a renewed prickle of fear.

"I'm authorized to pay Philadelphia prices."

"I've none for sale."

"Or take what I need." The British officer's tone

turned harsh.

"What's happening?" Cilla stood behind Charlotte, her hands pressed tight to her waist.

"They want horses." Charlotte glanced back at Cilla. "And your father refuses to sell—" Both girls gasped as a shot rang out, then another. Grabbing her skirt, Charlotte ran toward the door, shaking off Cilla's hand when it clutched at her.

"No! Charlotte don't go down there. Mother said to . . ."

But Charlotte heard no more as she flew down the stairs. The shots had stopped, but as she threw open the door and ran into the yard, a pistol muzzle swung up toward her. Now it was Elizabeth screaming *no* as she jumped up to block Charlotte. "She'll do you no harm," the older woman yelled, pushing Charlotte back toward the porch.

But Charlotte skirted her protector and faced the marine lieutenant. Her eyes dropped from his pistol to Alexander Knox sprawled on the grass by the front walk. Elizabeth had dropped down beside him, and was frantically stuffing her shawl against a wound on his right side. Blood seeped through, turning the paisley crimson, and Charlotte fought the urge to be sick, or worse yet, run.

"Are you their daughter?"

The marine lieutenant's words pulled Charlotte's attention away from Alexander and his wife, and she almost said yes. But her mind's eye still saw Elizabeth tending her wounded husband and she cringed at what else might happen. Already all but a small contingent of men had dispersed, and Charlotte could hear the whinnying horses as they were dragged from their stalls. She whipped her head around to see another group building a huge fire near the stables. They fed the flames straw and almost anything else they could drag from the outbuildings. All the marines moved methodically, efficiently, destructively.

"I asked if you were one of their daughters." This time the lieutenant's hand clamped about her arm.

"Leave her alone." Alexander Knox leaned on his wife, attempting to rise, and Charlotte jerked her arm free of the British officer.

"No!" she yelled. "You must stop this at once."

Now it was Elizabeth who reached for her, but Charlotte would have none of it. "Stop this, I say." The sickening smell of burning leather wafted her way, and Charlotte clutched the marine's jacket. "These people do not deserve this."

The marine tried to shove her aside and called for a subordinate to take her away, but Charlotte clutched tighter. "I'm not their daughter." Her words seemed to have no effect on the man. He pushed at her, obviously embarrassed by her display, and just as obviously wanting her gone, but she held on. He was young, his eyes a vivid green, and it struck Charlotte that at another time she might find him pleasing to the eye. But now he was ordering the destruction of the place she'd learned to love and she couldn't allow it. Marines moved toward the house, burning brands held high above their heads. Charlotte looked behind her and saw Cilla and the house servants being herded from the building.

"My father is General Winston of the Forty-ninth Foot Regiment." Charlotte blurted out the words.

A flicker of recognition crossed the lieutenant's eyes, and he ceased pushing her hands away, but he still did nothing to stop his men.

Charlotte took a deep breath and continued. The last time she'd admitted her relationship to the British military, it had caused her nothing but trouble. But this was different. She had a fleeting thought of what Charlotte and Elizabeth might think, but she couldn't let that stop her. "I'm the betrothed of Captain Matthew Levid." Certainly the lieutenant had heard of him. Every living soul on the bay had heard of him. Levid was one of Admiral Cockburn's captains, and his name had become synonymous with destruction among the Americans.

The lieutenant's eyes narrowed, and now it was he clutching her, his hands around her upper arms dragging her closer. "What are you saying?"

"It's true," Charlotte insisted, though she wasn't entirely sure. Who knew what Levid and her father had done once they discovered her missing—along with Captain Knox. "I'm Charlotte Winston. My father is in Montreal, and I'm engaged to marry Captain Levid. I was kidnapped in Montreal—" Elizabeth's gasp of surprise stopped her momentarily. "Not by these people. The Knoxes took me in. They're taking care of me until I can return to England."

The marine's fingers loosened, and he set Charlotte aside, his eyes raking down her slender form. Charlotte could see the doubts begin, so she rushed ahead giving them no time to form. "This family has been good to me. They've protected me, taken me in. You can't destroy their farm." Her voice was pleading, and a sudden insight told her that was not the way to handle this. She stiffened her shoulders. "My father, General Winston, would not want them harmed in any way." Her gaze traveled from Alexander, who now stood, stooped against his wife, then back to the lieutenant.

He flushed, his ruddy complexion darkening. Pointing to Alexander, he began, "He refused—"

"Wouldn't you?" Charlotte insisted. "But that

isn't the point. Captain Levid's displeasure is. And you can be assured, Lieutenant, he shall hear of this."

Charlotte had never considered herself a forceful person. The one other time she'd tried to use the name of her father and Captain Levid to intimidate someone, it had blown up in her face. Captain Knox had despised her for the relationship. But the British marine lieutenant did not.

He hesitated only a moment before calling out an order. His men withdrew from around the house. The others ransacking the barn ceased. "We're still taking the horses," the lieutenant informed her, his mouth grim.

"Philadelphia prices seems fair," Charlotte responded, surprised again at her boldness. She should be thankful that Oak Hill was spared the torch, but she couldn't stand to see the fine horses Jonathan's family had bred just taken.

At least with the money—if they got the money— they could replenish their stock. Besides, the murderous glint in Alexander Knox's eyes hadn't subsided, and even though his wound forced him to lean against his wife, Charlotte was afraid he might try something foolish if the British just took his horses. She chanced a glimpse at him, revising her assessment. He might try something foolish even if the British paid him for the horses.

The thought made her step forward. "You did offer Philadelphia prices, didn't you?"

The lieutenant's mouth tightened, but he nodded. Motioning for Alexander to follow, he marched toward the house. Cilla ran to her father's side and, together, she and Elizabeth helped him into the house. Charlotte could hear him muttering something about tearing the lobsterback limb from limb, but she also heard Elizabeth's words counseling restraint, and gave a sigh of relief.

Whatever the reason, his wife's words or his own realization that further resistance would be futile, Alexander negotiated with the lieutenant.

As Charlotte sat, straight-backed on a settee beside Cilla, she had no way of knowing if the price they settled on was fair. Certainly Alexander's murderous expression held no answer.

When the lieutenant finally stood, he moved toward Charlotte's side and asked her to join him in the hallway. Again, Charlotte was struck by his wholesome good looks and pleasant demeanor. If not for the war, he probably would be an ideal companion, but as it was, she hated him for what he'd put the Knox family through.

His manner as he guided her down the porch stairs was solicitous, and when he spoke, his voice was gentle. "I think it best that you come with us."

"And why is that?" His words took her by surprise. Not that leaving Oak Hill hadn't been something she'd considered since she blurted out her identity, but not with him.

The lieutenant's expression was incredulous. "This place is a hotbed of Yankee barbarism."

He looked so serious, Charlotte had to stifle a smile. "I don't imagine their conception of you is very flattering, either." The marine's scowl deepened, and Charlotte continued. "These people have been very kind—"

"So you said. However, I think it best you come with me. I can deliver you to Captain Levid."

"No." Charlotte realized her denial was too swift and definite, but the last thing she wanted was to be delivered to Captain Levid. "He is too busy to be bothered with me now," she countered, hoping he couldn't hear the way her heart pounded in her chest.

"I'm certain he doesn't approve of your circumstances."

"Oh, but he does." How easy it had become for her to lie. "He is quite familiar with the Knoxes, and knows where I am."

"I thought you said you were kidnapped?" The lieutenant's eyes narrowed.

"I was." Goodness, just because she could lie easily didn't make her good at it. Now what could she tell him? "I *was* kidnapped. But I escaped and came here because my betrothed . . . and father knew them, and I've gotten word to Matthew Levid." Charlotte swallowed. "He suggested I stay here." She swallowed again, realizing how difficult it was with her mouth so dry. "He knows where I am."

The British lieutenant studied her a long moment and Charlotte wondered if he could detect any sign that she was lying—outside of her farfetched story. She let out a sigh of relief when he turned and ordered his men to form ranks. Turning back to Charlotte, his eyes still harboring a skeptical gleam, he bowed. "I shall give your regards to your betrothed and tell him you're well."

Charlotte bit her lip to keep from screaming for him to forget he ever saw her, but instead she smiled and thanked him.

By the time the marines left, leading a string of Oak Hill's finest horses, Charlotte felt taut as a wire. Cilla touched her arm as she stood on the porch watching the dust settle, and Charlotte jumped.

"Why didn't you tell me?"

All manner of explanations streamed through her mind, but the truth was she'd been afraid to, and that's what Charlotte told Cilla.

"Afraid? I don't understand."

Charlotte glanced over her shoulder, then sat down

on the porch step. "You all treated me so well." She paused and took a deep breath. "I didn't think you'd . . . For heaven's sake . . ." She pulled up her knees, resting her chin on the angle. "Your country is at war with mine."

"But not with you, Charlotte." Cilla sat down beside her. "Is it true? Are you going to marry that butcher Levid?"

Charlotte shook her head, her chin rubbing the soft fabric. "No, I'm not going to marry him. But I was betrothed to him once, before . . ."

"My God."

These words had Charlotte staring at her friend who'd grown pale, her blue-gray eyes wide in her face.

"You were abducted." Cilla's hand fluttered to her mouth when Charlotte nodded. "By Jon?" This time Charlotte made no sign to admit or deny Cilla's words.

"But why? Why would Jon do that?"

"Oh, Cilla, it's so complicated." She couldn't tell Cilla about her brother Christopher, and truthfully didn't know what to say and what to leave out. "He didn't have much choice at the time."

"Well, he's going to have some explaining to do the next time he comes home." Cilla stood, brushing off her skirts. "I'm going in to see how Father's doing."

"Wait, Cilla." Charlotte rose and scrambled across the porch. "Let me explain to your parents. And please don't be too hard on Jon."

"For your sake I won't." Cilla went inside, leaving Charlotte alone with her thoughts.

There was no question now that she had to leave. Captain Levid would know her whereabouts, and though she had no misconceptions about his feelings for her, she also assumed he'd want revenge for her part in Jonathan Knox's escape.

She had to leave immediately, and Washington City across the bay seemed the logical place to go. Perhaps from there she could get to Canada, or, better yet, home to England. With this decision made she turned toward the door, pausing, her hand on the latch, when she heard a horse galloping up the lane.

The rider was as winded as his mount and barely paused as he wheeled the horse around. "The damn British torched the Brown place downriver!"

Cilla was beside her before the messenger disappeared from view. Charlotte turned, grabbing Cilla's hand. "He said the Brown place was set afire."

"My God, Libby!"

"We must do something." Charlotte began to shake, and tried hard to pull herself together. She hadn't even thought about the British going farther upstream to the next plantation—to Libby and Edward Brown's plantation. She started running toward the stables. "I'll see if there's anything left to hitch to a wagon. Tell your mother I'm taking William and Sam with me to fetch Libby and the girls."

Cilla protested as Charlotte knew she would, but paying her no mind, Charlotte entered the stables. She found the two freed black men who worked with the horses, cleaning up the harness and grain the British had tossed on the floor.

The stalls were empty, but Charlotte noticed a few horses, too old for military use, were still in the paddock. "Hitch the two best we have left to the wagon," Charlotte ordered. Later, climbing up in the seat beside Sam, with William in the back, they started out the lane.

By the time they reached the main road that ran

alongside the river, they were met by another rider coming from the east. He pulled up beside the wagon and tipped his hat to Charlotte. "I was just heading over to the Knox place to see how they fared. We got nothing but destruction down that way." He motioned behind him with a jerk of his chin.

Again Charlotte cringed at what the British had done. "Alexander is wounded, but I think he will be all right. They took almost all the horses."

"Don't doubt it. Admiral Cockburn's been all up and down this bay looting and burning. Damn water Winnebagoes!"

Charlotte nodded, coming to understand why the British detachment under Cockburn was nicknamed after a ruthless Indian tribe. "We're heading to the Brown plantation. We heard they were burned out."

"Yeah." The rider wiped a weary hand across his brow. "So were the Adams and the Criswells." He steadied his horse. "Keep an eye out. The English called for slaves to run away from their masters and join him." His gaze strayed to the two black men with Charlotte.

"Oak Hill has no slaves," she responded, then signaled for Sam to proceed.

"All the same you be watchful. I understand Captain Levid is still in the area."

"What?" Charlotte's hand stilled Sam as he flicked the reigns. She felt the color drain from her face, and knew the rider saw it, too. He leaned over his pummel and stared at her.

"'Twas Butcher Levid himself who came ashore at the Criswells. The whole group of them were under his command. Two schooners from what I can figure."

"Y-yes. I saw them earlier, but I didn't know it was his vessel."

"Lawrence Criswell said he marched up to the house as big as you please, demanding corn and meat for his men, then burned everything he couldn't take." He paused. "You sure you're all right? You're looking a bit pale."

"No, I'm fine. I have to get over to the Browns. Is someone helping the Criswells and Adams?"

"Yes. They're going inland to stay with Lawrence's sister."

Woodmore, the Brown's plantation, was worse than Charlotte imagined. Libby Knox Brown and her two daughters were out front under a giant elm, and Charlotte jumped down from the wagon seat before Sam could come around to help her.

Libby embraced her, and Sarah and Rebecca clung to her skirt. "Oh, Charlotte, they burned everything . . . everything. Edward couldn't stop them."

"It will be all right." Charlotte felt silly offering the hollow words, especially when she glanced about to see only the chimneys of the house standing, but she could think of nothing else.

"I hate them, Charlotte. I hate the British!"

"I know." Charlotte's hand soothed Libby's hair. What she didn't know was how Libby, how any of them, would react once they knew all about her.

"Oh, my God, Oak Hill. I didn't even ask." Libby pulled away, wiping her eyes on the back of her hand. "My parents? Cilla?"

"Elizabeth and Cilla are fine. Your father was shot—"

"Oh, no."

"But it isn't too serious. He's going to be all right."

Libby sank onto the soft grass, and Charlotte put her arms around the girls.

"And the house?"

"It's fine. They didn't burn anything." Charlotte

ignored Libby's questioning glance. "They did take all the horses, though. Except for these." Charlotte motioned toward the sway-backed horses hitched to the wagon. "Why don't you let me take you back to Oak Hill?"

"I shouldn't leave Edward."

"You're all going to need a place to sleep tonight. I'll wait till you're all ready to leave."

It was dusk before they headed back along the river road toward Oak Hill. Edward decided to stay so that he could start work first thing the next morning, but he insisted his wife and daughters go to Oak Hill. "I've slept out under the stars before," he told a weeping Libby. "See if your father can spare any men." As with many of the plantations in the area, most of Woodmore's slaves had run to the British and promises of freedom.

When they arrived at Oak Hill, Charlotte found Elizabeth in the parlor. Alexander, she was told, was resting. The bullet had only grazed his side, and though he was in pain, she expected a quick recovery.

Both Elizabeth and Cilla were very sweet, and thanked Charlotte again and again for going to Woodmore and bringing Libby and the girls home. They lamented with Libby about the burning of her plantation, and cursed the British. But they didn't say one word about the reason Oak Hill hadn't been burned. Nor did they mention Charlotte's connection with the enemy.

Yet it was all Charlotte could think about. Alone in her room that night, she tossed and turned, finally rising to pace between the hearth and window. Except for the chance of fate, Captain Levid himself might have come to Oak Hill today. She couldn't believe how close she'd come to disaster. And how close she still was.

Surely the marine lieutenant would tell Captain Levid she was here. Would he come back? Charlotte bit her lip and sank into the window seat. She had no idea what he or her father thought of her disappearance from Montreal, but surely they connected it with Jonathan Knox's escape. And now to find her a guest at Jonathan's home . . .

Pressing her forehead against the cool windowpane, Charlotte searched the star-sprinkled sky. What would Levid do to Jon's family if he returned? What would he do to her?

Jonathan Knox had come home.

Charlotte sat in the orchard, watching Libby's daughters chase butterflies, wondering if the rest of the family thought her rude that she didn't go into the house to greet him.

He'd heard about the carnage on the river, and sailed a small shallop to the dock this morning. Sarah had informed Charlotte, her tone serious, that he could only stay till the tide turned, for the *Revenge* was in danger of being trapped if they didn't stay in the bay. That had been hours ago, and Charlotte wondered if he'd gone yet when she sensed someone watching her.

Turning, she saw him, tall and dark, standing in the shadow of an apple tree. He looked so handsome, and Charlotte wondered if one of her secret wishes last night as she'd gazed upon the heavens was to see him once more. She flushed, her hands dropping to her side.

"Are you hiding from me, Charlotte?"

"No." The word was barely above a whisper, but Sarah and Rebecca heard her, and, spotting their uncle, gave up their game to run to him.

"Play with us, please," they cajoled, clutching his hands and making him laugh. But he shook his head, giving them each a squeeze.

"Not now. Run and play. I need to talk with Charlotte." Rebecca skipped away, but Sarah tried one more time, looking up at him, her eyes wide.

"Just chase after us once, Uncle Jon."

"Later maybe." Jon turned her around and patted her behind, sending her off in a fit of giggles to inform her sister that Uncle Jon would chase with them in a bit.

"You have a way with them," Charlotte said as she observed Jon watching his nieces. He turned, his eyes finding hers, Charlotte felt her knees weaken.

"Walk with me," he said, taking her hand.

"I can't leave the girls."

"We'll keep them in sight."

What could she do? In truth, she'd go with him anywhere. But that wasn't what he was asking. They wandered through the apple trees, skirting the bees that hovered about the ripening fruit. When they were out of earshot of the children, Jon stopped.

"Mother told me all that happened here," he said.

"I suppose they hate me."

"Hate you?" Jon's expression was incredulous. "Hell, Charlotte, you saved their home."

Not knowing what to say to that, Charlotte remained silent.

"They don't hate you, Charlotte. You surprised them, sure enough. Though Mother said neither of them had believed the story I'd given about you." Jon laughed and leaned his arm against the tree trunk. "They didn't have any trouble accepting that I abducted you."

"You told them that?"

Jon nodded, grinning at her expression. "I told

them the whole story."

"Everything?" Charlotte felt color flood her face.

"Well no, not everything." Jon cleared his throat. "But I did explain how you happened to be here." He paused. "And why I think you should leave."

Charlotte stopped shredding a serrated leaf and looked up. "You're right. I don't belong here."

"You don't belong here with Levid in the neighborhood," Jon corrected. His hand closed over her chin. "Unless you want to go with him?"

"You know I don't."

Jon let loose the breath he'd been holding. "Then I think you should go to Philadelphia. I have friends there who will be glad to keep you."

"Why are you doing this?" Charlotte had decided she'd gladly go with him anywhere, but sending her off to an American city wasn't the same thing. She knew what motivated her, but he was a different story. He was spurred on by revenge, of course. He made no attempt to suppress that from her. And patriotism. He loved his country and was willing to lay down his life for it. But what about her? Why did he care what became of her, put himself out for her?

"Why?" She wanted to know why, and he couldn't tell her. He lay awake nights, watching the lantern sway above his head, contemplating the same question. Why did he think of her constantly? Why, when he heard of Levid's raid, did his imagination dwell on visions of Charlotte boarding the Englishman's ship . . . willingly.

At great risk to himself he'd rushed home, partly to relieve his mind about his family, true. But also he'd come to assure himself that Charlotte was safe, that she still waited for him.

But that was no reason, so he gave her the one he'd used on himself. "I feel responsible for you."

"You needn't." Charlotte reached up to snatch a swaying leaf.

"Hell, Charlotte, I abducted you from Montreal, brought you here . . ." Jon paused. He wasn't about to bring up the main reason he felt responsible for her. He told her before that he wouldn't apologize for making love to her, but that didn't mean he didn't feel guilty about taking away her innocence. Even knowing she'd wanted him to didn't help. He'd pushed her all along.

His head dropped and he stared at his boot tips. "I owe you my protection."

Owe. Charlotte nearly cringed at the word. As it was, she barely kept her voice level. "You don't owe me anything." She knew what he was thinking. The abduction, his dragging her across the country, didn't mean a thing to him. He'd been desperate, his country was at war, and Charlotte had no doubt he'd do the same thing again if the need arose.

But making love to her, that was different. That had nothing to do with patriotic duty. That was an offense he thought needed amends . . . something he owed her for.

Jon's eyes shot up to meet hers. He raked his fingers back through his dark hair, his expression wary. "I don't have time to discuss this with you now, Charlotte."

Charlotte's brow lifted at his autocratic tone, but he ignored it, continuing his speech. "I'm leaving gold coin for you inside. Please take it with you, and use what you need. Hell, use all of it—I don't care."

"I don't want your money," Charlotte said, only to have her words ignored as well.

"I'll get a message to my friend in Philadelphia and he'll come for you . . . hopefully within a sennight."

He stopped and Charlotte folded her arms across her chest, feeling heat rise within her when the motion caused his gaze to drop. "Is that all?" she asked, her head cocked to the side.

Jon mimicked her pose. "I think so."

Fighting the urge to stomp her foot, Charlotte met his stare. She'd known he was arrogant, but this . . . "And how long am I to remain in Philadelphia? Until I return to England?"

Her last question was a risk, and she knew it. Charlotte couldn't fathom why she'd asked it except . . . Except she wanted him to say he didn't want her to go back to England. But he didn't. "Possibly" was all he said. Though his jaw clenched shut so tightly she could see a muscle in his cheek jump, he let his eyes drift out to where the girls chased a yellow butterfly.

"It's settled then," he said.

Charlotte looked up to see him staring at her, his expression unreadable. He stood, his hands clasped behind his back, and she wanted more than anything to melt into him. But she didn't. Instead she stiffened her shoulders. "Yes, I suppose it is," she answered, though she had no intention of going to Philadelphia.

# Chapter Nineteen

But that hadn't been all there was to it.

Charlotte pressed her forehead against the chilled glass and watched through the gathering dusk as spring rain drizzled into the muddy, puddled Washington City street. It was damp and dreary, and had been for days. Damp and dreary . . . and lonely.

But just closing her eyes could change all that. Charlotte's lashes lowered and she smelled the sweet fragrance of apples, heard children's laughter . . . saw Jonathan Knox as he looked that morning nearly nine months ago.

He'd stood so tall before her, his long, muscular legs encased in white breeches, his shoulders broad beneath the dark blue double-breasted jacket. A whirlwind breeze tousled his close-cropped raven hair and rustled the treetop leaves, sending rays of sunshine dancing across his face. His eyes were bluer than the backdrop of sky, and they held her in their spell until he turned on his heel, heading back toward the house.

Charlotte's breath had caught on a sigh as she'd followed his movements, the animal grace of his stride, knowing it was the last time she'd see him.

She'd had no intentions, even then, of going to Philadelphia.

He saw her as a responsibility, a problem needing to be solved, and she couldn't bear that.

He'd taken perhaps ten steps away from her along the crushed-shell path that led through the trees when he stopped. Charlotte didn't have time to wonder why when he turned, and more quickly than before covered the ground separating them.

Her gasp of surprise died on her lips as he clutched her against his hard body in a breathtaking embrace. One arm bound her waist, the other her shoulder as his large hand steadied the back of her head for his onslaught.

The kiss exploded onto her senses. No gentle prelude to passion, no shy do-you-want-me-kiss. His lips had demanded, his tongue, thrusting deep, parlaying with hers, had conquered. And she'd melted into him.

Her bones had turned to mush, and an overpowering ache had grown deep in her being. Later, Charlotte wondered what she'd have done if he'd dropped with her to the sweet grass and tried to make love to her. Surely she'd have stopped him with the children near by. But at the time she never even considered it. There was nothing in the world for her at that moment but him, and the feelings he inspired.

His lean, hard body, rigid with desire, the smell of his hair, and his taste. Still, after months away from him, she had only to close her eyes to taste him.

Charlotte's eyes sprang open. This was foolish—worse than foolish. Before, when Jon was but a fleeting image of a faraway pirate, she was able to control her daydreams. Maybe most of the time she chose not to, but it was there—the knowledge that she could.

But now she felt completely at the mercy of her

imagination, and her cruel mind would give her no peace from Jon.

"You must find a way to return to England," Charlotte mumbled to herself as she turned back into the room—the room where she'd lived for the past nine months. It was orderly and neat, with sunny yellow damask drapes and bedhanging, and a fireplace that took the damp chill off the spring day. She'd been lucky to find this boardinghouse on Pennsylvania Avenue, luckier still that Mrs. Peters, a widow with a soft heart for a stranded girl, ran it.

Because Charlotte *had* been stranded when she'd arrived in Washington City after her trip from Oak Hill. Armed with her resolve to burden Jon no longer, she'd questioned the Knoxes' servants until she'd found the name of a man who might ferry someone across the bay—for a price. Of course they'd had no idea she was asking for herself. But she'd contacted the man and arranged to meet him before Jon's friend could arrive to take her to Philadelphia.

More than once, as she sneaked out of the house at Oak Hill, and then crossed the bay in the leaky sloop, Charlotte had wondered about her sanity. Sometimes she still did.

Though her existence here was comfortable, Charlotte feared the only way to regain her peace of mind was to leave this war-torn country and return to the solitude of her home in Oxfordshire. She refused to believe she'd be even more lonely there.

But how to get to England was the big problem. There was certainly no nautical intercourse between America and England. More to the point American shipping was at a standstill. The English fleet had the Chesapeake Bay bottled up with a blockade that none but the luckiest privateer could run. And at this point in her life Charlotte didn't feel lucky enough to

343

try that. Besides, once into the waters of the Atlantic, the privateer certainly wouldn't set a course for England.

But perhaps there *was* a way.

Glancing once more at the note clutched in her hand, Charlotte laid it on the mahogany night stand beside a book she'd been reading. The *Life of Wellington* it was called, and though it was interesting, the text failed to hold her attention for long. *But tonight, when I return from the reception, I'll finish it,* Charlotte vowed to herself. Anything was preferable to letting her imagination run free.

Closing the door behind her, Charlotte descended the stairs. Three others shared the boardinghouse with Charlotte and Mrs. Peters. Two were men, brothers who ran a bookstore on Pennsylvania Avenue. They were jovial, interesting conversationalists; Charlotte secretly decided they read every book before they sold it—and they kept Charlotte supplied with the latest releases. *Life of Wellington* was a gift from them. "Something to remind you of home," they'd said on the accompanying card.

They, along with the other residents, a Mrs. Simpson, knew of Charlotte's desire to return to England. And even though their countries were at war, none of them seemed to hold it against Charlotte. Actually she'd run up against very little hatred of the British in Washington. Even Mrs. Simpson, whose husband was with Perry on the Great Lakes, seemed unaffected. And the Gordon brothers assured her that despite the war, *Life of Wellington* was selling very well.

"Oh there you are, dear."

Charlotte turned to see Abigail Peters emerge from her upstairs rooms. She was wrapped in a long, fringed shawl, and her gray curls were covered by a nightcap. "What's wrong, Mrs. Peters?" The face of the normally robust woman appeared flushed by fever and she leaned heavily against the doorframe as Charlotte rushed back up the stairs.

"It's nothing really." The older woman brushed away Charlotte's concern with a flick of her lace-trimmed handkerchief. "Just a touch of fever. No honestly, child, I don't need any help."

"Nonsense. You should be in bed." Charlotte led her back into the room, rushing ahead to turn down the coverlet. "Would you like me to send for a doctor?"

"No, no." Abigail sighed. "I'm sure that isn't necessary. I really do think this will pass soon." She settled her considerable bulk onto the mattress. "But I'm just sorry about tonight. I meant to tell you earlier, but I'm afraid I fell asleep."

"Tonight? Oh, you mean the drawing-room reception?" Charlotte tucked the covers under Mrs. Peters' chins.

"Yes, I won't be able to go with you as we'd planned."

Charlotte thought of the note on her bedside table. "It can't be helped. Your health is more important."

"But I know how you were looking forward to tonight," Abigail sniffed.

Charlotte could see the note as clearly as if it were in her hands. *I've a wonderful surprise for you. I will give it to you Wednesday night. See you then. Dolley.* "Please don't think any more about it."

"But the note from Mrs. Madison. You hoped she was able to arrange passage for you to England."

"If she has, I can find out about it another time. Let me ring for some tea."

"But what if Mr. Skinner could only arrange a prisoner trade for you at this time. You may be stuck here forever."

Charlotte chuckled, though she really didn't feel very lighthearted. Much of what Mrs. Peters said might be true. "You act as if you can't wait to be rid of me."

"Oh, never that, child." Her plump hand covered Charlotte's. "I just know how unhappy you are."

"I'm not really . . ." Charlotte couldn't bring herself to deny it. Though she didn't reveal this to her landlady, the cause of her unhappiness was not homesickness.

Jon.

An image of him came into her mind, and her eyes drifted shut, only to open again almost immediately. "I shall go to the President's house alone."

"Oh, no. I couldn't allow that." Abigail hefted her shoulders up. "I'll get up and dress."

"Don't be silly." Charlotte pushed her back into the pillows. "You're ill. And besides, there should be no problem with going alone." Charlotte wished she felt as confident as she sounded. Charlotte tapped her rounded fingernail against her front teeth. "Yes, it will be fine. I won't stay long—only until I can discover what Dolley's surprise is."

"I don't know." Abigail's small eyes were wary, but Charlotte saw her wavering.

"Believe me, there'll be no trouble."

"Do you think the President's wife can arrange for you to go back to England?" Abigail asked through her handkerchief.

"If anyone can do it, she can." Charlotte bent forward and hugged Abigail's shoulders. "I can't thank you enough for introducing me to her."

"Oh, posh." Abigail waved her handkerchief. "You know I enjoy going to her receptions. Taking you along just assured me attention from all the handsome young men.''

A soft rose blush colored Charlotte's cheeks. "Don't be silly. 'Twas you they swarmed around.'' This made Abigail laugh, and Charlotte joined in. Much to Charlotte's surprise, she *had* attracted the attention of several young men at the Wednesday drawing rooms socials she'd attended. Not that she cared. There was only one man who haunted her dreams.

As she'd hoped, her trip to the President's house was uneventful. The roads were wet and rutted from the earlier rain, the only vestige of which was a mist rising slowly about the poplar trees that lined Pennsylvania Avenue. The evening was exceptionally chilly for May, and Abigail had insisted Charlotte borrow her redingote. The long coat nearly wrapped around Charlotte twice, but she appreciated its warmth as she sank back into the gig lent her by the Gordon brothers.

President's Square across the street from Madison's house was dark. Charlotte couldn't see any of the militia, but assumed they were there . . . even on an evening such as this. They passed between the twin giant eagles guarding the drive, then waited in a line of coaches in front of the President's house.

Dolley Madison loved to entertain, and no invitation was needed for her Wednesday drawing room socials. It was the place to see and be seen, and apparently many residents of Washington City felt they needed a bit of entertainment on this particular Wednesday evening.

The mansion was bright with candlelight. Charlotte alighted from the gig, and as French John, the majordomo, took her coat, she immediately missed the warmth. Brushing the wrinkles from her gown, Charlotte hoped not too many people would notice it was the same one she wore last week, and the week before that. She'd had it made when Abigail Peters suggested the drawing room socials would be a good way to meet people who could help her return to England.

Charlotte hated to part with the coin the gown had cost, and though it was made as cheaply and simply as possible, it had still come dear. The supply of money Jon left for her at Oak Hill was quickly dwindling—of course he hadn't planned on her expenses to cross the bay and her room and board in Washington City—and Charlotte worried what she'd do when it was gone. The idea of offering herself as a governess had entered her mind recently and she had inquired of Mrs. Peters how to proceed with that. One thing she would *not* do was ask for more money from Jonathan Knox!

Not that he'd give it to her, Charlotte thought as she walked along the baronial hall with its great pillars. If he discovered she hadn't gone to his friends in Philadelphia, which he most assuredly had, he'd be furious.

"Which is fine with me," Charlotte mumbled under her breath. He was better off rid of her, and she . . . she was better off rid of *him*.

Sighing, Charlotte plastered a bright smile to her lips as the drawing-room doors opened. If only she *could* be rid of him.

The oval drawing room was magnificent, and as with each time she entered it, Charlotte paused to appreciate its splendor. Even with the crush of people inside, it appeared large. Tall windows at one end, framed by red velvet drapes, looked out over the terrace to the river below. Delicately curved chairs and sofas cushioned with the same red velvet were placed invitingly about the room.

348

Sitting on one of the chairs, leaning toward a gentleman who was talking, Charlotte noticed Dolley Madison. Dressed in a pink silk gown with matching turban, her dark curls peeking from beneath, she looked every bit the charming hostess. Charlotte gave her a small smile when she looked up, and was surprised to see the President's wife excuse herself from a group of admirers and head her way.

"I'm so glad you could come," Dolley said, taking Charlotte's mitted hands in hers. "But you're late," she chastised. "I'd all but given up on you."

"Mrs. Peters is down with a touch of influenza, and I wasn't certain I should come."

"Oh dear, nothing serious, I hope."

"No," Charlotte said. "I'm certain she just needs a little bed rest."

Dolley linked her arm through Charlotte's. "That's good. But please keep me informed if she should get worse. You know Jemmy had bilious fever last summer, so I'm quite knowledgeable about nursing the sick back to health. Come say hello to him now and then . . ." She cocked her head and smiled. "Then we must get to your surprise."

So soon? Charlotte had feared she'd have to wait until far into the evening before Dolley got around to telling her what it was. But even knowing she'd find out so quickly didn't appease Charlotte's curiosity. "Have you managed to get me an audience with Mr. Skinner?" John S. Skinner was the American negotiating with the British for a prisoner exchange—an exchange Charlotte hoped to be part of.

"Now, now," Dolley admonished as she led Charlotte through the throng of smiling people. "Don't be so impatient. I shan't make you wait much longer."

But because so many wanted to speak with the

vivacious President's wife it was much later when they again approached the door to the hallway. Charlotte had curtsied to the President and asked politely about his health. She'd also spoken with Sally Coles, Dolley's cousin. And through it all she wondered what the surprise could be.

"This way," Dolley said when they managed to make it into the hallway. "Goodness, there are a lot of people in there."

Charlotte smfiled. "It's because everyone is charmed by you that they all come."

"Do you really think so?" Dolley said with mock seriousness, then laughed. "Well, I know why you came. Are you ready?"

Charlotte nodded, but again Dolley hesitated. "You really are lovely. Yes, I truly can believe he loves you."

"Who?" Charlotte asked, puzzled. But Dolley simply opened the door to her private sitting room. The room was dimly lit, the only illumination coming from a fire in the hearth and the silver candelabra on the mantel. The candlelight danced over the portrait of Dolley painted by Gilbert Stuart and across the delicate furnishings, but Charlotte could detect no surprise.

She started to turn back toward Dolley, who still stood in the hallway, when a movement in the shadows by the windows caught her eye.

A gasp caught in her throat, and her fingers fluttered to her breast as Jonathan Knox stepped into the light.

Jon's eyes widened, then narrowed as he stared at the woman in the doorway. The light from the hall shone behind her, forming an aura around her slim figure, obscuring her face from his view, but he had no doubt it was Charlotte. What he didn't know was

350

how she'd come to be here . . . with him.

He'd come tonight at Dolley Madison's request to speak with the President about Admiral Barney's flottilla, and immediately upon arrival he'd been ushered into this room—to await the President, he'd been told. What seemed like hours had passed, and he'd come close to leaving several times. But he hadn't, swallowing his own pride for the chance to persuade the President to reinforce Barney.

Now, instead of the President, Charlotte stood before him. All he could do was stare.

"I think I'll leave you two alone for a minute." Dolley shut the door behind her.

The soft click of the latch galvanized Jon to action. He strode forward, stopping within touching distance of Charlotte. He could see her clearly now. The delicate oval face, dominated by her large dark eyes, the porcelain skin now tinted a glowing pink by the fire, the soft, fine curls—all urged him to take the extra step. To touch.

But he didn't. Resolutely he clasped his hands behind his back. "It appears I've found you."

"Were you looking for me?"

"Looking?" Jon stared into her eyes. "No," he said. "Not really." The expectant expression that lit her face vanished at his denial. His untrue denial.

Jon thought of his anguish when he'd received the letter from his parents informing him she'd left Oak Hill before his friend arrived to take her to Philadelphia. Of the torment he'd suffered wondering what had become of her. He imagined her dead and awakened from the nightmare in a cold sweat. He imagined her alone and wanting him, and wished he were free to search for her. He imagined her safe back in England, clung to that hope, because it was the only one that gave him any peace of mind. But even though he'd hoped for that, he asked about her wherever he went.

He'd mentioned her to Dolley Madison, he realized. He'd been waiting to see the Secretary of the Navy and she had walked by. Graciously she'd paused to say a few words to him. They discovered they had a mutual friend, and they'd discussed several other young ladies of her acquaintance. And then he'd blurted it out. "Do you know of a Charlotte Winston?" he'd asked in what must have been a lovesick voice.

"Charlotte Winston?" She'd paused, pursing her lips. "Why do you wish to know?"

He'd meant to shrug off her question . . . but he hadn't. The truth, the truth that had amazed him as he said it, spilled forth.

At that moment, the door to the Secretary's office had opened, and Dolley had bid him good day. Jon realized she hadn't answered his question, but was sure the answer was no. Until now.

Jon's gaze dropped from Charlotte's face to the gentle slope of shoulders, tantalizingly bare, to the gown that hugged her firm breasts and molded in soft folds to the rest of her body. The sight of her excited him, but it also made him angry.

The gown was silk, pale pink and shimmering. The style was flattering, sensual, with embroidery about the low neckline and hem. She looked beautiful and fashionable, and totally at home. Hell, she even knew Dolley Madison.

All this time he was worrying, fearing the worst, she'd been in Washington City enjoying society. A new thought came to him and his jaw clenched. Was she involved with another man? Someone must be paying for her expensive gowns.

Jon turned away, toyed with a brass inkwell on the

small lady's desk. "You seem to have landed on your feet."

"My feet?" Charlotte wasn't yet over the shock of seeing him standing before her. She never thought to see him again, yet there he was looking more handsome than any memory she could conjure up. When he'd mentioned finding her, she'd allowed herself a wild moment of believing he might love her, but he'd dashed that hope. And now . . . now, no one could miss the scorn in his voice. "What do you mean by that?"

"Oh, nothing." He managed to pull his attention away from opening and snapping shut the inkwell lid long enough to glance her way. "It's just that I understand now why you didn't wish to go to Philadelphia. Though I believe they have, at times, a rather exciting social scene. Nothing like Washington City, though. You made a good choice."

Charlotte forgot the joy of seeing him, the pain of his rejection, as anger took over. Stepping toward him, hands on hips, she demanded, "What are you talking about?"

He looked up, his dark brows lifting as he threw his blatantly male white-clad thigh over the corner of the small desk. "I'm talking about our agreement that you'd go to Philadelphia, and the fact that you came here instead."

"I never agreed to go to Philadelphia." Charlotte's voice was low but steady.

"Well, I sure as hell thought you did!" Jon stood, slamming the lid down on the inkwell with a snap.

"That's because you've done nothing but control my life since I met you!" She was as angry as he and intended to let him know it.

"Control?"

"Yes, control." Charlotte walked past him, her

skirts swishing softly about her ankles. Stopping at the tall window, she stared out at the night sky.

Raking his fingers through his hair, Jon scowled in disbelief at her slender back. "Hell, Charlotte, I haven't had control over anything since I met you." He took a deep breath. "I think you're safe in Philadelphia, only to receive a post from my parents saying you left before my friend arrived. No one knows where in the hell you—"

"I left a note."

"A note!" Jon's tone was incredulous. "All it did was thank my family for their hospitality. You didn't even—"

"How's your father?" Charlotte glanced at Jon over her shoulder.

"He's fine. The wound healed nicely."

"I'm glad."

Jon blinked, then continued. "As I said, no one knew where you'd gone and I—"

"And your mother? Is she all right?"

"Yes." He bit the word out between clenched teeth. "What about—"

"They're fine, too. Damnit, Charlotte, we were talking about your running off and hiding—"

"I didn't," she said, whirling around to face him.

"Well, what in the hell do you call it?"

Charlotte twisted back toward the window. She didn't trust herself to look directly at him. "I came to Washington City to see if I could find a way back to England." His curse made her cheeks burn. She swallowed back tears. Now her anger was tinged with sadness. "Well, what did you expect me to do?" she asked his image in the wavery windowpanes. "I was nothing but a bother to you."

He stepped closer. She could feel the heat from his big body envelope her, forcing away the damp chill, as he stood behind her. "Who said you were a bother?"

"You did." Charlotte sniffed, angry at her lack of self-control. This was no time to cry. "And now you say I control your life, so I'd think you'd be happy that I left."

"I wasn't." Jon took a deep gulp of air. "Damnit, Charlotte, why did you leave me like that?"

"I . . . had to go someplace." Charlotte turned her head, that motion putting her face mere inches from his. She could clearly see the hard planes of his face, the deep cleft on his square chin. His blue eyes were shadowed by long dark lashes as he looked down at her, but Charlotte knew they watched her intently as he waited for a reason.

"Why, Charlotte?" His breath fluttered the wispy curls near her ears.

Charlotte swallowed. She couldn't tell him the real reason. She just couldn't. Unrequited love for him sounded so melodramatic, so embarrassing. Just the sort of response expected from a woman who'd lived her life through daydreams—before Jon.

"Was it because of Levid? Because of what he means to you?"

Charlotte could hear the intensity in his voice, feel the restrained force in his hands as they grasped the indentation of her waist. "No," she whispered, closing her eyes and facing back toward the window. "He means nothing to me. He never did."

"But you were—"

"Going to marry him," Charlotte finished. "Only because my father insisted. I didn't know Matthew Levid—had only met him once. At that time I found him distasteful. Later . . . later, I found him repugnant. I want no part of him."

"That still doesn't explain why you came here to

Washington City. Is returning to England that important to you?"

His large hands spread, the fingers reaching around and joining over Charlotte's stomach. She took a deep breath to steady herself, found it did no good.

"Is it, Charlotte?"

"No."

Hot, damp lips touched her shoulder as the echo of her denial hung in the air. With a rasp of shivery whiskers, they moved up the curve of her neck, pausing just below her ear. "Charlotte." His breath tickled the fine hairs on her nape.

"Hmm?" She couldn't help leaning back into him.

"Have you any idea the torment I went through when I discovered you were gone?"

Probably near the same anguish she'd felt in leaving him, Charlotte thought, but only shook her head. The motion scraped his lips higher, and he bit gently on her ear before tracing the swirl with his tongue.

"I never meant to hurt you."

"Then don't leave me again."

Charlotte's knees weakened, and if not for the strong hands that now traced down her stomach, locking her back against his thick, throbbing hardness, she'd have crumpled to the floor. The heel of his hand pressed against her and her legs shifted.

"Charlotte." His voice sounded breathless and husky as she twisted her face toward him. His kiss was deep and hot, searing her, demanding her response. Her tongue shot into his mouth and he held it captive, sucking, tasting it with his own.

His mouth left hers to burn a path down her cheek, and Charlotte bent her head, eyes closed, to savor his touch. She moved, pressing her bottom more firmly

356

against him, and he groaned. "God, Charlotte, I want you."

She wanted him, too—more than she'd ever thought possible. Her lashes fluttered open and she stared at their mirrored image in the window. She writhed, and he enveloped her, his strong arms bracketing her. One hand trailed up her body while the other palmed her breast. He closed over the silk clad mound, relearning the shape and weight of it. In the windowpane the reflection of his large, dark hand against her pastel gown was wildly erotic. He squeezed. He enticed till her nipples tightened and pushed painfully against her chemise.

Her eyes lifted, met his, and held. Together they watched the ballet of their straining bodies. Together they moved closer to the brink.

The tapping at the door didn't faze Charlotte at first, but when Jon's hand stopped moving over her and she felt him stiffen, her breath caught.

"Charlotte. Captain Knox." Dolley Madison's voice drifted in through the wedge of light as she opened the hall door. "Some of the other guests are asking for you."

"We'll be right there, Mrs. Madison." Jon's words were slightly husky, but as the door shut with a soft click, Charlotte turned in his arms.

"Oh, my God. I'd forgotten where I was."

Jon grinned down at her shocked expression. "You have the same affect on me." His finger touched her cheek. "But I suppose we'd better join the reception."

"But I can't." Charlotte was so shaken emotionally she was sure it must show. Certainly her eyes shone brighter, her skin glowed. She clasped her hands anxiously over her hot face. "Everyone will know," she whispered.

"You look fine." Jon dragged her over into the light from the candles. "More than fine. Beautiful." His lips brushed against hers, but he pulled back with a wry smile. "I better not start that again."

Jon helped her pin up a few honey-brown curls that had come free, and watched as she brushed out nonexistent wrinkles in her gown. When she seemed satisfied . . . or resigned . . . he held out his hand and they opened the door. Dolley stood admiring a painting in the hallway. She took Charlotte's arm, smiled up at Jon, suggesting he might want to step onto the porch for some air, and led Charlotte back to the drawing room.

To Charlotte it seemed like hours before Jon appeared again. Though she'd stayed by Dolley's side—or was it the other way around?—and spoken with many people, her eyes had stayed riveted to the drawing-room door. Charlotte was close to wondering if she'd imagined the entire episode in the sitting room, when he appeared. Taller than most of the men in the room and splendidly turned out in the tight white breeches and dark-blue double-breasted jacket of his uniform, he took her breath away.

He stood at the doorway a moment, his eyes scouring the room, before coming to rest on her. Charlotte felt her cheeks burn, but couldn't look away. *Couldn't,* that is, until Dolley turned her about, introducing her to the editor of the *National Intelligencer.*

By the time he had finished telling Charlotte his views on everything from the war to the price of flour, a quartet began playing a lively waltz, and several couples had claimed the center of the drawing-room floor to try the newest European dance. Charlotte heard Jon's voice and pivoted about, a smile of welcome on her lips. But though he stole glances at her, Jon bowed over Sally Coles's hand as Mrs. Madison introduced him as a hero of Tripoli and one of Commodore Barney's brave captains.

Charlotte watched Jon escort Mrs. Madison's cousin to the dance floor. "Don't look so crestfallen, Charlotte," Dolley said from behind her fan. "You will get your turn at him."

Charlotte's "turn" came nearly forty minutes later when Jon again returned to the group of ladies. This time he took no chances, coming up on Charlotte from the side and asking her for the dance before the President's wife could intervene.

"What is she trying to do?" Jon asked as he placed his gloved hand to the small of Charlotte's back. He didn't hold her one bit closer than manners dictated, yet he could feel the heat and desire in her body, felt his own tighten in response.

"I believe she's trying to avoid a scandal." Charlotte looked up at him and couldn't help smiling at the fierceness in his narrowed blue eyes as he glared at Mrs. Madison. He glanced down toward her, and his expression softened.

"Have I been that obvious?"

"I . . . I don't know." She fixed her eyes on the gold epaulet on his shoulder. "Have I?" She heard his soft chuckle and her eyes flew to his face in time to see a decidedly wicked grin. Her own smile followed as he twirled her around the floor.

"Let me escort you home," he whispered close to her ear during the dying strains of the waltz.

"I can't. I borrowed a gig and it awaits outside."

"When may I see you?"

Surprise clouded Charlotte's expression when she angled her face to look up at him. What had become of her arrogant captain, the man who demanded and took what he wanted? Could he honestly be asking her permission to call—as if he were courting her?

"Charlotte?" They were almost to the group of ladies surrounding the President's wife, and still she hadn't answered, only stared up at him with that thoughtful expression knitting her curved brow.

Jon noticed Dolley Madison step forward, and he didn't have to wonder why. He imagined he stared at Charlotte like some lovesick youth, but he couldn't seem to stop, especially since she'd yet to utter a word. "Tomorrow?" he prodded as Charlotte was engulfed by the group of ladies.

Charlotte twisted, ignoring the subtle pull of Dolley's hand, and smiled at the captain. "Yes," she said, and though the din in the drawing room was great, she knew he heard her by the sudden flash of his grin.

# Chapter Twenty

"What's so interesting out on the street? Have the damn British arrived?" This was followed by a pause and a hoarse cough. "I'm sorry, Charlotte. You know I don't mean you."

Dropping the lace curtains at Mrs. Peters's bedroom window, Charlotte turned back toward the bed where her landlady lay nestled among the quilts. Ignoring the question about her vigil at the window, Charlotte sank into a chair she'd moved over by the bed. "No British . . . except me, of course. Secretary of War Armstrong doesn't think they have any interest in Washington City."

Charlotte shrugged as Abigail grunted her opinion of Mr. Armstrong and his views, then leaned over to touch the older woman's forehead. "How are you feeling? You were resting so peacefully, I hesitated to wake you this morning?"

"Better, I think, yet my throat still hurts."

"You feel a mite feverish, too," Charlotte commented. "Would you like me to send for the doctor?"

"No." Abigail hefted herself up against the pillows. "I don't need a doctor. But some tea would be nice. What time is it anyway?"

"Nearly eleven o'clock." Charlotte paused with her hand on the doorlatch. "What are you doing, Mrs. Peters?"

"Why, I'm getting up. Only a lazybones stays abed this late."

"Or someone who by all rights should send for a doctor." Charlotte retraced her steps, gently urging Abigail back against the pillows. "There's no need for you to rise. I've taken the liberty of discussing the menu with the cook, and chores for the day have been assigned." Abigail visibly relaxed. "And right now I shall go fetch you some tea. Does your throat hurt too badly to eat?"

Abigail shook her head. "Nothing but tea, please."

"Laced with a bit of whiskey and honey?" Charlotte's suggestion brought a smile to Abigail's wan face.

"You're a sweet thing, Charlotte. But pray tell me about last night before you go. Did you meet with Mr. Skinner? Have you found a way back to England?"

"No." Charlotte let the syllable linger, wondering how exactly to explain last night's surprise. But before she could elaborate, someone tapped on the door. Charlotte opened it to find Enis, one of Abigail's servants.

"Didn't want to disturb the mistress none, but there's a gentleman to see you, Miss Winston."

"There is?" Charlotte's hand pressed against her heart, trying to calm the wild fluttering. She resisted the urge to run to the window and look out, but then she hadn't heard a coach or even a horse stop near the house. She realized now that all through her conversation with Abigail, part of her had been listening.

"Who is it, Charlotte?" The question, spoken in Abigail's scratchy voice, made Charlotte look back toward the bed.

"I'm not certain. I'll stop back in later to let you know." After giving Enis instructions to fetch her mistress honey and whiskey-laced tea, Charlotte descended the stairs on wobbly knees. She shouldn't care so much if it was Jonathan Knox or not, she tried to tell herself. Last night had been like a dream, and she knew only too well how she could build dreams up in her mind.

But as soon as she stepped into the parlor and saw him standing there, her pulse quickened and she had to restrain herself from running into his arms.

Jon stepped forward, then stopped himself and shrugged, a self-conscious grin spreading across his face. "I wanted to come earlier, but I had to meet with the Secretary of War."

"Oh." Charlotte traced her fingers along the brocaded back of the chair she'd positioned between herself and Jon. "Was your discussion productive?" Her question sounded superficial, as if she really didn't much care, and the truth was she cared very much. But care or not, there seemed to be an invisible wall between them this morning. Was this courting? If so, she liked it better when he simply took what he wanted.

"I suppose so . . ." Jon began, then plopped down on the delicate sofa, burying his face in the palm of his hands. "Hell no, it wasn't productive." He let out a disgusted breath. "The British are roaming the bay at will." He paused, raking his long fingers down his face and meeting her eyes. "The government has no more money for ships. The *Revenge* is in Baltimore right now waiting for repairs that most likely won't be made. And damnit, I have to report back to Commodore Barney this afternoon."

"Today?" Charlotte couldn't help herself. She

skirted the chair and sank down on the sofa beside him. Before she had time to think, he'd grabbed her shoulders, pulling her across his hard chest, and pressd his mouth to hers. Gone was the mannerly gentleman who awaited her pleasure. He was replaced—if, in fact, he'd ever existed—by the captain she knew and loved. The man who, though kindhearted, took what he wanted.

And he wanted her.

The hands that clutched at, then molded, her buttocks told her he wanted her. The beautiful mouth that opened wide and wet and drank of her cried out his want. And his breath, husky and raspy in her ear, declared his need.

And, oh, she wanted him.

Charlotte clung to his shoulder, arching her breasts into his hard muscles as the melting inside her swelled and pooled. She sighed when he bit her soft lobe, groaned when he tongued the skin beneath her ear. "You can't leave today. Not today." Charlotte could hear the frustration in her voice, the near panic, that he'd disappear, leaving behind nothing but this awful ache.

Last night had been almost unbearable. As she lay in her bed reliving the moments with him alone, the feel of his hands, his mouth on her, she had to bite her lip to keep from moaning. But then she had hope of today and tomorrow and tomorrows after that. Now that dream was dashed.

"But you can't leave today," she whispered when his lips moved down her jaw. She'd just found him, how could he leave?

"Come with me." His words vibrated against her neck, sending chills down her spine. She'd go with him anywhere. But how?

Charlotte leaned back, forcing a sliver of space

between them, and searched his eyes. They were hooded, smoky dark, and Charlotte thought she might drown in them. "I don't understand . . ." she began, but his lips cut off her query and his hard chest crushed against her heaving breast.

"Now," he breathed. "Come with me now. I need to be alone with you." The moment he'd spoken his desire, Jon clutched her soft shoulders, lifting her body away from his and settling her back against the pillows. His hand rasped down across his chin and he heaved a deep sigh, laying his head against the sofa back.

Charlotte had the impression he was trying to gain control of himself and she tried to match him. But her pulse still raced and her body still longed for the release she knew only Jon could give.

She was so damn beautiful, Jon clenched his fists to keep from reaching out and hauling her across him again. But he wouldn't use force. Not of any kind. Not this time. This time the decision to make love or not would be hers. Just hers. And it wouldn't be complicated by anything—not even the fierce desire that raged between them.

For as much as his swollen body denied it, he wanted more than to bury himself deep inside her. He wanted her.

He slanted her a look, smiling when he saw her expression of bewilderment. Her gaze dropped down to the front of his breeches where a large, hard ridge strained the fabric, then flew back to his face. The stain of crimson in her cheeks caused his grin to deepen.

"What do you say?" Jon asked, his voice still husky. He tried to keep his eyes off her straining breasts with their hard-peaked nipples. "I have the use of a townhouse while in Washington City. It belongs to a friend. He's in the country for the summer. We could go there. It's close by," Jon added, deciding it didn't add undue pressure.

He cocked his brow questioningly, waiting for her response. For the longest time she simply stared at him, her dark eyes large, her mouth pensive. Finally when he decided she wasn't going to speak, she cleared her throat.

"We'd be alone?" Charlotte asked, her head tilting questioningly.

"Completely."

Her lashes swept down as she again surveyed his body, and though her face shaded darker, a tiny smile curled her lips. "How long do you suppose it shall take us to get there?"

Jon let out the breath beginning to burn his lungs and reached for her, burying his face in the side of her warm neck. "Ten minutes if we walk."

"And if we run?" Charlotte asked, suppressing a giggle as he pulled away, looking at her in mock astonishment.

"Why, Charlotte Winston, we must keep some semblance of propriety." He winked at her. "At least until we shut the door behind us."

And that's all the time he waited, Charlotte thought a half hour later when Jon backed her against the thick-paneled door of a federalist townhouse, taking her mouth in a kiss that promised further carnal delights.

Despite the haste they'd both felt, it had taken more than ten minutes to get to this point. First Charlotte had run up to Abigail's room to check on her and tell her she was going out. The older woman had been teetering on the edge of sleep, said she felt better, and luckily hadn't been alert enough to ask where Charlotte was going.

She escaped quickly, rushing down the stairs only to find Jon deep in conversation with Mr. Gordon, one of Mrs. Peters's tenants. To be fair, the conversation was decidedly one-sided, with Mr. William Gordon asking questions about the war and Jon giving short answers. Jon had caught Charlotte's eye once, rolling his own skyward as Mr. Gordon espoused his own theory as to what Napoleon's defeat would mean to the progress of the war.

"That's very interesting," Jon had commented, rubbing his jaw as if deep in thought. "I shall share your ideas with the Secretary of War when I—" With that, Jon had glanced at the mantel clock and mumbled an oath. "Goodness, how time gets away. If I don't hurry I'll be late, and I promised Miss Winston I'd escort her to . . ."

Where exactly he promised to escort her had been lost as he turned and hustled her out of the house. And then he had nearly run—striding so fast with his long legs that Charlotte had to protest before he slowed down. They'd turned off Pennsylvania Avenue onto Delaware, racing two blocks south to the redbrick townhouse.

"Mmm." Charlotte gave herself over to the purely sensual feelings Jon evoked. The smell of his big, powerful body, so earthy and erotic, surrounded her as surely as his chest and thighs held her captive against the polished mahogany.

"Mmm, what, sweet Charlotte?" Jon asked, his eyes twinkling as he reluctantly drew his lips from hers. Her mouth was cherry red and wet, and he took another taste before letting her answer, then decided he knew exactly what she meant.

Jon pondered the intensity of his feelings for her. He'd never wanted a woman like he wanted Charlotte. His fingers dug into her soft hair, dislodging curls as he braced her for the onslaught of his kisses. First deep and thrusting, then playful and nipping, Jon kept it up until she was arching against him and his hands were clutching at her bottom, pressing her nearer.

Charlotte wanted to touch him everywhere, and the memory of how his skin felt, warm and alive, made her bold. Her hands burrowed under his uniform jacket, under the linen shirt, sighing when her palms slid along his hair-roughened flesh. His stomach muscles tightened, and she smiled against his mouth, then began an earnest assault on his buttons. But his nankeen breeches were stretched to their limit by his manhood, and he was forced to shift before she could finish the task and feel the bold thrust of his flesh surging into her hand.

"Witch," he mumbled as he grabbed handfuls of her skirt, bunching it above her waist. His knee pushed between her legs, separated them, and Charlotte sagged against the door. His eyes were on her now, watching her as he slid his thigh up toward her moist heat.

He stroked, and she gasped, tightening her hands around him till he threw his head back, the strong tendons in his neck standing out like taut rigging in the wind.

And then he lifted her, in one fluid motion bringing her down around him in a possession that was deep and complete. Her legs wrapped around his narrow waist, her fingers dug into his wool-covered shoulders, and she melted around him.

"Oh, God Charlotte, you feel so good." Jon's hands tightened over her waist, lifting her slightly, then pulling her back against him as he thrust forward. She trembled, and Jon felt his control spiraling away. Her legs tightened, and where his breeches were pushed down, he could feel the soft skin of her inner thigh.

"Let it come, Charlotte." Jon wrapped an arm around her, his other hand finding the moist juncture of their bodies. She shivered. "Let it come." His finger found her, slid sensually as he swayed forward. "Let it . . ."

Charlotte stiffened. Then the shuddering release washed over her. Flattened against the door, she cried out, her breath coming in panting gasps as he rocked her back and forth.

His groan joined hers, echoing through the empty house as he exploded inside her. Jon's body pressed her into the door, his forehead rested against a panel, and he tried to catch his breath. He could feel her breasts heaving into his chest and he lowered her, pushing himself away and leaning on his forearms. "Are you all right?" he asked, looking down into her flushed face.

Charlotte could only nod. Her legs felt limp and she wasn't certain her voice still worked. But she didn't think she'd ever been more all right. She smiled, then sighed, which elicited a hearty chuckle from Jon.

"What?" Charlotte managed as he reached down and scooped her into his arms.

"Bed" came his succinct reply as he strode along the hall past the drawing room where draped white fabric covered the furniture. They were almost to the first landing when Jon paused, mumbling a disgruntled curse under his breath.

"What's wrong?" Charlotte stopped nibbling the side of his neck.

"Damn pants are falling down." He shifted her in his arms, giving her a shameless grin. "Do you suppose you could give them a yank?"

"A yank?" Charlotte laughed, her hand already forging a path down between their bodies. His skin was damp, hair-roughened, and hot.

"Not that," Jon shifted, but his voice was light with amusement.

"But I thought you liked me to . . ."

"Later," Jon assured the wide-eyed too-innocent face. "For now just pull up the pants or we're going to tumble down the damn stairs."

Charlotte considered suggesting he put her down, but then she didn't really want that. Besides, she was having too good a time exploring the heavily muscled columns of his thighs. And by the time she found the waistband of his breeches and pulled them slowly up, she discovered proof that he enjoyed it, too.

The room he entered was the only one on the second floor with an open door. From what Charlotte could tell by her brief tour, the house hadn't been lived in for some time. A faintly musty odor hung in the air and dust dulled the shine on the wide-planked floors.

"Whose house is this?" Charlotte asked as he lowered her onto the bed. The sheet and quilt covering it appeared clean.

"Joshua Harding," Jon replied, playing with the loose curls around her face. "We served together in Tripoli. When we got back he retired to the family plantation in Virginia. He doesn't use this place much. I don't think he's opened it up since the war began."

"But he lets you stay here?" Though Jon had used a key to open the front door, she hoped they weren't trespassing.

"He does indeed. Old Josh seems to think I saved his life once."

"And did you?"

Jon shrugged. "Actually, we saved each other's. But anyway, I have use of this house whenever I want it." His face dipped to kiss the tip of her nose, and his eyes sparkled with mirth as he proclaimed, "And I've never wanted it more."

Regardless of the physical evidence to the contrary when she touched him on the stairs, Charlotte thought Jon might be tired after their lovemaking in the hall. Nothing seemed further from the truth as he began unfastening the tiny buttons down the front of her gown.

His blue eyes turned smoky with desire, and Charlotte lay languidly on the mattress watching his face as he slowly uncovered her flesh. He lowered his head, touching his warm lips to a spot just below her collarbone, and Charlotte's arms fastened around his neck.

Longing shot through her that had naught to do with the passion he inspired. Her fingers wove through his hair, and she held him to her while Jon burrowed his hands beneath her, lifting her up against him.

"When must you leave?"

He sighed, the puff of air hot against her skin. "This afternoon. Four o'clock at the latest." In that moment he set back his departure time by over an hour. The thought of leaving her left him weak.

Her fingers tensed, then pressed into his silky hair. "That doesn't give us much time." Charlotte stared at the ceiling where a spider traced the intricacies of its web. Tears stung her eyes.

"I don't *want* to leave you." Jon's words were muffled as he kissed her shoulder.

"And I don't want you to go." Charlotte took a calming breath, blinking back her tears. "But you

371

must. So we shouldn't waste our time being sad."

"Oh?" Jon nuzzled the underside of her chin. "And what *should* we do with our time?"

By the time he'd finished removing her gown, and following the path of the fabric with his greedy mouth, Charlotte had little doubt what *he* thought should occupy their time. She took great pleasure in removing his clothing, dropping each piece over the side of the high tester bed until she had him gloriously naked.

The raging surface of their passion spent, Charlotte and Jon found time to explore the endless fountainhead of their intimacy. Jon marveled at her skin, soft and velvety as a rose. In its smell, that erotic mixture of woman and lavender soap, by the way, when he rubbed his jaw across her shoulder, the creamy white flesh pickened.

"Does that hurt?" he asked, bracing his forearms beside her head and staring down into her multifaceted eyes.

"No," she whispered. "It feels wonderful. Everything you do feels wonderful."

As if to prove her point, Jon nuzzled lower, tracing the center of one breast with his lazy tongue. "Do you like that?"

Charlotte didn't answer . . . couldn't, but then she didn't think he expected one, because he'd already taken the hard nipple into his mouth. And then maybe her body's reaction to his caresses was more eloquent than she could ever be. She arched toward him, sighing when, inside the moist heat of his mouth, his tongue teased the tip.

His mouth moved lower, his warm breath tickling her stomach. Charlotte felt herself slowly dissolving like sugar in hot tea as he inched lower. His movements grew more aggressive, his breathing harsher as his fingers stroked between her thighs, opening them for him.

His tongue was hot, so hot that it jarred any remnants of lethargy from her body. Wonderfully wet and wildly insistent, he probed and taunted, sending Charlotte's hands clutching, first the sheets, then his hair.

The waves of pleasure came quickly, overwhelmingly, shattering Charlotte in their intensity. She gasped for breath, still riding the crest of ecstasy, still feeling the tremors race through her, when he slid up her body and into her silken heat. His movements were anything but lazy now as he filled her, deeper and deeper with each bold stroke.

Charlotte thought herself surely spent, but found the passion only banked, eager to burst into flame again and again. When his body tightened, Charlotte wrapped her legs around his hips and cradled him to her, the only thought filling her mind, how very much she loved him.

"What?" Jon angled his head to look back at Charlotte as she stared at him. He leaned back against the bolster he'd made of pillows, and Charlotte lay sprawled on top of him. Her rounded breasts flattened against his chest, her legs tangled with his. Content, he existed in a state of semi-arousal that the feel of her soft back and hip beneath his caressing hand was fast changing.

"I don't understand." Charlotte smiled down at him.

"Why are you watching me so closely?" It was almost eerie the way she examined every inch of his face.

"I was just thinking, you're much more handsome

than he is."

Jon scrunched higher against the pillows. "Who?"

"The pirate."

"What pirate?" Now he sat up completely.

How silly could she be? Charlotte let her hand drift to Jon's cheek. Why had she said anything so foolish? And how was she going to explain? She glanced back up at his face, at the scowl that darkened his expression and decided she had no choice but to tell the truth. "He isn't real . . ." she began, then took a deep breath when he arched his brow.

"I spent a lot of time alone as a child, and sometimes . . . sometimes I would make up fantasies . . . daydreams, sort of, to keep me company." He still didn't understand. She could tell by his eyes. "I used to dream about a pirate. He looked a lot like you," she blurted out.

His brow arched higher. "You daydreamed about a pirate when you were a child?"

Charlotte felt heat surge up to her face. "No, actually I daydreamed about him when I was older." Charlotte knew the exact moment that understanding hit him. A wide grin covered his face. Before she could say anything he'd flipped her over onto her back, following with his own body.

"Why, Charlotte Winston, I'm shocked. You fantasize about a pirate."

"Not anymore," Charlotte countered, though she didn't think he believed her.

"And what does this pirate do to you in these daydreams?" His voice was full of mirth as he fanned Charlotte's curls across the pillow.

"Nothing."

"Charlotte?" He drew the word out as he tickled her ribs.

"No. Stop. I'll tell you." Charlotte tried to catch

her breath. She squirmed from beneath him, sitting on the side of the bed, her back to him. Why did she bring this up? But there was no help for it now. She swallowed. "Don't laugh."

"I won't."

Glancing back over her shoulder, Charlotte saw his expression was indeed serious, probably more serious than the discussion warranted, but she plunged ahead. "My mother was ill for years. My father was never home. And, well, we lived in a rather remote area. There really wasn't anyone to talk to, so I read, and . . . and daydreamed about the places in the books."

Charlotte folded her hands in her lap. "I became rather good at imagining, and soon I could just close my eyes and escape."

"You did that on the *Eagle*, didn't you? When I first pulled you into my cabin?"

Nodding, Charlotte peeked over her shoulder. "I'd always found it an effective way to block out unpleasantness. And it usually worked . . . until you."

"Was I that awful to you, Charlotte?" His voice was as gentle as the hand that reached out to brush her hair off her cheek. When she didn't answer, Jon leaned forward, pressing his lips to her shoulder. "I'm sorry."

"No. Don't be. It was the times, more than anything. And I should never have tried to sail for Canada. I just thought . . ."

"Your father?"

Charlotte stared off into the room. "I thought he'd want me there." As much as she willed it not to, her voice cracked on the last word, and Charlotte felt herself being pulled back against Jon's hard chest.

"Don't, Charlotte." Jon wrapped his arms around her, squeezing her warm body to his. "I'm sorry you had so much unhappiness. No. Don't talk, just listen." He cradled her head against his chest. "I wish I could change it. Make everything all right for you. But, God help me, I wouldn't have you staying in England, because then I'd never have met you." Jon took a deep breath, digging his fingers through her hair, and angling her face up toward his. Tears glistened on her lashes, and Jon wiped his thumb across the sparkling diamond tips. "I love you, Charlotte," he whispered. "I do."

"I love you, too." Charlotte thought her heart would burst. She touched the cleft in his chin, tilting his mouth down to hers.

Jon leaned back against the pillows, pulling her with him, wrapped securely in his arms. They lay like that, heart to heart, for endless minutes, relishing the closeness they felt.

"You know I told Dolley Madison I loved you."

"You did? When?"

"When I asked if she knew you." Jon looked down at Charlotte. "I inquired about you everyplace I went, but when I asked her, she answered my question with one of her own. 'Why do you want to find her?' she said."

"And you . . . ?"

"Said I loved you."

Charlotte nestled further into his arms. "I wondered why she set up our meeting."

"Thay's why." Jon brushed his lips across Charlotte's temple. "Are you all right?"

"Yes." She was more than all right, knowing Jon loved her.

"Good." He paused. "Now tell me about this pirate of yours," he teased. "Ouch!"

Charlotte let loose of the chest hair she'd pulled,

376

but he continued. "Come on, Charlotte. I want to know."

"Oh, if you insist." Charlotte let out a breath. "He was just a figment of my imagination who captured me occasionally, taking me off on his ship. Now are you satisfied?" But Charlotte could tell by the quirk of Jon's mouth that he wasn't going to let this drop.

"Where did he take you?"

"I don't know . . . The Caribbean," Charlotte admitted. "He looked like you."

"Except I'm more handsome," Jon pointed out with mock seriousness.

Suppressing a smile, Charlotte rested her elbows on Jon's chest. "Did I say that?"

"You most certainly did."

"Oh. Then I guess it must be true." She traced her fingertip along his collarbone.

"So what did this pirate do to you when he had you all alone?" Jon's hand played across her spine.

"Well, let me see." Charlotte cocked her head, enjoying their teasing interplay. "Sometimes he kissed me."

"Kissed you?" Jon's bark of laughter rumbled through his chest and into hers. "Doesn't sound like much of a pirate. You being so pretty, I would have thought he'd do a lot more than that."

"Actually he did ravish me occasionally."

"Ravish you?"

"Hmm." Charlotte inched up his body, rubbing against the part of him that boldly proclaimed his desire. "Of course, it was always very vague since I didn't know then exactly what comprised a ravishment."

"But you know now?"

"Oh, yes," she whispered. Charlotte let her hand

377

drift up his thigh. "You're an excellent teacher." To prove her point, Charlotte brushed her lips across his cleft chin, then spread her legs to straddle him. She sank down slowly, watching his face with passion-glazed eyes as she took him completely.

Her movements were wanton, and Jon fought to catch his breath as her body squeezed around him. Her hair tumbled forward and he grabbed a lock, pulling her down for his kiss.

"I think," Charlotte said against his mouth, "the pirate was always you . . . Always you."

"I don't want to leave you." Jon gave his boot a yank and looked up at Charlotte. She was using his comb, trying to redo the hair that had swept so gloriously down her narrow back.

"I know. But it can't be helped."

"Perhaps if you'd go back to Oak Hill . . ."

Charlotte turned away from the mirror. "I don't think I could get across the bay safely. Besides, I'm fine here with Mrs. Peters."

Jon stomped his foot into the boot. "You're probably right, but I still worry about you."

"And I you." Charlotte moved into the V of his legs, clasping his head when he lowered it to the valley between her breasts. "We shall just have to hope for the best and see what happens. But know that I will be awaiting you."

Jon looked up. "If the British attack Washington, I want you to get away. I'm leaving you enough money to go west, or south. Just don't stay and let anything happen to yourself."

"Do you think they'll attack here?"

"I don't know." Jon stood and walked to the window. The panes were dirty and rain-streaked. He shrugged. "Hell, no one knows what they'll do, or where they'll strike next. But I don't want you taking any chances."

"I won't." Charlotte joined him, looking out onto the peaceful springtime Washington street below. "I won't take any chances," she repeated when he draped his arm around her shoulder.

# Chapter Twenty-One

Rumors hung in the hot August air. Hung as thickly as the clouds of dust billowing behind overloaded wagons and coaches that rumbled down Pennsylvania Avenue.

Out of town. They were all headed out of town—escaping the British hordes. "Wellington's Invincibles" Charlotte had heard them called. They were the well-trained troops who conquered Napoleon and now were on their way to teach the upstart country a lesson in warfare.

By destroying the nation's capital? No one knew for sure. Charlotte had read the line from this morning's *National Intelligencer* over and over again as she sat by Abigail Peters's bedside. " 'We feel assured that the number and bravery of our men will afford protection to the city.' "

Charlotte hoped they were right. But she had a more immediate concern than her own safety. Jon was one of the brave men the paper spoke of. Word reached Washington City two days ago that Commodore Barney blew up his flotilla to keep the boats out of British hands. Jon was with Barney, and Charlotte spent a restless night and day pacing the floor before a messenger arrived with a hastily scribbled note. Penciled by Jon, and delivered through Dolley Madison, it contained only two lines: *I'm safe. Flee city. Love always, J.*

But how could she? Charlotte dropped into the chair beside the bed. Her smile showed more confidence than she felt as she looked over at Abigail Peters. "Can't you drink a little more broth?"

"I've tried, dear," Abigail said, and Charlotte instinctively leaned forward to hear her better. "But it is too hot to bother with eating."

Indeed it was hot, stifling, in the room, but Charlotte didn't dare open the window. The streets were clogged with dust, and Abigail would surely wonder about all the traffic on the road. Besides, Charlotte had stepped outside earlier, and there was not the slightest breeze.

After lifting the pewter mug off the night table, Charlotte spooned out some of the chicken broth she'd made. "Just eat a little more. Dr. Lindsey said you must regain your strength."

"Dr. Lindsey hasn't been by lately to see me."

*Because he left town*, Charlotte thought, but to Abigail she explained that he probably had more seriously ill patients keeping him busy. Actually Abigail didn't need the doctor. What she'd thought to be a minor fever in the spring was actually Potomac fever. But with the help of heavy doses of bark, she'd weathered the worst of it and was now recovering. But she was still weak—much too weak to travel.

A discreet tap sounded at the bedroom door, and Charlotte opened it, motioning the two men down the stairs before telling Abigail she'd return in a moment.

When Charlotte reached the parlor, the Gordon

brothers stood facing her. "We've finished filling the wagon with books," Henry said.

At a loss for what to say, Charlotte listened while William continued. "We have room for you and Mrs. Peters to come with us. We'll make room," he corrected himself.

"She's too weak to travel." What Charlotte left unspoken was that she wouldn't go without the older woman, but the Gordon brothers knew this. They'd discussed it before.

"Well, I guess we better be leaving then." This from William as he fingered the brim of his hat.

"I suppose so." Charlotte turned and led the two men into the hall. "You take care of yourselves, and let me know where you are." She opened the door.

"Blast it, Charlotte, we hate to leave you like this. If it wouldn't be for trying to save all the books, we'd stay with you."

"I know," Charlotte said, though she doubted William's words. Not that she blamed them. The Gordon brothers were scared. Everyone was. Goodness knows *she* was. And if things were different, if Abigail weren't so weak, she'd be long gone into the countryside. Mrs. Simpson was gone, as were Mrs. Peters's few servants. But worrying wasn't going to change things, and prolonging the Gordon brothers' departure wasn't going to help, either. "We'll be fine," Charlotte assured them. "Remember, I'm a British citizen."

"Well, just in case, we left a set of dueling pistols for you."

Charlotte glanced toward the hall table when William pointed. "They should keep you safe from . . ." William's round face turned red and he hurried through the door.

Charlotte pretended not to notice his discomfort.

But like everyone else, she'd heard the rumors. If the British took the city there would be rape and looting. "I don't believe that," Charlotte mumbled to herself as she shut the door. "I won't believe that."

Still, as she climbed the stairs, she felt uncomfortably alone. The Gordon brothers hadn't been much comfort, but they were better than nothing.

At the top of the landing she first heard it. Charlotte turned, dismissing the faraway rumble of thunder, then stopped. It didn't sound exactly like thunder. It sounded more like . . . Charlotte's eyes shut when she identified the sound as cannon.

But a moment later they snapped open. No more would she hide behind her fantasies.

The rumbling continued, off and on, into the sultry afternoon. Abigail was asleep by the time Charlotte got back to her room, so there were no questions to answer. Charlotte climbed the rickety steps to the attic, enduring the suffocating heat to get a better view of the countryside from the windows. With the heel of her hand she rubbed a clear spot on first the south window, then the west. Nothing.

The north view proved different. Charlotte stood watching the occasional puff of smoke drifting above the trees, wishing for a spyglass, or anything that would help her find out what was happening.

But there was no sign of how the battle went, no sign to indicate if the British would be conquering the American capital—and no sign of Jon.

With a sigh, she pressed her forehead to the grimy glass and prayed, fervently, passionately. "Please, please don't let anything happen to him," she murmured, brushing away the tears that trailed down her cheeks.

Finally, tired and hot, dirty from the attic, Charlotte descended to the second floor. The rumble of guns had stopped, replaced by an eerie quiet more terrifying than the earlier noise. Charlotte checked on Mrs. Peters, then went to her own room. Stripping off her soiled dress she washed quickly with tepid water from the pitcher, then dressed again in a flower-sprigged gown. She started toward the door, but something caught her eye as she passed the window. Pausing, she noticed a cloud of dust coming from the direction of the battle. As she watched it grew larger . . . and nearer.

Charlotte's heart hammered in her chest as she ran across the room, then down the steps. By the time she wedged open the front door, there were men in the street. Running. Though most of them wore no uniforms, she could tell they were Americans. They came in twos and threes at first, frightened, sweat-soaked men who repeatedly cast a wary eye over their shoulders.

"What happened?" Charlotte ran down the brick porch steps trying to get someone's attention, but they seemed not to notice. The sound of horses' hooves rent the air and Charlotte looked up to see a horseman galloping her way.

He yelled as he rode by, using the reins to slap his lathered horse. In the confusion of men about her, Charlotte couldn't hear all of what he said, but two words rang out loud and clear: "redcoats" and "rape."

Charlotte raced back into the house and slammed the door. She fumbled with the lock, finally managing to turn the key, then collapsed back against the hard wood. Her chest heaved, and she tried to calm her breathing.

"It isn't true. It isn't true," she told herself. But the facts did not lie.

The American Army was retreating through the

city and in no order at all. The men were panic-stricken, and that frenzy had got hold of her. She took a deep breath, pressed a hand against her heart, and tried to think rationally.

What should she do? What *could* she do? Slowly, Charlotte straightened her back and stepped away from the door. She'd go see if Mrs. Peters needed anything, and then she'd keep a vigil by the door. She could not become hysterical.

Besides, she knew British soldiers—her father was a general for heaven's sake. They didn't go around raping and pillaging. They just didn't. They were gentlemen. She had a sudden flash of Matthew Levid's sadistic smile, but shook her head to dispel it.

Then she caught sight of the pistols on the table. They were brass-trimmed and fancy, and she wondered idly if they were loaded—and if she could shoot one if she had to. Her mother's gardener had taught her how, but that was years ago. And she never shot at anything but targets he set up along the fence. They were innocuous enough—not like shooting a person.

Charlotte didn't think she could actually shoot a human being, yet a moment later, when a loud pounding began at the door, her hand grabbed up the pistol quick enough. She backed against the wall, the chair railing jabbing into her back, her heart beating a crazy tattoo.

"Charlotte!" More pounding. "Are you in there, Charlotte?"

"Oh, my God!" Charlotte ran to the door and fumbled with the lock, cursing its stubbornness before swinging the door open. "Oh, Jon!"

Jon burst through the doorway, grabbing Charlotte as she flung herself into his arms. He allowed himself a moment to hold her, breathing in the sweet fragrance of her, before putting her down. She still clung to his neck, and Jon kicked the door shut before taking her lips in a kiss he'd dreamed about all day.

"I've been so worried. Are you hurt?" Charlotte pushed out of his steely embrace to see for herself when he shook his head. His uniform jacket was missing, his shirt grimy and soaked with sweat, but he appeared to be in one piece. "Thank God," Charlotte murmured.

"Wait a minute." Jon continued to hold her at arm's length when she would have melted back against his chest. "What are you still doing here? Didn't you get my note?"

Charlotte swallowed. "Yes . . . I got it. But I—"

"You what? Don't you realize what's happened? Our army's been routed. For Christ's sake, they're out there running through the streets. You've got to get out of here." His voice rose and his fingers tightened with each word.

"I can't."

"Why the hell not?"

Charlotte would have laughed at the expression on his face if the situation weren't so serious. "Mrs. Peters isn't strong enough to travel, and I can't leave her here alone." Jon let go of her, and Charlotte missed the warm strength of his hands. After jerking away from her, he paced to the window, raking his fingers back through his hair. He turned about abruptly, motioning with his chin toward the pistol she still held.

"And what do you intend to do with that, Charlotte? Hold the entire British Army at bay with one pistol?"

Charlotte looked down at the gun in her hand then back up at Jon. Slowly she shook her head.

"You don't understand, Charlotte. You weren't there."

His voice faltered and Charlotte moved toward

him. "Was it so bad?"

"It was awful. A nightmare." For a moment he shut his eyes, reliving the debacle. "There didn't seem to be any leadership. Companies of men just placed anywhere. And the British kept coming at us. At first I thought we might hold. But then men started running, and nothing or nobody could stop them."

"But you tried, didn't you?" Charlotte touched his damp sleeve.

"Hell yes, I tried! My father fought to get our independence from England. I can't believe it's come to this."

"Maybe it's not as bad as you think." Charlotte wished there was something—anything other than saying empty words—she could do to lift his spirits. But the sounds of reality, of the American Army fleeing through the streets of the nation's capital, couldn't be denied.

Shaking his head, Jon smiled down at her. "Let's pray you're right. But in the meantime, I have to get you out of here. Now don't argue." Jon brushed his lips across Charlotte's. "I'll be right back." He reached for the door handle. "Lock this."

Long after the echo of the slamming door died, Charlotte stood staring out the parlor window. She saw no sign of Jon. He'd disappeared into the swarm of men clogging the dusty road.

He was safe for now, she could thank God for that. But what of the future? And what was she to do? Her hope that the American Army would keep the British from Washington City had vanished. By the looks of the men still filling Pennsylvania Avenue, they expected to be overtaken by red-coated soldiers at any second. But she couldn't leave Mrs. Peters. She couldn't.

The old woman's feeble voice interrupted her thoughts and Charlotte ran up the stairs.

"What is it, Charlotte? Tell me what's going on." Abigail Peters leaned up on her elbow and demanded an explanation as Charlotte opened her bedroom door.

"There's been a battle . . ." Charlotte began, not knowing how to soften the news. "I'm afraid the Americans lost and are retreating through the city. The British are expected . . . soon."

"Is there nothing to stop them?"

Charlotte shook her head. "Nothing."

It seemed to take Abigail a moment to digest this information, but when she did, her reaction was dramatic. Pulling herself into a sitting position, she announced, "We have to get out of here."

"But you're still so weak."

"Listen, Charlotte. My husband gave his life fighting the British back in '77, and I'm not about to stay here and watch them capture the capital. Fetch me some clothes."

"Wait a minute." Charlotte explained about Jon's visit.

"And you think he's coming back?"

"Yes. He said he would, and he wants me to leave." Charlotte turned when she heard the pounding. "That might be him now. Stay in bed."

Someone was beating on the back door this time, and Charlotte checked out the window before throwing it open. Jon pushed inside, then headed for the stairs, which he took three at a time. Charlotte followed, but he'd already disappeared into a bedroom. "Where did you get that wagon," she called up the stairwell.

"You don't want to know," Jon yelled back.

Before she turned on the landing, he was coming

back toward her dragging a mattress and blankets. Charlotte hurried back down the steps so he could get by her. "What are you doing?"

But he didn't answer, just went back out into the alley behind the house. A few minutes later, he was beside her again. "Where is Mrs. Peters?"

"I'm right here."

Charlotte gasped. The old woman had dragged herself from bed and now stood clutching the newel at the top of the stairs. Charlotte started up, but Jon edged past her, and in one easy motion scooped the old lady into his arms. "How would you like to go for a ride?" he asked, grinning down at her.

"If it means getting away from the damn British, I'm all for it."

Laughing, Jon started back down. "Get anything you need," he called to Charlotte, who'd already grabbed up the dueling pistols.

After settling Abigail in among the blankets, Jon turned toward Charlotte, pulling her off a short distance. "The side streets aren't too crowded . . ." he began. "I want you to head for Georgetown, farther west if you can."

"Aren't you coming?"

"I can't." Jon ran the pad of his thumb down her cheek. "My men are at the navy yard. I have to get back to them. See what we can do about slowing up the British."

He smiled, his teeth showing white against his dirt-streaked face, but it didn't hide his reluctance to leave her.

"I'll be all right," Charlotte said. "You just take care of yourself."

Jon nodded, then grabbed her against his chest. "Oh, God, Charlotte, I love you."

She wanted to cry—it was all she could do not to.

But a brave front was what he needed, and he'd get nothing less from her. He tilted her face, crushed his mouth against hers for a kiss that was as desperate as she felt. And then he released her, pulling her around to the front of the wagon and hoisting her onto the seat.

"You all right back there, Mrs. Peters?" he called, smiling when he heard her reply. Then Jon's eyes met Charlotte's and locked, his expression saying all the things they didn't have time to express with words. Without looking away, he reached out, slapped the horse's rump, and the wagon lurched forward.

The horse was Jon's and he didn't take well to pulling a wagon, or maybe it was Charlotte's inexperience that spooked him. By the time they'd traveled half a block, blisters burned on Charlotte's palms and sweat dripped between her breasts, but she was getting the hang of driving the wagon.

Ruts pockmarked the alley, bouncing Charlotte about on the hard wooden seat, and she couldn't imagine Mrs. Peters's discomfort. Charlotte wanted to look back but feared losing control of the wagon.

But they were getting away. Charlotte blew a wisp of hair off her face, and reminded herself of that. It wasn't far to Georgetown, and Jon thought they'd be safe there. Though the alley was relatively free of people, the crossroads ahead was jammed.

Worrying about how she'd pass through the throngs, Charlotte didn't notice the creak of the wheel till the wagon lurched to the side and she had to grab the seat to keep from sliding to the ground.

"Oh, no!" Charlotte jumped into the alley, running around to see what happened to the wagon. The sight of the wheel lying in the dust, and the axle digging into the ground, brought the sting of tears to her eyes.

"What's happened?"

Charlotte looked up to see Abigail pulling herself up to peek over the wagon side. "We've lost a wheel." Charlotte bit her lower lip. "I don't know how to fix it." Charlotte looked down the alley, then wiped her forehead with the back of her hand. "We have to go back."

Mrs. Peters didn't like the idea—and neither did Charlotte—but at least she didn't argue as Charlotte unhitched Jon's horse. Helping Abigail out of the wagon and onto Jon's horse proved difficult. The old lady had used so much energy for her show of bravado in the house that she could barely move.

It took Charlotte nearly thirty minutes to reach the back door, though they'd barely gone a block. At each step she expected to hear the clamor of the British assault, but there was still nothing.

When they reached the back door, Charlotte pulled Abigail off the horse, then slapped its hindquarters, hoping it might find its way to safety . . . knowing Jon wouldn't want the British to have his horse.

Once inside the house, Charlotte helped Abigail lie down on the couch in the parlor. Maybe after they both rested, she could manage to get her upstairs to her room.

"Do you have the pistols?" Abigail asked as dusk began to settle over the nearly deserted town.

"Yes." Charlotte motioned toward the table beside her chair where both guns lay. They were loaded. Jon had checked for her, but there was no other ammunition.

"Do you think they're coming?"

"I don't know." Charlotte's back hurt from holding herself so stiffly, but she seemed incapable of leaning back in the chair. Shadows lengthened in the parlor, but she didn't light any candles.

A loud explosion had her jumping to her feet and running toward the window.

"What is it?" Abigail called from the couch.

"I'm not sure." Charlotte peeked through a slit in the drapes. Dark smoke rose into the dusky sky. "It looks like it's coming from the lower bridge . . . or the navy yard." She had to remain strong. Worrying about Jon would do no good. But she couldn't stop herself. Snapping the curtains shut, she turned back toward the room. "I just don't know what it is."

Again quiet reigned over the house . . . the city. Charlotte could hear Abigail's breathing, the frantic pounding of her own heart. And then there was another beating . . . a fluctuating rhythm like the clomping of horses' hooves.

Growing steadily louder and nearer.

Silently Charlotte rose and moved toward the window. Her palms were sweaty as she gripped the fringe, inching the material back far enough to peek out.

Outside all was dark. She didn't know whether the other houses in the area were vacant, or, like herself, their occupants had chosen to snuff out their candles. Charlotte could see the outlines of several buildings: the Capitol to her left, Robert Seawall's house, Tomlinson's Hotel. And then as her eyes grew accustomed to the darkness, she noticed the group of men on horseback. They sat, facing toward the Capitol, apparently discussing what to do.

Then suddenly, the sound of musket fire pierced the air. Charlotte saw several men fall to the ground, then soldiers rushed toward the house across the street. She watched, her knuckles pressed to her mouth as they broke through the door.

"What is it? What's happening?" The volley of

gunfire awakened Abigail, and Charlotte took up the pistols and moved to her side.

"Someone fired on the British troops," Charlotte whispered.

"Did they kill any of them?"

"I don't know. Maybe." Charlotte sank back into the chair, clutching the pistol handle. But moments later she was up again, racing to the window as the British fired rockets at Robert Sewall's house. Then, as she watched, the southern sky lit up with shooting flames. Something large was burning in the direction of the navy yard.

Charlotte hardly had time to react to that when someone started pounding on the front door. Glancing quickly at Mrs. Peters, Charlotte headed into the hall. She took a deep breath, hid the pistol in the folds of her skirt, and cracked open the door.

Five soldiers stood illuminated by a torch on the front porch. The first stepped through the doorway, looking from side to side. "We've orders to search this property," he said. "Are there any men here?"

"No. Only myself and my elderly landlady, and she is very ill." Charlotte tried to keep herself from shaking as she answered, but she was very frightened. And there was something oddly familiar about the soldier's voice. She couldn't quite place it, but she'd heard it before. Narrowing her eyes, she studied his profile as he looked toward the parlor. And then it hit her.

He turned and she lowered her head, staring intently at the floor. "Are there any firearms on the premises?"

"No . . . I mean yes . . . I . . ." The sweat-slicked gun nearly slipped from her hand as Charlotte tried frantically to decide what to say. But the British soldier was having no part of it.

Grabbing Charlotte's chin, he jerked her face into the light. "Which is it?" he began, only to stop, his eyes widening. "It's you."

Instinct alone made Charlotte lift her hands to fight off the lieutenant's rough treatment. She realized her mistake quickly, but not before the lieutenant caught the gleam of brass of the gun stock. He knocked it from Charlotte's hand, pushing her back against the wall and holding her there with his forearm.

"If it isn't Captain Levid's betrothed," he said, a sanctimonious grin on his face. "Funny, but the captain wasn't at all happy that I'd spared you and the Knox plantation when last we met. As a matter of fact, he was quite angry—actually chastised me for my error in judgment."

Charlotte fought to catch her breath as he leaned more weight upon her chest. Was he going to kill her right here? Just when she thought she might pass out from lack of air, he loosened his grip. Charlotte opened her mouth to speak but he jerked her forward, and out the door. "I think Captain Levid would like to see you for himself."

Baltimore was in a frenzy of preparation. Only forty miles up the bay, this seaport felt strongly that they'd be the next hit by Cochrane. By the twenty-eighth of August the citizens were digging a line of fortifications about the city. And Jon was preparing to sail the *Revenge* down the broad, shallow Patapsco River.

If the British *did* attack he didn't want his ship bottled up in the harbor and lost—better to be free to sail the bay, striking as he could.

"For the sake of the men, at least, you should show

more enthusiasm." Adam Burke leaned against the hard oak tavern wall and eyed Jon over the tankard rim.

Jon took a swallow of rum, ignoring his friend, then gave up the ruse and slammed his fist against the scarred table. "I am enthusiastic, damnit. It's just—"

"You're worried about Charlotte," Adam finished for him.

Jon blew air through his clenched teeth. "It's stupid, I know. But I can't get it out of my head that something has happened."

"You sent a messenger." Adam leaned forward on his elbows. "There's nothing else you can do."

"I know." Jon shrugged. I'm sure she's all right. Hell, she's probably back in her boardinghouse by now wondering why I made her leave."

"And waiting for you to come back," Adam added.

Grinning, Jon shook his head. "We're both going to have to wait a while for that. Let's just hope we can get into the bay before Cochrane moves on Baltimore."

"Aye, it's—"

"Captain Knox, sir."

Both men turned as Mr. Jenkins, the sailor Jon had sent to Washington City, interrupted Adam. "I've been looking for you and they told me at the dock you were here at this tavern."

"You have news for me?"

"Yes, sir."

Jon grabbed the envelope the tar held out and tore open the seal. He began to read, his expression growing more intense with each word. He stood, the parchment clenched in his hand, a nerve throbbing in his cheek. "We need to get back to the ship."

"What is it? Is the note from Charlotte?" Adam

followed his friend out into the steamy night air.

"It's from Mrs. Peters . . . Charlotte's landlady." Jon paused a moment to rein in his anger. "Charlotte was in Washington City when the British came . . . something about a broken wagon wheel. Anyway, Charlotte was taken . . . by Levid."

"My God." Adam stopped in his tracks, trying to digest the news. "But why?"

"I don't know." Jon headed down Water Street toward the dock. "But he has her."

Adam grabbed Jon's sleeve. "Wait a minute. I'm sorry. I liked her, you know I did. But there's nothing you can do. You don't know where he's taking her, and even if you did, he has the whole damn British Navy to back him up."

Jerking his arm free, Jon turned on Adam. Jon's tone was flat, but his eyes shone in the dim lamp light. "I know where he's headed. The bastard left a message. A message for me. He's going to Oak Hill."

# Chapter Twenty-Two

Oh, how she hated boats.

Charlotte rested her head against the bulwark and squeezed her eyes shut tight. But no sweet reveries flashed through her consciousness. She could pretend nothing save the harsh reality that surrounded her.

Her stomach, queasy at best, lurched as the *Scorpion* rolled on a swell. Pressing her fingertips to trembling lips, Charlotte glanced toward the bucket pushed discreetly beneath her bunk. But experience told her a sudden lunge to the pail wouldn't be necessary . . . for now at least.

Was she gaining her sea legs . . . or had she finally resigned herself to the inevitable? For Charlotte knew that fear and worry played a principal role in her affliction.

She was Captain Levid's prisoner. Of course, he didn't call her that. When he introduced her to Admiral Cochrane, she was his charming betrothed, liberated from the clutches of the enemy, and longing to see the peace and tranquility of English shores.

Charlotte dropped her forehead to bent knees, chastising herself for allowing, nay *participating*, in that farce. But the echo of Captain Levid's threats had filled her mind, and she knew it would only make matters worse for her to contradict Levid's story to the admiral.

Not that she had much opportunity. Captain Levid had escorted her onto deck to watch as the admiral's launch brought him from his flagship. After a brief introduction, Levid had ordered Charlotte below—to rest, he said.

And there she remained for over a sennight, tucked away in a small cabin, day and night, night and day. A sailor brought her food, minimal water to wash with, and nothing more.

"At least I've had no further encounters with Matthew Levid," Charlotte murmured. But in her mind she wasn't certain that even listening to his harangue about her behavior wouldn't be preferable to this forced isolation, for in her solitude she could do nothing but worry about Jon.

A tapping at the door drew Charlotte's attention and she looked up to see two sailors tugging a brass tub into her cabin.

"What's this?" Scrambling to her feet, Charlotte eyed the men as they wedged the oval-shaped hip bath between the bunk and wall. There was barely room to move about in the tiny cabin, yet two more sailors entered carrying buckets of water which they sloshed into the tub.

"With the captain's compliments," one of them said before they all backed out of the doorway.

Charlotte's gaze traveled to the door, where the metallic clank of key turning lock sounded, then back to the tub. It was far from full, the undulating water barely covered the scooped bottom, but it offered relief from the discomfort of her own uncleanliness.

Who cared if it came from Captain Levid? At this point, Charlotte decided, she'd accept a bath from the devil himself. Quickly stripping, Charlotte stepped into the tub, gasping when the chilly water closed over her foot. Gooseflesh crawled over her skin as she settled down and made fast work of scrubbing herself. She used her chemise in lieu of a towel and hurriedly searched through a sea chest containing some clothes gathered for her when she left Washington City.

Her hair soaked the collar of her mint-green gown, but Charlotte didn't care. The bath was wonderful, but she didn't like how vulnerable she felt being naked—not that she was anything but vulnerable anyway.

As if to prove her point, another knock sounded, followed quickly by the entrance of a young midshipman. He seemed embarrassed, blushing a deep scarlet when Charlotte turned, her hands held high in the process of pinning up her damp curls.

"The captain wishes to see you," he said, showing a sudden compelling interest in the planked deck.

"If I could have a moment more . . ."

"He requires your presence now, miss."

"I see." Charlotte stuck a pin in her hair and followed the young man down the passageway.

"Well, well, Charlotte, I see you've taken advantage of the bath I sent. I knew you would."

Charlotte made no response as the door was shut behind her. The captain's cabin was much larger than the one she'd come from—and it had windows. Though the light hurt her eyes, Charlotte ignored Captain Levid, training her gaze instead on the row of transom windows. To her surprise she could see trees and a shoreline through the leaded panes.

"You're wondering where we are, no doubt. Go

ahead and look." From behind his desk Levid motioned Charlotte across the cabin with his hand. "I think you'll recognize it."

Charlotte studied Captain Levid through narrowed eyes. He leaned back in his chair, a glass of Madeira cupped nonchalantly in his palm, and he seemed to be enjoying himself immensely. At her expense? Charlotte had no doubt. But that didn't stop her from moving toward the windows lining the back wall of his cabin.

The *Scorpion* was sailing up a river, she could tell that. The banks were lined with pines and oaks, and occasionally a cultivated field reached down near the shore. Tobacco and corn grew in the late-summer heat. It looked a pleasant enough waterway, but Charlotte couldn't place it, and started to tell Levid so when something caught her eye.

A pier.

It jutted out into the shallow current, frightening in its familiarity.

"I see you recognize our location at last." Levid took a sip of wine, then smiled into Charlotte's puzzled face.

"What are you doing here?"

"Oh, come now, Charlotte. I think you can guess. This is where Jonathan Knox lives. As a matter of fact I believe we just passed his wharf. Oak Hill, is it not?"

Charlotte abruptly looked away, unable to stand the sight of his smirking face. There could only be one reason he'd take the trouble to come here, and that was to destroy it. His next words confirmed her suspicion and brought her stare back to him.

"Deceit saved Oak Hill once—yours, Charlotte. But it won't this time."

"These people have done nothing." Charlotte

clutched at her skirt, balling the fabric into a tight wad. "Why would you do this?"

"Ah, you plead so prettily, my dear. I think I rather like to see you this way. But alas, it will do no good. You see, I've already planned my course of action. Would you like to hear it?"

"No." Charlotte turned back toward the window as he stood and began moving toward her.

"Are you quite certain?" His brow wrinkled. "I think you might find it interesting."

Charlotte pressed against the glass as she felt Levid's presence behind her. He seemed to enjoy her discomfort, sandwiching her between his body and the window.

"I suppose I'll have to tell you my little scheme anyway." His hot breath fanned the tiny hairs on the back of Charlotte's neck and she cringed. "You see, I'm quite proud of my ploy, and you are such an integral part of it, my dear." Charlotte flinched when his fingers touched her shoulder.

"As you probably know by now, I plan to burn Oak Hill. But then that's only as it should be. And not the most interesting part. That concerns Captain Knox himself. Ah, I thought that might gain your attention," he said when Charlotte jerked her head around.

"There's nothing you can do to Jonathan."

"My, what a passionate defense of your lover. But ill-advised. It's a pity I can't take you on deck to see, but I don't think that would be wise. However, if I did, you'd understand why we passed Oak Hill." His fingers tangled in her hair and Charlotte twisted her face away, ignoring the pain. "We're following the good captain's schooner—the *Revenge,* is it? Never mind, you needn't answer. I know all about it. I also know we have it trapped."

"You're lying."

Levid's laugh was harsh and as cruel as the hand he used to grab hold of her chin. "Lying, am I? Well, we shall all see soon enough. Your friend, Captain Knox, is determined and tenacious. I'll give him that. But I'm afraid he's overextended himself this time. By coming after you he's lost everything."

"What do you mean, coming after me?"

Levid smiled and his hot breath enveloped Charlotte. "I left a message for Captain Knox in Washington City. And thanks to your convincing performance for Admiral Cochrane—you really did look quite ill—we're supposedly making a stop on my way to Baltimore. A stop where you will be delivered to a Federalist family with British loyalties. Thus our little side trip up the Manakin River."

"But of course leaving you will prove to be impossible after I encounter the infamous Captain Knox. And I'll have to take you with me. But not before I destroy Oak Hill . . . and Captain Knox."

His words fell on her like iron weights, each more crushing than the last. Charlotte shut her eyes. If ever a situation demanded her to escape, it was this one. The roll of the ship churned her stomach, or perhaps it was the smell and feel of the man pressing against her. But she couldn't just give up and retreat into her dream world. Reality wouldn't allow it. She must do something to save Jon and his family. She must think of *something*.

A loud rumble vibrated through the ship, and Charlotte's eyes flew open. "Good. We must be within range of the *Revenge*. Soon, Charlotte, soon." He bent forward, his mouth pressing down on hers in a nauseatingly wet kiss. His fingers tightened in her hair as he shoved her against the wall.

The heels of her hands dug into his chest as

Charlotte tried to twist her face away. She hated him, hated him with all her being. He finally pulled his mouth away, leaving his disgusting taste behind, and she spit at him.

One of Levid's hands tightened around Charlotte's throat. The other wiped the spittle from his chin. His pale eyes bulged with malice. "You'll pay for that, Charlotte. When I've finished with you there won't be a second you won't regret your actions."

Charlotte gasped for air, her hands clawing at his. "I'll never marry you. Never!"

"Marriage." Levid barked the word. "I've no interest in marrying some American's whore. But I will have my fill of what Knox finds so appealing. Who knows." Levid's fingers loosened their hold and Charlotte sucked in a grateful breath. "I may even let him watch . . . before I kill him."


"Return fire!"

Jon watched the gunners load the two carronades he'd had dragged from the main deck and run out the cabin windows. Now he could fire on the *Scorpion* from astern. And he could keep moving up the river.

"We're out of range, you know." Adam stood at Jon's shoulder, his face grave.

"I know."

Adam glanced back toward the already grime-covered tars as they swabbed out the bores in preparation for another volley. He was a doctor, certainly no naval tactician, but even *he* knew they hadn't a chance of hitting anything. He also knew, for all Jon's prowess as a seaman, he wasn't thinking clearly—hadn't been since that night in Baltimore when he received word of Charlotte's abduction.

His friend was more distraught than he'd ever seen

him. Not that they'd discussed it. Jon hadn't said a word to anyone. And that's one of the things that bothered Adam. Even when Christopher and the other men were impressed, when Jon blamed himself for the deed, he talked his feelings over with Adam. But not this time.

On that night when he received the message from Levid, Jon had boarded the *Revenge* and sailed. He didn't report for orders. He simply left Baltimore and crossed the bay for the Manakin River.

Adam tried to talk to him. But each time he went to Jon's cabin he found the captain seated at his desk, poring over charts, too busy to do more than glance up and hastily dismiss his friend.

When they reached Oak Hill, Jon sent Adam ashore to warn his family. And though Adam appreciated the chance to see Cilla and make sure she and her parents got safely away from the plantation, he wished Jon would have gone, too. His parents might have talked some sense into him. But Jon remained on the schooner. And now he was firing at the *Scorpion* with no hope of hitting her.

Adam cleared his throat, following Jon through the cloud of acrid smoke to the passageway. "Perhaps we should save the shot till they're closer," Adam suggested. He was worried, and some of that emotion spilled over into his voice. But the *Revenge* was trapped in the river, and soon they'd run out of navigable channel. But Jon kept them sailing forward.

Jon stepped out on deck and grabbed his spyglass, focusing it on the *Scorpion*. "I know what I'm doing, Adam." He lowered the glass, blowing air through his teeth. "At least I hope I do."

"I've always trusted your judgment at sea, Jon, but for God's sake . . ." Adam lifted his hand in supplication, only to drop it again. "Levid's going to think you've lost your mind."

"No." Jon leveled the spyglass again. "He's going to think I'm trapped, and that I'm running scared." Jon turned, his eye catching Adam's. "And he's going to follow. Mr. Taylor!" Jon barked the name, and the young officer stepped forward. "Begin draining all the water we carry."

As the sailor left to carry out the order, Adam rubbed his chin. "You're getting rid of the water?"

"Aye. If my plan works, we can take on more. If it doesn't . . ." Jon shrugged.

Adam raked both hands back through his hair. "Exactly what plan are you talking about?"

Jon folded his arms across his chest. "The plan to trap Levid." And he hoped, by God, the plan to rescue Charlotte. "By draining off our water we'll raise the *Revenge*—not a lot, but hopefully enough. Between that and our shallower hull, plus the fact that I know the shoals in these waters pretty well, we should be able to run the *Scorpion* aground."

"And attack her." Adam felt a huge weight lift off his shoulders. Perhaps Jon did know what he was doing.

"Aye, attack her. And board her. And defeat the bloody bastard once and for all."

Jon unrolled a chart, then skimmed the shoreline with narrowed eyes. He ordered sails trimmed to slow the *Revenge*. "I want her alongside us," he told Adam, and both men watched as the *Scorpion* gained on them. When the two ships were side by side, yards apart, Jon moved to his helmsmen.

"The next order I give, you are to repeat at the top of your lungs. Loud enough to be heard on the enemy ship. Then do just the opposite. Understand?"

Jon waited till he thought the *Scorpion* nearly leeward of a charted shoal, then yelled, "Hard to starboard! We'll ram the British bastard!"

The order was repeated by the helmsman. Captain Levid on the *Scorpion*'s quarterdeck heard and ordered his vessel starboard to swerve away from the *Revenge*. But the American schooner turned larboard, and too late Captain Levid realized his mistake.

By midafternoon Charlotte had exhausted herself pacing Captain Levid's cabin. If there was something she could do to avert the disaster Levid described to her, she didn't know what it was. He'd gone on deck to see the fall of Jonathan Knox firsthand. And Charlotte had put her mind upon coming up with a solution. But she couldn't.

She sank to her knees beside the bunk and prayed. She beseeched God for a miracle, one that would save Jon and his family, one that would—

The sudden lurching of the ship sent Charlotte sprawling across the cabin floor. Wondering how they'd encountered such a huge wave in the river, Charlotte grabbed hold of the headboard and waited for the vessel to right itself. It didn't.

The floor continued to slant at a forty-degree angle as Charlotte pulled herself to her feet. But a moment later, with the sound of cannon fire pounding in her ears, she dove back onto the deck.

"Keep your aim high," Jon yelled above the din of battle. "Shell the deck." His words were punctuated by the sound of splintering oak as the *Scorpion*'s mizzenmast crashed.

So far, things had gone as he planned. Egged on by the seemingly frightened *Revenge*, the *Scorpion* had boldly dogged them up the river. If anyone on board the British ship had preached caution, apparently

Levid had ignored them. And then the *Scorpion* fell for his trick with the orders and lay stuck on a shoal.

Jon gave the enemy little time to think about anything except protecting themselves as he'd opened up all his guns on the leeward side, raking the beached ship with fire and grapeshot. Squinting into the shrouds, Jon noted the marksmen picking off the British tars as they scurried about.

Grabbing up his spyglass, Jon searched for any sign of Captain Levid or Charlotte. He hoped she was safe below, and that he could get his men aboard the *Scorpion* before anything happened to her. But as he scanned the deck he spotted Levid. He was near the main mast, shouting orders, and Jon felt his jaw clench in rage.

The *Revenge* inched closer and Jon ordered the tars manning the grappling hooks at the ready. He tore off his jacket, taking one last look at Levid, then stuffed his pistol into the waistband of his breeches and grabbed his sword. Leaping off the quarterdeck, he was the first one over the side.

The *Scorpion*'s decks were slanted and slippery with blood, the air thick with saltpeter and brimstone. Jon slashed his way through several British sailors, his gaze focused on the mainmast. Around him men screamed in pain as the fight raged.

A British marine blocked his path, and Jon sent his sword on a flashing arc down over the man's shoulder. Shoving him out of the way, Jon pushed toward the mast, but when he reached it, Levid was gone.

Wiping sweat from his brow, Jon jerked his head around, searching for some sign of his nemesis. He caught a flash of braid-decorated jacket heading toward the hatch and followed.

Scrambling down the ladder, Jon saw Levid

running along the passageway toward his cabin. Racing after him, Jon burst through the door just as Levid grabbed Charlotte about the waist and shoved her in front of him.

"Let her go, Levid!" Jon ground out the words as he aimed his pistol at the British captain's head. But he knew he couldn't shoot. For Levid had an almost identical piece jammed in Charlotte's ribs.

Apparently Levid knew it, too, because he merely scoffed, dragging Charlotte toward the back of his cabin. "Oh, I think not, Captain Knox. Miss Winston only makes our confrontation more interesting. Don't you think?"

Jon inched away from the door. Above them the battle raged, but it all seemed foreign, faintly dreamlike. His consciousness tunneled, focusing on the pistol and Charlotte's eyes, dark and trusting in her pale face. "She has nothing to do with this." The deadly calm of his tone surprised Jon.

"No?" Levid sounded mildly amused. "She lied for you, treasoned herself for you . . . whored for you."

Jon stepped forward, but halted when Charlotte groaned, Levid's pistol gouging her side, and Jon stepped back. His heart beat against his ribs and he swallowed, forcing himself not to look at Charlotte. "My men are all over this ship. You have no way out. Let her go and I'll make certain you're paroled right away."

"Ha! This from the man who vowed to kill me."

"I mean it." Jon moved forward again. "You have my word. Now let her go."

Charlotte felt Levid's arm loosen, and thought for one ecstatic moment that he planned to do as Jon insisted. But his evil laugh shattered her hopes and his words rang like a death toll in her ears. "A better idea is to kill you both. Your whore first."

"Noooo!" Jon's roared denial rang through the cabin, drowning out the metallic cocking of the hammer. He leaped forward, a vision of Charlotte's startled face frozen in his mind, at the same moment the door burst open.

Levid jerked, firing wildly toward the doorway, then crashed to the floor, Jon on top of him.

Charlotte landed with a thump against the desk. She pulled herself up and looked frantically toward Jon. He fought with Levid, rolling wildly on the floor, first one on top, then the other. They grappled for Jon's pistol, and Charlotte gasped as the gun twisted in their hands.

She lurched forward to do something . . . but what? Her gaze swung to the door and the body lying halfway in the cabin. Adam. He'd been shot and lay bleeding on the wooden deck. Her mind registered that at the same moment she noticed the pistol clutched in his fingers.

Flying to his side, she grabbed it, twisted back, and took aim. Levid lay on his back, his feral eyes on the man above him, the pistol slowly turning toward Jon's head.

The explosion recoiled her against the wall and rang in her ears.

"Charlotte! Charlotte!" Strong arms wrapped around her, and she collapsed against Jon's hard chest. "Talk to me. Are you all right?"

"Yes, yes. Oh, Jon, yes." Charlotte didn't know whether to laugh or cry as he lifted her chin to look into her eyes. For one awful moment as she pulled the trigger, Charlotte couldn't be certain whom she would hit. But now Jon was holding— Her eyes widened. "You're hurt."

"No, it's not my blood."

"Good." Charlotte sank back against him, then

411

jerked away. "Oh, my God. Adam."

Jon's gaze followed her gesture toward the door, then rushed over, dropping to his knees in time to hear his friend groan.

"He's not dead?" Charlotte tore off a section of her chemise and stuffed it into the ragged hole in Adam's shoulder. Just then Adam's eyes fluttered open.

"What happened?" Adam tried to sit up, but stayed flat on the floor, his face wincing in pain.

"You were shot. And you saved our lives." Jon nodded toward Charlotte and she smiled when Adam turned his head. Jon hunched forward. "Let me pull you back in here. I'll leave Charlotte a gun, but I better get back on deck."

"No need to." Adam grabbed Jon's arm. "It's over. The British surrendered to Mr. Taylor. Your men are seeing to the prisoners."

Head back, Jon breathed a sigh of relief, his eyes closing. But they immediately snapped open. "Wait a minute. What are you doing down here? Why aren't you in the surgery?"

Adam's smile was sheepish. "I couldn't let you have all the fun. Besides, I was looking for you." He shifted, gritting his teeth against the fire in his shoulder. "I wanted to tell you the reason we overpowered the British so quickly. We had some help from their crew."

"*Their* crew? But who on their crew would help us?"

There was a commotion in the passageway behind Jon. He turned to see the cause as Adam lifted his good hand, pointing, and answered with a mumbled, "Him."


Charlotte had sought the garden as a refuge from

the excitement in the house. It wasn't that she didn't share everybody's joy. She did. But she didn't really belong inside. It was a family celebration . . . and she wasn't family.

They all were listening to Jon's brother tell of his ordeals on the British ship, and how he and the rest of the impressed sailors had jumped their captors when Jon's men attacked the *Scorpion*. She smiled. Jon and his family were so happy to have Christopher back with them . . . alive and well.

Trailing her fingers along the tiny green boxwood leaves, she took a deep breath of rose-scented air, then sighed. Charlotte was so deep in thought she didn't notice the footsteps crunching along the crushed shell path till they were nearly upon her.

Turning, Charlotte looked up at Jon. He paused perhaps five feet from her, and stared. "Do you want to be alone?" he asked, his expression somewhat cautious for him.

"No." Charlotte smiled. "I just . . ." She lifted her hand, then let it drop. "It was noisy."

Jon chuckled softly. "My family can be a little boisterous. Especially with Libby's children here." Jon reached out and plucked a yellow rose from the trellis. "I thought you might be upset . . ." He carefully stripped the thorns. "About what happened. I know we haven't had time to talk, I haven't even thanked you for—"

"It's all right." Charlotte smiled. "I'm not upset." She probably *should* be upset, and maybe it would hit her later. After all, she'd killed a man. But right now, knowing the alternative might have been Jon's death, she felt only relief.

"Are you sure?" Jon handed her the rose.

Charlotte nodded, lifting the blossom to her nose and breathing deeply of its sweet fragrance. "How is your brother doing?''

Jon laughed. ''He'll be fine as soon as Mother stops forcing food down him.''

''He's *still* eating?'' Charlotte asked with mock amazement. Ever since The *Revenge* docked at Oak Hill and Elizabeth saw her younger son, safe but woefully thin, she'd worked at remedying the situation.

Jon laughed again, and Charlotte's heart seemed to expand with love for him. ''I'm so glad you found your brother.''

''I am, too. He gave the British a false name, he told me. Captain Levid never did know who he was.''

''Levid was just trying to hurt you with stories of your brother's death.''

Jon nodded, then his eyes caught hers. ''Charlotte, I—''

''And how is Adam doing?'' A useless question, for she knew very well how he was. But it suddenly hit Charlotte that with his brother found and Captain Levid dead, Jon's link to her was gone. True, the war still raged—if rumors could be believed, General Cochrane was on his way to attack Baltimore—but that didn't mean Jon had to keep her here.

Right now he seemed slightly annoyed as he stared at her. ''Adam is fine. A terrible patient, but Cilla can handle him.'' He crossed his arms. ''And to forestall any further questions, let me assure you my father is well, as is Libby, her husband and two daughters. Did I cover everyone?''

Charlotte studied the tips of her blue satin slippers. ''I believe so.''

''Except you.''

''Me?'' Charlotte glanced up. ''I already said I was fine.''

''Perhaps I should clarify myself.'' Jon traced a

stray curl resting on Charlotte's cheek. "I meant to say *us*."

Charlotte looked up into his indigo-blue eyes and her pulse quickened. "Us?"

Jon bent to kiss her parted lips, then stopped himself. Jerking around, he raked his fingers through his hair. "I know you had it in your mind to return to England. I mean, hell, you've told me that often enough, but—"

"I don't have to go back." Charlotte took a step toward him.

"You don't?" Jon glanced over his shoulder.

"No. I mean it's my home and everything but I—"

"Damnit, Charlotte, I don't want you to go. I love you. Stay here and—"

The force of her lips crushing against his cut off Jon's words as Charlotte hurled herself into his arms. He enveloped her in his embrace, kissing her over and over again—her lips, her nose, the tip of her chin. "Marry me," he whispered against her cheek. "Marry me now." He punctuated his request with another kiss, this one deep and hungry and leaving Charlotte feeling slightly bereft when he pulled away.

But he didn't go far, and when she answered "yes" against his lips, he lifted her into the air.

"You will?" he asked, smiling up at her.

"Oh, yes," Charlotte assured emphatically as he lowered her to the ground, sealing their happiness with a kiss.